Enticing Her Love

The Steeles at Silver Island

Love in Bloom Series

Melissa Foster

M&F

Cover Design: Elizabeth Mackey Designs
Cover Photography: Sara Eirew Photography

PRINTED IN THE UNITED STATES OF AMERICA

A Note from Melissa

I am thrilled to bring you Sutton Steele and Flynn Braden's love story. Not only do they have scorching chemistry and great banter, but coming from big, complicated families, they truly were fated to be together. Flynn is adventurous, a bit gruff when holding in his feelings, and he loves as hard and deep and loyally as all our beloved Bradens do. Sutton didn't stand a chance against her off-limits boss, and I had so much fun watching them fall in love and find their happily ever after with two of my favorite families. I hope you love them as I do. It is important to note that I have taken many fictional liberties while writing this story and do not recommend anyone take a trip into the Amazon rainforest without a trained professional.

If this is your first Melissa Foster book, while interconnected, all Love in Bloom stories are written to stand alone with no cliffhangers or unresolved issues, so dive right in and enjoy the funny, steamy, emotional ride.

For avid fans of my Silver Island families, don't worry, there are many more Silver Island stories coming. Get ready to fall hard for Wells Silver as he fights his way to his happily ever after in FLIRTING WITH TROUBLE, the first book in the Silvers on Silver Island series, available at your favorite online book retailers and my online bookstore.

Be sure to check out my online bookstore for preorders, early releases, bundles, and exclusive discounts on ebooks, print books, and audiobooks. E-books can be sent to the e-reader of your choice and audiobooks can be listened to on the free and easy-to-use BookFunnel app.

Shop my store: shop.melissafoster.com

I have many more steamy love stories coming soon. Sign up for my newsletter so you don't miss them.

www.MelissaFoster.com/Newsletter

SILVER ISLAND

Fisherman's Wharf

Seaport

Wildlife Refuge

Rock Harbor

Brighton Park

Seaport Primary

Rock Bottom Bar & Grill

Trista's   Happy End

Silver Island Airport

Rock Harbor Primary

Lover's Cove

Top of the Island Winery

The Bistro

Silver Monument

Silver Island Community College

Silver House

Majestic Park

Brighton Bluffs

The Sweet Barista

Scoops

Silver Island High

Silver Harbor

Sunset Beach

Silver Haven Primary

Fortune's Landing

Marina

Silver Haven

Fortune's Cove

Chaffee

Bellamy Island

Cuddlefish Cove

Chapter One

SUTTON CLOSED HER eyes as the warm liquid slid down her throat, a feeling of complete and utter bliss overtaking her. *This* was what she wanted. What she craved. She'd take hazelnut coffee over a man any day. It was sweet and hot and never failed to satisfy. She heard footsteps approaching and opened her eyes, clutching her mug between both hands. Her chest tightened as she scrutinized the steps, just as she did every time she was alone in the break room. That was what working for survivalist Flynn Braden did to her. She had to mentally prepare to be in the same room with him as if she were going to war. The footsteps were fast and light, not the heavy, determined steps of her rival.

She breathed a sigh of relief when her research assistant and friend, Andi Pennington, walked into the room.

"Hey, boss," Andi said cheerily. She tucked her long blond hair behind her ear and pushed her glasses to the bridge of her nose. "Do I look green to you?"

Sutton studied her for a moment. "No, why? Are you feeling sick?"

"No, just incredibly jealous. I wish I could fit in your suitcase and go to Ecuador with you."

Sutton was a reporter for the *Discovery Hour* show on the

World Exploration Network. She and her infuriating boss and their film crew were leaving at the crack of dawn tomorrow to stay with an indigenous tribe in the Amazon rainforest.

"I wish you could come, too. I tried to get Flynn's approval to add you to the trip, but he said it wasn't in the budget." Andi would have been a great buffer between her and Flynn.

"Thanks for trying." Andi poured herself a cup of coffee. "The trip sounds amazing. I just reviewed the itinerary again. The shot list flows well, and Flynn knocked the write-up out of the park." The write-up was a general outline of the topics they would cover in the show. "He incorporated a lot of the research we did, especially yours. I just passed him in the hall, and he said we did a fantastic job."

"That's great." Sutton heard the sarcasm in her own voice. She'd give just about anything for an ounce of the kudos he gave everyone else.

"Oh no," Andi said with a disappointed expression. "He hasn't said anything to you, has he?"

"Not a word."

"*Ugh.* I swear that man has it out for you." Andi lowered her voice. "But between you and me, I agree with Leni. I can never tell if he's looking at you like he wants to kill you or…you know." She waggled her brows.

Leni was one of Sutton's younger sisters, a PR guru. Flynn's brother Seth, a business mogul, was one of Leni's clients. Leni swore Seth was as easygoing as Flynn was a pain in Sutton's ass. She had been following the Flynn-Sutton drama since Sutton had started working there. Not that Sutton had shared the Seth-Leni connection with Flynn. Other than when he was barking orders, the man barely said two words to her.

"My money is on kill," Sutton said. She'd been a fashion

editor with big dreams, a double major in journalism and English, and no reporting experience when the founders of the parent company, LWW Enterprises, had given her a shot and promoted her to the reporter position with *Discovery Hour*. She'd busted her ass to prove herself worthy of the job. Nearly a year and a half later, she'd done just that. Except in the eyes of her boss, who she was sure had been trying to get her fired since day one.

As if his ears were burning, Flynn strode in, all rugged and broad shouldered, with shaggy scruff that said he had better things to do than shave and collar-length sandy hair. Sutton's entire body tensed up. His black T-shirt stretched tight across his broad chest and muscular biceps as he raked a hand through his hair, his midnight-blue eyes locking on her. The air thickened with tension, sparking with electricity so sharp and hot, it felt combustible.

His gaze shifted briefly to Andi. "Andi," he said not unkindly, then returned a tight jaw to Sutton, eyes boring into hers. "*Steele.*"

The bite in his words brought out a hiss of her own. "*Braden.*" She knew what to do with lust-driven heat, but this frustration-driven energy was sharper and hotter than anything she'd ever known.

"I'd better run," Andi said. "I'm meeting my sister for drinks. Have a great time on the trip." She hugged Sutton, whispering, "*You might be right,*" and hurried out of the room.

Flynn's eyes remained trained on Sutton. "Having second thoughts about going on this trip?"

"Not in the least. I just hope you can scare off predators as easily as you scare off people." She turned to leave as the VP of their division, Karen Malterson, walked in. The sharp brunette had a reputation for being cutthroat but fair, and Sutton had nothing but respect for her. Although Sutton rarely saw Karen, when she did, she'd noticed that Karen either seemed to be observing her or oblivious to her.

"I've been looking for you two," Karen said. "I'd like to speak to you in my office."

Sutton's stomach pitched. Had Flynn finally succeeded in getting her fired?

In the time Sutton had worked there, she'd been called into Karen's office only twice. Once was during the first week she'd worked there, when Karen had welcomed her to the division, and again a few months ago, when Karen had questioned her desire to go into the rainforest for their current assignment.

Flynn hiked a thumb over his shoulder. "I was just about to—"

"Whatever it is can wait," Karen said firmly. "My office. Now." She spun on her heel and walked out.

Flynn gritted out a curse, glowering at Sutton as if *she'd* caused the interruption to his schedule.

Jackass. She headed down the hall, leaving him to stew on his own, but his determined footfalls sounded behind her, and she felt his presence looming like a villain as they entered Karen's office.

"Close the door," Karen directed.

Flynn did as she'd asked. "Is something wrong?"

"Hopefully not for long. Take a seat." She nodded to the chairs across from her desk and went to sit behind it.

Sutton lowered herself to a chair, feeling nauseous.

"I've noticed tension between you two, and I'm concerned it will affect the show." Karen paused, as if waiting for a response.

Shitshitshit. There was no way Flynn would get canned over this, so Sutton lied to save her ass. "I'm not sure what you think you've seen, but things are fine between us, right, Flynn?"

He didn't spare her a glance, his jaw ticking. "There's no tension."

"Then it sounds like I made the right decision," Karen said. "I've changed your assignment. You'll no longer be spending time with the tribe. The show is now focusing on the two of you surviving three nights—seventy-two hours—in the Amazon rainforest."

"What?" Flynn snapped. "It took *months* to get the tribe's approval. The show is *set*, focusing on the culture of the tribe and the conditions they live in, the challenges they face with the encroaching extractive industries, deforestation, poachers, and drug runners. You can't just throw all that away for *this*." *This* came out with so much venom, Sutton startled.

"It's *done*," Karen said with finality. "The leader has agreed to let you travel within their territory without a guide or a tribal member."

Flynn's eyes narrowed. "Do you have *any* idea how dangerous the rainforest is? How the hell am I supposed to keep the crew and *her* safe?" He dropped *her* like a curse. "None of them are trained for this. It's a fucking death warrant."

"I agree with Flynn," Sutton said anxiously. "I'm *not*—"

Karen held her hand up. "Let me remind you how hard you both fought for this assignment. Sutton, when I met with you about the dangers of the rainforest and the possibility of you getting lost, hurt, or worse, you said you had done your research and knew the dangers, and you trusted Flynn to keep you safe. And, Flynn, when I addressed those concerns about Sutton and the crew, you insisted you had the expertise to ensure their safety. You promised to make sure the crew didn't leave the camp without a tribal member and to stick by Sutton's side every minute. I'm holding you to that. But I'm not unreasonable."

Sutton exhaled loudly. "Oh, good. I thought you were seriously sending us in with only Flynn to keep us all safe."

"I *am* serious," she said. "I'm not unreasonable in thinking Flynn should be responsible for you *and* the crew, which is why the crew will not be joining you on this trip. There's no need to risk more lives than absolutely necessary. Sutton, you'll be reporting as usual, and, Flynn, you'll be filming, and the camera will have a shotgun mic. I'm counting on you to keep her safe. But the ball is in your court. Are you two up for the job, or do you want to walk away from *Discovery Hour*?"

Sutton couldn't breathe.

Flynn continued staring at Karen, the muscles in his jaw clenching. Sutton half expected smoke to come out of his ears. If he refused to do the assignment, she wouldn't have to, and she might even get a new boss in the process. So she held her tongue.

He gave one curt nod and bit out, "Absolutely," then turned those serious eyes on Sutton.

"Sutton?" Karen asked.

Hell no was on the tip of her tongue, but Flynn's eyes held a challenge, and when she opened her mouth, "*I'm in*" came out.

Chapter Two

SUTTON DIDN'T KNOW which she wanted more, to give Karen a piece of her mind for sending them on this ridiculous trip, to smack the hell out of her infuriating boss, or to sleep for twelve hours straight.

She and Flynn were at the Guayaquil airport in Ecuador, awaiting the last leg of their twenty-plus-hour trip. What was Karen thinking, sending them into the rainforest alone, like some sort of freaking team-building mission with wild animals and deadly insects and poisonous plants? She'd told them there would be gear waiting at the Coca airport for them, including a satellite phone, two tents, a hatchet, a machete, a lighter, a flashlight, a net, two canteens, and a first-aid kit.

How about a gun and full-body armor?

It was the freaking Amazon rainforest for Pete's sake.

Sutton was terrified about the trip, but she wasn't about to let the man who was afraid of nothing in on her secret. Not that Flynn had shared any of his experiences with her. Just the opposite. He never talked about himself. Everything she knew about her boss came from researching him *before* she'd met him.

She'd learned he was the youngest person, at twenty-one, to win *Wilderness Warrior* by outlasting thirteen other contestants in Kenya, Africa. Rumor had it, when they came to extract him, he refused to leave, wanting to prove to himself how long he could last there. He'd also survived a month in the jungles of Indonesia by himself, tracked polar bears in Alaska, climbed Mount Everest, and accomplished many other near-impossible, dangerous feats. He'd banked a million dollars from the reality-show win and had gotten all sorts of notoriety, but then he'd disappeared for a number of years. By the time he'd emerged, he was no longer a headliner. There were all sorts of theories about why he'd disappeared, and people thought that made him mysterious. The media had even dubbed him the *lost boy*. But Sutton couldn't care less about where he'd gone or why. All she cared about was why he was such a jerk to *her*, always pushing her to dig deeper, even after she'd practically dug to China, and never offering any words of praise.

She and Flynn had traveled together many times over the past year and a half, but it was always with a crew. Spending hours trapped in airplanes and airports with him was a new kind of hell. She'd rather be buried alive with tarantulas than spend three days with him anywhere.

She thought about where they were heading. She'd re-searched every little thing about the Amazon rainforest and what they would face during their visit with the tribe. Once she'd learned they'd be roughing it alone, she'd taken an even deeper dive into the dangers that lurked there. The rainforest was home to some of the largest species of tarantula.

Suddenly her pain-in-the-ass boss didn't seem so bad.

But he was bad enough.

It was his fault there was tension between them in the first place. She'd had it with him and his unyielding demands and lack of niceties. Which was why she was focusing on her phone and attaching her résumé to an email that could hopefully get her an interview for her dream job as a reporter for Global News Now (GNN), one of the country's leading news outlets, and get her out of her current untenable situation. Her finger hovered over the send icon, but she hesitated, thinking about the people she enjoyed working with at the World Exploration Network and the founders of LWW, who had given her a shot at reporting. Sutton had a bond with them through the Ladies Who Write sisterhood, which was like a sorority for women who liked to write, at Boyer University, where they'd all gone to college. The founders were older than her, but they'd not only founded the sisterhood prior to starting LWW Enterprises, but they'd eventually gone on to buy the house where the girls had lived at Boyer and had since helped many of them find their way in the professional world. She didn't want to let them down.

She didn't want to let herself down, either.

Reporting for *Discovery Hour* was always supposed to be a stepping stone to becoming a cutting-edge reporter headlining global issues. She took a bite of a peanut butter cracker, her comfort food. She'd brought a supply of them. Lord knew she'd need some kind of comfort for the hell she was about to be put through.

She glanced at Flynn standing by the coffee counter talking with a barista. He raked a hand through his hair, flashing the easygoing smile that softened his hard edges. That smile never seemed to come Sutton's way, ratcheting up her frustration.

Fuck it. She was done with his crap. She sent the email and thumbed out a text to Leni.

Sutton: *I did it!*

Leni: *Define it. Quit? Killed? Screwed?*

Sutton finished her cracker, thinking about how many times they'd played the kiss-marry-kill game when they were younger and how often Leni had wanted to kill the boys on Silver Island, where they'd grown up, while Sutton had usually tried to negotiate more options. Today she didn't need more options. *Just give me a weapon.* Although it wasn't like she hadn't thought about screwing Flynn a time or two…*hundred.*

Sutton: *None of the above. I sent my résumé to GNN.*

Leni: *Hold on while I nix the body bag I just ordered.*

A shadow fell over Sutton. She looked up as Flynn lowered his big body into the seat beside her and said, "Updating your will?"

"I took care of that when I first started working with you." She pocketed her phone. "I was just making sure the hit man I hired is still on board."

He half scoffed, half laughed. "Hope he's better at his job than you are at yours."

She narrowed her eyes, too tired to mince words. "Were you born a dick, or did it take years of practice?" She'd never said anything quite as blatant as that to him, and Flynn was quiet for so long, she wondered if she'd crossed a line that *would* get her fired. Just as she was about to backpedal, he spoke.

"Probably both."

She breathed a sigh of relief. "For your information, I'm worth my weight in gold. You're just too blind to see it."

His dark eyes swept over her. "Nobody's going to get rich on that."

She rolled her eyes.

"You know, you could cancel the hit man and save a few bucks by doing the deed yourself. Or are you afraid to get your hands dirty?"

"I'm not afraid. I just don't think I'd look good in an orange jumpsuit."

"Good thinking. Here." He handed her a cup of coffee.

"I don't want your coffee."

"It's yours." He held up his other hand, showing her another coffee cup.

That was a first. She eyed the proffered cup skeptically. "Is this like a last meal? Did you pay the barista to poison it?"

He shoved the cup into her hand. "Just drink the damn coffee."

"Okay, but if my hit man fails and I don't return home from this trip, you'll have to deal with my siblings. You should know Archer is itching for a reason to kill you." She had three brothers and two sisters. Her older brother Archer was a beast of a man with a hair trigger. He was overprotective of all of them, but he was especially watchful over Sutton and Jules, the only two siblings who didn't have a twin.

He scoffed. "The winemaker? I'm not worried."

"Then you really are a stupid man." She sipped the coffee and was shocked by the sweet taste of hazelnut. "How did you know how I like my coffee?"

"You're not exactly quiet about your love of hazelnut. After you practically made out with the food and beverage guy for bringing you hazelnut creamer at that archaeological site in Portugal, I saw him pay off the girl he worked with so he could bring you your coffee every morning."

"I *hugged* him, and he did not pay anyone off."

He sat back and kicked his long legs out, crossing them at the ankles. "I saw what I saw." Wrapping both hands around his coffee cup, he rested his head back and closed his eyes.

When he wasn't looking at her like she was in trouble with

the principal or saying something cutting, she could *almost* pretend he wasn't a hard-ass jerk. "I can't believe you're not angrier about this assignment."

"Who says I'm not angry?"

"You don't seem bothered."

"What do you want me to do, stomp my feet like a toddler when my boss says something I don't like?"

"Is that supposed to be a dig at *me*?"

"You didn't hear that from me." He sipped his coffee.

She rolled her eyes. "I don't know why I bother talking to you." She took another drink, so grateful for the warm deliciousness, she couldn't hold it in. "This is really good. Thank you."

"You were looking pretty feral," he said gruffly. "I didn't want to be on the receiving end of you losing your shit and figured it might take the edge off."

Mouth opens, hard-ass jerk returns.

SUTTON WAS TOO bleary eyed to be bothered by the sheeting rain when they finally landed in Coca, Ecuador, at five thirty a.m. They collected their massive waterproof backpacks and the gear bag the company had sent, grabbed a quick bite to eat, and caught a taxi for the ride to the airstrip where they were meeting the pilot who was going to fly them into the rainforest.

She gazed out the window at the stunning views of the mountains in the distance as they drove through Coca, a town known as the gateway to Ecuador's Amazon rainforest because of its proximity to the Coca and Napo Rivers. Taking in the colorful concrete buildings lining the roads and the lush foliage, she wished they had time to explore the area and was hit with a familiar wave of gratitude for the chance the company had taken when they'd hired her. Her trouble with Flynn aside, she'd traveled all over the world, seeing and learning about people and places she'd never imagined having access to, and through *Discovery Hour*, she shared that knowledge to help raise awareness about plights that might otherwise go largely unnoticed. She'd also learned a lot from Flynn about in-depth reporting, presenting the news, and understanding and working with different cultures. Despite their strained relationship, it would be hard to leave all that behind.

It was a long, silent ride to the airstrip, and it rained the whole way. The one-story concrete building beside the airstrip had seen better days. Sutton pulled the hood of her raincoat over her head as they grabbed their backpacks from the trunk, but it promptly flew off. She squinted against the rain. "I imagined getting here and sleeping in the sun for a few hours, not drowning in a downpour."

"We're going to a *rain*forest, not the desert." He strode toward the building.

Toying with the idea of burying *him* alive with tarantulas, she followed him into a crowded waiting room. Speaking in Spanish, Flynn told the two dark-haired men behind the counter that they were looking for Santiago Macías. The older of the two men rose to his feet, standing eye-to-eye with Sutton at five eight. Flynn towered over them at six three or four. In Spanish, Santiago introduced himself as their pilot, offering his hand and a warm smile, and proceeded to explain that he couldn't fly in this weather but said they could wait with the others until there was a break in the rain.

Sutton asked how long the other people had been waiting. When he said several hours, she looked at Flynn. "If that's the case, maybe we can give him our phone numbers so he can call when it's safe to fly, and we can find a nearby hotel where we can shower and get a few hours' sleep."

"We finally agree on something." He presented the idea to Santiago, who agreed and told them there was a hotel run by a friend of his less than a mile away and offered to drive them there.

After exchanging numbers, they followed him out to an old, rusted truck. Sutton slid onto the center of the bench seat, and Flynn packed his large body in beside her, squishing her between him and Santiago. She couldn't *wait* to have some breathing space.

Beyond exhausted, she said, "How good does a hot bath, plush towels, and a comfy bed sound right now?"

"It won't suck," Flynn said.

A few minutes later, they turned onto a narrow dirt road and into the driveway of a small house that wasn't in much better shape than the building at the airstrip. The yard was a mix of dirt and grass, and there was a small HOTEL sign out front. Sutton knew better than to judge a book by its cover. They grabbed their packs, thanked Santiago, and headed inside to the reception desk.

"Hola," said a plump woman with friendly eyes and tawny skin. She introduced herself as Ana, and they asked if she had two rooms available.

Sutton's stomach sank when she said there was only one room available.

What had she done to deserve this kind of punishment?

Flynn must have seen something in her expression, because

he said, "What's the matter, Steele? If you can't handle sharing a hotel room, maybe I should get you a ticket home."

She glowered at him. "You'd like that, wouldn't you?" She forced a smile for Ana and in Spanish said they'd take the room. After Flynn paid for the room, Ana gave them the key and directed them down the hall.

Flynn unlocked the door, and Sutton could do little more than stare at the postage-stamp-sized room with peach walls, one double bed, a small dresser, and just enough space to walk between the bed and a beige love seat that was missing an arm, like a misplaced piece of a sectional sofa. There was no door separating the bathroom from the bedroom. A maroon sink stood against one wall beside a small shelving unit with towels and travel-sized bottles of what she assumed were shampoo and body wash. Just beyond the sink was a toilet alcove with saloon-style shutter doors that were almost a foot off the floor. To the left of that was a step-down shower, separated from the rest of the room by only a shower curtain.

"So much for a hot bath," Sutton said.

Flynn walked into the middle of the room, making it feel even smaller. "The couch looks comfortable enough."

"Good, then you won't mind sleeping on it." She dropped her backpack by the dresser.

"You're kidding, right? Look at the size of that thing. Which of us do you think would sleep better on it?"

"What's the matter, Braden? Can't hack the accommodations? Maybe I should get you a ticket home."

He scoffed.

She eyed the bathroom. She could move the shelves next to the shower so she didn't have to put her clothes on the floor, and get undressed behind the shower curtain. That would be easy enough. Having grown up with a gaggle of siblings, she wasn't shy by any means, but Flynn was the last person she wanted to hear her going to the bathroom.

She turned to him. "I don't suppose you'd be willing to take a walk while I get cleaned up, would you?"

"In this weather?" He looked amused as he sat on the love seat and took off his boots.

"*Fine.*" She pulled out her phone and strutted to the toilet, cranking up "Mean" by Taylor Swift as loud as her phone allowed to mask the sound of her going to the bathroom. After she was done, she washed her hands and went to move the shelves, but they were heavier than they looked, and she struggled to tug them across the floor.

Flynn walked over and stood at the entrance to the bathroom. His feet were bare, and *huge*, which made her traitorous mind think of that old wives' tale about the size of a man's feet relating to the size of his package. Her gaze traveled up his tree-trunk legs.

"Need help redecorating?"

Startled by his deep voice, she realized she was staring at the formidable bulge behind his zipper and tore her gaze away. What the hell was wrong with her?

"Nope." She wasn't about to give him the satisfaction of feeling superior in any way.

He watched her struggle for a minute before shaking his head and walking away. She finished moving the shelves and set clean cotton shorts and a comfortable shirt on them, then hung a towel over the shower rod. She stepped behind the curtain to undress. She turned on the water and scooted away from the icy spray. It took forever for it to become tepid, but she closed her eyes, trying to relax as it rained down over her.

How was it possible to be so tense while she was too tired to see straight?

She didn't have to search far for the answer. He was probably sprawled out on the bed right now, just to annoy her. She took extra time washing her hair, appreciating the luxury of running water and a clean shower, which she knew she'd long for once they were in the rainforest. She rinsed out the shampoo and opened her eyes, coming face-to-face with an enormous spider. She screamed and bolted out of the shower, smacking into Flynn's granite chest, causing her to scream even louder.

His arms circled her. "What's wrong?"

"Spider! It's a spider! It's huge. It's—"

"Sutton, *stop screaming* and pull yourself together."

His authoritative tone broke through her fatigued hysteria, and she became painfully aware of his hot hands on her bare back, her naked body pressed against his exquisitely *hard* frame, and just how good he felt.

"*Sutton,*" he growled, his arms locking tighter around her.

She looked up, and his eyes drilled into her, primal and hungry. Flames engulfed her from the inside out.

His jaw clenched, and he uttered a curse. "You okay?"

Shitshitshit. Was she so exhausted, she was seeing things? "*No.* I'm naked in my boss's arms. How do you think I am?"

"It's probably not the best way to go after a raise."

"Shut up!"

His lips twitched with amusement.

"You think this is *funny?*"

"I'm so damn tired, I don't know what to think. Other than I have no idea how you're going to handle the rainforest if you can't handle a spider."

"I *expect* spiders to be in the rainforest, not in the shower! I need a towel."

He loosened his grip, stepping toward the towel.

She clung to him. "Where do you think you're going? You are *not* seeing me naked."

"Are we pretending I can't see your ass from up here?"

"Yes! Stop looking!"

He sighed exasperatedly and belted his arm around her, crushing her against him and lifting her off her feet as he stepped closer to the shower. He snagged the towel and draped it around her.

"Thank you." She secured it over her chest. "Can you *please* kill that spider?"

He pulled open the shower curtain and turned off the water. "You must have scared it away. I don't see it."

"What?" She peered around him. "Are you sure? It was right above the lever—"

"You mean that crack with the stain around it?" He pointed to a discolored spot on the wall the size of her hand.

"*No.* There was a spider." Embarrassment consumed her as she searched the walls and ceiling for the damn spider she was no longer sure had even existed.

"Three days with you in the rainforest should be fun. Come on, Steele. You should get some sleep before you start seeing werewolves or vampires."

"I'll take Jacob or Edward in the rainforest over you any day."

Chapter Three

FLYNN STARED UP at the ceiling listening to the rain falling outside the open window, trying *not* to think about how Sutton's terrified scream had set off his protective urges. Or how the sight of her naked, and the feel of her in his arms, had made him damn glad she'd used all the hot water. But *not* thinking about those things was impossible, given that she was currently snuggled against him, using his chest as a pillow, one long leg resting on his thigh and her hand dangerously close to his all-too-interested dick.

Did she have to smell so fucking sweet?

A big-ass spider crawled into view on the ceiling. *Fucking spider. This is all your fault.*

He should have stayed on the couch, but it was about three feet too short, and the rain was exacerbating an old rock-climbing injury, making his shoulder throb. He was used to that painful annoyance and never let it slow him down, but sleep was essential to maintaining his mental fortitude while in the rainforest. Sutton had been sleeping so soundly when he'd gotten out of the shower that, an hour later, when he was still awake on the couch and she was snoring, he'd thought it was safe to slip onto the other side of the bed and catch a few winks.

He hadn't expected her to move a muscle, much less wrap herself around him like a koala to a tree.

Out of all the blondes in the world, why did he have to be so damn attracted to *her*? It made no sense. Nobody gave him as much grief as she did. She was tenacious as a tick, and she never withheld her opinion no matter how objectionable, but there was no escaping the physical attraction that had gripped him like talons the first time he'd lain eyes on her, and it had been pissing him off ever since.

He'd never forget the day the tall, slender smokeshow with porcelain skin and dainty features that were impossible to look away from had blown into their offices dressed to the nines like his sister's old News Anchor Barbie, turning the heads of everyone in the place. Sutton had been confident, eager, and as green as a blade of grass. LWW was all about female empowerment, which was one of the reasons he'd chosen to work for them. He respected strong, smart women, like the women in his family, but Sutton's first words to him—*So, the lost boy found a home*—had grated on his nerves. He'd been sure they had a diva on their hands who would be afraid to get her perfectly manicured nails dirty. He'd told management as much, but they'd been dead set on giving her a shot.

Sutton Steele had been trying his patience from that moment on, and now she was drooling on his chest.

She stretched, arching her back and purring like a cat. Her hand landed on his chest. He gritted his teeth against the feel of her delicate fingers trailing tentatively over his skin.

Her eyes flew open, and she shot up to her knees, her visual shock and anger hitting him like daggers. "What are you doing in my bed?"

Not what I'd like to be doing. Shoving that unwanted

thought away, he wiped her spittle from his chest. "Getting drooled on. You might want to…" He touched the corner of his mouth.

Looking appalled, she swiped at her mouth. "Shouldn't you *ask* before getting into a woman's bed?"

"You were snoring, and you'd been hallucinating spiders. I thought you'd appreciate the sleep, not use me as a body pillow."

She made an annoyed sound and climbed off the bed, breathing fire, and looking cute as hell in cotton sleeping shorts and a black tank top with FUELED BY FACTS AND COFFEE written in gold script across her chest. "You're such an ass. That naked-spider incident was *not* an invitation." She stalked into the bathroom and began furiously brushing her teeth.

"Get over yourself." He rose to his feet. "I needed to sleep."

She rinsed her mouth out and stalked into the bedroom. "*I* should get over myself?" Snagging her hairbrush from the dresser, she flipped her hair to one side, brushing it with a vengeance. "That's rich, coming from Mr. Know-It-All."

"What's that supposed to mean?"

"You act like you're some kind of *Discovery Hour* god and have *all* the answers."

"And you think I *don't*?"

She tossed her hairbrush on the dresser and planted a hand on her hip, her eyes blazing with challenge. "I think you're a sanctimonious jerk who can't stand the idea of me getting ahead."

"You'd better *hope* this sanctimonious jerk has all the answers. I created this show from the ground up. The success of the program depends on *me* getting it right." He stalked toward her, taking in the shock of that truth in her widening eyes. "I busted my ass and paid my dues, earning the right to hold this position, but you wouldn't know anything about that, would you? You got here because you were sorority sisters with the LWW founders." The second the words were out, he regretted them. Even if they were true, exhausted or not, he knew better than to let her get to him and allow his patience to snap. Then again, she had a way of getting under his skin and causing him to forget a hell of a lot more than his manners.

Her eyes narrowed, hurt and anger coalescing in them, sending a stab of guilt right through him. She closed her mouth, shoved her phone in her pocket, and her feet into her Tevas. "At least you finally had the balls to say it out loud."

"Sutton—"

"Don't bother trying to deny it." She put the strap of her crossbody pack over her head. "I knew you hated me. I just couldn't figure out why."

Jesus fuck. "I don't *hate* you, and I'm sorry for what I said."

"Why?" she challenged coldly, but the hurt in her eyes shone through. "We both know it's how you feel."

"I'm sorry for the way it came out, but you're right. It's exactly how I felt when you were hired and you strutted in with your glamour girl designer clothes and sky-high heels."

She lifted her chin. "At least you're an honest sanctimonious jerk."

"I don't believe in lying, and you're too smart to think nobody would figure out how you got the job without any experience."

"I don't care what people think. I didn't beg for the job. I had the education, the drive, *and* the talent. The only thing I lacked was experience, and you know damn well they wouldn't have given me the chance if they didn't believe I could do it.

And another thing. You want to talk about busting ass? I've been doing that and *more* every day since I started working for you. But do I get a pat on the back or a *good job, Sutton?* No. You praise everyone else for jobs well done, but you just ride me harder, like nothing I do is good enough."

"Do you want to know *why* I push you so hard?"

"Because you hate that you haven't been able to get me fired yet." She pulled clean shorts out of her pack.

His jaw ticked. It was true he'd wanted her gone at first, but Sutton was a force of nature when she wanted to be, and she'd been chipping away at his misconceptions ever since. "My job is to get results. I push you because when you're given an assignment, you get the job done. But light the right fire under your ass, and you go above and beyond, pushing yourself to do a phenomenal job."

"If that's true, then you suck as a boss. Turn around so I can change." When he did, she said, "What kind of person doesn't give credit for a job well done?"

"If you want to be mollycoddled, you're working for the wrong man."

"I don't want to be mollycoddled," she fumed, her voice muffled, as if she were pulling on her shirt. "I'm talking about showing me some appreciation. It's called encouragement."

He heard her zip her shorts and turned around, stepping closer. "What do you call giving you harder, more interesting assignments than any rookie reporter deserves?"

She lifted her chin, but her brows knitted.

"I've encouraged you every step of the way, just not in the manner you want me to, with cheers and pats on the back. Well, guess what, Steele? You wouldn't be doing half the assignments I've come up with if I treated you that way."

His phone rang, and he snagged it from the dresser, putting it to his ear. "Yeah?" He listened as Santiago spoke swiftly in Spanish. He was ready to fly, but they had to leave right away. Flynn told him they'd be right there and ended the call, turning his attention back to Sutton. "We have to head to the airstrip. Santiago's ready to go. I suggest you change into long sleeves and long pants. Remember to put on bug repellent, and tuck your pants into your boots." He dug his clothes out of his backpack.

"I'm fine in these," she snapped as she rolled up her wet clothes from earlier and put them in a laundry sack.

"If you want to leave all that skin for the bugs, that's up to you, but we're not going to have much daylight to set up camp. And if you step on a snake with nothing covering your ankles, you'll be in real trouble."

She huffed out a breath and started rummaging through her backpack. "I hate it when you're right."

"Don't forget bug repellant on your skin *and* on your clothes." He turned his back to her and dropped his shorts.

"What are you doing?" she snapped.

"Putting on repellant and long pants." He sprayed his legs and boxer briefs.

"I'm *right* here."

He glanced over his shoulder, catching her staring at his ass. "Nobody's forcing you to look." Her cheeks pinked up, and that was a *fine* look on her, but she spun around, stealing it away as he finished changing. He hooked the GPS to his waistband and put his other clothes in his backpack. "Get rid of those crackers and anything else you shouldn't have brought."

"No way. I need them."

"We don't have time to argue, Sutton." He grabbed her

backpack and dug through it.

"Hey!" She charged over and grabbed his arm as he withdrew a large ziplock bag full of peanut butter crackers and granola bars.

"We're supposed to be living off the land." They were given strict guidelines not to bring any food, water, or other survival supplies.

"We could *starve* out there," she snapped.

"Is that what you're going with? Because you know damn well we can survive three weeks without food." He threw the bag of food into the trash can and peered into her pack, spotting a package of something else and pulling it out. "Instant protein coffee? Are you fucking kidding me?"

"Coffee is *life*." She lunged for it, her hand landing on his chest as he lifted the bag out of her reach.

"Sounds like you need a better life." He threw the coffee into the trash. "Where's the hazelnut creamer?"

She scowled.

"Give it up, Steele. It's no good to you without coffee."

She angrily unzipped the body pouch and took out a handful of single-serve creamers. "You're *not* going to like me when I'm hungry and uncaffeinated."

"I don't like you now, remember? Get changed. We've got to go."

Chapter Four

THE SMALL BUSH plane vibrated and whirred as Flynn captured breathtaking views of the river snaking through the dense rainforest. He was glad it had stopped raining by the time they left the airstrip. He was able to get video of Sutton and Santiago as they embarked on this leg of the expedition. Sutton had barely said two words to him after leaving the hotel, but she'd mustered surprisingly good spirits for the camera prior to takeoff.

With wilderness biologists for parents and a grandfather who was both an archaeologist and a paleontologist, Flynn had been going on adventures like this his whole life. While preparing to stay with the indigenous tribe for their original assignment, he'd studied the area and had consulted with one of his grandfather's friends, who had been documenting life in the Ecuadorian Amazon rainforest for more than fifty years. They had mapped out the areas around the tribe to make sure they wouldn't accidentally traipse into locations inhabited by illegal miners, drug traffickers, and the like, or uncontacted tribes. He was looking forward to exploring, but he wasn't happy to have lost the opportunity to stay with an indigenous tribe. That experience would have allowed them to experience ancient culture and history firsthand. Now he was stuck making a fucking reality show with a woman who thought he was the devil.

The plane tilted hard to the right, shaking as it descended toward a grassy patch. Sutton grabbed his hand, her fingernails digging into his flesh. He turned off the video camera and looked at the woman who was always in control. *Except apparently around cracks in a bathroom wall and tilting bush planes.* Their eyes locked, the blaze of heat that seemed to live between them as present as the fear in her colorless face. She yanked her hand away and clung to the edge of her seat, knuckles blanching. His gut seized at her discomfort.

Did she dislike him so much she couldn't admit to being scared?

Fuck that. Like it or not, they were in this together, and he wasn't going to let her feel lost or alone on this expedition. He reached over and pried her fingers from the seat, taking her hand in his. She tried to pull it away, but the fear in her eyes was still there, so he held on tight as the plane descended. "Focus on *me*. It's almost over."

She didn't look away, but those beautiful hazel eyes narrowed and her mouth opened like she was going to make a smart-ass comment just as the plane touched down with a hard, bumpy landing, causing a shocked sound to shoot from her lips. The plane came to an abrupt stop, drawing another fearful sound. She yanked her hand free and turned away, busying herself with preparing to disembark.

He gave her space to calm down, but she still looked shaken after they climbed out of the plane. "You okay, Steele?" he asked as the pilot unloaded their gear.

"*Fine.*"

He knew damn well she was far from fine. She was about to walk into a forest that could swallow her whole. On top of that, she was embarrassed about grabbing his hand on the plane and still pissed about the conversation that had gone down at the hotel. That was a lot to deal with. Too much to handle in the next sixty seconds, so he focused on the one thing he could have an immediate impact on—diffusing her embarrassment. "Thanks for holding my hand. I was rattled up there."

Her eyes flicked to his, and her lips twitched like she didn't know if she should be amused or accuse him of lying.

He lowered his voice like he didn't want Santiago to hear him as he handed Sutton her backpack. "I hate these tiny planes. But if you tell a soul about what just happened, I'll personally feed you to a jaguar."

"You're kinder than me." She shouldered her pack. "My plan is to bury you alive with tarantulas."

"Damn. That's harsh."

"So are *you*," she said cuttingly, and walked away.

Now, there's a view worth filming. He turned on the camera and filmed her heading toward the brush. But they had a show to make, so he cut it short, calling out, "Hey, Steele. Where do you think you're going?"

She turned around, looking at him like he'd asked a stupid question. "I thought I'd take a dip in the pool, maybe grab a cocktail, and with any luck, catch a Magic Mike show."

"Magic Mike will have to wait." He held up the camera. "We have our own show to make."

"You filmed us taking off, and the whole trip here."

Not the whole trip.

"Get over here, Glamour Girl. Let's get a shot of you with the plane taking off behind you, and you can tell the world how excited you are to be embarking on a grand adventure with a hot filmmaker."

"I thought you didn't believe in lying." Without so much as a smirk, she headed for Santiago, turning on the charm for the pilot.

Flynn explained their plan, and they thanked him for flying them out. As Santiago climbed back into the plane, Sutton said, "Aren't you going to be in the intro with me?"

"I don't get in front of the camera," Flynn said. "That's your job."

Santiago started the plane, and Flynn watched Sutton getting into position a safe distance away. She put her hair in a ponytail, did a few mouth stretches, and cleared her throat.

"Ready?" he called out.

She inhaled deeply, blew out the breath, and nodded, putting on a killer smile.

"We'll go on three." Flynn began videoing, with Sutton center screen, and waved to Santiago, giving him the okay to take off, then holding up three fingers on his free hand. When the plane was on-screen but far enough away that the noise wouldn't drown her out, he silently counted down as he lowered his fingers—*Three. Two. One*—and pointed at Sutton.

"What does it really take to survive the Amazon rainforest? That's what I'm in Ecuador to experience firsthand. I'll be spending the next seventy-two hours living off the land, with no assistance from the outside world, no food or water, and one ornery cameraman, who also happens to be my boss, survivalist Flynn Braden, who claims to know his way around the jungle." Her eyes sparked with mischief.

Damn, she was good. The audience would eat that up.

"Join me on this exciting expedition, and see if I fall prey to wild animals or lead them to Flynn. I'm Sutton Steele and *this* is *Discovery Hour*."

Her smile remained in place as he silently counted down again. As soon as that third finger went down, she was gone, strutting toward the forest.

This ought to be fun.

He hung the strap of the camera around his neck, pulled out the machete, and went after her. "It's a rainforest, not a jungle, and if you think I'm going to let you walk into it by yourself, you're wrong." When she didn't stop walking or even acknowledge that he'd spoken, he said, "Just like you're wrong about me hating you."

"If how you treat me is the way you treat people you like, then I feel sorry for your enemies."

"I don't have enemies. Have you ever stopped to think about how you act toward me?"

"I'm too busy fending off your disapproving looks."

Unwilling to take part in more of a pissing match with her, he ground his back teeth and stepped around her.

"Of course *you* have to lead the way," she said exasperatedly.

He stopped and looked at her. "Do you know how to spot deadly plants? Tarantula nests? Big cat scat?"

Her eyes widened a little, but the confidence in her voice didn't falter. "I did my research."

"I know you did, and I'm sure you did an excellent job of it, but for once in your life, trust me. When it comes to this place, nothing prepares you like experience." Karen hadn't needed to remind him that he'd promised to stick by Sutton's side every minute and that she was holding him to it. He was holding himself to it. He stepped closer, speaking low and evenly so she would hear every word. "Everything in this forest wants to kill us, including the weather. If you want to get out of here alive and well…" Stopping himself from saying, *I suggest you let me lead*, he went with, "I suggest we do this together. In case one of us misses something."

The seriousness he was hoping to see finally rose above the anger in her eyes. "Okay."

"Let's take a second to catch our breath and prepare. We need to keep our ears and eyes open. Look before every step you take, but always be aware of what's lurking around you. In an hour, whether you like it or not, all your senses will be heightened, as will your anxiety. We'll need to look for wells of collected rainwater in leaves and rocks, and you don't want to move anything with your hands. We need to find a couple of long sticks."

"There's one." She reached for a branch on the ground, but he grabbed her wrist, stopping her. "You just said we need sticks."

"That's right, but if you pick that up and end up with aggressive ant bites or piss off a snake that's hiding under it, you're in trouble. Think of the rainforest floor as one giant cobweb just waiting to suck you in and never let you go. Before you pick up anything, scrutinize it. Look around it for signs of what might be under it. Look for marks on the ground that could indicate a creature large or small is nearby. Remember, animals slither, burrow, climb, hang, fly, and swim. They sting, bite, and spit, and in some cases, just touching something can kill you or make you very sick. In other cases, like with snakes, you can cut their heads off and hours later they can still bite and kill you."

New fear rose in her eyes. She inhaled deeply, swallowing hard, and nodded. "Okay."

"This place is no joke, Sutton. There are illegal miners, drug runners, poachers, and uncontacted tribes who know outsiders are trying to take over their land. They'll kill you with poison darts before you have a chance to flash that pretty smile of yours and explain why you're here. I've mapped out the area, and we should be safe from the criminals and other tribes, but you can never count on that safety. I'm sure I'm going to sound like a sanctimonious ass a lot of the time while we're here, and it's okay if you hate me for it. I'd rather get us through this safely than be on your favorite-friend list."

Those keen eyes narrowed. "I don't think you're in danger of landing on that list, but I do appreciate you keeping me safe."

SUTTON WAS HOT and sweaty and her heart hadn't stopped racing since they got on the plane. It felt like they'd been walking for hours, and it had rained for a good part of it. It had finally stopped a little while ago, but everything was wet and buggy, and the deeper they went into the forest, the more terrified *and* awestruck she became.

One of the things she loved most about reporting was that while she was on camera, all other thoughts and worries fell away, and she became solely focused on the subjects she was covering. She had a feeling that would not happen here. If she wasn't watching her step or their surroundings, she was looking up and around for the source of noises, which were constant and came from every direction. There were screeches, chirps, birds singing, and rustling along the forest floor. She'd startled at birds taking flight and plants brushing along her hands. Thankfully, they hadn't seen any big cats or their scat, although

Flynn said big cats were elusive and rarely seen. That made her feel better *and* worse. She imagined big cats hunting them, biding their time for the right moment to pounce. She tried to shut down those thoughts, but just knowing the man-eating cats were out there was enough to make her want to stick close to Flynn. The man wielded the machete like it was an extension of his arm, and he was a walking knowledge base on the rainforest, showing her which plants to avoid, stopping to gather edible flowers, plants, and mushrooms, explaining how he knew they were safe to eat, and showing her where animals had traipsed.

Despite her fear, she was as impressed and thankful for how much he knew as she was mesmerized by the beauty of the rainforest. Tall trees loomed around them like lanky giants, their umbrellas allowing only streaks of sunlight to illuminate the mist hanging in the humid air. Spiders and bugs crawled on the greenest leaves she'd ever seen, and thick, woody, moss-covered vines hung from trees in loopy tangles like giant snakes. There were vibrantly colored butterflies and other winged insects all around them, and it seemed no two were alike. Then there was the earthy, damp smell hanging in the air. There was something appealing about that pungent smell, so different from the fabricated scents of her daily life.

Flynn stopped abruptly and stepped closer. "Look up there." He pointed to two small monkeys with orange along their necks and chests running along the branches above them and watching them. "They're golden-mantled tamarins."

"They're watching us. I want to say they're cute, but are they dangerous?"

"No. They're just curious. I'd like to get your initial thoughts on video for the show."

"Yeah, definitely. It's amazing seeing them in the wild instead of behind an enclosure in the zoo."

"They don't belong in zoos. You can talk about the monkeys first in case they decide to take off."

"Okay. But if a puma eats me, promise me you won't let my parents see the video."

"Deal. But just a heads-up. If something eats me, my parents will probably want to see it."

"If something eats *you*, I'm not sticking around to film it and become its dessert."

"Fair enough." He laughed softly. "Hold still."

As he reached for her face, she panicked. "*What is it?* A spider? A bug?"

"Just dirt." He wiped her cheek.

The breath rushed from her lungs in relief. "Thank you."

He stepped back to get the video camera ready. "It's good that you're scared, Sutton. You're more likely not to let your guard down and do something that could get you into trouble."

"I don't think it's possible to let my guard down in here."

"Let's hope it stays that way, and for the record, I'd never hold that fear against you."

She was about to make a smart-ass remark when she remembered what he'd said earlier. *Have you ever stopped to think about how you act toward me?* "I appreciate that. Do you want me to do a brief intro telling viewers where we are, so they know we're deep in the rainforest, and then skip it for the rest of the time we're here?"

"That's a good idea. We can always add something later if we need to. Let's get to the good stuff."

He actually smiled, and it wasn't smirky or fake. It was the kind of smile that said they'd finally agreed on something and he was glad about it, rather than just relieved by it. That made her feel the tiniest bit less stressed as he counted down to start filming and pointed at her.

"We're coming to you from deep within the Amazon rainforest, where two golden-mantled tamarin monkeys are frolicking on branches above us and checking out the intruders." She pointed to the tree, and he moved the camera in that direction, lingering for a few seconds before returning to her. "As you can imagine, everything here is wet, and there's vegetation on every surface. We have to watch where we step and use sticks to move things so we don't surprise snakes or other animals." She held up her stick. "I'd like to invite you to take a moment to listen to the plethora of sounds serenading us."

She was quiet for a long moment. "There's never a lull in the noises of birds, animals, and insects. The dangers here are very real, but beyond the lush greens that cover the rainforest is a rainbow of vibrant colors. We passed flowers and plants that were shocking pink, deep purple, bloodred, and sunny shades of yellow. The rainforest is as magnificent as it is terrifying. It feels like we've stepped into another world, and in a way, we have. To a time when humans didn't monopolize so much of the earth. Governments can claim ownership of this land, but make no mistake, this is not *our* rainforest. Those monkeys, and all the other creatures who live here, own this land. We *are* the intruders, and we'll do our best to leave it as beautiful as we found it."

She stopped talking, but he kept the camera on her. She waited at least twenty seconds before finally saying, "Are you going to stop filming?"

"Yeah. *Sorry.*" He turned the camera off and put the strap around his neck. "That was fantastic."

She was stunned. He *never* complimented her like that. "Are you just saying that because I gave you shit for not showing any appreciation or encouragement earlier?"

"Hell no. That was raw and passionate and *real*, and like I said, Steele. I encourage you, just not the way you want me to."

He sounded sincere, and looked it, too. Something unexpectedly bright bloomed inside her—and that annoyed her. She didn't like that she wanted his praise, but didn't everyone like hearing that they were doing a good job? Their earlier argument came back to her, giving her pause. He *had* given her tougher assignments than newbie reporters were usually given, and she had no idea how he could have known it, but she had always responded well to a challenge. The jerk was right, and *that* annoyed her, too.

"You're starting to look like you want to kill me again," Flynn said. "Let's get out of here and find a place to make camp. We still need to find a water supply and food."

As they headed deeper into the forest, she said, "We'd have food if you hadn't thrown away my crackers."

"Let it go, Steele."

Chapter Five

"I KEEP MISTAKING those woody vines for snakes." Sutton pointed ahead of them to a hanging vine that formed a loop close to the ground and wound around the trunk of the tree.

"And here I thought you just liked the feel of my arm." She'd been grabbing his arm every time she startled. Not that he was complaining. He was glad she felt safe enough with him to realize she could rely on him. "Those woody vines are called lianas, and they're actually a classification of how something grows, like a tree or a bush or shrub. They can reach more than seven hundred feet long."

"That's huge."

"They actually serve a purpose." He swung the machete to clear a plant from their path. "The soil is shallow, and the vines help hold up the trees. Unlike the strangler fig, which starves them."

"What's a strangler fig?"

"See the tree over there that looks like it's being hugged by a tree with octopus arms?" He pointed to a strangler fig.

"We've passed a few of those. They're kind of pretty."

"You'll see a lot of them here. The outer tree is the strangler fig. Animals poop out their seeds in the branches of other trees.

They germinate and become vines, making their way down the tree to the soil, where they suck up all the nutrients. As the vines grow, they attach to the tree, and eventually they starve the trees they're hanging from. When the host tree dies, you'll see the stranglers with a hollow center."

"I think I saw one when we first came into the forest."

"You'll see many more while we're here," he assured her. "Mother Nature is pretty cool."

"She's got a wicked sense of humor, that's for sure."

As they pushed past a waist-high plant, a stream came into view. "And she just made my day. Check it out."

"Can we drink that?"

"No. You can't drink any water that's touched the plants or ground here until it's purified. We don't know what animals, insects, or bacteria it's come in contact with. But we're not taking the stream water. It's the rainwater that's pooling in the rocks that we want."

"Let's go." She started to head in that direction, and he grabbed her hand.

"Slow down. Remember, animals need water as much as we do, so before we plow ahead and take what isn't ours, let's look around and make sure we're not getting in any creatures' way. Look for big and small animals, especially snakes." He grinned. "And those nasty viperish vines."

"Very funny."

He chuckled and they scanned the area before making their way to the rocks. "We need to be creative to gather the water so we don't waste it, and we'll purify it once we make camp. I think it's important that we film this for the show."

"Absolutely."

"I can give you directions and you can explain it to the

audience while you do each step, but that gives you time to mentally prepare."

"And that's bad?"

"It's not bad, but it's not raw. I think it'll come across better if they experience it in real time with you. Let the audience see your successes and your failures."

"Is that why you're not getting on camera? To avoid exposing your failures?"

He gritted his teeth. "*No.* This isn't about me. You're the reporter. I'm just here to keep you safe, film the show, and prove to my boss we can share the sandbox. Think you can play nice and take directions from me while we film so they get something authentic? Or should I turn off the sound and do a voice-over later?"

She gave him a deadpan look. "Give me a little credit."

"Okay, but keep in mind that calling me a dick is not audience appropriate."

"Damn, *really?*" she said sarcastically. "What about jerk?"

He wiggled his hand in a so-so fashion, earning a smile. He got the canteens out of the gear bag and handed them to her. "Here we go, Glamour Girl. But can you please call it a rainforest and not a jungle?"

"Yes, of course. I have no idea why I even said that before."

"Viewers learn from us. We want to educate them correctly."

"Yes, I *know*," she said defensively. "*Jungle* is a descriptor, not a scientific term. It doesn't refer to a specific ecosystem the way *rainforest* does. In here, there's not much sunlight because of the thick canopy of trees, and even though it seems like there's a lot of growth on the rainforest floor, there's not compared to a jungle, which has more sunlight, more vegetation, and more growth on the ground. Here, most of the action happens up there." She pointed up. "In the jungle, it happens down there." She pointed to the ground.

He was amused and impressed. Then again, she had yet to disappoint him on an assignment. "Someone did her homework."

"Of course I did, and by the way, in my research, the rainforest was often called a jungle."

"If you read information written fifty years ago, that was the term that was used. Anything since then must have been written by misinformed people."

"Which is exactly why you said something." She nodded, as if she was realizing he wasn't just being a pushy ass. "Got it."

"A'right then, Steele. Let's do this." He lifted the camera, waiting for her to flash that killer smile, which meant she was ready to report. He silently counted down and pointed at her.

"One of the scariest things about being in the rainforest is that you can starve to death or die of dehydration. A person can go three days without water and three weeks without food. After only a few hours of sweating profusely while trekking through the rainforest, I'm famished and so thirsty, I can't imagine making it through the night without a drink. We've gathered some edible plants and flowers, and we've just come across small pools of rainwater that have gathered in the crevices and valleys of large rocks."

Flynn panned to the pools of water, the largest of which was only about six inches long and four inches wide, and then panned back to her.

"We don't know what types of bacteria this water might have come in contact with, so we're going to collect it in our canteens, and we'll purify it once we set up camp. Flynn is going to guide me through this process, and you get to come along for the ride. Okay, Flynn, where do we start?"

Sutton never hemmed or hawed on camera, but she usually had time to prepare. As pissed as he was about being in the rainforest, if they hadn't been there, he might never have gotten to see that she was a natural at impromptu reporting. There weren't many people who could pull that off without seeming uncomfortable or ill prepared. That opened doors to the types of stories they could cover.

"Why don't we start with the largest pool of water. You'll need two big leaves that you can use as a funnel."

"That should be easy. Look at all these leafy plants." She motioned around them. "But the rainforest is tricky. We can't just pluck a leaf from a plant without first visually inspecting it to be sure there are no nasty creatures lurking about. Let's see what we can find." She looked over the leafy plants to her right and crouched to inspect beneath the leaves, quickly stumbling backward, eyes wide. "I think we'll skip that one."

"What's wrong with it?"

"There's a *huge* spider on the bottom of that leaf."

"Let's get a look at that spider." He got a shot from under the leaf. "That's a scary-looking dude, but it's not a spider. It's a tailless whip scorpion. They're nonvenomous but quick moving—" The scorpion jumped off the underside of the leaf, and Flynn stepped back. Sutton screamed, grabbing the back of his shirt as the scorpion took off into the brush. "It's all fun and games until a scorpion shows up."

"*Ohmygod.* Are you still filming?" she asked in a panic.

"Of course." He turned the camera on her. "Now you can get that leaf."

"Right." She forced a smile, but her eyes said he'd pay for

that later. She scanned the ground again before reinspecting that leaf and another and tearing them from the stems. She held them up with a real smile this time. "Two scorpion-free leaves."

"Excellent. Now comes the tricky part."

"And you thought avoiding the scorpion was tricky," she said to the camera.

Damn, he liked this side of her. "Being careful not to tear the leaf, you're going to roll one of them into a funnel and put the thinner side in the canteen. Make the other side as wide as possible. That's the side you'll use to collect the water." He waited for her to make the funnel.

"How's this?"

"Perfect. You'll want to position the wide end of the funnel at one end of the crevice, in the water, and then use the other leaf like a scoop, slowly pushing the water into the funnel."

"That might be easier if you helped me."

"It would be easier, but you can do it."

She scowled, quickly catching herself, and turned it into a camera-ready grin as she got into position and said, "And that's just one reason I might have to feed Flynn to the wild animals."

She probably thought he'd edit that out, but her frustration, and the look of determination on her face while she collected the water, was what made this footage stand out. When she'd collected all she could, he said, "See? You barely lost a drop. How do you think you can get the last little bit that's left?"

"Why bother? There are two other pools of water."

"Because while it's not much water, you'll be thankful for every drop tomorrow."

She studied the small amount of water in the crevice, brow furrowed. "I can't get it with the leaf, and I can't use the leaf like a straw because we can't put the water in our mouths." She looked at him curiously.

"One way to do it is to use your shirt to soak it up, then drain it into the canteen."

"Will that work when there's so little water?"

"There's only one way to find out."

"Okay, let's try it." She used the hem of her shirt to soak it up and was able to only wring out a few drops, but the light in her eyes told him she was glad she'd done it. "Look at that. It worked. What else you got, Braden?"

And you can't understand why I push you.

Chapter Six

"STUPID TENT. I swear they make these things as difficult as possible to put together," Sutton grumbled to herself, wresting with the freaking tent poles while Flynn went to find a log he could split to see if the inside was dry enough to burn. They were supposed to have *two* tents. But there was only one in the gear bag, which she was going to give Karen hell for when they got back. If that wasn't bad enough, they'd sent the hardest tent in the world to put together. Every time she got the plastic tubes together, they popped out and the tent smacked her in the face. When it flew up for the fourth time, she threw it on the ground and heard a chuckle. She spun around, shooting a death stare at Flynn as he videoed her. "Are you freaking kidding me? I thought you were out getting wood."

"This was too good to miss." He laughed and continued videoing.

"Would you put that thing down and help me?"

"But this is so much more fun."

She stalked over to him, glowering. "Know what's *not* fun? Being hungry, thirsty, and *wet* and thinking *you're* going to get wood so we can get more comfortable. But I'm still wet, and you have no wood."

Laughter burst from his lips, deep and throaty, his beaming smile lighting up his entire face, making him look even hotter, which pissed her off.

"*Why* is that funny?"

"Do you really need me to explain?"

She realized her mistake and tried to scowl, but she couldn't keep a straight face. "Shut up. You know what I meant, and *stop* filming!" She yanked the camera from him, but the strap was still around his neck and he flew forward, their bodies crashing together, which made him laugh harder and annoyed her even more as she lost her balance, her arms flailing. He swung the camera on its strap over his shoulder with one hand, catching her with his other around her waist, and crushing her to him. Laughter broke through her frustration, and she buried her face in his shirt.

Even hot and sweaty the man smelled good. The kind of good that took her mind to darker places. She imagined his naked, glistening body pressing down on hers—

"If you wanted to be close to me, all you had to do was ask." His voice was teasing and gruff at once.

Cheeks burning, she kept her face hidden against his chest. "I hate you right now."

"Well, that's a damn shame, isn't it?" His hand flattened against her back, and his tone softened. "You know, it's okay *not* to hate me, Steele."

The way he said it, she wasn't sure if he meant he was a good guy and to cut him a break, or something deeper. She looked up at him to try to figure it out, and their eyes connected with that sizzling heat that fractured her thoughts and had her fingers curling tighter into his shirt. Their laughter silenced, his smile smoldering. His lips were *right there*. Had they always been so perfectly bowed and tempting? For the second time today, she was all too aware of how good he felt, and *that* startled her out of her reverie.

What the heck was wrong with her? She needed to get her head on straight. The rainforest must be making her delirious. That was the only logical explanation for the desire pooling inside her. Forcing herself to step out of his arms took more effort than it should, as if the forest itself was winding around them, drawing them together. "I think I'll stick to disliking you, at least until you give me a dry place to sleep."

"Now, there's some motivation." He cocked a grin and headed for the tent. "These things can be pesky."

"More like *impossible*." She watched him expertly set up the tent in a matter of minutes.

"Let's make sure there are no tears or creepy-crawlies before we put our gear in it." He crawled inside the diminutive tent, inspecting the seams and sides.

"How are we both supposed to fit in that thing with all of our stuff?"

"There's plenty of room."

Maybe if we were conjoined twins.

He climbed out of the tent, and as he zipped it closed, she said, "Don't zip it. We need to put our stuff inside."

"We need to make sure our gear has no critters on it before putting it in the tent, and I don't want any unwanted visitors getting in while we do that."

"Good thinking."

They checked their gear, and after it was safely put away, she felt a modicum of relief.

He grabbed the machete and his walking stick. "Let's go find some chontacuro worms for dinner."

She'd read about the fat worms that were harvested from chonta palm trees, but the thought of eating them turned her stomach. "As delicious as that sounds, I think I'll enjoy a vegan meal tonight. I'm good with flowers and plants. I'll contemplate diving into those delectable worms tomorrow."

"Tomorrow I'm hoping we can catch some fish, but you've got to be starved."

"Honestly, I don't have much of an appetite tonight. But I'm happy to film you finding and eating worms."

"Nice try. I'm not getting on camera, but I will eat them after *we* gather them. There's not much daylight left. Let's find a place to use as a bathroom. You'll definitely want to go before it gets dark. But if you have to go at night, let me know and I'll stand guard."

"There's no way I'm going to the bathroom after dark." She followed him into the forest.

"I grabbed a bunch of moss along the way to use as toilet paper."

"No, thank you. I brought biodegradable wipes. You're welcome to use them."

He frowned. "That's cheating, Steele."

"Cheating would be staying in a resort and spending an hour here filming, or bringing bottled water and ready-made meals. Look at me." She held out her arms. "I'm sweatier and grimier than I've ever been. I'm starving and thirsty and every noise makes my heart race. I'm going to drink the disgusting water and eat God knows what to survive, but I draw the line at getting bugs in my cooch. You're a guy. You just whip it out and go. I have to squat, and who knows what might jump up and bite my ass or worse. I brought unscented facial and body wipes, too, so my face wouldn't break out and I wouldn't feel gross all the time. But don't worry, I also brought ziplock bags. I'm not going to leave either type of wipes behind and ruin the rainforest."

"You brought ziplock bags? What else are you hiding?"

"*Nothing.* You threw out my other necessities."

"Peanut butter crackers and coffee are not necessities. They're luxuries. Are you sure there's no kitchen sink in your backpack?"

"Very funny. I brought a Snugpak, because I thought it would be uncomfortable sleeping in a hut with the tribe, but it's not like I'm hiding it."

He lifted his brows in question.

She rolled her eyes. "It's an ultralight sleeping bag that has built-in netting to cover my face so no snakes or spiders can get to me at night."

"I know what a Snugpak is. I just can't believe you brought one. We're supposed to be roughing it."

"Look around you, Braden," she said loudly. "We're searching for a safe place to pee in the rainforest. This *is* roughing it, and I asked Karen if I could bring the Snugpak. She said it was fine."

"Didn't you grow up on an island? Didn't you ever go camping there?"

"*Yes*, but the island isn't like this. I roughed it many times on the beach."

"And by that you mean, what? You fell asleep in the sand after a party and didn't make it home?"

"No."

He cocked a brow, poking at something on the ground with his stick.

"Fine. *Yes*, but it *was* roughing it. It gets cold at night by the ocean, and there are sand flies, and we have foxes and other wild animals. It's not a walk in the park."

He stifled a laugh.

"Okay, maybe it *is* a walk in the park compared to this, but it wasn't like there were bathrooms on the beach."

"You had to run home, didn't you?"

"*No*. We peed in the water or held it until morning." She lowered her voice. "Or we went to whoever's house was closest."

"And the truth comes out. I thought you were tougher than this, Steele, but if you're comfortable misleading the audience, you can use your wipes. Just be sure to carry them out."

She should feel victorious, but he had a valid point that she hadn't thought about. He was right. It was cheating. She didn't want to mislead the audience, and she was surprised to realize she didn't like disappointing Flynn, either. "Are you going to narc on me to the audience?"

"That's not my job. If you're comfortable with the world thinking you roughed it when you used wipes on your tender tush, that's on you." He walked around a bush and checked out the surrounding area. "This'll work as our bathroom. I'll dig a hole. If you poop, cover it with a leaf."

"I am not pooping in the same hole as you."

"Everyone poops, Sutton."

"You're not putting anything in my poop hole."

He laughed.

"*Ohmygod*." She shoved him, laughing.

"Who knew you could be this much fun?"

"*Please*. Anyone who knows me could have told you that, but you're better at bringing out my claws than my fun side."

He started digging a hole with the stick. "In that case, I'll talk about your poop hole more often."

AS MUCH AS Sutton had been dreading spending this time with Flynn, by sundown she had to admit that he wasn't as jerky as she'd thought he was. Or rather, as he had been before the trip. He'd not only dug separate holes as their bathroom areas, but he'd also left a trail of bright pink flowers leading to hers, and more around it. He'd made a joke about making sure she knew which one was the ladies' room, but it felt like an olive branch. He also promised to stand guard every time she went and insisted she take the hatchet with her in case anything crept up on her. His protectiveness and sense of humor were a nice, unexpected change of pace that made it easier for Sutton to let her guard down.

As much as she hated to admit it, she liked this Flynn Braden, with his sexy smiles, lighthearted comments, and caveman skills, and that rattled her in a whole new way. There was comfort in the familiar feelings of disliking him. They had made it easier to ignore her attraction to him. But she didn't know what to do with this new affinity for her boss. She shouldn't notice the way those sexy smiles made his eyes crinkle at the corners or how he moved through the forest with hawklike vision and the power and stealth of a panther, and she definitely shouldn't like the way his rough laugh made her stomach quiver.

But it was hard not to notice those things when he was treating her differently in other ways, too. He'd pushed her in the past, and he'd taught her things, but not in this friendly, patient, we're-in-this-together manner. She'd made careless mistakes when they'd first set out, and instead of snapping at her, he'd taught her why she needed to do things differently. He'd quickly proven that he had in fact earned the right to act like he had all the answers, because he did have them. He made her feel safe, and not only did he know how to handle every situation, but he was taking the time to make sure she did, too.

They were sitting by a crackling fire, which they'd made in a hole lined with rocks, and it seemed every insect, moth, and butterfly was drawn to the flames. She'd thought everything was too wet to burn, but Flynn had a solution for that, too. He'd shown her how to use the hatchet to chop off a section of a fallen tree and had videoed her doing it for the show. She was proud of being strong enough to help. He split the log and showed her how to carve off shavings from the dry center of the wood to use as kindling. They used larger, center pieces of drier wood to keep the fire going, and his primitive method of purifying water was brilliant, too.

They gathered rocks and placed them in the fire. Together they hollowed out a bowl-shaped area in the fallen tree and poured their water into the hollowed area. They used sticks to pick scalding rocks out of the fire and put them in the water. As the rocks cooled, they swapped them with others from the fire until the water boiled, and then they kept it going for two full minutes. They refilled the canteens using the same methods they'd used earlier. If she hadn't seen the water boil with her own eyes, she wouldn't have believed it possible.

She looked at him sitting beside her, his elbows resting on his legs, hands clasped together, his tousled hair hanging over his forehead. He looked as comfortable as if he were sitting by a bonfire in a yard or on a beach, while she startled at every noise and every bug. For the first time since they'd begun working together, she was curious about who he was and how he'd become a survivalist. The sounds of things scampering along the forest floor had her grabbing his arm and spinning around, scanning their surroundings. "What was that?"

"Not a big cat."

"How do you know?" The panic in her voice was palpable.

"Because they're stealthy, and whatever that was, was in a hurry and moving away from us."

"You can tell all that from that brief sound?"

"Yes." He rubbed his right shoulder, then bent his right elbow and moved that arm in a circular motion, like he was stretching it.

She'd seen him do that a few times today. "Are you okay?"

"Yeah. Fine. I just pinched something. Are you getting hungry yet?"

She was starving, but she was trying to convince herself she wasn't. They'd eaten most of the flowers and plants they'd picked, and she was surprised that they hadn't tasted that bad. They'd found a handful of chontacuro worms in a rotting tree and were currently roasting them on sticks with the mushrooms Flynn had gathered. The thumb-sized worms were as fat as slugs with black heads and tan, ridged bodies.

"No. I'm fine," she lied.

He eyed her with amused disbelief.

She looked over her shoulder toward a shuffling noise. The noises felt different at night, more pronounced, but that was probably just her fear taking hold, and there was a constant high-pitched sound, as if the forest were filled with cicadas.

"Looking for your hit man?"

"*No.* We had a chat while you were digging our bathroom facilities. I told him to wait until tomorrow to make the hit."

"Does that mean your hatred for me is wearing off?"

"You wish. I need something to stave off the wild animals if they show up tonight."

He grinned. "Now you're thinking like a survivalist."

"Don't let this go to your head, but I have a pretty good teacher." She watched him move the skewers away from the fire and set them on a rock to cool. "You're really going to eat those worms?"

"Yes, and so are you."

"*No*, I'm not."

He gave her a look that said she was being stubborn. "You've probably expended more energy today than you have in weeks, and you'll need your strength for tomorrow."

"I'll be fine. I do yoga, and I've gone a night without eating before."

He raked his hair away from his face. "I heard you earlier, griping about yoga not giving you the muscles you needed for traipsing through the rainforest."

She hadn't realized he'd heard her bitching. "That's because I've been doing yoga for a few years, and I considered myself fairly strong until I had to carry that heavy backpack through the rain for hours. But just because I wish I was stronger doesn't mean I need to eat grilled worms."

"I think you did great today. You really pulled your weight, and those worms are loaded with protein and vitamins. They're a lot better for you than those processed peanut butter crackers you eat all the time. Natives claim these worms are a cure-all for a list of things from coughs and asthma to gastritis and arthritis."

"None of which I have, thank you very much."

He picked up a skewer and studied the worms. "It's okay. I get it, Glamour Girl."

"What's *that* supposed to mean?"

"Just that you're cool as long as there are butt wipes and a Snugpak, but you're not very adventurous at heart."

"How can you say that? Look where we are."

"You came against your will to keep your job."

That was true. When she'd convinced Karen to let her go into the rainforest, she'd thought they were staying in a hut with a tribe of hunters to keep her safe. "So? I'm still here, aren't I?"

"Hey, I get it. You don't mind the viewers talking behind your back about how you couldn't hack the hard stuff, and that's okay."

Her competitive spirit kicked in, and she narrowed her eyes. "There's *nothing* I can't hack."

"Prove it." He popped a worm into his mouth, chewed it up, and swallowed it down with a taunting lift of his brows.

"I know what you're doing."

He leaned into her side, speaking playfully. "Come on, Steele. Show the world what you're made of before it's too dark to see." He reached for the camera.

It was hard to say no when she wasn't hating him. "You get some sort of sick pleasure out of annoying me, don't you?"

"I guess I'm just a glutton for punishment." He lifted the camera. "No intro. Just get to the heart of it. On three."

"*Wait.* You're not giving me time to think of what to say."

"That makes it better. Go with what you feel. *One. Two. Three.*" He pointed at her.

"As you can see, it's nearly dark, and it seems like every insect in the forest has come to join our cookout." She motioned to the insects swarming around the fire. "I've given up trying to swat them away. There are too many to worry about.

I've decided to peacefully coexist with them. Unless something harmful lands on me—then all bets are off."

Flynn's approval showed in his smile, and she tried not to notice how good that looked on him.

"We've just finished roasting the chontacuro worms we harvested earlier." She held up a skewer. "I'm told these little guys have healing properties, and they're packed with vitamins and protein. Let's see if they can heal my annoyance at my pushy boss who won't let me get away without eating one. Here goes nothing."

She pulled one of the worms off the skewer, prayed she wouldn't throw up on camera, and popped it into her mouth. She held her breath, hoping she looked as casual as Flynn had when he'd eaten one, but as she bit down, cracking through the crunchy outer shell, she felt herself wincing at the mushy, warm center spilling out. She managed to chew it quickly and swallow it down, and was surprised she didn't feel the urge to gag. "That was not bad. It tastes kind of like fried pork rinds mixed with something mushy and woodsy."

"Could you eat them every day?" Flynn asked from behind the camera.

"If my choices were to eat them or die, I definitely could. Although it would probably taste better with salt and other seasonings." She smiled. "That said, I don't think I'll be seeking them out after we leave the rainforest. Assuming we make it through the night." She looked around the darkening forest, trying not to flinch as something howled in the distance. "I'm not generally afraid of the dark, but I'd be lying if I said I wasn't wishing for a hotel room with a nice hot shower and four protective walls." She shielded her mouth with her hand and lowered her voice, as if sharing a secret with the viewers. "Stay tuned to see if I roast my boss next."

Flynn waited a few seconds before turning off the camera. "That was great. What did you really think of the chontacuro worms?"

"I was honest. It wasn't nearly as bad as I thought it would be."

"Good. Are you glad you tried it?"

"I want *so* badly to say no, but *yes*, I'm proud of myself, and I can't believe I'm saying this, but I'm glad you pushed me to do it."

"Ha! See? There is a method to my madness." He offered her more worms.

"No, thanks."

"Come on, Steele. You know you're still hungry." He waved the skewer in front of her.

"I'm stuffed," she said with a laugh.

He popped a worm into his mouth. "Mm-mm. Tastes like steak."

He pulled another off the skewer and goaded her until they were both laughing, and she gave in and ate one more. He finished the rest of them and licked his fingers. "Now, that was tasty."

"You're such a weirdo. Would it be awful if I used a tiny bit of our water to brush my teeth?"

"Why? You got a date?" he teased.

"*Please.* The men I know are hardly worth brushing my teeth for. I haven't even gone on a date in six months." She couldn't remember the last time she'd had sex. But she didn't miss it. She hadn't been with that many men, but she'd been with enough to know they always left her unsatisfied and feeling a little empty.

"It's been three times that for me."

She couldn't tell if he was kidding or not, and although she was curious, she didn't want to get into a dating discussion with Flynn, so she let it go and said, "Probably because you sleep with worm guts in your teeth."

Chapter Seven

AS DARKNESS CREPT in, Sutton's senses were on high alert. Not just from the dangers lurking in the forest, but from Flynn's close proximity beside her on a log by the fire. Without the buffer of animosity, everything felt intimate. Even brushing their teeth had taken on a strange closeness. She tried to focus on the insects fluttering around them and not the quickening of her pulse every time their arms or legs touched.

"Look at us, getting along like old friends," Flynn said.

"I wouldn't go that far." Sutton didn't want to touch any of her old friends, and it was all she could think about doing with him. "How did you learn so much about survival?"

"It's in my blood."

"What does that mean? Were your ancestors tribesmen?"

"No, but that would've been cool. My grandfather is an archaeologist and paleontologist, and my parents are wildlife biologists, although my mom has worked as a wildlife photographer since my oldest sister and brother were born. They've always stressed the importance of learning from nature and understanding it, so we can nurture it rather than destroy it."

"Those are great lessons."

"Yeah, and they gave us every opportunity to learn from

them. My parents wanted it all. Their careers, family, travel, and they wanted us to have it all, too, which is why we traveled with my father for his assignments."

"Wow. How often did you travel?"

"Most of the time. We had our home base in Ridgeport, Mass, but we lived overseas for months at a time until I was eleven, when my older sister and brothers put their feet down about traveling so much. We also visited my grandfather on some of his expeditions, which I loved. I used to think he was a real-life Indiana Jones. He even has a cool name."

"What is it?"

"He goes by his middle name, Bradshaw Braden. Tell me that's not every bit as great as Indiana Jones."

"It is a great name. Why does he go by his middle name?"

"Because when he was young, a bully found out what his middle name was, and I guess he thought it was funny and made fun of him, so my grandfather told everyone to call him Bradshaw to show the little jerk that he didn't care what he said, and it stuck."

"Good for him. That takes guts."

"He's still a tough old bird. I can't imagine what he was like as a kid."

"Are you close with him?"

"Very. When I was a teenager, after we settled in at Ridgeport and stopped traveling so much, all I wanted was to get back out there and see more of the world, so my parents let me travel with my grandparents. It was *awesome*. My grandmother is amazing. She takes everything in stride, and my grandfather never treated me like a kid. He taught me about everything he was doing. He believes kids are never too young to learn how to do things right."

"That explains how you knew so much when we did the story on the archaeological site last year."

"Yes, it does. I could ask him anything as a kid. Still can. Nothing is off-limits."

"He sounds like my grandmother. She's always been my confidante."

"Yeah?" His intrigued blue eyes found hers, and that new familiarity took hold, momentarily stealing her thoughts.

"Mm-hm."

"It's nice, having someone older who you trust and can be completely honest with. We talked about everything from girls to staying on a solid path and not getting lost in drugs and drinking. He's always been big on life lessons. He used to say, *Boy, stay grounded in the things that matter, and you'll never be lonely. Family, helping others, and doing what you can to help keep this beautiful earth we've been gifted from being destroyed.*"

"My grandmother's like, *Honey, you only live once. Go out there and have some fun.*"

He laughed. "Sounds like she and my grandparents would get along well."

"Your grandparents sound really special. Are they still active?"

"Very. My grandfather's always cooking up some scheme, driving my grandmother crazy with trips and ideas for archaeological excursions. He's made some incredible discoveries over the years, like a thousand-year-old mummy at a site in Peru and the skeleton of a theropod dinosaur."

"Wow, exploring really is in your blood."

"Yeah. When we were young, we traveled all over the globe. South America, Asia, you name it, we've probably been there. We've lived in homes and tents and huts. We spent a lot of time in the Torricelli Mountains of New Guinea, where my father discovered the northern glider back in the eighties, and the year before I was born, he and my mother spotted a new species of tree kangaroo in the same mountains. The golden-mantled tree kangaroo."

"That's wild. Is that kangaroo related to the golden-mantled monkeys we saw?"

"No. Golden-mantled just refers to the coloring across their shoulders."

"I can't imagine growing up on the move like that. Was it hard to make friends when you traveled? How did you go to school?"

"Are you doing a story on me, Steele?" he teased.

"*Sorry.* It's just that on the island, community was as much a part of my life as my own family was. We went to school with the same kids every year and hung out with their families. I can't imagine not having that."

"It was all I knew, and I loved it, so I didn't see it as hard or feel like I was missing out. My mom homeschooled us when we traveled remotely, and there were kids in some of the places we went, but even when there weren't, I was never bored. I had my brothers and sister, and I was a curious kid. I wanted to know the *why*s and *how*s of everything. According to my mom, I came out of her womb asking how I got here. I'm pretty sure I drove my older siblings nuts. I was so fascinated by the places we went and the things we saw and did, I assumed everyone was. I didn't want them to miss out on anything, so I was always rambling about it."

She wondered if that was part of the reason he pushed her so hard, to make sure she didn't miss out on anything. But she wasn't about to ask and open up that can of worms when they were finally getting along, so she asked about his family, which she was curious about. Leni had told her a little about Seth, and she knew his brother Clay played for the New York Giants, but she'd never been interested enough to go looking for more information. "How many brothers and sisters do you have?"

"One sister and three brothers. Big families are kind of a Braden thing."

"When I interviewed your cousin Zev, he said something similar." One of her early assignments had been to interview Zev Braden, a treasure hunter who had discovered a sunken pirate ship off the coast of Silver Island. Flynn had come down with the flu and hadn't gone to Silver Island with her.

"That's right. You interviewed Zev when I was on my deathbed. He's my second cousin, by the way."

"You weren't dying. You had the flu."

He chuckled. "What about you? Are you from a big family? You've mentioned a couple of siblings."

"Big families are a Steele thing, too. I have two sisters and three brothers."

"Look at that. Something else we have in common. Do they drive you nuts with group texts?"

"Yes! Is that a big-family thing?"

"I guess. It's pretty funny sometimes."

"Ours, too. Where do you fall in the lineup?"

"I'm number four. Victory is the oldest. Her real name is Victoria, and then come Seth, Clay, me, and my youngest brother, Noah. What about you?"

"I'm number three. Jock and Archer are twins. They're the oldest, and Jock's real name is Jack. Then there's *me*, and then Levi and Leni, who are also twins, and my sister Jules, the group-texting queen, is the youngest."

"There are two sets of twins? Your parents must have been run ragged."

"I honestly don't know how they survived Jock and Archer. They were always doing crazy stuff, like making flight suits and jumping off roofs. And they pranked everyone. They still do."

"They sound awesome."

"They have their moments." She adored her siblings, but her family had experienced more than their fair share of heartache, and it had been tough. "Are your brothers and sister survivalists and into exploring, too?"

"Some more than others. Vic loves her creature comforts." He leaned against Sutton's side. "But she could hack it out here with me as long as she had her dream fairy, which she's had since she was a kid to keep bad dreams away, and a Snugpak and butt wipes."

"Sounds like my kind of person."

"You'd like her. She's a trip, and she's tough. When she was in her twenties, she fell in love with her boss, who was in his early forties, and she married him."

"That's a big age gap. My brothers would have been all over that."

"We were, but there's no telling Victory what to do. If you tell her to go right, she'll go left just to prove she can."

"Sounds like Archer. Do you like her husband?"

"I did. He was great. He treated her like gold, and she adored him. Unfortunately, he passed away several years ago from a heart attack."

Her chest constricted with memories of her own family's tragedy. "That's horrible. She must have been devastated."

"We all were. Harvey was a big part of our family. Vic was so crushed, she tried to push us all away the first few months after he died, but we didn't let her. *I* didn't let her. I was a pain in her ass, showing up on her doorstep and refusing to leave. I don't know if I did the right thing or not, but it felt right at the time."

Sutton swallowed against the guilt she usually kept tamped down but was clawing its way up to the surface. "Trust me, you did the right thing. Whatever happened would've been worse if you'd let her shut you all out."

"You sound like you have experience with that kind of thing."

"Unfortunately, I do. Jock lost his fiancée and their baby in a horrible car accident, and his fiancée was Archer's best friend. We had all grown up together on the island." Sutton didn't know *why* she was opening up to Flynn. Maybe it was because they had this in common and she knew the heartache that went along with it and the fortitude it took to move past it. Or maybe it was because there in the darkness, it felt like they were the last two people on earth, and talking about something so personal, something she hadn't shared with others, was making her feel even closer to him, and she liked that. He stirred so many emotions in her, and she liked that, too, even though she knew she shouldn't.

Whatever the reason, the words kept coming, and she didn't want to stop them. "Archer blamed Jock, and Jock felt so guilty, he let him. He wasn't even driving when it happened. It was awful. Jock shut us all out and rarely came back to the island for more than a decade. It tore my family up. Things are better now, but it was tough for a long time, and so much happened during those years. Jock became a caregiver for an older gentleman whose name was also Harvey. He's the one who gave Jack the nickname Jock. I moved to Port Hudson, Leni went away to school and moved to New York, Levi got a girl pregnant and she didn't want the baby, so he and his daughter, Joey, moved off the island and he was raising her by himself. Jules opened her shop. We all started our adult lives. It's strange to have that happen when your family is in such a discombobulated state."

Flynn put his hand on hers, his compassionate gaze wrapping around her like an embrace. "I'm sorry your family went through that. Grief can really mess people up."

She had the urge to rest her head on his shoulder and take comfort in the closeness. It had been so long since she'd wanted that, but he was still her boss, so she struggled against it, sliding her hand out from beneath his and swatting a bug flying near her face. "It sure can."

"How old were you when that happened?"

"Nineteen. I was in college. I feel guilty about that because I wasn't home to help my sisters through it. I wish I had done for Jock what you did for Victory. Maybe it would've saved all of us years of heartache."

"Or maybe it would've caused a rift between you two. It did for me and Vic. Talk about tension. There was a lot of it between us for a long time."

"That stinks. What happened? Did you back off?"

"You of all people know I don't give up just because people give me shit, and I *never* give up on people I care about."

He held her gaze, as if his words had a deeper meaning. But they couldn't, could they? *Do I want them to?* She realized with a start that she did and tore her gaze away, focusing on the fire instead of him. "How is Victory now?"

"She's doing well, but I don't know if she'll ever let herself fully move on. She took over their entertainment management company, Blank Space Entertainment, and has basically buried herself in work ever since."

"I can understand that, but don't give up hope. Look at Jock and Archer. They finally faced their demons. They're getting along and living life to the fullest again. The reason Jock came back to the island and finally confronted Archer was because he fell in love with an amazing woman, who is now his wife, and her little girl, who he adopted. Daphne and Hadley—she's four and so freaking cute—changed everything, and Archer's getting married in a few weeks. I never thought any of that would happen."

"According to my mother, love is the most powerful impetus of all."

"I've never been in love, but I've watched my brothers and sisters take the plunge, and I have to say. I think your mom is right."

"She usually is."

He held her gaze so long, her nerves ignited, and she grasped for something to say. "Is there still a rift between you two, or are you closer now?"

"No. We're good. I'm close to all of my siblings, but Vic's probably closest to Seth. They have similar personalities."

"So he'd be okay out here with a Snugpak and butt wipes, too?"

"He would, but he doesn't need them. He likes to get his hands dirty, and he's very athletic. I meant he and Vic have that older sibling mentality. They color within the lines and like things mapped out. It works for them. They're both very successful. I told you about Vic, and Seth is a business mogul. He founded BRI Enterprises, a major retail conglomerate, and he co-owns a number of restaurants, but he's also a big-ass dork."

She heard the tease in his voice and bumped his shoulder with hers. "That's *mean*."

"No, it's not. He is a dork. Black-framed glasses and all. He wears plaid shirts with patterned sweaters that don't match, and he's all about analytics and bottom lines."

"None of that makes him a dork. It sounds like he's comfortable in his own skin and smart."

"If he were here right now, he'd tell you he's a dork. Just ask Leni. Doesn't she do Seth's PR work?"

She was surprised he knew that and realized with a nugget of discomfort that he probably complained to Seth about her the same way she complained to Leni about him. *Ugh.* Why did that bother her? She shouldn't care if he complained about her, but she did.

In an effort to combat those feelings, her snark came out. "*Yes*, and she has only good things to say about him. In fact, since he's single, I might have to look him up when we get out of here."

FLYNN TRIED TO ignore the unexpected stab of jealousy he felt, but the more Sutton let her guard down, the more he liked her, and the more he wanted to strip it away.

She poked at the dying embers in the fire pit with a stick. "And your other two brothers? Could they hack it out here?"

"Why? Do you want to look them up, too?" He said it teasingly, but the thought of her hooking up with one of his brothers grated on his nerves.

"I don't know yet. Tell me about them, and I'll decide."

Great. Now he was stuck talking about his brothers to the one woman he wanted to get closer to. He briefly contemplated making them sound not so great, but he wasn't that much of a jerk. "I'm sure with the right preparations and training they could handle it if they had to, but Clay is a quarterback for the Giants. He'd never chance injuring his throwing arm in a place like this, and Noah's a marine biologist. He lives in Colorado, and he's partnered with some of our cousins in an in-door/outdoor discovery center for kids called the Real DEAL, which stands for Discover, Experience, Appreciate, and Learn. He'd definitely be into a trip like this. When we were kids, he'd follow me around. If I went exploring, he was right there with me. If I was sitting under the stars reading with a flashlight at night, chances were, he'd plop down next to me, and I was reading to him."

"Hold on there, Braden. Are you saying you have a sweet side?"

He scoffed. "Hardly."

"Reading to your little brother is a sweet thing to do. It's okay to admit that you have a sweeter side. Or at least you did toward him."

"I'd do anything for any of my brothers or Vic, whether I like whatever it is or not." He wasn't about to admit to being sweet. If anything, he was a little bit of a dick when he was caught in a corner, as he'd proven with how he'd treated Sutton.

"Whatever. I still think it was sweet. Hey, you know what? We should think about connecting Noah with Andi. She's working on her PhD in marine biology. I'd hate to lose her as a research assistant, but she's too smart to be pigeonholed, and maybe he has something for her in her field."

"I've already mentioned her to him."

Her eyes widened. "You *have*? Does Andi know that?"

"No, but why do you look so surprised?"

"Because we work together every day, and before this trip, if you weren't barking orders at me, you barely said two words to me. But you praise Andi for her work, and you've gone out of your way to recommend her for a job. That doesn't seem strange to you?"

"Not at all." *I'm not attracted to Andi. Getting to know her doesn't hold the same threat as getting to know you does.* "She mentioned she was studying marine biology, so I reached out to my brother. It wasn't a big deal, but Noah doesn't have any positions available right now, so you shouldn't mention it to her."

"I won't." She fell quiet, worrying with her hands, like she was stewing over something.

"Spit it out, Steele. What's on your mind?"

"It's just…I'm trying to figure out why you're such a jerk to me all the time."

He'd known she'd bring it up sooner or later. He'd been hoping for much later. Like never. "I'm your boss."

"That's not an excuse. Most bosses aren't jerks."

"I told you why I push you."

"I get that you push me to do a better job, and you're right. I do work harder when I'm challenged. But it's more than that." Her voice escalated. "You come into the break room or pass me in the hall, and you physically change. You get your back up like I'm the enemy."

"You're not the fucking enemy."

It started raining, and she groaned. "Are you *freaking* kidding me?"

"Welcome to the rainforest. Let's get this fire out." They rose to their feet and used the sides of their boots to push damp dirt onto the smoldering embers. "That's good. We should use our raincoats to collect rainwater overnight."

"*Damn it.* I should've thought of that."

"Instinct leads you to get out of the rain. It takes stepping outside of that to think like a survivor. You'll get there."

"Here's my instinct." She opened her mouth and tipped her face up to the sky, catching the rainwater in her mouth.

He laughed. "That works, too."

They stretched their raincoats between four logs, using rocks to hold them in place, and left the middles drooping to collect the rain.

"In the morning we'll put the water in the canteens, and once we light a fire again, we'll purify it. We should do this every morning before we leave camp, too, to catch whatever rain falls while we're gone."

"Good idea. I should've brought a bucket instead of a sleeping bag."

"You'll know for next time." He snickered at her eye roll. "Brush yourself off to make sure there are no bugs on you before we go into the tent. I'll check your back." He moved behind her. "Take your ponytail out. I'll check your hair, too."

"Great. Now I'll be thinking about bugs in my hair all night."

She pulled out her hair band, and her long blond hair tumbled over her shoulders, thick, shiny, and so alluring, he wanted to wrap it around his fingers and show her exactly why he was trying to keep a modicum of distance between them. Fuck. Those thoughts were going to get him in trouble if he wasn't careful. He tried not to notice how soft her hair was as he sifted through it, plucking out dirt and a few bugs.

"Are those *all* bugs you're taking out?"

"No. It's mostly dirt."

"*Mostly?*" She eyed him over her shoulder, rain wetting her long lashes.

She looked so beautiful and vulnerable, he wanted to take her in his arms and kiss her fear away. "Don't worry. I won't let anything get to you."

"Thanks," she said softly.

He threaded his hands into her hair, massaging her scalp as he checked for clingy critters, trying not to think about how good those silky strands felt. She breathed a little harder. "Am I making you uncomfortable?"

"*No,*" rushed from her lungs. "It just…It feels good."

Fuck yeah, it does. "Are you saying I'm good with my hands, Steele?"

"Don't let it go to your head, but you missed your calling."

"Too late. My ego is blowing up." He imagined her rolling her eyes. "Don't roll your eyes at me."

"How can you possibly know I did that? You can't see my eyes."

He couldn't resist grabbing hold of those silky strands and turning her head so she was looking over her shoulder at him. Either he was seeing things, or that little tug had caused a spark of desire. Fuck, he liked that. "Tell me I'm wrong."

She stifled a smile.

"I guess I know you better than you thought." He went back to massaging her scalp, taking his time despite the rain, enjoying the soft sounds of appreciation she made and the way she leaned into his touch. Oh yeah, she was into him. This was dangerous. He gathered her hair in one hand, holding it over her shoulder, as he leaned in and spoke into her other ear. "All clear. I'm going to check out the rest of you now."

"*Uh-huh.*"

He had no idea how two syllables could sound so lustful and tried not to think about it or about the feel of her body through her thin shirt as he brushed the dirt off her shoulders and back. But memories of her wet and naked from the hotel room pressed in on him, making him want so much more. When he reached her waist, her breathing hitched. *So damn sexy.* He didn't want to stop touching her, but he didn't need to get sued for sexual harassment. Placing his hands on her hips, he drew her back against his chest and felt her heart hammering. "Do you want me to keep going and do the rest, or do you want to do it?"

She looked over her shoulder, their gazes colliding with the impact of a lightning storm. "I want you to get *everything* off me."

Holy hell. He wanted to take that literally, and the look in her eyes said she wanted him to, too. But she'd fucked with his head just enough for him to doubt himself, so he erred on the side of caution.

As he brushed the dirt off her ass, trying not to notice her soft curves, she sucked in a sharp breath, breathing harder with his every touch. Moving lower, he wiped off the backs of her hips and thighs, feeling the tightening of her muscles and hearing every sexy little gasp as if magnified. It was fucking torture.

When he finished cleaning her off, he stepped away and turned around, trying to regain control of the desire coursing through him. He took off his shirt to shake it out, and her soft hands touched his back. "Sutton, you don't have to—"

"I want to," she said breathily.

He had no idea if there was dirt on his back or not, and he didn't care, because her touch was electric. She took her sweet time, too, running her warm hands over his shoulders, lingering on every muscle, tracing them, as if she were memorizing him. Her hands trailed down his back and along his sides. His jaw clenched at the desires mounting inside him. She didn't stop to ask about wiping the dirt off *his* ass, and the minute her hands were on it, his dick wanted in on the action.

"That's good. Thanks," he gritted out, stepping out of her reach and shaking out his shirt.

Her gaze traveled to his chest and down his abs, leaving fucking flames in their wake. As if she caught herself staring, she tore her gaze away and headed for the tent. "I can't believe people live like this."

He wanted to say, *Fighting an attraction that has been building for a year and a half? Yeah, it's fucking torture.* But he kept that to himself and took the appropriate route. "Because of the bugs?"

"The bugs, the rain, the constant fear of what's lurking around you."

"I don't see a lot of people living here."

"The *tribes*," she clarified. "I know the importance of retaining their cultures and remaining in the rainforest, but some of them don't even wear clothes. I can't imagine running around here naked."

That's funny. I like imagining you running around naked.

He gritted his teeth.

It was going to be a long damn night.

Chapter Eight

THE RAIN AND other night sounds were nearly drowned out by Sutton's anxious breathing. She'd directed Flynn to turn his back in the small tent and had used the body wipes she'd brought to clean herself up before changing into a clean shirt and cotton pants to sleep in. She'd offered Flynn some wipes, and he had to admit, it was nice to wash up. Although he hadn't asked her to turn her back while he used them or when he'd changed into sweats. She'd chosen to do that all on her own. He didn't bother with a shirt, knowing he'd be hot enough sleeping next to Sutton. She'd used a flashlight while writing in her journal, and he'd wondered if that was her nightly ritual. He'd hoped after that she'd feel more comfortable and be able to relax. But he was worried about her. She was zipped inside her sleeping bag like a mummy and still flinched at every little sound.

"You okay, Steele?"

"No. I thought I'd feel safer in this thing, but I feel trapped and it's freaking me out. Are you sure nothing can get into the tent?"

A sharp set of claws could tear that tent apart in seconds, but that wasn't what she was asking, and he wasn't about to make her more nervous. "As sure as I can be. If anything gets in, it'll probably go after me first, since I'm so sweet."

She laughed softly, then groaned and unzipped her sleeping bag, kicking it off with a loud exhalation. "That's better. It took me a solid two months to learn how to quiet my mind when I first started doing yoga, but then I mastered it. I really thought it would help while we were here. But my mind is like a dungeon of worries."

"Wild animals might have something to do with that."

"*Ha ha.* Just so you know, if anything creepy gets in, I'm hiding behind you."

"Damn, and here I was thinking you'd sacrifice yourself for me." He went up on his elbow, gazing down at her. As his eyes adjusted to the darkness, he tried to distract her from her worries. "Tell me more about your family."

"They're nothing like yours. Growing up, we lived a pretty simple life on the island, and while there were life lessons and the rest, the only thing my grandparents taught me was how to make wine and sunbathe in my bra."

"That's a great combination. I bet the guys you grew up with loved it, but why bother with a bra?"

"Are you kidding? I'd've been the talk of the island if I went topless."

"I meant, why not wear a bikini top?"

"*Oh.* Well, when I went to the beach I did, but sunbathing with the Bra Brigade is a tradition."

"You just keep getting more interesting, Steele. What's the Bra Brigade?"

"It's a group my grandmother started with her girlfriends when they were growing up. They've been sneaking away to remote places on the island to sunbathe in their bras since they were teenagers. Over the years they recruited their daughters and daughters-in-law and granddaughters and friends."

"So this Bra Brigade is a big deal?"

"Kind of."

"I'm picturing a line of women marching down the sidewalk like ducks in a row, with towels over their shoulders and beach bags—"

"We're not an army. Did you not hear the part about *sneaking away*? We don't want people to see us. It's like a secret club. We go out to the cliffs or to one of the private coves."

"A secret club sounds much cooler than marching ducks. You know all the thirteen-year-old boys are armed with binoculars just waiting for the Bra Brigade to pick a spot. They probably stake out street corners and sit in windows with walkie-talkies. As soon as they see movement, they're like, *I've got a visual* and *ten-four on the cliffs.*"

She laughed. "Is that what you were like as a kid? A spy?"

"Isn't every young boy? Look at the payoff. Not only would I see you and probably all your friends in your bras, but I'd also see older women."

"Were you seriously into older women at thirteen?"

"I was into boobs, and they had some nice ones."

They both laughed. Something rustled outside the tent, and Sutton gasped. "What's that?" She shifted closer to him.

"Nothing you have to worry about. Tell me more." He didn't want her to be scared all night, and whatever was making the noise was retreating from the tent. "I can't imagine Archer is cool with the idea of you prancing around in your bra. You make him sound like he'll kill anyone who comes near you."

"Not just me. My sisters, too, and don't mess with my mom or my grandmother, because he has zero patience for that."

"Who would mess with your mom or grandmother?"

"Nobody smart. My mom is a big, beautiful woman. She'd give a stranger the shirt off her back—"

"And ask them to join the Bra Brigade?"

"Probably, or at least feed them dinner and get to know every little thing about them. But because she's big, sometimes people who don't know her can be assholes and make comments."

The sadness in her voice tugged at him. "That sucks. I'm sorry she has to deal with that."

"Me too. She's so confident and loving, and she really is beautiful inside and out. People on the island adore her, but we get a lot of tourists, and sometimes kids are mean. I remember one time when we were young, my family was barbecuing on the beach with our close friends the Silvers and the Remingtons—"

"The Silvers of Silver Island?"

"Yeah. Their family is a big deal. Their ancestors founded the island, and they own the Silver House, a fancy resort on the island. But they're really down-to-earth, good people. Alexander Silver and Roddy Remington are the reason my parents met and fell in love. My dad isn't from the island. He met them when he was in college, and the summer after their freshman year, they invited him to come back to the island with them. He came for the summer and met my mom. She was sixteen, but that's a story for another time." She laughed softly.

He looked forward to hearing it.

"Anyway, back to Archer. We were on the beach with all our friends, and this group of kids walked by. They were probably fifteen or sixteen years old, definitely tourists, and I guess one of them called my mom fat. I didn't hear him, but

Archer, who was thirteen at the time, took off after them like a bat out of hell. He tackled the kid who'd said it and broke his nose. The other guys in the group went after Archer, and of course my father and his buddies and all the boys from our families ran over. I'll never forget the look on Archer's face as they dragged him away. If looks could kill, that kid never would have made it off the island. Archer was hollering at him, *You ever talk about my family again and I'll kill you.*"

"The dude sounds loyal but mildly out of control. Not that I don't appreciate that type of loyalty."

"He used to be pretty bad, but his fiancée, Indi, has mellowed him out quite a bit. Now they have a safe word."

"I don't need to know about your brother's sex life."

She swatted him. "Not that kind of safe word. If he starts going off the rails, she says *bananas*, and it stops him in his tracks long enough to slow him down and make him think before pummeling someone."

"I'd hate to see what he'd do to someone who said something bad about Indi."

"I don't even want to think about that. But as gruff as Archer is, he also has a softer side."

"What does that look like? Only giving a guy a black eye?"

"No. I mean a *real* softer side. He's done some really sweet things for us."

"Like…?"

"Well, I've wanted to be a reporter for as long as I can remember. I was that weird little girl whose idols were Barbara Walters, Tom Brokaw, Anderson Cooper, and Connie Chung. I didn't realize they were journalists until I was a little older, and of course, that became my goal."

"That's adorable."

"I'm glad you think so. When we were kids, all the other little girls wanted to play games, but I wanted to play reporter, so Archer made me a cardboard television and wrote *Silver Island News* above the hole he'd cut out for the screen. He covered the dining room table with a sheet and put the box on top of it and a chair behind it, where I could sit, and it would look like I was on TV. Then he surprised me with it and watched me report the Silver Island News every afternoon."

"Damn. That is sweet."

"I told you. He did other things, too. When I went away to college, he came with me and stayed for two days. He made sure I got settled in and knew how to get to my classes. We walked all over the campus and through town. He wanted to make sure I knew how to get everywhere, and he pointed out places he thought I should avoid or be careful of at night."

"Did you listen to him?"

"Yeah, I did. I wasn't the kind of person who went looking for trouble. Growing up on a small island where everyone looks out for each other is very different from attending college in Port Hudson. I had a little culture shock."

"Were you afraid to go away from home?"

"No. I wanted to. I had big dreams. But I appreciated the extra time Archer took to make sure I was comfortable. After he went back home, he texted me a few times every day to make sure I was okay."

"He wanted you to feel safe. That's the mark of a good big brother." He had a newfound respect for this man he didn't know.

"He did the same for Leni when she went to school."

"What about Jules?"

"She never went away to school, but she has a special place

in all our hearts. She was diagnosed with cancer, a Wilms tumor, when she was only three, and she had to have a kidney removed. They were able to get all the cancer out, and it hasn't come back, thank God, but it was scarier than being in this rainforest."

The heaviness in her voice made him want to put his arm around her and pull her close, but he held back, knowing it would make it even harder to resist doing more. "I can't imagine how awful that was."

"I hope you never have to. Jock wouldn't leave her bedside until she was fully recovered, and Archer was a mess. He'd always been her savior, scaring away the boogeyman and all that, but he couldn't save her from cancer, which made it really hard for him to be around her."

"That's rough, carrying that kind of responsibility. What about you?"

"I remember being terrified because what kid wouldn't be if their baby sister was going through that? But I've always been kind of practical, too. Our parents told us the doctors were taking good care of her, and I believed them. I knew I couldn't fight the disease for her, but I could help Jules be happy. I wrote her stories about a little girl who was stronger than she ever believed she could be and overcame all sorts of obstacles. I'd draw pictures of Jules conquering whatever the story was about, and I'd leave the stories tucked beneath her pillow while she was sleeping. I'd get up at the crack of dawn every morning and sit outside her bedroom, waiting for her to wake up. Then I'd just happen to walk in when she found them. I can still see her sweet little face surrounded by wisps of golden-brown hair. She'd go, *Sut! The story fairy came! Wead it to me!* Every time we got to the end of a story, she'd say, *My happy end!*" Sutton laughed, and a tear slid down her cheek.

His chest constricted, and he reached over, wiping the tear with the pad of his thumb. His hand lingered, caressing her cheek. "It appears Sutton Steele has a sweet side, too."

"For Julesy I do."

"Sounds like you're a great big sister. Did you ever tell her you wrote the stories?"

"No."

"Why not?"

"Because she believed in the story fairy, and I didn't want to steal that from her."

He'd been attracted to many things about Sutton, but he had no idea what to do with the feelings her love for her siblings stirred. "Do you think she's figured it out?"

She shrugged. "If she has, she never said anything to me about it. But she named her gift shop the Happy End."

"A nod to her big sis. I love that."

Something howled in the forest, and she froze, eyes wide. "What was that?" she asked shakily.

This time he didn't hold back. He put his arm over her, pulling her against him. "Probably a monkey."

"*Geez,*" she whispered. "Don't the animals ever sleep?"

"There are just a lot of them." He tried to find something to take her mind off the animals. "So, you're the oldest girl, born after twin boys. I bet you were treated like a princess by your parents."

"If I was, I don't remember it. Levi and Leni are only two years younger than me, so all I remember is growing up with twin bookends and a baby sister who had cancer."

"What was that like?"

She was quiet for so long, he didn't think she was going to

answer.

"Touchy subject?"

"No. I'm just thinking. I can't remember anyone ever asking me that before. People always say it must've been fun growing up with such a big family, and it was. I love my family. My parents are amazing, and my brothers and sisters are the best. My mom would read to me most nights, and my dad always found a few minutes to sit and talk with me, but sometimes I felt a little lost among my siblings, which is probably why my grandmother and I are so close."

"I can understand that. Did your grandmother live close by?"

"Yes. She lives in the carriage house behind my parents' house. When I was little, she'd invite me over in the evening for tea parties. It was just the two of us. She'd serve tea in fancy teacups, and serve cookies, and we'd watch the news together. I'd talk about wanting to be a reporter, and sometimes I'd practice, and she'd tell me how great I was going to be. She used to say that people believed what we showed them, and if I believed in myself, others would, too."

He imagined her as a lanky little girl, hazel eyes wide with excitement as she mimicked her favorite reporters. "Sounds like a smart woman, and you obviously heeded her advice."

"I took my cues from her and my mom. They're two of the most confident women I know, *and* my grandmother is a fellow fashionista, so I figured she knew what she was talking about."

"Sounds like being a glamour girl runs in your family."

She smiled up at him. "You should see my grandmother. She's more of a glamour girl than I am. She wears her hair in a stylish blond pixie cut and has a closet full of designer clothes. She *never* goes out without makeup and being fully accessorized.

My mom has a good sense of style, and Leni always looks well put together. Jules can't help but look cute in anything she wears. But my grandmother and I really *love* fashion, and not to show off or for anyone else's benefit. It's just something we're passionate about for ourselves. Some people spoil themselves with trips or fancy cars. For us, it's fashion. For as long as I can remember, the week before school started, my grandmother would tell my mom we had to run an errand, as if we were staying on the island. Then we'd take the ferry to Cape Cod and get our nails done and shop all afternoon."

"It sounds like your relationship with her is a lot like mine with my grandfather."

"I think so, too. That's why being the first granddaughter brought into the Bra Brigade *was* a big deal for me. I got special time with my grandmother, and it felt good to have something the other kids didn't. That sounds crappy, doesn't it? Since we had tea parties and a shopping trip once a year, too. But it wasn't like the tea parties were every night."

He felt a budding connection taking root and held her tighter. "Not at all. By the time I came along, my parents were already at the stage where they let me do things they never would have let the older kids do. I know what it's like to"—*feel like the lost boy*—"want something of your own."

"Who would've thought we'd have that in common? For me, that feeling was often overridden by not wanting to be a burden on my parents. The boys were wild, Leni was tough, and Jules had been sick. They had enough to worry about, so I kind of blended into the background, got perfect grades, and did as I was told. My dad even called me his little angel. He still calls me that sometimes."

"That's a cute nickname, but you're *not* someone who

blends in."

"What's that supposed to mean?"

"You're not a wallflower. You're opinionated, and behind that ball-busting confidence is a huge heart. You go the extra mile for the people who need it, and all those things make you stand out."

"I went the extra mile for my baby *sister*."

"Not just for her. When Ted's wife had a baby, you got everyone to say congratulations on video and sent it to them with that basket full of baby stuff." Ted was one of their cameramen. "And when that office intern had her appendix out last year, you put together a care package and passed a card around the office for everyone to sign."

She was quiet for a second. "What makes you think that was me?"

"Because nobody did those things before you came on board, and you gave me hell for taking too long to sign it. You stand out, Sutton. That's a good thing. Why are you denying it?"

"I don't *know*. Why do you care?"

"God, you're maddening. You want praise, but you argue when I give it to you. *Fuck it.* You want to know why I care? Because maybe I wish you *would* blend in, but everything about you is striking. Your looks, your personality, the way you carry yourself, the way you stand up for yourself and for others. I can't imagine you *not* standing out in any situation."

"You mean because I annoy you," she snapped. "No wonder you look at me like you want to kill me."

"Are you fucking with me right now? You think I look at you like I want to kill you?"

"It's not like you don't have a reason. I know you're pissed that you have to keep me safe while we're here."

An incredulous laugh fell from his lips. "Jesus, Sutton. That's not why I'm pissed."

"Yeah, right." She looked away.

"You want the truth?"

She glowered at him. "No. *Lie* to me."

"That smart mouth of yours has been fucking with me since the day we met."

"And yours hasn't fucked with me?"

"Do you get off on challenging me?"

"As much as you get off on ordering me around. Do you know what it's like knowing I'm a burden to a guy who can't stand the sight of me?"

"Okay, *enough* of this bullshit. It may not seem like it to you, but I feel like I've seen nothing *but* you for a year and a half, and I see a hell of a lot more of you than just the arguments we have. The reason I haven't taken more time to get to know you prior to being forced into this situation is because I'm so fucking *attracted* to you, I can't be near you without wanting you. Every time you challenge me, I want to grab you by the hair and kiss that scowl off your beautiful face. And I'm not pissed because I have to keep you safe. I wouldn't trust your life in anyone else's hands. I'm pissed because being here with you makes keeping my hands to myself a million times harder."

"Then *don't*."

"Don't *what*?" he fumed.

"Keep your hands to yourself."

He scoffed. "So you can sue me for sexual harassment? You'd like that, wouldn't you?"

"You're an idiot." She grabbed his face, tugging his mouth to hers.

Holy fuck. She kissed him as hungrily as he devoured her, their connection scorching, setting his entire body ablaze. But there was more at stake than getting off with the woman he craved. He tore his mouth away, both of them breathless, and growled, "Just so we're clear, you're not going to turn this around and sue my ass, are you?"

"*No.* Now stop talking and kiss m—"

He crushed his mouth to hers. He'd fantasized about kissing her for so long, he couldn't hold back, and he intensified his efforts, kissing her rougher, more possessively. Her mouth was sweet and hot, and she was so fucking eager, matching every thrust of his tongue with one of her own. Kissing her was like finding gold in undiscovered territory, and he wanted to *explore.* He pushed a hand into her hair, wrapping the thick locks around his fingers, earning a sensual moan. Every slide of their tongues had her moaning and writhing, sending *want* and *need* burning beneath his skin, unleashing a year and a half of pent-up desire.

He shifted over her, grinding his rigid cock against her center as they devoured each other. She rocked her hips, fingernails digging into his flesh. He reveled in her hunger for him and slowed them down to savor it, kissing her deeper, more sensually, drawing longer, more lustful sounds. He was powerless to slow their mounting passion, and she was right there with him, surrendering to it, clawing and groping as they ate at each other's mouths.

"*Fuck*, Sutton. You feel so damn good." He fisted his other hand in her hair, crushing his mouth to hers in a punishingly intense kiss, earning one needy sound after another. Those noises, her taste, and the feel of her soft curves beneath him were painfully exquisite. He wanted to possess every inch of her.

He'd known kissing her would be out of this world, but this was unlike anything he'd ever experienced. Kissing Sutton Steele was fucking nirvana.

FLYNN'S FINGERS TIGHTENED in Sutton's hair, sending an intoxicating sting of pain and pleasure spiking through her. Another moan escaped, drawing a guttural growl from him that made her entire body flame. His kisses were raw and passionate, all consuming. She'd never been kissed so hungrily, so thoroughly, and she greedily took everything he gave. She was dizzy with desire, clawing at his back and arms, grinding against his hard length, and wanting so much more. As if he could read her mind, he shifted slightly and pushed his hand beneath her shirt, palming her breast. She hadn't been touched in so long, her breath rushed from her lungs.

His eyes blazed into her. "*Stop?*"

"No. Please don't."

His wicked grin made her body shudder with desire. "Then I want this off."

He pulled her shirt off, openly drinking in the sight of her bare breasts. She had a fleeting thought about him being her boss, but their mouths fused together, obliterating her ability to think at all. He took her nipple between his finger and thumb, squeezing just hard enough to send rivers of heat slithering down her core. She moaned, arching beneath him, and then he was kissing a path down her neck. His hot breath hit her breast a second before his lips and tongue wreaked havoc with her sanity. She clung to him as he kissed and licked painfully close to her nipple, his tongue sliding around it, making the taut peak ache and burn.

"*Flynn*," she begged, burying her hands in his hair and holding tight.

"I like your hands on me." His eyes went volcanic. "Don't be gentle."

Holy cow. This man…

She tightened her fists in his hair, earning the sexiest growl she'd ever heard. He continued his sensual torture, licking, kissing, and sucking each of her breasts without touching her nipples. Lust coiled tighter and hotter inside her with every touch of his lips, every slick of his tongue, until she was barely breathing. He recaptured her mouth in a brutal kiss, pressing his hard cock against her neediest parts. He rocked and gyrated, putting mind-numbing pressure where she needed it most as he deepened their kisses, igniting every nerve in her body until she was trembling, on the verge of losing it. How was that even possible? Most men couldn't find that magical spot with a map, much less get her there that fast, fully dressed.

He trapped her lower lip between his teeth and tugged, sending a bolt of heat between her legs. She whimpered needily.

"You're so fucking sexy." He reclaimed her mouth, his cock working the best kind of magic through their clothing. Her panties were drenched, and she was hanging on to her sanity by a thread. He shifted off her.

No. Come back.

His hot lips came down over her breast, sucking her nipple to the roof of his mouth as he pushed his fingers beneath the waistband of her pants and left them there, scalding and tempting.

"*Touch me*," she pleaded, and felt him smiling against her

skin as he pushed his big hand into her panties. She'd never been so thankful for loose cotton pajama bottoms.

"I've wanted to touch you for too damn long," he rasped. His thick fingers slid over her clit, sending scintillating sensations skating through her. "*Mm.* So ready to come for me, baby." He lowered his mouth to her breast again, grazing his teeth over her nipple as he drove her out of her mind with his fingers. She closed her eyes, heart racing, every inch of her vibrating. Desire pounded through her veins, billowing inside her until it throbbed beneath her skin. He sucked her nipple *hard* and pushed his fingers inside her, taking her higher and higher, until she was whisper-begging, "*Can't take it…please…ohgod…*" He pressed his thumb on her clit, sending an orgasm crashing over her like a bullying wave. Swells of pleasure consumed her and "*Flynn—*" flew from her lungs like a prayer. Her inner muscles pulsed around his fingers as she rode his hand like it was made for her pleasure.

Just as she started coming down from the peak, he sent her soaring again. She pulled at his hair, hips bucking with every surge of pleasure, until she collapsed on the hard ground, trying to catch her breath. His mouth came coaxingly down over hers, and he breathed air into her lungs. One hand threaded into her hair, while his other slid up her belly, cupping her breast, teasing her nipple with feathery touches that had her body twitching with aftershocks. When he kissed his way down her breasts and stomach, she grabbed his arms. "Wait." She'd used her body wipes to clean herself up, but it wasn't the same as bathing. "I feel dirty."

A slow grin slid into place. "I *like* you dirty."

"*Flynn.*" She laughed. "I mean—"

"I know what you mean, and I don't give a fuck. I want my

mouth on you."

Even in the dark, she could see him looking at her like she was the only thing on earth he wanted.

He pressed a kiss just above her belly button. "I want to taste you when you come."

Her body screamed, *Yes, please.* "I want that, too."

She'd never had her pants taken off so fast. As Flynn's mouth made her body sing, she didn't care what was outside the tent. Desire burned inside her with every slick of his tongue, every graze of his teeth, filling every crack and sliver until she ached with the need to come.

"So fucking sweet." The lust in his voice drew a moan. She fisted her hands in the sleeping bag beneath them as he lifted one of her legs over his shoulder, feasting on her. His scruff abraded her inner thighs in an intoxicating mix of pain and pleasure. Her desperate sounds filled the tent as he quickened his efforts, using his hands and mouth to send her careening into oblivion. "*Ohgodohgod*—" The world spun away, her body quivering and quaking. Flynn was relentless in his pursuit of her pleasure, giving her a repeat performance that drew wild sounds from her lungs, leaving her breathless and boneless.

He kissed all around her sex and inner thighs, slicking his tongue along her sensitive flesh. She was vaguely aware of him putting her underwear and sleeping pants on her, kissing her body as he crawled up it. He brushed his lips over hers. Her eyes fluttered open as he whispered, "Damn, Sutton," and his mouth came down over hers in an unexpectedly tender kiss that had her melting against him.

"That was incredible." She was too blissed out to move. "Give me a minute to get my brain to function, and then I'll scramble yours."

He smiled and kissed her again. "No need. I'm used to going to bed hard from thinking about you. This is a thousand times better. Thank you for trusting me."

His words burrowed deep into her chest as he helped her put on her shirt and gathered her in his arms, spooning her, his body cocooning hers. "You're safe with me." He kissed her cheek. "Get some sleep."

"You do have a sweet side," she whispered.

"Stop telling yourself lies, and get some sleep."

She snuggled into him and drifted off to sleep wondering what lies she'd have to tell herself tomorrow.

Chapter Nine

SUTTON AWOKE FEELING achy from hiking with a heavy backpack, too warm, and damp. Not the good kind of damp. The kind of damp caused by humidity, not by Flynn, who wasn't in the tent. She had no idea when he'd gotten up, but the fact that he wasn't beside her made her stomach knot up as last night came rushing back in vivid, heart-pounding detail. She'd been so worked up, she hadn't thought twice about taking that first kiss, and *wow*, could he kiss. She could still taste him, still feel his hands and mouth on her, and still hear his gruff voice, thick with lust and unspoken promises. *I'm so fucking attracted to you, I can't be near you without wanting you…So ready to come for me, baby…So fucking sweet.* Her body ignited anew.

What is wrong with me? What was I thinking, coming onto my boss?

Coming on *my boss.*

Oh God…

She squeezed her eyes shut, thinking about how incredible it had been to be close to Flynn. He made her feel more than anyone ever had, and that was *before* they'd gone beyond kissing. She'd never been a moaner, but she couldn't have held those sounds back last night if her life had depended on it. Flynn's deep voice rumbled through her mind again—*You're safe with me. Get some sleep*—and she was overcome with a different type of warmth. She *had* felt safe in his arms, and she'd slept better than she had in months, despite being in the middle of the rainforest with who knew what lurking outside the tent.

But now she was alone in that tent, which said a lot, didn't it?

She heard Flynn walking around. He was probably pacing off his regret. But what if he wasn't? What if he felt the same precarious connection she did and had escaped the tent to deal with his emotions?

The thought made her heart race even faster. What if he wanted to do it again?

What if she did?

Do I?

She closed her eyes against the *yes* echoing in her head and began mentally working through the pros and cons of hooking up with Flynn.

I broke my no O streak. Pro.

I broke it with my boss! Definite con.

He admitted to being attracted to me since the day we met. She didn't know if that was a pro or a con.

He could have been pretending just to get me to fool around. That was a definite con.

Ugh. That was getting her nowhere.

She had to go out there and face the music, but what did she want?

More.

More of that connection, more talking and getting to know each other. More of those unbelievable kisses and all the delicious touching that had followed. But he was her boss, and that wasn't even a gray area. That was a clear off-limits zone, which sent reality crashing down on her. What she wanted didn't matter, because if anyone found out, they could both lose their jobs.

With that sucky reality in her head, she used her body wipes to clean herself up, put on bug spray and clean clothes, and shoved her feet into her boots before heading out of the tent. The raincoats they'd set up were hanging from a tree branch, and there were smoldering embers in the fire pit. She spotted Flynn crouched beside the log where they'd purified the water last night, and her pulse quickened. His hair hung over his forehead, a royal-blue long-sleeve shirt straining against his biceps. He wore tan cargo pants tucked into boots, and he was pushing water through a leaf funnel into a canteen.

He looked up, and a slow grin crept across his handsome face, sending those butterflies into flight. "Hey, Steele. How'd you sleep? You look rested."

"Um…good. Yeah. I'm good." He was acting like nothing happened, which made her feel awkward. They couldn't just ignore what they'd done. That would make it even more awkward, so she gathered her courage and said, "So…*that* happened."

He closed the canteen and pushed to his feet, brows knitted. "Can you be more specific? A lot happened yesterday."

"*Flynn.*" She shot him an imploring look.

"What?" He closed the distance between them. "Are you talking about eating worms or using the makeshift ladies' room?"

"Oh my God. Can you…?" She crossed her arms. "I am *not* going to spell it out."

"If it wasn't those things, then I guess by *that* you meant when we kissed?"

She rolled her eyes.

"No?" He leaned in so close, their chests brushed, and he lowered his voice. "Do you mean when I touched you?" He ran his hand down her arm, and even through her shirt, it brought rise to goose bumps. "Or when I had my mouth between your legs and you came so hard and loud, you probably scared off all the dangerous animals?"

Great. Now she was the good kind of damp. *Bastard.* He looked amused. Was this a game to him? She lifted her chin, holding his gaze. "I don't think any of that is what Karen meant to happen when she sent us here."

He drew back, standing taller, eyes serious. "I'm sure you're right."

"It can't happen again. You're my boss, and we could both get in trouble."

"Okay. It won't happen again." He gave a curt nod, as if sealing their deal. "We've got two canteens of purified water and a lot of ground to cover and filming to do. Why don't you go brush your teeth, use the bathroom, and do whatever else you need to before we go looking for breakfast."

That's it? She'd gone through a litany of emotions and he wasn't bothered in the least? So he was just having fun? She was a hookup? Of course she was. *I really am an idiot.*

"You should bring your sandals in your pack when we leave camp. There's a river a few miles from here where we can fish. You'll need to go in the water, and I'm sure it'll be rocky. I don't want your feet to hurt."

"What makes you think my feet can't take a few rocks?"

He cocked a grin. "I've seen your pedicured toes, Glamour

Girl."

She wondered if that was another reason he wasn't interested in more than having a little fun, because he still thought of her as a glamour girl. The fact that she even wondered about it annoyed the heck out of her. He was her boss. He could get fired. What more of a reason did he need?

Shoving thoughts of what they'd done down deep, she locked them away, spun on her heel, and went to pee in the stupid hole in the ground.

AFTER FORAGING FOR more chontacuro worms for breakfast, which Sutton had been too hot and irritated to eat, and Flynn had eaten raw, they filled their daypacks with supplies and headed out to find the river. Sutton followed behind Flynn as they made their way through the dense forest. She must be getting used to the rainforest noises, because she wasn't as jumpy as she'd been yesterday. Flynn let her use his personal video camera to film. Seeing the rainforest through the lens of a camera gave her an entirely different perspective, making her feel slightly removed from it and, at the same time, even closer. In between watching where she was stepping, she focused on spotting colorful birds, playful monkeys, and industrious insects. Anything to keep her eyes off Flynn's back. His shirt was so snug, it showed every muscle as he swung the machete, guiding them through the forest.

After what felt like several hours, though time blurred in the rainforest, so it was probably only an hour or two, he stopped walking and said, "You've got to see this." He took her by the wrist, pulling her in front of him. With a hand on her hip, he drew her back to his chest and lowered his face next to hers, speaking quietly and pointing with his other hand. "See that hole in the ground?"

How was she supposed to concentrate on anything *but* the feel of him, when other than his earlier tease about last night, he was back to the tight-jawed, order-giving guy she knew so well? She couldn't afford to get lost in that confusion. "Yeah."

"Look just above it and to the left, at the tree about ten feet back."

"What am I looking at?"

"Follow the trunk up to the first branch, and you'll see a tree boa."

Visually tracing the line of the trunk, she spotted the amber snake lying in the crook of the branch and held her breath, fear prickling the back of her neck. "Aren't they aggressive?"

"Yes. Very." Flynn's hand curled tightly around her hip. "But we're far enough away from it. You're safe."

You're safe with me. The chains she'd used to trap those memories rattled, and she struggled to push them away again, but one memory from yesterday broke through. *I was so fascinated by the places we went and the things we saw and did, I assumed everyone was. I didn't want them to miss out on anything.* That was all this was. Flynn's excitement and his need to share it.

"Are you up to getting it on camera?" he asked.

Was the universe testing her? She was so used to him giving orders, his question threw her for a loop, making a small part of her wonder if last night had meant something to him after all. It bothered her that *that's* where her head went, and a bigger part of her, the smarter, more rational part that'd had to fight with him every step of the way for the last year and a half, took offense to his question.

"Of course I'm up for it." She stepped out of his grip and handed him the camera. "Let's do this."

His jaw ticked, and he stepped back to frame the shot with the other camera. "I'll zoom in on the snake when you call it out," he said gruffly.

She put on her reporter face, and when he pointed at her, she forced herself to be ultra-professional. "There's no lack of life in the rainforest. For novices like me, much of the wildlife blends into the scenery. Lucky for us, for experienced survivalists like Flynn Braden, it's like playing Where's Waldo. Over my right shoulder, coiled on the branch of a tree, is an amber tree boa, not to be confused with the emerald tree boa, which is a heavier, thicker snake. Tree boas aren't venomous, but they are aggressive. I'm glad there's some distance between us." She rattled off several facts about the species and told the viewers where they were heading next. "Let's see what else we can find." She held her smile until Flynn lowered the camera.

"That was great, but you don't have to mention me in these clips."

"I don't want to mislead the viewers into thinking anyone could wander into the rainforest and be safe in a place like this. You see things I don't, and you have skills that are keeping us alive and well. I know you don't want to be on camera, but do you prefer I don't mention you, either?"

"No." He raked a hand through his hair, tension tightening his jaw. "I just didn't want you to think you had to."

"I don't. And, honestly, I don't really think when I do these clips. I just say what comes to mind. I figure you'll edit out a lot of it anyway." Her stomach growled loudly.

"Bet you're wishing you'd eaten those worms now. Let's go catch some fish."

Other than giving a few directives to watch her step, Flynn didn't say much the rest of the way to the river, and the silence amplified the tension between them. She'd liked the window of friendship they'd found, and it bothered her to think he'd opened up to her with an endgame. But she couldn't reconcile that thought with the Flynn she'd gotten to know last night.

When they came out from under the umbrella of trees, it felt like they'd entered another world. The sun beamed down with all its bright, wonderful glory on the river snaking between the overgrown banks. Just ahead of them was a small rocky area, the only spot along the river's edge that wasn't covered with trees and brush. Sutton looked up at the sky, overcome by a sense of freedom, and spread her arms out to her sides, breathing deeply. "I didn't realize how much I missed seeing the sky. Isn't it beautiful?" She spun around and saw Flynn holding up the camera. It took her a second to realize he was already filming her. She snapped into reporter mode. "Clearly we found the river, and I'm a little excited." She rubbed her hands together. "Time to catch some fish. The water is murky, but I cannot *wait* to get wet."

Flynn flashed a wicked grin.

"In the water," she clarified. "I cannot wait to get *in the water*."

He laughed and stopped filming.

"You're awful, Braden."

He put his pack on the rocks and set the camera on it. "I believe *incredible* was the word you used last night, and I prefer it."

She was thankful for the levity, and her heart told her to

lean into it. But that particular organ wasn't as resilient as the rest of her, so she stifled that urge, shrugged off her day pack, and pointed at him. "Do *not* go there."

He held his hands up in surrender. "I wasn't going anywhere. I can't help it if you have a dirty mind."

"Uh-huh." She walked toward the water. "I know that smile."

"Don't go in yet, Steele." He beat her to the water's edge, blocking her from going in.

"I just want to put my fingers in."

"I know you do, but let's take a minute to get our bearings and make sure there are no visitors waiting to rush into the water with us. Anacondas are slow on land, but they're wicked fast in the water. And trust me, you don't want to be ambushed by a caiman."

Where was her head? Thank goodness he was using his. "Right, of course."

"Once we're sure we're clear, then I'll go in first to make sure there aren't any surprises waiting for us."

As they walked around the periphery, Flynn scanned the brush and looked all around, in between, and behind large rocks and trees, under giant leaves, and in the grass, indicating Sutton should do the same in case he missed anything. She had a feeling that man never missed a damn thing.

When he was satisfied that they were safe, he headed for the water.

"What are you going to do if there's a snake or caiman or piranha in there?"

"I guess we'll find out." He took off his shirt and shoes, then unbuttoned his jeans.

"What are you doing?"

As he stripped them off, he said, "Getting in the water."

"Naked?"

"I was going to wear my boxer briefs, but if you prefer…" He started to take them off, too.

"*Stop!*"

He laughed. "Make up your mind, Steele."

"Do *not* go in there naked. Something might bite your junk off."

He grabbed his crotch. "Just the thought of that hurts."

"Seriously, Flynn. Why didn't you bring a bathing suit?"

He shrugged. "I didn't think about it."

"Are you sure you should go in? Can't we catch fish from the shore?"

"With our fishing rods?" He looked amused. "I'm not worried, Sutton. Piranha attacks on humans are rare. They're not starving in these conditions, and I'm not bleeding profusely, so they won't be interested in me. I'm also kind of looking forward to wrestling a caiman or an anaconda. I'll be fine."

"You're crazy. At least take the machete with you."

"Nah. It'd just hinder me." As he walked into the water, he said, "If anything happens to me, you stay out of the water, no matter what. Got it?"

She nodded and held her breath, frantically searching the water as he waded in waist deep, his watchful eyes scanning his surroundings. "Feel anything?"

"No." He spun around. "Shit."

"What's wrong?"

"I—" He fell back in the water and disappeared below the surface.

"Flynn! *Flynn!*" She ran to get the machete and sprinted toward the water in full panic just as he broke the surface.

"What happened? Are you okay? *Getoutgetoutgetout!*"

He laughed.

"*Wha…?*" Her panic turned to fury. "You bastard! You almost gave me a heart attack! How could you do that to me?"

"How could I not?" He cracked up and pointed to the machete. "What were you gonna do with that?"

"Whatever I had to! *Jesus.* I thought something got you." She waved the machete at him. "I should hack off your trouser snake and use it as bait."

"*Hey.* It was a joke, and I happen to be fond of that body part."

"That was a horrible joke. Do I have to remind you that there are very real threats here?" she said as he trudged out of the water, his excruciatingly hot body glistening in the sun. Water dripped down his pecs and abs, and *sweet mother of all things drool-worthy*, dark, wet cotton clung to what looked like an anaconda in his boxer briefs.

"Eyes up here, Steele."

Her eyes flicked to his, embarrassment burning her cheeks. "Are you kidding me? How am I supposed to ignore that thing when it's practically waving hello?"

He eyed his dick and smirked. "It's a Braden curse."

She rolled her eyes.

"But that's not appropriate boss-employee talk, so we probably shouldn't go there." He stepped closer, and her traitorous nipples rose to greet him. "I'm sorry I scared you. How about you put down that weapon?"

She hadn't realized she was still holding the machete up like she was going to use it. She tossed it onto the rocks, grumbling, "I wish I could make you do the same."

"What was that?"

"Nothing."

"Ready to take your pants off and get wet?"

More than ever. But she wasn't about to tell him that. "How is *that* appropriate boss-employee conversation?"

FLYNN GRITTED HIS teeth. He shouldn't have phrased it like that, but after last night, everything felt bigger and more intense—his feelings for Sutton, his need to protect her, and his desire to do a hell of a lot more than they'd done—and he was having a hell of a time reining himself in. "We're here to fish, remember? Fish live in the water, and we're both going to get wet if we're going to catch anything."

She parked a hand on her hip, a challenge glittering in her gorgeous eyes. "You know damn well that's not what you meant."

"Do I?" He cocked a brow. "Get those boots off, Steele. Let's get started."

He went to get the net out of the pack. When he turned around, she was standing barefoot on the rocks, pulling her shirt off, revealing a sexy pink-and-white bikini top. His jaw tightened as she shook out her hair, and it cascaded over her shoulders. "Of course Glamour Girl brought a bikini." *Shit.* He hadn't meant to say that out loud.

"Is there something wrong with that?" She shimmied out of her pants.

She was all soft curves and long, lean legs, more beautiful than anyone he'd ever seen, bringing memories of last night, when he'd thought they'd grown infinitely closer. He knew backing off from a physical relationship was smart. Even if it killed him. If anyone found out, he'd probably be the one to get fired, but she'd worked her ass off, and he didn't want to screw up her professional reputation, either.

Fuck my life.

She was glowering at him as if she was waiting for a response.

"No. I'm sure this river sees plenty of itsy-bitsy, teeny-weenie, pink-and-white checkered bikinis. Get your sandals on."

She crossed her arms. "You didn't need yours."

"My feet are calloused. Yours are soft."

Her brows knitted. "How do you know? And don't say because you saw my painted toes."

"Your delicate little heel touched my back last night when we were doing that thing we weren't supposed to be doing."

Their gazes held, and her cheeks pinked up. "*Fine.* I'll wear them."

He turned his back to her, studying the river, unwilling to let his desire for her cloud his need to protect her. "You need to keep your eyes and ears open while we're in the water."

"I know." She stepped beside him.

"Stay near shore. They sent a twelve-foot net, which we'll stretch between us and drag through the water. If you feel *anything*, your goal is to get to land. Okay?"

She nodded. "Should we film this?"

"Shit. How did I forget that? Hold this." He handed her the net and grabbed the tripod out of the pack. He set it up on the bank, so it captured about halfway across the water, hoping to avoid getting himself in the shot. When he was done, he took the net from Sutton and handed her one end of it before heading into the murky water. She started to follow him, but he held up his hand. "Stay there."

"You just said we both have to be in the water."

"We do, but I don't want you in there any longer than you have to be." When he was waist deep, he scanned the surface and the riverbanks, praying nothing surprised them, and motioned for her to get in. "Stay close to shore as we move through the water."

"Okay." She walked in slowly. "It's warmer than I thought it would be, and *so* dirty. Are you sure this is safe?"

He couldn't be sure anything was safe in the rainforest, but he wasn't going to tell her that. "The indigenous people have been fishing this river for ages." His senses were on high alert as she waded in up to her thighs. She was so damn brave, she blew him away. "That's far enough. You okay?"

"As long as I don't think too hard about what I can't see under the surface."

"Sorry, babe, but you *need* to think about what's under there."

"I know. I am. Don't worry."

"A'right, then, let's do this. Try to stay even with me."

As they dragged the net through the water, her eyes remained trained on the water in front of her, while his skated around them, over both riverbanks, and behind them, all the while keeping a pulse on the net, feeling every hitch and sway.

"Did you fish like this growing up?" she asked.

"Yes, and a hundred times since."

"I never thought of my life as small, but it seems that way compared to yours."

"There's nothing small about your life, Steele. Look where you are and where you grew up. People would pay big bucks to grow up on an island and be the star of one of the hottest discovery shows out there." The net caught on something, and he stilled, holding up his hand, warning Sutton to stop so he could focus. His pulse sped up, feeling her worried eyes on him as he measured the stillness of the net to determine whether it was stuck in the undergrowth or in something dangerous. He breathed easier when there were no signs of life struggling against it. "It's okay. It's just undergrowth." He moved along the net, lifting until it freed from its tethers.

"That was nerve-racking," she said as they started walking again.

"Are you okay to keep going?"

"Yes." Her eyes remained trained on the water. "Can I ask you something personal?"

"Go for it."

"Last night you said you knew what it was like to want something of your own in a big family. Is that why you went on *Wilderness Warrior*?"

"I'm sure that was part of it. I was an arrogant kid, and really competitive with my brothers. Seth is brilliant. He started making money hand over fist when he was in college, and don't ask me how, because he's got brains that I can't keep up with, and Clay had already paved his way into the NFL. I wanted to show them I could be a success, too."

"I can understand that. What was the other part? The money?"

"Hell yeah. A million dollars is a lot of dough. But I didn't want to use the money to party or dick around. I wanted to explore and raise awareness about the plights of others." He wanted to tell what his grandfather called heart-driven stories.

"Then why did you disappear after you won? Didn't you get

a ton of sponsorships and special guest spots on shows and podcasts?"

He looked at her, weighing his answer. The sun beat down on her back, and her brows pinched in concentration as they moved slowly through the water. It was hard to believe he'd been so wrong about her at first. She wasn't just another pretty face. She had grit, and she never backed down. That confidence and determination were the sexiest things he'd ever seen. He'd give anyone else a half-ass answer to the question she'd asked, dodging the reason he'd gone into hiding, but for the first time in as long as he could remember, he wanted to share the truth. He wanted Sutton to know the real him, just as she'd been showing him who she was. "Because it turned my life into a circus."

She seemed to mull that over as they trudged through the water. "In what way?"

"I wanted to do something good, but the media turned me into the *it* guy. A pretty face the public would be drawn to."

"Aw, poor Flynn was too handsome for his own good."

He scoffed. "I didn't say I believed it, but companies wanted to pay me to travel and promote whatever they were selling, or to say I was exploring some cool remote place when they were really going to put me up in a fancy hotel and drive me out to a fucking forest or a desert for a few hours to pretend I was doing something important in a place like this. It was bullshit."

"I don't know, Flynn. I wouldn't mind a cushy deal like that."

"C'mon, Steele. You can't tell me you're not enjoying this fine Ecuadorian spa. I'm kind of loving our mud bath."

She smiled. "It's a good one, but a little wine and cheese would be nice."

"Okay, here comes the whine." He spoke in a whiny, child-like voice. "*I don't wanna walk through the water anymore.*"

She laughed.

"And here comes your cheese. Hey, beautiful, did you do something to my eyes? Because I can't take 'em off you."

She winced. "That was cheesy."

"Ya think? Still hungry for more? If being sexy were a crime, you'd go straight to jail."

"Please stop." She laughed.

"So, what do you do for a living besides take my breath away?" He loved hearing her laugh and seeing that smile light up her eyes, so he rattled off a few more cheesy lines.

Ten minutes later they were still laughing as they volleyed cheesy lines and gathered the net to see if they'd caught any fish.

"How does it feel to be the king of cheese?" she asked.

"Not as good as it felt to be between your knees" came out before he could stop it. *Shit.*

"Flynn!" She swatted his arm, but she was still laughing.

"Sorry, but you should know by now that I tell it like it is."

"Well, stop being so honest."

"So, you like liars? That makes sense." He started opening the net.

"Why would that make sense?" she snapped. "I don't like liars."

"Just that you're lying to yourself if you think you could take a cushy job and feel good about lying to the public." He started weeding through the net, pulling out leaves and other debris.

She sighed. "It was just the idea of a spa. A comfy bed, a clear bath, and a back massage sound really good right now."

"I get it, but you'd be bored shitless fake reporting. Hold

this for a second. I want to get the camera." He handed her the net, and her eyes bloomed wide.

"Ohmygod. The *camera*. We have to edit out what you said!"

He'd planned on editing out the things he'd revealed about himself, as well as the not-safe-for-work comments, even though he was pretty sure they were too far from the mic for it to have picked up their conversation. But she was adorable when she was freaking out, so he played it up. "I don't think the audience would mind hearing a few cheesy jokes."

"Not that! The part about my *knees*." She whispered the word *knees*.

"I thought we were on the same page about honest reporting." He chuckled as he went to get the camera. Turning the camera on her, he pointed to the net.

Like the professional she was, Sutton turned her scowl into a smile and did what she did best. "We've just pulled the net out of the river. The water was warm and too muddy to see under the surface, which made every step a bit nerve-racking, and the riverbed was rocky and weedy. I'm glad I had my sandals on." She paused, as if that comment was meant for him. "But I'm even happier that there were no giant snakes or hungry caiman waiting for us. Let's see if we caught any fish." She pulled out a few reeds and held them up for the camera. Peering into the net, she fished around with her hand, removing leaves and twigs. Her eyes widened, and she gasped. "We got one! Look!" Pride shimmered in her eyes as she lifted the net, showing the audience a fish tangled in it. "It's only about four inches long, but that's more than we had five minutes ago!"

Sutton's pinched brow told Flynn she was trying not to make faces as she freed the fish from the net. It wiggled out of her fingers and fell to the ground. "Whoops! He's a feisty little guy." She picked it up by the tail and showed the audience again before setting it aside and working through more of the netting. She pulled out a small branch and made a surprised sound. "We got another one! This one's bigger. After only a day and a half in the rainforest, I'm practically salivating over these fish." She fought with the netting and the squirming fish, held up the fish for the camera, and then set it with the other one.

She pushed to her feet, her tone turning serious. "When we entered this beautiful, terrifying rainforest, I had tunnel vision and saw myself as prey. All I could think about was how many predators there are and the varying shapes and sizes of them, from spiders and poisonous frogs to venomous snakes and wild cats. We won't even talk about what happens if you eat the wrong plants. I'll always be prey to many things that live here, but today I feel powerful and resourceful. Today I became a predator, too."

Flynn remembered the first few times that life-changing feeling had hit him and was hit with a rush of happiness for Sutton.

AFTER CATCHING AND cooking several more fish, they were sitting on the rocks with full bellies and smiles on their faces. Well, Flynn was sitting on the rocks. Sutton was sitting on her day pack. Why seeing that made him happy, he had no idea. It was just one more thing about the woman who was as tough as she was feminine that intrigued him.

"I would kill for an iced hazelnut coffee right now." Sutton turned her face up to the sun and closed her eyes. "What do you miss most?"

"Not much." The truth was, he didn't miss a damn thing, because nothing back home compared to spending time with Sutton. Even if last night was all the intimacy they'd share, and the rest of their time together was spent just getting to know each other better, he knew two more nights would never be enough.

She shaded her eyes, studying him. "Really?"

"We've got food, great company, and sunshine. What else could I want?"

"Running water, a comfortable bed, a reading light."

If he had the first two things, he wouldn't have her, but the third suggestion piqued his interest. "Are you a big reader?"

"Yes. Always have been. What about you?"

"I bring a book with me everywhere I go."

"You do?" She looked astonished.

"Yup. I've got one back at the tent."

She sat up and leaned forward, eyes dancing with excitement. "So do I. What book did you bring?"

"*Gulliver's Travels.* What did you bring?"

"I have hundreds of ebooks on my ereader. I'd rather hold a book in my hands, but I'm a mood reader, and with my luck, I'd have chosen the wrong one. Why did you choose *Gulliver's Travels?*"

"I take it on every trip."

"Like a good-luck charm?"

"Exactly like that. I had a leather book cover that zips up made to protect it. My grandfather gave it to me when I was a teenager. He gave me all of my favorites: *My Side of the Mountain*, *Hatchet*, *Lord of the Flies*, *Treasure Island*, *Tom*

Sawyer, Huck Finn, Around the World in Eighty Days. If it's an adventure book, I probably own it and have read it a million times."

"I *love* those stories."

He couldn't believe his ears. "You've read them?"

"All except *Gulliver's Travels,* and I never finished *Around the World in Eighty Days,* but now I'm putting them both on my reading list. I told you I was a weird little girl. I used to make up news reports about the books I read, and those were more interesting than others."

"I don't think that's weird. I think it makes you even more intriguing." The smile that earned lit him up inside. "What else do you read? Do you have a favorite book?"

"My favorites change depending on my mood, and I read just about everything." She leaned back on her palms. "I love women's fiction and steamy romance. Especially the ones that really tear my heart out."

He cocked a brow. "That doesn't sound like an enjoyable escape."

"I hate drama in my real life, but in books I want all the feels. I want to laugh and cry and swoon. And when I read suspense and adventure, I want to be on pins and needles and have to use my brain to figure out whatever the main characters are trying to overcome or unravel. But I don't like reading horror, unless Jock wrote it."

"Your brother is a writer?"

"He's not just a writer. He's an amazing writer. His first book, *It Lies,* hit number one on the *New York Times* bestseller list for sixteen weeks, and all the big publishers had a bidding war over his second book, *Eyes on You,* which was on the list for twelve weeks."

"*Whoa.* That's impressive. How many books has he written?"

"Only two, and he's started a third. He didn't write during those difficult years when he and Archer weren't talking."

"It sounds like Daphne and Hadley did a lot more than just bring your family back together. It sounds like they opened his creative well."

"They did, and I think he did just as much for them. Jock adores them so much. You should see how he looks at Daphne, and Hadley used to scowl at everyone. It was so freaking cute. Now those scowls are rare, which is better, of course, and her smiles are golden. I'm really happy for them." She gazed out at the water, as if she were reflecting on that happiness. Then she took a deep breath, sitting up straighter, and said, "You know, they have a pretty good chef at this spa. That was a tasty meal. I might come back to this waterfront restaurant."

Her rapid subject change made him wonder if it was hard for her to think about those difficult years, so he tried to lighten the mood. "It didn't compare to what I had last night."

"Flynn!" She swatted at him, and missed.

He laughed. "You're the one who opened that can of worms."

"I did *not.*"

"Oh no?" He cocked a brow. "Who took the first kiss?"

Her jaw dropped, and she snapped her mouth shut, but she couldn't hold in a laugh. "I blame Karen for that indiscretion."

"That's a good strategy. I'll go along with that."

"She's the one who sent us here unsupervised."

"What are we, toddlers?" She looked so relaxed, leaning back on her palms, long legs crossed at her ankles, her pretty pink toenails on display, and he was having such a good time, he was tempted to spend the whole afternoon right there in the sunshine, earning more carefree laughs and sweet smiles. But he had something special he wanted to show her, so he pushed to his feet and offered his hand. "Come on, Steele. We've got exploring to do."

"Where are we heading?" She squinted up at him as she took his hand, and he pulled her up to her feet.

"Wherever the day takes us."

Chapter Ten

"CAN'T YOU JUST shimmy up that tree like a monkey, swing out on the branch, and hang from your knees to grab them?" Sutton asked.

It was raining, and they were deep in the rainforest again, looking up at yellow passion fruits dangling several feet above their heads from a maracuyá vine.

"What if there's a snake up there in that mass of leaves by the juncture of the trunk and the branch going in the other direction?"

"Then I guess you'll shimmy back down."

He gave her a deadpan look. "And if I'm up there and something comes after you down here?"

"Then you'll have to Jackie Chan it and flip out of the tree to save me." She grinned.

"You think that's funny, huh?" He grabbed her ribs.

She squealed and spun around, laughing. "Come on, *Mowgli*, get up that tree."

"You're gonna get it now." He lunged, grabbing her ribs with both hands. She squirmed and laughed, trying to break free. "You're mine now, Steele." He tickled her, and she howled with laughter.

"In your dreams, *Mowgli*!"

He swept an arm around her, hauling her against him, both of them laughing. "What're you going to do now, smart-mouth?" He had her hands and arms trapped against her sides. "What's your endgame?"

"To get my mouth around something big and juicy," she said sassily.

He knew by the glint in her eyes that she was fucking with him, so he decided to give it right back to her. "You've seen how big it is. Think you can handle it?"

Her eyes narrowed. "I've handled bigger."

I doubt that. "How do you feel about being on top?"

Her eyes widened, and she blushed a red streak, but her eyes never left his. *So fucking hot.*

"I…*um*…like it."

"I was hoping you'd say that." He placed his hands on her waist, trailing them down her hips as he crouched in front of her. "A'right, baby. Let's go. Right here, right now. Show me what you've got, and you know I'll get you there."

She breathed harder, lust rising in her eyes. "Here?"

"We don't have all day, Steele. Let's go. Get on my shoulders."

Her brow wrinkled. "On your—"

"Shoulders. What were *you* talking about?" He watched understanding dawn on her, irritation replacing the lust he'd seen, and he laughed.

"You're such an *ass*."

"We've already established that. Now stop bitching and climb on."

"Are you sure you can hold me?"

"Woman, I could hold three of you. Now get your fine ass

moving."

"That's not very appropriate talk for a boss," she teased as she climbed onto his shoulders and grabbed his head to steady herself.

"I'm pretty sure having my face buried between your legs wasn't appropriate either, but shit happens." Her thighs squeezed around his head, and *man*, did that give him ideas.

"*Shh, Braden.* We're not talking about that."

"I won't talk about it." He moved beneath the branch. "But you've got quite a grip with those thighs, so you know I'm going to think about it."

"*Flynn.* I need to concentrate."

"Sorry. It was a compliment. Your thighs must get quite a workout."

"Not the good kind," she grumbled, muscles flexing as she rose off his shoulders, trying to reach the dangling fruit.

"That's it. Work those muscles."

She wobbled, and gasped. He quickly wrapped his hands around her thighs, steadying her, and tried to ignore the pinch in his shoulder. "I've got you."

She sank down to his shoulders again, holding on to his head. "Don't let me fall."

"Babe, you could be wrapped around my head in the other direction while I take my fill, and I still wouldn't let you fall."

"You should add that skill to your résumé." She rose off his shoulders again, reaching for the fruit.

Damn, he liked her sense of humor. "How do you think I got this job?"

She laughed, and he felt her rising higher. "I'm *almost* there." Her voice strained with her stretch.

"I'll get you there." He put one hand on her ass, keeping the other on her leg.

"Not *that* kind of almost there!"

"You really do have a dirty mind." He pushed her ass up, lifting her higher, using his other hand to steady her.

"*IgotitIgotitIgotit!*" She sank back down to his shoulders.

"I told you I'd get you there."

"*Ha ha.* It's heavier than I thought it would be."

He chuckled. "You know the fourteen-year-old in me would say *that's what she said.*"

She leaned down with a big-ass smile. "So would the twelve-year-old in me." She handed him the small oblong fruit. "Hold this. I'll get the others so we have enough for later and tomorrow."

"A'right. Now it's a party."

She collected several passion fruit, and as he helped her down, she said, "That was fun."

"We make a good team."

"When we're not driving each other crazy." She surveyed their stash, looking over the fruit, picking each one up and squeezing it. "Some are harder than others."

He cocked a brow.

"You're such a guy." She shook her head.

"Sorry. I don't know where all that's coming from. I'm not usually like this."

"Sounds like I'm bringing out the kid in you. That's got to be better than when I piss you off."

"I don't know about that. I like you when you're feisty." Their gazes held, and that thrum of electricity grew stronger. He cleared his throat and looked away in an effort to redirect his brain.

"How do we eat these?" She held a piece of fruit in front of his face.

"I'll show you. Let's find the ripest one." He felt each of them and picked up the softest. "They're filled with seeds that are encased in pulpy juice, and that's what you eat." He broke it in half, exposing the white, spongy layer beneath the skin and the seeds in the center, and handed her half. He tipped the other half up to his mouth and ate the seeds.

She followed his lead. "*Mm*. It's sweet and tart."

"They're good, aren't they?" He opened another one and gave her half.

"*So* good. The seeds are crunchy, and the pulp is like gel."

"The wonders of the rainforest." After they finished eating the second one, they stowed the rest of the passion fruit in the daypacks. "Let's go see what else we can find."

"Want to see what's through there?" She motioned up a hill through the brush to their left.

"I think we should stick to this direction."

"But there might be something cool over there."

"It looks like good stalking ground for big cats, if you ask me. There's a bit of a hill. They'd have a great view of their prey down below."

She put up her index finger. "On second thought, I think we can skip that direction."

As they made their way through the forest, they stopped to film a sloth hanging out in a tree and, later, a slew of leaf-cutter ants carrying vegetation to their underground colonies, brightly colored caterpillars, enormous centipedes, howler monkeys, and spider monkeys.

"Is that a tarantula nest?" Sutton pointed to a hole in the ground with webbed silk around the entrance.

"It sure is. Good spotting."

They took a minute to film it, and Sutton gave a stellar performance. As Flynn lowered the camera, he heard the sound of running water.

"Which wa—"

"Shh." He held his hand up.

Sutton moved closer to him, grabbing his arm. "*What is it?*" she whispered, frantically looking around. "*Something big?*"

"No. Listen." He was quiet for a second. "Do you hear water?"

Her brows knitted, and she listened intently. "I think, *maybe.*"

"Let's check it out." The sound grew louder as they neared its source.

"That sounds like a lot of water," she said excitedly.

He let her lead, falling a step behind and lifting the camera to catch her initial reaction for himself more than the show, though he was glad for the excuse, because there were few things as beautiful as an excited Sutton. She pushed through a thicket of plants and stood stock-still. Flynn lifted the camera higher, filming the sun beating down on a waterfall surrounded by rocks, lush plants, and colorful flowers.

"Flynn, look!" She spun around, radiant with her sun-kissed cheeks, eyes dancing with delight, and a beaming smile that hit him square in the center of his chest. "Oh! You're filming. Give a girl some warning next time."

"And miss that spectacular reaction? Not a chance, Steele. Go on. Do your thing."

She didn't miss a beat, and he followed her toward the water, filming her as she told the audience about how the air felt cooler and smelled fresher. "Even the birds sound magical, like something out of a fairy tale. This could *almost* make me forget the dangers that lurk here." She went into detail about waterfalls being a natural source of negative ions, which had positive effects on mood and were known to help some people breathe easier.

All Flynn knew was that being around Sutton used to make it hard for him to breathe, but lately she'd become his waterfall, and he was not doing a good job of keeping that attraction under wraps.

She finished her segment and didn't wait for him to stop filming before whipping off her shirt. "Put that thing away. Let's make sure there are no creepy monsters waiting for us and go in!"

Someone is learning.

As they walked around the perimeter, Flynn went through the same careful inspection he had at the river, checking out the plants, grasses, crevices of rocks, and the surrounding brush.

"This is beautiful, isn't it?" Sutton asked as she peered around a plant. "Do you think it's…?" Her brow furrowed. "Wait a second. How did you know to film me?"

"I always film you."

"Yes, but you weren't taking the video camera *out* when I found the waterfall and turned around. You were *already* filming."

"We heard water," he said as he looked under a plant.

"Barely. I wasn't even sure I heard it, but you made a bee-line for it." She cocked her head, eyes narrowing. "You knew this was here, didn't you? That's why you wouldn't go explore that hill with me, isn't it? You said you had mapped out the safe areas and the river. It's all starting to make sense."

"You caught me." He motioned to the waterfall. "Welcome to your *au naturel* water treatment, Ms. Steele. This spa doesn't have plush robes or fancy wine, but the views are great, and I hear the company isn't half-bad."

She smiled. "When he's not barking orders or trying to make me blush."

"Yeah, well, you need to be pushed, I need to keep you safe, and you're fucking adorable when you blush." He needed to stop saying personal shit like that, but he longed to be closer to her, not drive more distance between them. "Most people would have cried uncle the first night here. But not you. You're fierce, and confident, and you've got a big-ass chip on your shoulder and something to prove, which I'm sure I contributed to."

She held up her index finger and thumb an inch apart, mouthing, *Little bit.*

"That's probably not going to change, but I was hoping being at the waterfall might help you feel less like a trapped animal and would be more along the lines of the lifestyle you're accustomed to. Not that you're a diva. I didn't mean that. You're…" *Jesus, Flynn, get your head out of your ass.* "Fuck it. I don't know. You're like Sam in *My Side of the Mountain.*"

"Are you comparing me to a twelve-year-old boy?"

"Mm-hm. Yeah, I guess I am." He rubbed the back of his neck. "That probably wasn't the best choice."

"I've been called worse."

"Good. *Wait.* Has someone been talking shit about you? Because I'll put a stop to that real quick."

"Only you."

"I don't call you names or talk shit about you," he said defensively, noticing too late the tease in her eyes. He ground his back teeth and tried to focus on what he was saying. "Anyway, what I meant by you being like Sam was that you're tenacious. You make up your mind to do something, and no matter what challenges you face, you don't give up. That's admirable, and I have no fucking clue where I was going with this, but here we are, so as long as there aren't any critters in that water, you can get undressed and enjoy it."

SUTTON COULD DO little more than watch Flynn strip down and crouch by the water's edge in his boxer briefs, scanning the water for threats. Every peek she got into the heart of the man behind her hard-edged, complicated boss made their attraction more difficult to ignore. She was having a hard enough time trying not to think about last night or how much she wanted more, and this sweet gesture made it even harder to deal with. She was as touched by his bringing her there as she was by the compliments he'd given her. Although she was surprised he'd gotten his back up at the idea of someone talking shit about her. Why would that bother him when he didn't seem bothered in the least by the idea of last night being a onetime thing? It wasn't like he needed to protect her outside the rainforest.

She watched him get in the water, his expression serious as he moved around, checking every inch, disappearing beneath the surface and behind the falls, looking at every rock, every plant. Keeping her safe. *I wouldn't trust your life in anyone else's hands…Being here with you makes keeping my hands to myself a million times harder.* His words still rang as genuine in her head, warring with the way he'd acted like he didn't mind not touching her again.

"All clear, Sut."

His deep voice brought her back to the moment. He was treading water in the middle of the plunge pool, smiling like life was simple. Maybe it was for him, and she was just overthinking. Surely when they got back to Port Hudson and their normal lives, this needy ache for him would dissipate.

"Are you coming in, Steele?"

"Yeah." She pulled out her elastic hair band, feeling the heat of his stare as her hair tumbled free and she climbed into the cool, clear, refreshing water. "*Ah.* This is heavenly." She swam underwater to him, and when she broke the surface, she floated on her back. "I feel like we've found a hidden treasure."

"This whole rainforest is a hidden treasure."

"It is. A scary one, but a treasure just the same." She felt his eyes on her again and had the strange thought that the pieces of him he'd been revealing to her were like hidden treasures, too. She began treading water. Their legs touched, and it sent a shiver of awareness through her. His lips twitched, those enticing blue eyes holding her captive. Her nerves prickled, and she dove underwater to break the connection. When she came up for air, she splashed him and swam away. He caught her foot, and she squealed, yanking it free and turning to splash him again, but he splashed her first, making her giddy with delight.

"You're in for it, Braden!" She splashed him hard, and a battle ensued. They swam around laughing and splashing, egging each other on. When he lunged for her, she gulped air into her lungs and dove underwater. He followed, his face an inch from hers underwater, eyes boring into her, that electric current searing between them despite the cool water. *Kiss me,* whispered through her mind, and his gaze intensified, as if he'd heard it. Her lungs burned, and her body flamed. Sure she was losing her mind, seeing what wasn't there, she broke through the surface to escape the heat of him, but he followed her up and snagged her around her waist.

"Where're you going, Steele?"

The feel of his hot, hard body intensified the lustful ache inside her. "Anywhere I want." She broke free and treaded water.

"You do make me feel like a kid again."

That tweaked her heartstrings, because at the moment she felt that way, too, and she realized how different they both were right now. The warnings weren't blaring in his eyes as they had been upon their arrival, and she was sure hers probably gave away how much she wanted him. She tried to distract herself from the anxiety that caused and said, "I'll have to leave a good review for this resort."

"Maybe take off a star for the accommodations."

"You don't like our luxurious suite? Do you want to borrow my Snugpak tonight?"

He shook his head, a low laugh tumbling out. He rolled his right shoulder back and rubbed it with his left hand.

"Is your shoulder still hurting?" She wondered if she'd made it worse by climbing on his shoulders to get the passion fruit.

"It's fine."

"What did you do to it?"

"It's an old climbing injury. I tore my rotator cuff a couple of years ago when I was climbing with Seth and Noah and some of our cousins."

"Were you barking orders at them, and they shoved you off the mountain?" she teased.

"They probably would have liked to do that a time or two, but no. It's just an overuse injury. I had it repaired, but it acts up in damp weather."

"Then why are we *here* of all places? You choose our assignments. We could've gone anywhere, and you set up the trip to stay with the tribe in the rainiest place possible."

"Because it's not a big deal. It doesn't stop me from doing anything. It just hurts sometimes."

"Well, you deserve a spa day more than I do. I'll massage it for you." She moved closer, fully aware that touching him was not going to help calm her desires, but it could help his pain, and it might even tell her whether he felt something more toward her or if she was imagining it.

He waved her off. "It's okay. I'm good."

"If you're worried it'll make you seem less manly if you let me help you, you're wrong. Everyone needs help sometimes."

He scoffed. "I'm not worried about that."

"Then stop being stubborn. You brought me to this beautiful waterfall. It's the least I can do." She didn't give him a choice. She closed the gap between them and began rubbing his shoulder, kicking her feet to stay up. Touching him without the cover of laughter or teasing brought their ever-present sexual tension into focus, and there was no escaping the way it enveloped them like a cape, drawing them closer. She felt him tense up, saw the muscles in his jaw tighten, and knew he felt it, too. "Am I hurting you?"

"*No.*" The word dripped with restraint. "You don't have to do this."

"I want to. You're so tense, you need it. I wish I could get better leverage, to really get in there and work the muscles."

He cursed under his breath and grabbed her by the waist, pulling her against him and guiding her legs around his body. His skin was hot, his chest deliciously hard, and when their eyes connected, a storm of lust and restraint brewed in his eyes. Did he see the same in hers? Her heart was beating so fast, she was sure it would burst through her chest. She tried to concentrate on massaging his shoulder, but he was keeping them both afloat, and with every kick, his erection brushed between her legs.

Neither spoke as she continued rubbing his shoulder. She couldn't look away from the hunger in his eyes, her breath catching with every taunt of his erection. The air pulsed, thick with desire. Without a word, he belted his arm around her, moving toward shallower water. She slid her arms around his neck, reveling in the feel of his muscles flexing against her, his heavy breath coasting over her cheek as his feet found the bottom, and he stopped walking. Her body was on fire, despite the cool spray from the falls kissing her skin. She wanted *Flynn* to kiss her. His lips were right there for the taking, but she didn't want to be the one to make the first move this time. Nervous about doing just that, she went back to rubbing his shoulder. "Is it helping?"

His eyes narrowed. "Not really."

Why were they punishing themselves? Nobody would know what they did while they were here. She didn't know if he was holding back because he was her boss or for some other reason. Could he be missing her cues? God, this was torture. She'd never wanted anyone this badly. The heck with it. She threw caution to the wind, speaking seductively. "Is there a better spot? Do you want me to go *deeper*?" She heard the quiver of desire in her own voice as she rubbed her body against his.

His eyes flamed. "I'm trying to play by your rules, Sutton. But your rules suck."

Thoroughly confused, she said, "Rules?"

"That what happened last night can't happen again."

"They're not *my* rules."

"Well, they sure as fuck aren't mine."

"You took off before I even woke up. I figured I'd save myself the embarrassment of you not wanting me and say it before you could."

His jaw clenched. "I left the tent because I was as hard as fucking stone, and I didn't want to make you uncomfortable."

"*Oh*" fell stupidly from her lips.

"*Jesus.*" He rocked his hips, pressing his erection firmly against her. "Does it feel like I don't want you?"

She couldn't suppress her smile as she shook her head. "But you're still my boss, so…*what happens in the rainforest stays in the rainforest?*"

"I like the way you think, Steele." He grabbed the back of her head, and their mouths fused together, tongues battling, teeth gnashing, moans coalescing. She ground against him, unable to get close enough. He kissed her harder, forcing her mouth open wider. His scruff abraded her skin, every swipe of his tongue amping up her desire. She pushed her hands into his hair, holding tight, the way he'd liked it last night. He gritted out, "*Fuuck*," and reclaimed her mouth. His hand moved between her legs from behind, stroking her through her bikini bottom, driving her out of her freaking mind. "You fucking kill me."

"Don't die yet," she pleaded.

"Not a chance." He pushed his fingers beneath the thin material, sliding through her wetness. "Even underwater I can feel how slick you are for me." He pushed his thick fingers inside her, and "*Yes*" rushed from her lungs at the glorious intrusion. He recaptured her mouth, and she moved with him as they devoured each other, his rough fingers stroking over that magical spot, drawing desperate sounds from someplace deep inside her. Her desire mounted, prickling her limbs and pounding through her core. She broke the kiss, panting out, "*Oh God*," clutching his shoulders as she chased her release.

"That's it, baby. Give that tight pussy what it needs. Then I'm going to fuck you like I've been dying to all day." His dirty talk unearthed something primal in her, and she clawed at his shoulders, fingernails digging into his flesh as she ground against his hand. "You're so fucking sexy," he gritted out, and sank his teeth into her shoulder, sending an erotic mix of pain and pleasure spiking through her. She cried out as she spiraled over the edge, consumed with mind-numbing sensations that went on for so long, she was sure she'd set a record.

When she finally came down from the high, she couldn't wait a second longer to feel him inside her, and she pushed at his boxer briefs. "Take 'em off. I want *all* of you."

He made quick work of stripping them both naked, and tossed her bathing suit and his boxer briefs onto a rock. "Get over here, you sexy thing." He tugged her into his arms, kissing her mesmerizingly slowly and enticingly deep as he lifted her, her legs circling his waist. The broad head of his cock pressed temptingly against her entrance. She tried to sink onto it, but he held her still, hungry noises escaping her lungs and filling his as he rocked his hips, teasing and taunting, until she was trembling with need. She tore her mouth away. "*Flynn*, give me that anaconda."

He smiled against her lips. "Always rushing." He dragged his scruff along her cheek, speaking into her ear. "I've been thinking about your tight pussy wrapped around my cock for so long, I'm not going to want to pull out. Are you protected?"

"*Yes.*" She'd been so intent on having him, she hadn't even thought about mentioning it, and it struck her that even in the throes of desire, he was still watching out for both of them.

His mouth covered hers rough and demanding as he buried himself to the hilt in one hard thrust. She gasped, clinging to him as fiery sensations consumed her. She felt every blessed inch of him. His thick length filled her so completely, pleasure radiated through her core. He ground his hips, stretching her, holding her ass so tight, she was sure he'd leave handprints, and that turned her on even more. She grabbed his shoulders as he lifted her, sliding her along his shaft painfully slowly, then took her impossibly deeper, continuing in a toe-curling rhythm. "Fuck, baby. You are so damn tight."

"Feels good. *Faster.*"

His mouth came coaxingly down over hers, kissing her passionately, *seductively*, but he didn't quicken his efforts. He slowed his pace, intensifying every tantalizing sensation, each thrust taking her higher, until her entire being was on fire.

"*Jesus*, Sutton. You take me so good."

The greedy pleasure in his voice was an aphrodisiac, and she wanted to hear more of it. She'd never known what was missing with the men she'd been with, but now she knew it wasn't any one thing. It was *everything*, and Flynn was a master at all of it. The way he handled her, his control, his filthy mouth, those eyes that burned through her. He brought out something dark and dirty in her, and she didn't hesitate to use it, countering, "You *fuck* me so good."

He growled against her lips. "I knew I liked that mouth of yours."

Continuing his masterful seduction, he played her body like no one ever had. His hips moved in small circles, controlling their pace, every stroke of his cock along that hidden spot leaving her breathless. Pressure mounted inside her like a volcano ready to blow, and *good Lord*, he liked her mouth? His mouth was wreaking havoc with her. His tongue plunged deep and fast, in contrast to the torturously slow beast between her legs, magnifying every sensation. She could barely breathe for the electricity pulsing beneath her skin, but she could *taste* his desire, *feel* his restrained power, and she wanted it *all*.

She wanted to make him lose his mind *for her*.

Determined to reclaim a modicum of control, she clung to his shoulders, moving faster, riding him harder. He gritted out a curse, hips jackhammering, water splashing around them. He tugged her head back by her hair, sending white-hot shocks through her core, and sank his teeth into her neck, catapulting her into a world of cataclysmic explosions. "*Flynn—*" He continued pounding into her, heightening her pleasure, until she cried out again, the loud indiscernible sound echoing around them.

His fist tightened in her hair. "Open your eyes."

She did, and his hungry eyes pierced through her. "I want you to *see* me and remember who's making you feel so good."

"As if I could forget?"

His eyes flamed, and their mouths collided in a feast of need and greed as he drove into her so hard, she knew she'd feel him for days, and she relished the thought of it. He fucked her faster, *rougher*, so perfectly, another orgasm came crashing down on her. Her hips bucked as her inner muscles clamped around his cock. "Fuck, Sutton," he growled, slowing them down. "*Fuuck.*"

"*Don'tstopdon'tstopdon'tstop.*" She was already chasing another high, so lost in them, she didn't care if she was speaking in tongues.

"I'm not going to stop. I'm going to fucking lose it." With a sinful, guttural sound, he pounded into her. She clung to him, his every muscle corded tight, and his next thrust sent them both over the edge. His name flew from her lungs as he gritted out hers like a curse. She felt every jerk of his cock, every gust of his breath, as they rode out their pleasure. When she collapsed, boneless against him, his chin fell to his chest, and those strong arms that had held her up gently cradled her.

"*Jesus*, Sut." He buried his face in her neck, pressing a kiss there.

"Hm?" was all she could manage.

He slid his hand up her back and into her hair, giving a playful tug. "I have a feeling we're in big trouble."

She whispered, "Thoroughly fucked."

"Catch your breath, sweetheart. We're just getting started."

AFTER A SECOND round of incredible sex, Flynn sat by the water keeping watch as Sutton lay on her stomach on the rocks writing in her journal. Her hair was gathered over one shoulder, one leg bent at the knee, her foot bobbing slowly toward the ground and then back up. The afternoon sun glistened on her back, and that sexy pink-and-white bikini was begging to be stripped off by his teeth.

She was even more beautiful when she was sated and relaxed like this, while he was flying high, like a wild animal that had been restrained from the only thing he'd wanted and had finally broken free. Now that he knew what she felt like wrapped around him as she shattered in his arms, he craved even more of her. A deeper connection. He had two days to fill his well. Two days to capture the moments like this, when her guard was nowhere in sight.

Pushing to his feet, he turned on the video camera, panning from her gorgeous head to her adorable feet. She was engrossed in whatever she was writing, her pen sailing across the page. "Doodling my name?"

"Hardly." She didn't turn around or stop writing.

"Yeah, that would be juvenile. You're a reporter, far too detail oriented for that. I'm guessing it's more along the lines of"—he raised his voice an octave—"*Flynn Braden is so hot. I can't wait to get down and dirty with him again.*"

She closed the journal and rolled onto her side, shielding her eyes from the sun. Her smile faltered. "You're filming this? Are you crazy? Delete it!"

"Chill." He didn't stop filming. "This is my personal camera, and damn, Steele. You're sexy when you're pissed."

"Then you must think I'm sexy often."

You have no idea how right you are. "Have you made your pros and cons list about us yet?"

"Wouldn't you like to know?"

"I'll take that as a yes. How'd I do?"

She sat up, wrinkling her nose adorably, and held out her hand, wobbling it from side to side.

"Seriously? Let me help you. *Pro.* Never has trouble getting wood."

"I wrote something about you being a dick. Does that count?"

He pointed the camera at himself as he lowered himself down beside her. "That's how she says she loves me." Keeping the camera at arm's length, he filmed both of them. "Sutton Steele, what kind of advice do you have for anyone who might come to the rainforest with their boss?"

A rascally spark flickered in her eyes. "Come *to* the rainforest, or come *in* it?"

Man, she was amazing. "Your choice."

"If you've got only one tent, make good use of it. It'll help you sleep." That flicker in her eyes turned seductive. "And if you find a waterfall, make even better use of it."

He leaned in, kissing her passionately.

She swatted at the camera. "Turn that thing off."

He arched a brow. "What if we want to watch it later?"

"What happens in the rainforest stays in the rainforest, remember?"

He set the camera down and shifted over her, kissing her smiling lips. "So you don't want to watch me taking this sexy little bikini off with my teeth?" He bit her bikini strap, tugged it, and snapped it against her skin.

She bit her lower lip, eyes narrowing.

"Pros." He kissed her neck. "It would be hot, and we can delete it after, leaving absolutely *no* cons."

"Promise to delete it?"

"You've got yourself a deal, Steele."

Chapter Eleven

"WHAT DO YOU think, babe? One more time," Flynn said greedily in the dark tent. They had been insatiable for each other all day, having sex three times at the waterfall, and he'd lost count of how many times since. He thought a few times would be enough to calm his raging desire for her, but they were greedier and more passionate every time they came together, and she—*they*—were addicting.

"*Mm.*"

"Need a break?"

She shook her head. "Just a kiss."

He leaned over and kissed her smiling lips. "Hands and knees, sexy Steele." She'd proven to be an eager, willing lover, and she not only liked when he used his teeth, tugged her hair, or told her what to do, but she got off on it and enjoyed giving it right back, which was hot as hell.

"Getting creative again?" she asked as she sat up.

"I need to pad my résumé somehow." He ran his fingers between her legs, and she exhaled, eyelids fluttering. "I can fuck you harder and deeper from behind."

"Then what are you waiting for?" she asked just above a whisper.

That's it, baby, challenge me. He fisted his cock. Those hungry hazel eyes zeroed in on him as he gave himself a few tight strokes.

She licked her lips. "Are you going to share, or am I your visual inspiration for a solo flight."

"Do I look like a fool to you?" She'd been his inspiration for so long, her face, her body, and the way she walked and talked were imprinted in his mind. He wasn't about to waste the real thing. Besides, he could use some additional visuals for the solo rides he'd endure when they left here. "Bring that sexy mouth over here. I want your lips wrapped around my cock before I fuck you."

"Funny, I was just thinking the same thing."

He went up on his knees, and she wasted no time, wrapping her hand around his dick and slicking her tongue over the head. "*That's it.* Let me see those pretty eyes." Her eyes flicked up to his while her tongue slid over his slit. "Stroke me, baby." She did as he asked, licking him from root to tip, and fisted his cock again, stroking him as she teased the head with her tongue. He buried his hands in her hair, and her eyes flamed. "Suck it. I want to feel you squeezing and stroking as I fuck your mouth."

He didn't have to ask twice. She was as hungry for this as he was, sucking hard, stroking tight, moaning so loud, it vibrated through him. Pleasure glowed in her eyes. He was tempted to come in her mouth, but he had a bone-deep *need* to be buried inside her again. To hear her whimpers and moans and feel her tight heat taking him. Gritting his teeth to stave off his release, he drank in the sight of her devouring his cock for another minute before tugging her back by her hair and saying, "That's going to happen a lot before we leave here." He took her in a smoldering kiss, teasing between her legs, getting off on her moans and needy sounds.

He kissed her softer and drew back, loving the lustful haze gazing back at him. "On your knees, sweet thing. I need to fuck you now." Thinking about what she'd said when they'd first started fooling around in the tent—*You need to pull out. I'm not traipsing around this rainforest with you know what dripping down my legs*—he added, "I'm looking forward to coming all over that beautiful ass of yours." He'd already come on her stomach, thighs, and tits and had filled with greedy pleasure each and every time, knowing he'd branded her inside and out. He kissed her again. "Now get up on your hands and knees and we'll continue our debauchery."

"I like these fringe benefits," she said as she lifted her gorgeous ass in the air for him, her silky hair trailing down her back.

"Look at you, so damn beautiful." He knelt behind her, running his hands over her ass, and gave one cheek a smack. She glowered at him over her shoulder, showing the fierceness he craved. "Don't pretend you don't like it, Steele."

He aligned their bodies, bending over her back to press a kiss to her shoulder as he thrust slowly into her. When he was buried deep, he stilled, loving her desire-drenched exhalation and the way her pussy squeezed greedily around him. "Feel good, baby?"

"God, yes," she said breathily.

"Let's make it feel even better." He wrapped his arm around her, palming her breast and rolling her nipple between his fingers and thumb as he moved his hips, earning a hungry moan. He squeezed her nipple.

"*Ah*" fell sharply from her lips. "*Again.*"

Loving the way she craved him as much as he craved her, he

squeezed harder, pumping his hips faster. Her pussy tightened around his dick, and he wrapped her hair around his other fist. "*Yes*," she said in one long breath. "How can I be…so close…so fast?"

"We're combustible." He rose up, keeping hold of her hair and grabbing her hip, driving into her harder and deeper, her pleasure-filled sounds fueling his passion. Their bodies grew slick with sweat, the sound of flesh on flesh ringing out around them. He released her hair and wrapped his arm around her, his fingers finding her clit like heat-seeking missiles.

"*Oh…Flynn.*"

He quickened his efforts, earning more needful noises. Her thighs flexed. "*I'm gonna—*" Her long, surrendering moans wound around him as she gave herself over to the ecstasy they created. He stayed with her, jaw clenched tight, fighting off his own release as she sailed down from the peak.

"Hold tight, baby." He quickened his thrusts, watching her body swallow his cock, hips pounding against her ass. "I love seeing you take me so deep." She sank down on her elbows, taking him deeper, intensifying everything. He wrapped one arm around her again, giving her what she needed as he pounded into her, sending her into the throes of another orgasm. Her pulsing pussy hurled him right up to the edge of madness. Heat scorched down his spine, and his balls drew up. He gripped the base of his cock, pulling out just as his orgasm hit like a bullet train. Gritting out her name, he came on her ass, branding her again. Pummeled by a tidal wave of pleasure, he grabbed her hip, riding it out as her sweet, sated sounds etched into his mind.

He collapsed over her. "Damn, Sutton, that was…" He scrambled to find a word impactful enough to describe what he felt, but he felt too much. Being with her was all consuming in a way that obliterated every other form of pleasure.

"*Perfect,*" she said softly.

He trailed his hands down her trembling hips, unable to believe that after all this time of fighting his feelings, they were *here.* He was suddenly hit by the level of trust she'd given him. Not just by sharing her body but by being in the rainforest with him in the first place, trusting him to keep her safe. Silently vowing never to abuse that trust, he kissed her back and reached for a wipe, gently cleaning her up. He put the used wipes in a ziplock bag with the others and lay next to her, pulling her against him.

She nestled into his side like she belonged there, and it felt like she did. He'd kept walls around his heart for so many years and had been fighting his feelings for Sutton for so long, he almost didn't recognize the stirrings in his chest. But he *did*, and he didn't want to shove them down deep or run as fast and as far as he could from them. He wanted to revel in them. To revel in *her.*

She sighed dreamily. "This trip sure turned out different than I expected."

"That makes two of us." He kissed her temple, hugging her against his side.

"I don't usually do things like this."

"Seduce your boss?"

"I did *not* seduce you." She laughed.

"Who took the first kiss?"

She smacked his stomach. "Shut up. You were taunting me well before that."

"If that's what you need to tell yourself to sleep at night."

"*Flynn.*"

He laughed. "Has it really been six months since you've been with someone, or have you been seducing other unsuspecting men?"

"Definitely the latter. Haven't you heard? I've been working my way through the office. I started with the mailroom guys and worked my way up the ladder. Now that I've conquered you, I'm ready for the big leagues."

Loving the way she played along, he said, "I thought I read something about that on the men's room wall, but I wasn't going to say anything."

"I earned that gossip. What about you? How long has it really been?"

The fact that she hadn't answered him did not go unnoticed, but he let it go for now. "Since I seduced the mailroom guy?"

"Sure, we can start there."

He had a moment's hesitation about revealing the truth and decided to play it safe by being honest but not too specific. "More than a year."

"It's been more than a year since you've had sex?" She leaned up, gazing down at him assessingly. "Are you messing with me?"

He held up his right hand. "I've got the calluses to prove it."

She laughed and lay back down. "Why so long? I mean, you were kind of a dick to me. I'm glad I know why now, but you've always been nice to everyone else, and I've seen the way women look at you. I'm sure you've had plenty of opportunities."

"It's not a priority."

"What about dating? Is that a priority?"

"Not really."

She was quiet for a minute. "Was it ever a priority?"

"Sex or dating? Actually, it doesn't matter. The answer is the same. When I was in college, sure, both were as important as school and doing the things I enjoyed in my free time with family and friends."

"When did that change?"

"After I won the reality show."

"When you became the *it* guy? Why would that turn you off to sex and dating?"

"It didn't at first. I played the field for a while. Then I met a girl who I thought was pretty special. But I was getting tired of being in the spotlight. I was brought up to take pride in whatever I did, and I didn't feel that. I didn't like knowing people were pursuing me for superficial reasons. Whether it was for my status, money, or looks didn't matter. It was all bullshit, so I started going out less and turning down the pretty-boy jobs. After a few weeks of the girl I was seeing pushing me to accept those offers, I realized that was why she was with me. It's a shitty feeling to put yourself out there and think you're connecting with someone only to realize it was all a farce. That's when I said fuck it all and took control of my life. I ended that relationship, finished out my contracts, packed my shit, and got the hell out of the country."

"And that was it? Women have taken a back seat since then?"

"I'm no saint, but yes. Everyone took a back seat except my family."

SUTTON'S REPORTER BRAIN kicked in. "What does that mean?"

"Are you asking about women?"

"I guess, but also in general."

"It means I learned to value myself and what I want. I'm a commitment guy. I like relationships, but I wasn't in a position where I felt I could trust people's motives. So I stopped trying to connect with women for anything more than sex, and it's been a long damn time since I've even looked for that."

"At least fifteen minutes," she teased, giving herself a moment to process what he'd said.

"Yeah, well, you broke my dry streak, that's for sure."

"But *we're* connecting, or at least it feels like we are." She felt him tensing up.

"You're different, Sutton. This thing between us has been building for a long time, and we have to work together when we go back. I think in this circumstance, it's best if we understand each other and where we're coming from."

It stung to hear him say it so matter-of-factly, but that was their reality. "Where did you go when you left the country? From what I read about you before we started working together, it seemed like nobody knew where you went."

"I can't tell you all my secrets. What if I have to go into hiding again? You might sell me out to the tabloids."

"We could pinkie swear that I won't."

His chest rocked with his low laugh. "I knew if I didn't take steps to disappear, it would never stop. I had the money to make it happen, so I went where I knew people would help me get it done. After a few international stops, I had a new identity to travel under the radar."

"Like in the movies."

"It wasn't anything like in the movies. I hated it. I hated giving up who I was for even a minute, but I would've lost my mind if I'd stuck around."

"Nobody recognized you?"

"I was the it guy in the US, but twelve and a half years ago it wasn't that hard to disappear once I was off US soil. I stayed off the main travel routes. My cousin Ty's father is ex-military, and he connected me with an old buddy of his in Indonesia who got me a boat to New Guinea, where I met up with one of my father's friends. He helped me get what I needed to stay on an uninhabited island, and that's where I ended up."

"Uninhabited, like this?"

"Similar, but with no deadly plants or animals."

"Why didn't you take us *there* for the show?"

"Trust me, you'd be bored. I stayed long enough to clear my head and get my bearings. Then I got the hell out of there and stayed with a Vanuatu bush tribe for a couple of years, which was something I had always wanted to do. Once the hype about me died down, I continued traveling under my fake identity. I went to the places I had been wanting to go, and eventually, I started using my real identity again."

"Don't let this go to your head, but I'm kind of in awe of you right now. I would never be brave enough to do what you did."

"I've seen you step up to the plate enough to know that if you felt like you were losing yourself, you could do whatever it took to save your sanity."

"You have more faith in me than I do."

"You've proven yourself over and over. Not just here, but on every assignment."

"Was that a pat on the back, Mr. Braden?"

"I'd give you a slap on the ass if I didn't think it might send you inching away. Now, let's get back to you for a minute. You never answered my question. Has it really been six months since you've been with a guy?"

"Did I screw you senseless? It's only been about half an hour."

"All right, smart-ass. I just told you my secrets. You can tell me one of yours."

Her fingers trailed over his chest. "It's been longer than six months."

"Why?"

"Because like for you, sex isn't a priority, and I don't want to settle. I want what my parents and my brothers and sisters have."

"Which is?"

"This will sound funny since you didn't want to be the world's *it* guy, but my parents and my siblings and their significant others treat each other like they're *it* for them. Like the sun and the moon and the stars all pale in comparison, and nobody else in the world could fill their shoes. When you're around them, you can feel their love for each other. That's what I want. To be somebody's *it* girl."

"What's stopping you from getting out there and meeting someone?"

"A couple of things. I hate dating apps, and meeting smart, interesting single guys is impossible unless you hang out where they do. I don't know where they spend their time, but I don't hang out in bars, or anywhere, really. I've been a little busy trying to prove myself to my infuriatingly pushy boss."

"Sounds like an asshole."

"He can be. But it turns out he has a nicer side, too, and

he's pretty good with certain body parts."

"So you're into him for his dick?"

She gasped, feigning shock. "I'm not that kind of girl. I was going to say his *brains*."

He shifted onto his side, bringing them nose to nose. "That's an organ, not a body part."

"I meant his *hands*. He knows how to wield a machete, and—" His hand slid between her legs, and her thoughts fragmented.

"And?" he urged.

"And get wood."

"Wood, huh?"

"He's really good with wood, and I like his mouth, too."

"This mouth?" He brushed his lips over hers and bit her lower lip, tugging as he increased the friction between her legs, sending pinpricks of pleasure all the way down to her toes.

"*Yes—*"

He pressed his hard length against her leg. "But not his cock?"

"I can take it or leave it." Desperate for more, she reached between them and palmed his length.

"Seems to me you're better at taking it."

"As true as that is, I need other body parts right now."

"Just tell me what you need, babe. I am happy to oblige."

"This episode of *Getting Randy in the Rainforest* is to be continued. I need your feet on the ground and your eyes on the forest, so I can pee."

He laughed and touched his forehead to her shoulder. "You're killing me, Steele."

"Sorry," she whispered.

"No need to be." He kissed her tenderly, and as he drew

back, his expression turned serious. She imagined the protective part of his brain shoving his libido to the side, barking orders, as he reached for her clothes and said, "I'll be right there with you, but you need to be on full alert, and don't forget the hatchet."

Chapter Twelve

AS THE SUN crept over the tent the next morning, Flynn awoke hot, hard, and happier than he'd been in years. Sutton was fast asleep in his arms, making the cutest snoring sounds. *My little spoon.* With that dangerous thought, he tried to concentrate on all the things they had to do today. They'd skipped dinner last night, and with one more night in the rainforest and a long trek out, they needed sustenance. He mentally mapped out where to forage for food and tried to come up with a few ideas for filming, which was difficult when all he really wanted to do was stay in the tent with the beauty in his arms. But he didn't think that would go over very well. *Sorry, Karen. We have no footage from day three. We were too busy doing dirty things to each other.*

That gave him pause. No woman had ever distracted him from work the way Sutton did. He was frustrated with himself for allowing it to happen, but at the same time, warmer emotions battled their way to the forefront.

Sutton made a sleepy sound and turned in his arms, eyes closed, a sweet smile playing at her lips as she cuddled as close as she could.

He hugged her against his side, kissing the top of her head.

"What's that smile for?"

She opened her eyes, tipping her face up. "I was just dreaming about hazelnut coffee from the Beanery, and a hamburger and fries from the Beehive." The Beanery was a coffee shop and the Beehive was a café. They were both in Port Hudson.

"Your dreams are very different from mine."

"Where's that Portuguese coffee guy when I need him?"

Jealousy flared in his chest, just as it had when the guy had brought her coffee while they were on that assignment in Portugal. "You don't need *him*."

"Yes, I do," she grumbled.

He gritted his teeth.

"Are you *jealous*?"

He gave her hair a playful tug. "Don't mock me, Steele. I didn't like seeing you hug him then, and I don't want to think about it now."

She smiled. "Forget the coffee guy. Aren't you hungry? I'm starved. I would kill for a chocolate–peanut butter milkshake and some of Dawn's red-velvet cupcakes, or her cookie-dough-stuffed brownies. Or those cheesecake bites she makes. *Mm.*"

Andi's older sister, Dawn, hosted an LWW baking show called *Just Desserts*, and she often brought goodies in for Andi and their team to enjoy.

"If you ate all that sugar, you'd be even hungrier an hour from now. We can get some chontacuro worms and passion fruit and head back to the river to catch more fish. I'll make you a feast."

She buried her face in his chest. "No more *worms*."

"You're cute when you're cranky." He ran his fingers through her hair. "I've got some breakfast sausage you can have, but it doesn't have much nutritional value."

"You're the reason I'm starving in the first place." She sat up and pulled on her boots.

"I didn't hear you complaining last night."

She gave him the side-eye and left the tent mumbling something about needing to pee.

"Wait for me," he called after her, shoving his feet into his boots.

"I've got the hatchet!"

He went after her, catching up a few steps from her potty hole and tugging her into his arms.

"*Flynn*," she complained.

"You're hungry and tired, which means you're even more vulnerable to every danger out here. You can be sick of me or annoyed with me or pissed off at me. All of that is okay, but I'm still not going to let you put yourself in danger."

She huffed out a breath. "No, I *can't* be any of those things at you."

"Why not?"

"Because I can't see you as a dick anymore. You're protecting me even while I'm tired, hungry, and cranky."

"Babe, please see me as a dick and use me to your heart's content."

She laughed and buried her face in his chest.

"There's that smile I like so much." He patted her ass. "Go pee. I'll make sure you're safe."

"Don't listen," she admonished.

"I know the rules."

Her expression softened. "I'm sorry I'm crabby. My head hurts."

"You haven't had caffeine in two days, and after how much we sweated last night, you're probably dehydrated. We'll get you fixed up. You know," he said playfully. "Orgasms are great for headaches."

"If that were true, then I shouldn't have a headache for a year." She strode over to the hole in the ground. Her gaze shot back to him, surprise and delight shimmering in her eyes. "When did you put more flowers here?"

He'd done it after she'd fallen asleep last night. "I didn't. It must be the poop-hole fairy."

"I see your wings, Braden. You're setting the bar pretty high. How is any other guy ever going to measure up?"

"If flowering your poop hole is your measure of male worthiness, we need to talk." Just the thought of her with another guy pissed him off. But the fact that *she* was thinking about it? That cut like a knife.

"I SPEAK FIVE languages." Flynn swatted a bug off his arm. "I was president of my high school science club, and the first time I kissed a girl I threw up." It was late afternoon, and they were playing Two Truths and a Lie, and Sutton was doing an excellent job navigating as she led them back to camp after a great day.

The guayusa-leaf tea he had made for Sutton contained natural stimulants and had helped ease her headache, putting her in a much better mood. They'd foraged fruit for breakfast and had spent the morning exploring in the rain. They filmed monkeys, snakes, birds, insects, and lizards, medicinal trees, edible plants, and more. When it stopped raining, they'd gone to the waterfall and had ended up driving each other out of their minds. *Twice.* Sutton had lain in the sun with her head on his lap and had dozed off as he'd read *Gulliver's Travels* to her. She'd needed the rest, and he found he loved those quiet, comfortable moments of closeness as much as their intimate ones. After more exploring, they'd returned to the river to catch fish for dinner before heading back to camp.

"That's too easy," she complained. "There's no way you threw up the first time you kissed a girl."

"Wanna bet?" He had no trouble sharing embarrassing stories about himself with her, which should feel uncomfortable, since he never shared personal stories with anyone. But he was having fun, and he was enjoying learning more about her, like how her favorite color was blue because she felt most at peace when she was near the water, that she'd lost her virginity in college to a guy she'd dated for a month, and her favorite season was fall because she had an affinity for sweaters. She looked damn good in them, too.

She glanced over her shoulder, amusement dancing in her eyes. "That's a story I *have* to hear, but then what's the lie?"

"I speak four languages, not five."

She tossed him an eye roll and turned back, wielding the machete. "Tell me about the kiss. How old were you? Did you puke *while* you were kissing her? Because that would be gross."

"I was thirteen, her name was Maggie Montrose, and no. Not while kissing her."

"I need visuals. What did she look like?"

"She was cute. She had curly red hair and freckles, and she wore glasses. She always had a book with her, and I remember she dog-eared the pages. I gave her crap for that."

"You were pushy at thirteen?"

"I guess so."

She ducked around a branch. "So where did the kiss happen?"

"At a school dance. I was so nervous, I must've downed ten glasses of soda before we kissed."

"Was she your date?"

"No. I was too nervous to ask her, but we told each other we'd be there, and I planned it all out in my head for days before the dance. I was going to ask her to dance and then go in for the kiss on the dance floor."

"Oh no. *On* the dance floor?"

"Yup. I was doing well, too. I got up my nerve and held my breath as I went in for the kiss. I was still holding it when we stopped kissing, and I guess I was still so nervous, I forgot to breathe. I thought I was going to pass out. I *wish* I had passed out, but I hurled right there on the dance floor."

"*Aw.*" She laughed. "Now I feel bad for thirteen-year-old Flynn. I bet you didn't get many kisses from Maggie after that."

"I didn't want to kiss *anyone* after that, but Clay straightened my ass out."

She glanced over her shoulder with a furrowed brow. "Did he teach you to kiss?"

"No. He hooked me up with one of his female friends, and she taught me how."

"No wonder you like older women. Did she teach you *all* the bases?"

"Not all of them. But that's enough about me."

"Come on, don't be like that," she goaded. "Let me in on your boyhood secrets. I told you about when I lost my virginity."

"There's nothing to let you in on. She let me feel her up, and that was almost enough for me to embarrass myself by creaming in my pants."

She laughed. "That would have added insult to injury."

"Enough rehashing my most embarrassing moments. It's your turn."

"Okay, let's see." She swung the machete to move a plant out of the way. "I got my tonsils out when I was four, I have more than thirty handbags, and I'd like to personally thank the girl who taught you how to kiss." She turned around with a playful smile and dragged her forearm across her sweaty brow. "Thanks to her, this time with you hasn't been that bad."

"Is that right?" As he reached for her hand, his gaze caught on a snake coiled on the ground just inches behind her left foot. Instinct kicked in, leveling his voice and his heart rate. "*Sutton. Don't move.*" Her face blanched with his icy command as he slowly took the machete from her with his right hand, removing the hatchet from the holder at his waist with his left.

"*Flynn...?*" Panic riddled her voice.

"*Shh. Don't talk.*" His eyes remained trained on the snake. "Don't move, and you'll be fine." He fucking hoped it was true, but it was a deadly bushmaster poised to strike. The bushmaster was a pit viper, and their bite was one of the deadliest in the world even with treatment. They produced such large quantities of venom, and their striking speed was so fast, they could kill just about anything that crossed their path. Its broad head hovered menacingly above its thick body. Flynn had one shot, and if he fucked it up, one of them was going to get bitten and would likely not make it out of there alive. "I'm going to move," he said just above a whisper. "Do *not* so much as flinch."

"'Kay," she whispered shakily.

The snake eyed him. *That's it, motherfucker. Look at me, not her.* Gripping the machete tightly, in the space of a breath, he took a purposeful step to her left while simultaneously lifting the machete, placing his right booted foot between Sutton and the snake, and bringing the machete down with all his strength behind the snake's head as it lashed out. He pushed Sutton away, sending her stumbling.

"*Flynn!*"

"Stay *back*." His hand shot out. *Fuck. Fuck. Fuck.* The snake's fangs had punctured his boot, and the severed head was hanging from it. He could barely hear past the thundering of his heart and concentrated on slowing down his heart rate. He tried to focus enough to feel something more than the burn of adrenaline and figure out if the fangs had punctured him.

"Your foot!" Sutton cried.

"Stay there. I'm fine." *At least I fucking hope I am.* He pushed his foot down inside the boot, the sole sinking into the ground. He closed his eyes briefly, bringing all his focus to his feet. Thank God he didn't feel puncture wounds. He slid the tip of the machete under the curved fangs, prying them off his boot, and used the flat edge of it to fling the severed head several feet away. He picked up the snake's body and hurled it into the brush, not wanting it anywhere near Sutton. Only then did he pull her trembling body into his arms, pressing one hand to her back, the other cradling her head. Relief engulfed him like a cloak. "It's okay. You're okay. It can't hurt you anymore."

"But are *you* okay? Check your foot." Her tears wet his cheek.

"I'm fine. It didn't get me. I'd feel it." He kissed the top of her head, holding her tighter, needing the connection as much as she did. He wasn't used to caring about anyone this much, and he didn't know what to do with the emotions swamping him. "You're okay, sweetheart." *Thank God you're okay.* "You're safe. I've got you."

Chapter Thirteen

SUTTON HAD BEEN terrified when Flynn's voice had gone cold and he'd told her not to move. It had taken every ounce of her willpower not to run, and in the split second when he'd moved behind her and she'd heard the smack of the machete and the visceral, animalistic noise that had erupted from Flynn, her heart had nearly stopped. But nothing compared to the fear that had gripped her when she'd seen the snake's severed head hanging from Flynn's boot. Flynn didn't even look scared, while she could barely hold her shit together. He'd been hypervigilant after that, and those eagle eyes hadn't missed a thing since, guiding her away from even the smallest of potential dangers, from spiders to holes in the ground.

She thought they'd both be able to breathe a little easier when they reached the campsite and could talk about what had happened, but Flynn had gone into some kind of silent warrior mode, checking every inch of their site with a fine-tooth comb, splitting wood, building a fire, and cooking the fish and mushrooms they'd brought back for dinner, all with a pinched expression and tension riddling his entire body. Her attempts at conversation while they ate were met with only nods or shrugs. She had a feeling he was upset with her for not paying more attention when she'd taken the lead, and he had a right to be, but if she had to watch him clench his jaw, poke the fire, or circle the campsite one more time, she was going to lose her mind.

"I'm going to take a piss." He pushed to his feet, his gaze skating around the perimeter of the campsite as he strode determinedly away.

Too agitated to sit still, she got up and shook out her hands, hating the fear that still riddled her, that she'd disappointed Flynn, and that she'd nearly cost at least one of them their life. She paced by the fire, trying to figure out how to get through to him.

Flynn eyed her as he came back into camp. "What do you need?" he asked gruffly.

"I need you to talk to me. I'm *sorry*. I know I messed up. I was having so much fun, I got caught up in that stupid game and fell into a false sense of security—"

"*Stop it*," he barked, tension rolling off him. "You didn't do anything wrong."

"Yes, I did! You trusted me to take the lead, and I almost got us killed."

"*No*, Sutton," he growled. "Keeping you safe is *my* job. I never should've let you take the lead. You haven't been trained for this. I know the dangers of this place. I know what to look for. I should have had my eyes peeled the whole time, and—"

"You trusted me to take the lead, and I was proud of that. But you're right—you shouldn't have let me take the lead."

"*No*," he fumed. "That came out wrong. You should be proud. *I'm* proud of you. You've come a hell of a long way, but I had my eyes peeled for trouble when you took the lead, and *that* should have kept us safe. That's how you learn. You lead with the support of a trained professional, and I wanted that for you, but *I* fucked up. I got sidetracked and let my fucking guard down. I should've been looking five steps ahead of you at all times." His jaw clenched and his hands curled into fists, pain riddling his features.

"Then it's both our faults. You can't take full responsibility. I was in front, and that stupid snake was *right there*, and I didn't even see it."

"*Damn it*, Sutton. It's *not* your fault." He hauled her into his arms. "I can't stand the thought of anything happening to you."

Shock stole her voice. His arms tightened around her, and he kissed the top of her head. She told herself not to make too much out of that. They'd gone through something traumatic, and that did strange things to people's emotions. But the longer he held her, the more she needed to know the truth. "Because you don't want to send me home in a body bag and be a person of interest in the investigation, or—"

"I'm just glad you're safe, and I've got you all to myself for one more night."

She closed her eyes. *One more night*, echoed in her head.

"I'm sorry I was a dick."

"You weren't a dick. I'm just scared, and you just shut me out, and…" Her throat thickened. "I hate that."

He leaned back, taking her chin between his finger and thumb, and tilted her face up. A sea of worry looked back at her. "That's what tore your family up for so long."

She nodded, surprised he'd put the two together.

His jaw clenched again. "I'm so fucking sorry. I'll try not to do that to you again. I know you're scared, and I'm sorry." He kissed her softly. "It's been a hell of a day. One of the best and one of the hardest I've ever experienced."

"Me too."

"I'm beat, and I just want to be close to you. Is that okay?"
She nodded, tears dampening her eyes. "I want that, too."

His arms circled her again, and he held her for the longest time. Then they put out the fire and went through the necessary steps to make sure they were safe for the night before settling into the diminutive tent. Neither spoke as they stripped off their dirty clothes. Sutton went up on her knees in her T-shirt and underwear and turned away to use the cleansing wipes, but Flynn touched her arm, stopping her.

"Let me." He went up on his knees and took the wipe from her hand, gently cleansing her face and neck. His gaze was soft and caring, his touch as intimate as it was firm, as if she was something precious to be treasured. "You really are so beautiful."

The way he said it, low and thoughtfully, made her blush. "I'm a mess."

"The most beautiful mess I've ever seen." He set the dirty wipe down and grabbed another from the package.

"You don't have to—"

"Just let me do this." His jaw ticked. "After tonight, you'll have all the time in the world to take care of yourself."

They didn't speak as he took off her shirt and washed her shoulders and arms, all the way down to the tips of her fingers. He washed along her collarbone, caringly caressing his way down her body. She closed her eyes, soaking in the feel of the cool cloth moving over her skin in stark contrast to the heat taking root between them. When he slipped her underwear down her legs to cleanse her, he wasn't touching her sexually, but it felt even more intimate than if he were. She could barely breathe for the emotions stacking up inside her as he moved behind her, giving every inch of her body the same careful—*loving?*—attention, as if he were memorizing the feel of her.

When he was done, she reached for the package of wipes to do the same for him, but he shook his head and kissed her. "If you touch me like that, I'll be all over you. Lie down, babe. I'll be there in a second."

She didn't bother putting on clothes to sleep in. She wanted to lie naked with him, and as she lay down, she was too far away to see much of him in the darkness, but she could tell his movements were purposeful and efficient. So different from the way he'd touched her.

When he lay beside her, he pressed his lips to her forehead for a long time before gathering her in his arms and holding her tight. He exhaled like he'd been waiting all day for this very moment, and within the confines of his strong body, she felt like she'd been waiting, too.

"Thank you for trusting me," he whispered. "Try to rest, babe. We've got a big travel day tomorrow."

She didn't want to think about that exhausting trip or that this was their last night together. The last time she could lie in his arms. She kissed his chest, and he ran his fingers through her hair, hugging her. Why did this big-hearted, complicated man have to be her boss? She'd never met anyone like him, had never felt so safe and wanted. That sounded strange even to her, given where they'd started and the fact that this was all they'd have, but that didn't stop her from wishing they had more time together.

SUTTON DIDN'T KNOW when she'd dozed off or how long they'd slept, but she awoke to the caress of Flynn's hand down her hip. As her eyes adjusted to the darkness, they found his, awakening the desire that was always simmering between them. He brushed his lips over hers once, *twice*. Need stacked up inside her as he did it a third time, rolling her onto her back and lowering his big, warm body over hers. His cock nestled between her legs. She was as entranced by the emotions in his eyes as she was by the feel of him, so good and right and familiar.

He grazed his scruff along her cheek, whispering, "*Sutton*," low and gruff and greedy. Her entire body flamed. He kissed her cheek and laced their fingers together, moving her hands above her head and holding them there. He used his knees to spread her legs wider, teasing her with the head of his cock. She writhed and panted and was just about to beg for more when his mouth came mercilessly down over hers, and their bodies came together, igniting a rush of sensations. "*God*, Sutton," he growled, his voice drenched with emotion.

She didn't know how he managed to speak. She couldn't have strung two words together if her life depended on it. But she could move, and *holy mother of sex gods*, so could he. Driven by something bigger than lust or greed, more powerful than urgency, their bodies moved in perfect harmony. He released her hands, pushing one hand into her hair, cradling her head. His other hand slid beneath her knee, lifting it, opening her wider for him and taking her deeper. Every thrust took her higher, brought her emotions closer to the surface, until she was so full of them, she felt them in every exhalation.

"*Christ*, you feel good," he gritted out against her lips.

"Don't pull out this time."

He leaned up, brows slanted. "You sure?"

"I want to feel you come with me."

"You have no idea how much I want that." He reclaimed her mouth with renewed passion, but his thrusts were slow and deep, so different from before. Each one felt purposeful, powerful, drenched with emotion. They clung to each other, their kisses turning feverish. Their moans filled the tent as their bodies took over, thrusting, grinding, groping. Sutton sensed they were both trying to outrun the inevitable, to escape the end of what had only just begun. She closed her eyes against that reality and abandoned all control, losing herself in Flynn. She got swept up in the taste of his mouth, his rugged scent, and the weight of his body bearing down on her. Her inner muscles coiled tighter, tantalizing sensations rasping up her limbs, billowing in her chest. Their passion magnified like an inferno. His hand fisted tighter in her hair, setting off a flood tide of pure, explosive pleasure. "*Flynn*—" flew from her lips and "*Sutton, baby, Sut*—" cut from his as they rode the turbulent tides of their climaxes, until they collapsed, spent and blissfully sated, in each other's arms.

Chapter Fourteen

SUTTON GAZED OUT the airplane window Sunday afternoon as they neared the end of the final leg of their journey home. They'd been on the go for more than twenty-four hours. It had rained on their trek out of the rainforest, and they'd waited hours at the landing site for the rain to abate so Santiago could pick them up. Sutton didn't mind the rain. It had given her more time with Flynn, and she'd secretly hoped it might rain long enough to buy them a night at that crappy hotel by the airstrip. But they didn't get that lucky. Their ever-efficient travel coordinator had thought ahead and had booked them on a late flight out of Ecuador. Sutton had catnapped at the airports during layovers, but Flynn had been watching over her like a hawk, and as far as she knew, he hadn't slept since their last night in the tent. She warmed with the memory of waking up yesterday morning the same way they'd fallen asleep, tangled up like strangler figs to trees.

She stole a glance at him, sitting beside her reading. She didn't know how he was functioning, but it seemed like he was always self-possessed and in control. After how close they'd gotten, she'd thought, or *hoped*, they'd remain close as they traveled. But from the minute Santiago's plane had appeared in the distance, it had seemed like Flynn flicked an internal switch from playful and sensual rainforest lover to distant boss. Or maybe to a protective travel partner, the way he was watching over her, but they were definitely back on their own sides of that invisible line between boss and subordinate. He wasn't gruff or mean. He was just *appropriate*. She knew it had to be this way, but she hadn't expected it to leave her numb with longing for him.

The announcement to stow their belongings and prepare for landing rang out. Flynn got up to put his book in his small backpack in the overhead compartment, his gaze drifting her way. She didn't have anything to stow, and shook her head. She was too tired to read and too numb to write in her journal. She had no idea how *that* had happened so fast. And with Flynn of all people. A week ago, she'd wanted to be as far away from him as physically possible, and now she wanted nothing more than to fall into his arms. She couldn't stop thinking about their last kiss, which they'd shared just before seeing Santiago's plane. Afterward, Flynn had said, *How does it feel knowing this rainforest will forever hold our secrets?* He'd said it matter-of-factly, like he was sealing their deal. She'd somehow managed to keep the sting of that agreement locked down and had replied, *I hope it's better at keeping secrets than my sisters are.*

She gazed out the window again as Flynn settled into the seat beside her, telling herself that once she got some rest, she'd feel different.

"Glad to be almost home?" he asked.

"Yeah. It'll be nice to get back to Port Hudson, where the biggest threat is a speeding car that I can see coming from a hundred feet away." *Instead of a six-three protective sex god with heart-slaying ninja skills.*

163

Brows knitting, he nodded and placed his hand over hers, leaning in so close, she could practically taste him. "I'm really glad I got to know you, Steele. You're an incredible person and a talented reporter."

He squeezed her hand, blue eyes pinning her in place with the hungry look she'd come to crave. *Finally.* She readied for the kiss she'd been dying for, but in the next second he released her hand and sat back, leaving her reeling.

Oh no. Nonono.

She had never pined after a man before, and she was not going to let him turn her into that kind of girl. It was time to reclaim her…*whatever* it was that made girls stupid. If Sutton knew how to do one thing well, it was faking it until she made it. Hell, that was how she'd gotten through her first six months as a reporter.

Gathering willpower like a shield, she said, "It's about time you realized that." She forced a victorious grin and looked out the window before the hurt could wipe it away.

FLYNN WATCHED SUTTON thumbing out a text as they waited for their backpacks to appear on the conveyor belt. She'd gone into the rainforest a bright-eyed, snark-mouthed glamour girl, and she'd come out looking like an unkempt Jane who had gotten ravaged by Tarzan. She'd washed up and put on clean clothes at the airstrip, but that glimmer of heat had remained in her eyes for too damn long. Thankfully, she'd finally gone back to having a stiff upper lip. He'd needed her to, because looking at her doe eyes on the plane had nearly done him in. As much as it sucked to leave behind what they'd had, it had to be done.

"Family checking on you?"

"Andi." She pocketed her phone. "I wish our bags would come out. They're taking forever."

"Got a date?"

"Yes, with a hot shower and clean sheets." She eyed him. "Are you itching to pitch a tent in your backyard?"

"Something like that." He spotted their backpacks and snagged them off the conveyor belt, handing Sutton hers and shouldering his own. "I've got my truck. Do you need a ride?"

"No, thanks. I left my car here."

Text me when you get home so I know you're home safe hung from the tip of his tongue. Gritting his teeth against the unfamiliar urge, he nodded curtly, said, "See you Tuesday, Steele," and got the hell out of there.

Chapter Fifteen

AS WAKEFULNESS CREPT in, Flynn fought against it, rolling over and reaching for Sutton. His hand landed on an empty space, and his eyes flew open. "*Sut—*" His rustic three-bedroom cabin came into focus, and his groggy brain remembered they were back in New York. *Fuck.* He scrubbed a hand down his face, glancing at the clock as he threw his legs over the side of the bed and sat up. *2:07 a.m.* He must've gone out like a light, because he'd showered and lain down to read, but his book was still on the nightstand.

He grabbed his phone as he climbed from his bed and opened the doors to the deck. A cool breeze swept over his bare chest. His cabin was situated on several private lakefront acres in the mountains just outside Port Hudson. He hated feeling penned in, so he'd had accordion-style doors made that ran the length of the walls for the master bedroom and living room, opening to decks that cantilevered over the water.

As he stepped outside, the gentle sounds of the water took him back to the waterfall, bringing images of Sutton, naked and writhing against him. His dick jerked with the memory.

He inhaled the crisp mountain air and glowered down at the recently horny body part. "That's *not* happening." He wondered what Sutton was doing. Sleeping? Journaling? Reading?

Thinking about me?

Dude, get a grip.

They'd opened Pandora's box. He walked to the far side of the deck, sat on the top step that led to a walkway connecting the deck to the boathouse, and powered up his phone. He'd sent his family a group text when he'd gotten home—*Back home safe and sound. Going to crash*—and now their responses rolled in.

Dad: *Glad you're safe, son. Call us when you're settled and rested.*

Clay: *Good thing I got my harem out of your cabin this morning.*

Mom: *Clay! Love you, Flynn. I can't wait to hear about your trip.*

Seth: *Did Sutton make it back, too?*

Noah: *Maybe Sutton offed Flynn and she sent that text from his phone to throw us off.*

Victory: *Dibs on his cabin!*

Noah: *You'd have to leave the city to enjoy it, Vic.*

Seth: *Guess Vic didn't read Clay's message.*

Victory: *Ew. Scratch that.*

Seth and Noah sent laughing emojis.

Clay sent a devil emoji.

He smiled at their banter. It was too late to respond to any of them except Seth, who was a night owl. He opened a new message to his oldest brother, thumbing out, *You up?*

His phone rang, and Seth's name appeared on the screen. Flynn answered on speaker. "Hey, bro. How's it going?"

"Not bad. I figured you'd be dead on your feet."

"I crashed for a few hours, but you know I'm not much of a sleeper."

"Right. How was your camping trip?"

He smiled at Seth's minimization of their trip. "Different than expected."

"No shit. I still can't believe Karen saddled you with that last-minute change. Did you and Sutton play nice? How'd you make out?"

"Prime choice of words, asshole." Seth had been giving him shit about Sutton since she'd first started working for him.

Seth's low laugh came through the phone. "I know you were hell-bent on getting her fired, but despite your constant denial, I swear there's always been more to it."

"You think you've got it all figured out." Flynn pushed to his feet and paced, worried about what his self-made billionaire brother who stuck to a strict code of business conduct would think of him if he told him the truth.

"Tell me I'm wrong. Don't laugh it off or thwart the question like you always do. Just *tell me* I'm wrong."

Flynn raked a hand through his hair. He couldn't make himself lie to the brother who had always had his back. "Yeah, about that. The company fucked up. We only had one tent."

"Oh, *man*."

"A fucking *pup* tent."

"Are you kidding me?" He laughed again. "That must've made it *hard*."

"*Seth*," Flynn warned.

"What? I meant hard to keep a professional distance." He barely got the words out without laughing.

"You're an asshole."

"I'm not the one who slept with my subordinate."

"And you don't think I feel like shit about that?" He ground his back teeth against that statement. He didn't regret sleeping with her. Not one iota. But she *was* his subordinate, and that was flat-out wrong. "I don't know why I thought I could talk to you about this."

"Because you *can*," Seth said more seriously. "I'm just giving my kid brother shit. I can't believe you took that risk, but I've seen it coming for months. Anytime someone mentions her name, you look like you're going to shred your skin like the Hulk."

Felt like it, too.

"I've tried to get you to open up to me about it, but you're so damn obstinate."

Flynn clenched his jaw. *How could I open up to you about it when I was lying to myself?* "I think you need better glasses."

"Ah, I see Denial is with us. Man's best friend. He shows up when you least expect it and sticks with you through thick and thin until you damn near lose your mind. Want to talk about it?"

"Not really. Just know that I didn't make the first move."

"That'll help a little if she sues you, but it's not going to win the case."

"She's not going to sue me. She's not like that. We knew what we were doing, and we agreed that whatever happened there stayed there. We're done messing around. Come Tuesday it'll be business as usual." *Whatever the fuck that means.*

"Good luck with that, Hulkster. Just remember, workplace hookups rarely end well."

"Then it's a good thing we're done. You know I don't like complications in my life, and I have no patience for drama. Listen, man, do me a favor. Can you keep this between us? I don't need to catch shit from Clay or Noah."

"So, it's safe for me to tell Vic?"

"Fuck no."

Seth laughed again. "You know I won't tell anyone."

"Thanks." He was too agitated and hungry to stay on the phone. "Listen, I'm starved. I've got to go rustle up some food. Thanks for the therapy session."

"Anytime, brother."

Flynn ended the call and went inside. He walked through his bedroom into the main, open living area and headed for the kitchen. Maybe some food would take the edge off. The sandwich he'd gotten on the way home from the airport hadn't nearly been enough.

He opened the fridge and stared at the nearly empty shelves. *Shit.* He grabbed a bottle of water, making a mental note to hit the grocery store in the morning, and went to the pantry, which was just about as bare. Being a fairly clean eater who cooked his own meals had its downfalls in the snack department. He grabbed a box of crackers and a jar of peanut butter, thinking about Sutton and those damn prepackaged peanut butter crackers she'd hoarded in her bag and how furious she'd been when he'd tossed them in the trash. He'd seen her eating them when she worked late in the office and when they were on assignments, like she had an endless supply.

He snagged a plate and knife and went into the living room, setting his meager feast on the rough-hewn coffee table. As he opened the accordion-style doors to the deck, night sounds trickled in, keeping Sutton in the forefront of his mind. On the surface, they were wildly different. She'd walked out of the airstrip bathroom looking like a million bucks, despite not showering, and while he'd washed up, he wasn't about to go crazy for a twenty-plus-hour travel day. He imagined her packing her bags before they'd left for Ecuador, picking out a travel outfit for the return trip and stashing it away, not to be touched until they were on their way home. She would probably spend her day off tomorrow—*well, technically today given the time*—getting her hair and nails done and having lunch with her girlfriends or sisters, while he'd catch up with his family on the phone, but he'd be happy not to see a single person.

Except her.

Damn, he missed her already.

He sat on the couch eating peanut butter cracker sandwiches, telling himself to stop thinking about her. He took a swig of water and rested his head back. His gaze landed on a spider on the wall, and the image of Sutton running out of the shower screaming and crashing into him came rushing back. He laughed and took a picture of the spider, then thumbed out a text to her.

Flynn: *I think your friend followed me home.* He added the picture of the spider.

His thumb hovered over the send icon. *What the hell am I doing? What happened in the rainforest had to stay in the rainforest.* Did that include inside jokes? He thought about her seeing the text in the morning and either blushing, laughing, or giving him shit for it. All three sounded damn good to him.

"Fuck it." *Hello, Denial, my old friend.* He hit send and set his phone on the cushion to slather peanut butter on another cracker. His phone vibrated with a text a minute later.

Sutton: *Why do all guys think one inch is equal to three? That spider is way smaller than mine was.*

Flynn: *You mean your shower stain?*

An eye roll emoji popped up.

Sutton: *You were too busy looking at my ass to see it.*

Flynn: *You're not wrong.*

She sent a smirking emoji.

Flynn: *Actually, I saw your spider on the ceiling that morning in the hotel while you were snoring in my ear.*

Sutton: *SEE! I told you I wasn't hallucinating. I knew there was a spider!*

Sutton: *You could have told me you saw it.*

Flynn: *That wouldn't have been nearly as fun. Why are you awake at this hour?*

Sutton: *I slept all day and woke up starving a little while ago. You?*

Flynn: *Same.*

He sent her a picture of a peanut butter cracker sandwich.

Flynn: *Jealous?*

She sent a picture of two empty packages of peanut butter crackers.

Sutton: *What else you got?*

Flynn: *I think you know the answer to that.* He added a winking emoji.

Three dots danced on the screen. He waited with bated breath for her snarky retort, but the dots disappeared. His gut clenched. He shouldn't have gone there. He started to type an apology, but a picture of batteries popped up.

Sutton: *All of the pleasure. None of the hassle.*

Flynn: *Are you using images of me for inspiration?*

Sutton: *I left those in the rainforest and googled your brothers.*

He scoffed.

Sutton: *What are you doing?*

Flynn: *Not myself.*

She sent a laughing emoji.

He took a picture of the view of the water and sent it to her.

Sutton: *You live on the water? Lucky! It's so pretty.*

Flynn: *I'm contemplating taking my boat over to Silver Island and scoping out the Panty Parade.*

Sutton: *You mean the Bra Brigade? I'm starting to worry about you. Being interested in older women is one thing, but my grandmother?*

Flynn: *I didn't mean the BB. I meant the Panty Parade. You probably weren't part of that group. It's for women who prefer men over battery-operated boyfriends.*

Sutton sent a cracking-up emoji.

Sutton: *I skipped that group and put together a group called the Pleasure Platoon, for women who enjoy both.* She added a hot-faced emoji.

He chuckled, enjoying their banter a little too much. He was *this close* to suggesting they give her fellow Platooners something to talk about and ended the conversation before he made that mistake.

Flynn: *There you go, being inappropriate with your boss again.*

She sent an emoji with a raised eyebrow.

Flynn: *Maybe you should give those batteries a rest and get some sleep.*

Sutton: *But I'm not done with your brothers yet.*

Three more hot-faced emojis popped up.

Flynn gritted his teeth, thumbing out, *Good night, Steele.*

Sutton: *It's going to be a VERY good night.*

A smirking emoji popped up.

"Fuck." He tossed his phone on the couch, stripped off his sweats on his way outside, and dove into the lake, hoping the cold water would obliterate thoughts of her touching herself to images of his brothers.

Chapter Sixteen

SUTTON HAD THOUGHT she'd sleep like a log last night, but after texting with Flynn, she'd slept fitfully. Her dreams were full of the rainforest, revisiting the sounds and fears, rendering her anxious and rattled, and reliving the sexy times with Flynn in vivid detail, which left her hot, bothered, and beyond frustrated. She'd spent the last half hour trying to figure out why he'd reached out last night. It was driving her nuts. She was glad he had, but it was like he'd known she was lying in bed thinking about him.

Irritated with herself for ruminating over him, she set down her phone and went to take a shower, focusing on her to-do list, at the top of which was a trip to the Beanery for about a gallon of hazelnut coffee before her nail appointment. Thank goodness she'd thought ahead and had booked a mani-pedi. Her nails look like she played in the dirt for a living.

As she stepped beneath the warm shower spray, her mind skipped back to the waterfall and Flynn, his mouth on hers, their naked bodies pressed together. *No. No. No. He is not on my to-do list. Groceries. Focus on groceries. And laundry. I have to do laundry.* That made her think of Flynn stripping off her bathing suit and the feel of his rough hands exploring her body. She futilely tried to fight the heat those memories brought, but it was like trying to stop the wind, so she gave herself over to them, moving her hand between her legs. Flynn's deep voice whispered gruffly in her ear. *Even underwater I can feel how slick you are for me.* She closed her eyes, picturing his handsome face and desire-filled eyes, working herself right up to the verge of release, feeling his thick fingers inside her, hearing his gruff voice coaxing her along. *That's it, baby. Give that tight pussy what it needs.* She quickened her efforts, letting the memories flow, until his name tore from her lungs. She pressed one hand to the cold tile, her body quivering and quaking. Eyes closed, she savored his image as she rode out the orgasm thoughts of him had brought, which sadly, weren't anywhere near as satisfying as the man himself.

SHE WAS RUNNING late when she finally headed out the door for her nail appointment and was met by a young guy ascending her porch steps. "Hi. Can I help you?"

"I have a delivery for Sutton Steele."

"That's me."

He handed her a coffee carrier from the Beanery with two to-go cups in it. "Enjoy."

As he headed for his car, she called after him, "Who sent this?"

He glanced back at her and held up his palms. "I have no idea. I'm just the delivery guy."

"Thank you." She headed to her car and climbed in, wondering who had sent the coffee. Part of her hoped it was Flynn, but it was more likely one of her sisters or Andi, who were all very supportive of her coffee addiction. She transferred one cup to the cupholder and took a sip from the other. Sweet, warm hazelnut brought a smile. Her phone chimed with a text. She put the cup in the cupholder, hoping it was Flynn and hating herself for wanting it to be him.

She saw Leni's name on the screen and decided there would be absolutely, positively no more foolish hoping. She read her sister's text as she started the car.

Leni: *I'm glad you and Flynn didn't kill each other, and I'm dying to hear about your trip, but I have a crazy week. Catch up over dinner Friday? Can you meet me in the city?*

Sutton: *Yes!*

Leni: *Perfect. Enjoy your coffee and pampering.*

Of course Leni had sent it.

Sutton: *I am. Thank you!*

She headed into town for her appointment, and a little while later her phone chimed when she was at a stoplight. Hope crept in again, despite her determination to slay that troublemaking emotion. She managed to will it away before grabbing her phone.

Jules: *Hi! Do you have plans for lunch?*

Jules made a habit of stopping by to see Sutton whenever she was in the area to meet with a distributor for her gift shop, but she didn't usually give her notice.

Sutton: *Just a date with my washing machine. Why? Are you going to be close by?*

The light changed, and she went on her way.

THE COFFEE CARRIED Sutton through her nail appointment and her errands, but nothing distracted her from thinking about Flynn. After she finished putting away her groceries, she headed into the laundry room, where she'd dumped her filthy backpack last night. She checked her phone for the umpteenth time, telling herself she was looking for Jules's reply, *not* checking to see if she'd missed a text from Flynn. It was true. Jules had never texted back. But that was typical for her youngest sister, always flitting from one thing to the next. Sutton envied Jules's spontaneity, even if she sometimes left her hanging, because more often than not, Jules made everyone smile.

Unlike Flynn, who also hadn't texted and was unknowingly frustrating her.

She turned on the washer and withdrew a handful of clothes from her backpack. As she tossed each one into the washer, she stopped cold at the sight of Flynn's royal-blue shirt, remembering how he'd looked in it the morning after they'd first fooled around. The image of him crouched by the log where they'd purified water, looking ruggedly delicious with his hair hanging over his forehead, came rushing back to her. She closed her eyes, bringing the shirt to her nose, and inhaled his earthy scent. A pang of longing moved through her.

Her phone chimed, startling her from her reverie, and her hopeful heart weaved that chime and the shirt into a sign—only to deflate at the sight of Andi's name on the screen. She definitely needed a distraction from thoughts of Flynn.

Or rather, to squash those thoughts altogether.

Andi: *Can I stop by to drop something off? I only have a minute. I'm on my way to the eye doctor.*

Sutton: *Sure.*

Andi and Dawn shared a townhouse in the same complex as Sutton. She tossed Flynn's shirt into the washer with her other clothes and was emptying the rest of her things from her backpack when the doorbell chimed. She gathered her journal and toiletries, including the unopened butt wipes she'd decided not to use so as not to trick the viewers, dumped them into the laundry basket, and carried the basket with her to answer the door.

"Hi," Andi said, looking cute in pale green skinny jeans, a white button-down, and a taupe cardigan. "I needed to see that you were alive and well with my own eyes."

"It's good to see you. Come in." She set down the basket and hugged her.

"I can't. I have to get to my eye appointment." She held up a gift bag. "Dawn and I made you cookie-dough-stuffed brownies last night. We figured you might be having withdrawals."

"You are the best! Thank you!" Sutton took the gift bag and hugged her. "You have no idea how much I fantasized about these while I was away."

"You deserve them after surviving the rainforest and all that time with Flynn, which I want to hear all about, but I have to run or I'll be late. See you tomorrow at the office?"

"For sure." Sutton was nervous about seeing Flynn again, but she wasn't about to share that with Andi. "Thanks again for the brownies. I'll text Dawn to thank her."

"Great. You should eat them all. You look like you lost weight."

"Yes, *Mom*. See you tomorrow." She waved, and as Andi headed back to her car, she closed the door. She carried the laundry basket into the kitchen and set it down beside the table so she could open the brownies. When she lifted the lid, the scent of freshly baked brownies had her practically salivating. She chose the biggest one and took a bite, closing her eyes to savor the taste as it melted in her mouth. She ate half of it before texting Dawn.

Sutton: *Girl, you've outdone yourself. I was having withdrawals, and these brownies are to die for. Thank you for thinking of me.*

She finished the brownie and was eating a second one when Dawn's response rolled in.

Dawn: *I'm glad you're enjoying them. Andi told me about the last-minute change to the trip. She was worried sick about Flynn being a jerk to you. But you know how I feel. Jerk or not, sign me up for a rainforest getaway with that man, and I'm so there.* She added three flame emojis.

Dawn had never made any bones about having the hots for Flynn. Jealousy gnawed at Sutton, but she couldn't let on about it, even to her friend. It was too risky since Andi worked with them.

Sutton: *Maybe you should bake him chontacuro-worm brownies.*

Dawn: *I don't know what those are, but hey, if that's what he's into, it obviously does his body good.*

A hot-faced emoji popped up.

Dawn: *Enjoy the brownies. I have to get back to the set. I'm making Gâteau St. Honore cake today. YUM!*

Sutton: *I have no idea what that is, so put it on the list of things you should make for me.* She added praying hands and a red heart.

She finished her second brownie, and her phone vibrated again, this time with a family group text.

Jules: *FaceTime in 2 minutes!*

FaceTime? Sutton scrolled through her messages to see if she'd missed one from Jules about setting up a video call, but there weren't any missed texts. Then it dawned on her. *This* was why Jules had asked if she was free for lunch.

Maybe thirty seconds later, her phone lit up with the incoming call, and Jules's bright eyes lit up the screen. Her golden-brown hair hung past her shoulders, the top layer pinned up in a ponytail in the middle of her head like a fountain. That had been her signature look since she was little. She was sitting with her husband, Grant Silver, who was eight years her senior and treated her like gold. His shaggy hair and beard were a shade darker than hers, and his eyes no longer held the shadow of a man who had lost too much. He had, in fact, lost too much during his military career and after. While Jules could never bring back the comrades or the limb he'd lost, Sutton knew he had her younger sister to thank for the happiness looking back at her.

"Hi, Sutton. You look *amazing!*" Jules exclaimed.

Everyone thought Jules was dramatic, and she was, but Sutton also believed her little sister, who had taken a brush with death, felt everything deeper than most people did, and she simply gave weight to those emotions. It was just one of the things Sutton adored about her.

Grant lifted his chin. "Hey, Sutton. Glad you're safe."

"Me too. I've missed you guys."

Her parents' warm smiles appeared on-screen, as Daphne, Jock, Levi, Leni, and their grandmother joined them. Everyone talked at once, and Sutton tried to keep up as Leni told them her fiancé, Raz, was in LA for meetings this week and was sorry to miss their call, and Levi said his fiancée, Tara, a photographer, should join them any minute.

"It's great to see everyone," Sutton said.

"How are you, darlin'?" her father asked. "You got some sun on your cheeks. It looks good on you."

"Thanks, Dad. I'm doing okay. Just a little tired," Sutton said.

"Of course you're tired," her grandmother said. "You've been traipsing around a jungle with that good-looking jackass boss of yours."

"*Mom*," Sutton's mother chided, her long auburn hair and bangs framing her pretty face.

"*Pfft.*" Her grandmother waved a hand dismissively. "I call it like it is. Sutton, sweetheart, if you're into jungle boys, I have a friend at *bingo* who would fill out a loincloth nicely, if you know what I mean."

Everyone knew her grandmother, and many of the original Bra Brigaders, frequented a strip club on Cape Cod called Pythons when they claimed they were playing bingo. They all stifled their laughter as their mother glared at their grandmother. "Mom, *please.*"

Tara's pretty young face appeared on-screen.

"Hi, babe," Levi said.

"Hi. Sorry I'm late," Tara said. "I had a photo shoot that ran over. Welcome home, Sutton. Joey made me promise to tell you she misses you."

"Tell her I miss her, too, and I'll see her at Indi and Archer's wedding."

"Where are Archer and Indi? Has anyone talked to them?" Jules asked. "I told them we were calling at noon sharp."

"They're probably in their boat making waves at the marina," Levi said, making everyone chuckle.

"I'm sure they'll be along any minute," her mother said, just as Archer's and Indi's faces appeared on-screen. "Speak of the devils."

"Sorry we're late to the party," Indi said, smoothing her tousled hair. "You can blame Archer for showing up at my work and cornering me in my office."

"He gets that overactive libido from his grandfather," their grandmother said.

Archer grinned smugly. "I'm not sorry about that."

"You have *no* shame," Sutton teased.

"For loving my fiancée? Why would I?" Archer smirked.

"Can't you keep it in your pants for one afternoon?" Jules complained. "How would you like it if I showed up late all the time because I was having sex with Grant?"

"I'd love it," Grant said, pulling her into a kiss.

Archer glowered at him.

Their father held his hands up. "This is too much information for some of us."

"Speak for yourself, sonny boy," their grandmother said. "I'm all for a healthy sex life."

"As if we haven't all caught you and Mom making out in the pantry, Dad?" Leni said.

"Or the laundry room," Jock added. "That scarred me for life."

"Don't forget the living room. Remember that, Leni?" Sutton said, reminding her about the time they'd walked in on their parents feeling each other up on the couch.

"I only wish I could forget it," Leni said, and she and Sutton laughed.

"Finding them in the supply room at work was a little scarring, too," Daphne chimed in. "Sorry, Steve and Shelley."

"They still frequent that room?" her grandmother asked. "Grandpa and I caught them there many times. Then they got creative, going out to the vines and the work shed—"

"Jesus, Dad. Not my vines," Archer complained.

Their father chuckled.

"Don't forget the bathroom," Levi added.

"That was *us*, not them," Tara said, and everyone laughed.

"Oh, right. *Shit*. Sorry, babe," Levi said.

"I guess you all come by it honestly," their father said, and lifted their mother's hand, kissing the back of it.

"Okay, enough making me blush," her mother said. "Sutton, sweetheart, I want to hear all about your trip. Did you have a good time?"

A little too good. "It wasn't like I was at a spa, Mom. It was terrifying out there."

"Because of nature or Flynn?" Leni asked.

"Do I need to put that guy in his place?" Archer asked gruffly.

"*No.* He was actually pretty great," Sutton said.

Archer's eyes narrowed. "How great?"

Sutton gave him a deadpan look. "We were in the middle of the rainforest, where nearly everything could kill us. He watched out for me, and he taught me a lot."

"Does that mean he didn't act like an ass?" Leni asked skeptically.

"If he knows what's good for him, he didn't," her grandmother said. "In the office our girl has to be professional, but there are no holds barred in the jungle."

In more ways than one.

"He had his moments," Sutton said. "We both did, as anyone would in those circumstances. If anything, you should thank him for keeping me safe. He saved my life. I was inches from a deadly pit viper, and he put himself between me and the snake and cut its head off." The fear she'd felt in the moment rushed in, and her words tumbled nervously out. "Did you know that snakes can still bite and kill you after their heads are cut off? The damn thing—the severed head—went after him, and its fangs got stuck in his boot. I thought…" She shook her head, unwilling to go there.

The girls gasped, and her brothers uttered "damn" and "holy shit."

Her mother's hand covered her heart. "Oh, sweetheart. I can't imagine how scary that was. I'm in a panic just hearing about it."

"It was horrible, but he knew just what to do, and he didn't hesitate. One second we were laughing, and the next he was dead serious and taking action. He was incredible."

"It sounds like we owe that man heaps of gratitude," her father said.

Everyone concurred.

Indi turned to Archer. "How come you've never saved me from a snake?"

"Baby, you don't need saving. You like my snake," Archer said.

"*Ew*," Jules said, and they all laughed.

"Tara almost bit it on the sidewalk the other day, and I totally caught her. That's almost as cool, right?" Levi said proudly.

"Bit your snake?" Leni teased.

"*No!*" Tara blushed.

"It's more like a worm," Jock said, earning more laughter.

Sutton listened to their banter, thinking about how many

years their family had lost and how wonderful it was to be close again. As she watched her parents, and her brothers and sisters with their significant others, teasing and one-upping each other, she ached for the kind of true love they'd all found. There had been moments in the rainforest when she'd thought maybe she and Flynn were headed for that type of bond. But now she knew they weren't, because her siblings and their significant others would fight to the death to be with each other, and Flynn had been able to turn off any feelings he'd had and walk away. Last night's texts gave her pause, but there was a world of difference between a fun friendship with a white-hot sexual connection and soul-deep love.

She told them more about the trip, purposely leaving out the part about having only one tent. "Being there changed how I see myself and what I am capable of. Foraging for food and water gave me a good dose of perspective, making me even more grateful for everything I have."

"Like hazelnut coffee," Leni and Jules said in unison.

"I meant the basics, like food and water and a bathroom, but yes, coffee, too."

"Sutton, honey," her mother said. "Since Flynn was better on the trip, are you still thinking of leaving the show?"

"Of course she is," Archer said emphatically. "They risked her life sending her to that damn rainforest. She never should've gone."

Sutton glared at him. "Thanks for the vote of confidence."

"Seriously, Archer," Jules snapped. "Sutton can do anything she puts her mind to."

"I didn't mean because she can't handle it. It was irresponsible of them to send her there. She's not trained for pit vipers and whatever else is in that place," Archer explained.

"You're not wrong," Sutton conceded. "But I'm not trained to go to any of the places they send me. To some extent, that's what research is for—although no amount of research could give me the skills I'd need to survive in the rainforest by myself."

"That's what I'm talking about," Archer said.

"But they didn't send me alone, Archer, and they wouldn't have sent me with Flynn if they didn't believe he had the skills to keep me safe. After seeing him in action, I can see why they trusted him."

"Does that mean you want to stay with the show?" her father asked.

"No." *I slept with my boss, and I have a feeling tomorrow is going to be horribly awkward, which adds to my reasons for leaving.* "I'm just saying that I'm glad I'm going on tough assignments and seeing the world. GNN hasn't gotten back to me yet, but the job they have available sounds like what I've always wanted, so if they get back to me, I want to follow it through and see where it leads." She tried to ignore the dull ache in her chest at the idea of not seeing Flynn every day, despite knowing things would be awkward.

"I think that's smart," her father said. "Don't sell yourself short."

"I agree with your father," her mother said. "I wish the job wasn't in California, but I'm a firm believer that fate has a way of guiding us through big life decisions."

Sutton was on the fence about fate for many reasons, one of which was what had happened between her and Flynn. Why would fate finally lead her to a man she ended up really liking, and feeling connected to, only to leave her worse off than she'd been in the first place? "Mom, if that were true, shouldn't fate have stepped in and taken Jock's and Archer's hands sooner than the decade it took for them to find their way back into each other's lives?"

Jock and Archer exchanged a guilty glance, but their mother's loving expression didn't change as she said, "Some things take more time than others. I have to believe that everything our family went through had to happen in order for us to become whole again. If they'd tried sooner, maybe one or both of them wouldn't have been ready, and it would have made things worse."

"We'll never know about that," her father said. "But there's one thing I know for sure. It took that long for our sweet Daphne and our little love Hadley to find Jock, and those beautiful girls fueled his heart in a way nothing ever had, and in the end *that* is what led him here."

"For what it's worth," Daphne said softly, "I wish I had all the years with Jock that Hadley and I missed out on."

"Me, too, babe," Jock said.

"Jock and Daphne are righter than rain in a drought," their grandmother said. "So you can rest assured that in this complicated, wonderful life we're given, whatever is supposed to happen will happen, and it will happen when it's supposed to, no matter how hard you fight against it."

And just like that, Sutton's thoughts returned to Flynn.

Chapter Seventeen

BY MIDMORNING TUESDAY, Flynn had worked his way through most of the emails and phone messages that had come in while he was out of the office, he'd met with the post-production/editorial team, who caught him up to speed on previously filmed episodes that were in various stages of production for upcoming shows and had handled about fifty other things. Including answering dozens of questions about his trip from just about everyone he saw. He didn't mind sharing his experiences, but he couldn't think about the trip without mentally veering into dangerous territory. The beautiful subject of which was standing at the break room counter with her back to him, wearing a sheer white blouse, a figure-hugging tan skirt, and high heels that made her legs look impossibly long.

He wasn't surprised to see Sutton pouring hazelnut creamer into her coffee, but after how many times they'd ravaged every inch of each other, he'd thought the bone-deep ache for her would have dissipated by now.

Man, was he wrong.

She took a sip, assumably unaware of his presence, and tipped her face up, making a humming-moaning sound. He had the urge to slide his arms around her waist and whisper dirty promises until she was wet and needy, and then fulfill every single one of them.

Grinding his back teeth against those troublesome thoughts, he walked into the room. She was standing in front of the cabinet where they kept their mugs and glasses. When he stepped behind her, their body heat instantly filled the gap between them. His chest brushed her shoulder as he reached over her to grab a glass. "Thinking about me again, Steele?"

She turned, that familiar thrum of heat now a raging inferno. Pink cheeks be damned, a challenge gleamed in her gorgeous eyes. "Dream on, Braden."

Back on the same page. Fucking perfect.

Had she always clutched her coffee mug so tightly between both hands, or was she struggling against their new normal, too? He tried not to overthink that, and noticed her white-tipped fingernails were freshly polished. He wondered what color she'd chosen for her toenails, and immediately gave himself hell for thinking about it. "I see Glamour Girl is back. You sure cleaned up nicely."

"Thanks. It felt amazing to be pampered. Not that our Ecuadorian spa didn't have its own benefits." Their gazes locked, and there was no escaping the flash of lust in her eyes.

Those moments are etched in my mind, too. "They're once-in-a-lifetime memories. I'm glad we have them."

She lifted her chin in the way she did when she was steeling herself against something. After how close they'd gotten, he hated being on the other side of it again, but he knew they were doing the right thing.

"Me too." She glanced at the doorway. "Have you seen Karen?"

"Not yet. Have you?"

She shook her head. "Andi said she had meetings out of the office this morning." Her expression turned serious, and she lowered her voice. "I've been thinking. We probably shouldn't tell her there was only one tent. It'll just raise questions."

"I hadn't planned on mentioning it."

"Good." She exhaled with relief.

He didn't like her feeling uneasy about what they'd done. He wanted to tell her as much, but if he broached that subject, he'd have a hard time keeping the rest of his feelings to himself. Instead, he tried to bridge the gap with a safer subject. "I'm about to start reviewing the footage. Do you want to join me and check it out?"

"Really? I never get to see the raw footage of our shows."

"We don't usually have to film without a crew, either. Special circumstances call for special exceptions."

"Then, *yes*, definitely. I'm anxious to see it."

As they headed down the hall, he fought the urge to put his hand on her back and say all the things he felt. In his office, he moved a second chair in front of his computer and started the video, revisiting the airstrip for takeoff. To his surprise, as they watched, the tension fell away, and soon they were joking about the never-ending rain and their *glamorous* hotel suite.

As the plane descended on-screen, Sutton said, "When I saw the tiny clearing where he was going to land, I was sure we were goners."

"Really? You hid it so well."

She bumped him with her shoulder. "Thank you for helping me through that."

"I'll always have your back, Steele. Even when you're furious with me for throwing out your crackers and coffee."

"You don't mess with a woman's snacks or caffeine."

"So I've learned." This time when their gazes met, there was a hum of a different kind. One of trust and friendship. He was glad that had remained. As they watched the clips and chatted about their trip, he was just as taken with her on-the-fly reporting as he'd been in the rainforest. "That right there is your calling."

"Risking my life every second with my ornery boss slash cameraman?"

He'd prefer it that way. They made a great team, and it was a lot more enjoyable watching her in action without any preparation. "If that's what it takes to get you to report like that? Hell yes."

"You see that much of a difference?"

"Don't you?"

"I don't know. I'm my own worst critic. I was in a heightened state of anxiety and excitement. I feel like I did a good job, but I also kind of look like I'm on speed."

"No, you don't." He laughed. "You were unscripted. You look excited and interested with a reasonable amount of fear, which makes it authentic."

She looked at him for a long moment, her gaze warm and reminiscent. "Thank you. That means a lot to me."

Yeah, well, you mean a lot to me. "I'm just being honest."

They continued watching. When they came to the clip with the tamarin monkeys, she gasped and smacked his leg. "Did you see that? Stop the video!"

He paused it, forcing himself to keep a straight face. "What?"

"Go back." She frantically motioned with her hand for him to hurry as he rewound the video. "*Stop!* Right there!" She pointed to a big cat sleeping on a branch a good distance behind her. "Is that a jaguar? That's a *jaguar*. Ohmygod. We could've been killed!"

He chuckled. "It's an ocelot, and it's sleeping."

"Did you know it was there? Did you see it when you were filming?"

"Yes."

She smacked his leg again, looking appalled. "Why didn't you tell me?"

"Because I knew you'd freak out, and that would've put us in danger."

"We *were* in danger."

"Ocelots don't usually attack humans, and the fact that it was there meant its biggest threats, which are larger wild cats like jaguars and pumas, weren't nearby."

She shook her head, gaping at him. "You must have nerves of steel. You never gave me *any* indication that it was there." Her brows knitted. "What else didn't you tell me about?"

"Nothing that wouldn't have put us in danger if you'd freaked out."

"That means there *was* more," she said angrily.

"Would it have been better if a wild cat had come after us or a snake had dropped out of a tree on you?"

"*No.* Could that have…? Never mind." She shook her head and held her hand up. "Don't tell me."

"I'm sorry I kept a few things from you, but I was trying to keep us alive."

"I know. I get it." Her expression softened. "It just drives home a point I've been thinking about."

"What point is that?"

"You've traveled all over the world and you've done crazy, dangerous things. It'll probably sound stupid to you."

"I've never heard anything stupid come out of your mouth, Steele. I'd like to hear what you have to say."

"It's just that I feel like being there changed me. I don't know how to describe it, but I feel different."

Being with you changed me. "That's not uncommon after a harrowing trip. What feels different?"

"In some ways everything." She paused, that reminiscent expression returning for a long beat, before being pushed away by something a little more distant. "When I was getting my nails done yesterday, I realized that here, there's a sense of safety and power and stability. I don't mean like I'm someone special. I mean as a society. We're taught to work hard to buy things and gain recognition. It's like the more we have, the safer we feel, but none of that matters in the rainforest. It's a whole different existence. It showed me how vulnerable we really are and how insignificant all that other stuff is."

"I understand that, but what does it mean for you, personally?"

"I don't know. That's just it. I feel different, but it's not like I'm going to stop striving to be the best I can be at whatever I'm doing, or stop getting my nails done or give up my favorite coffee."

He laughed. "You wouldn't want to go hog wild."

"Exactly." She smiled, but then her brows knitted, and she lowered her voice. "But seriously, Flynn. It's like we left a different world. It feels weird not being scared every second, or surrounded by that hot, damp air. Even being able to see the sun without trees in the way, and hearing my own thoughts instead of a symphony of animal sounds is strange. And *this…?*" She motioned between them.

Somehow he knew she wasn't referencing what they'd done,

but rather how strange it was for her to be talking to him like this, trusting him on this level outside the rainforest, where everything was different.

"How could seventy-two hours have such a big impact?" she asked.

This was more dangerous territory, because her eyes implored him to understand that now she was talking about a much bigger question, so he tried to answer carefully. "You connected with nature"—*and me*—"on a level most people never will. You relied on it to sustain you, and we relied on each other for everything. It was us against the elements. That changes people. I'd worry more if you didn't come back feeling different."

"Do *you* feel different? Or have you been on so many excursions, you're used to it?"

Trips like that affected him, but it was Sutton who had left an indelible mark. "Like I said, those experiences change a person."

THEIR GAZES HELD, a silent understanding of *we're not going there* hanging between them like a sad neon sign. Sutton hadn't intended to say any of those things, but she was glad she had. She'd come to work anxious about seeing Flynn, worrying everyone would take one look at them and know they'd slept together. It almost made her wish she'd had more one- and two-night stands, so she would have experience in faking this type of thing.

But there was no going back, and she somehow knew even if

she'd had experience, it would be nothing like what she felt toward Flynn. She'd heard him approaching the break room when she was getting her coffee. But she hadn't wished him away like she used to. Despite her worries, she'd *wanted* to see him, and her anticipation had magnified with his every determined footstep. When he'd stood in the doorway, she hadn't needed to look to know it was him. Their connection had blazed a path between them. Even now, with that uncrossable line separating them, she felt their connection trying to coil around them like a snake.

At least now she knew where she stood. She needed to cut that snake's head off, but *needing* to and *knowing how* to were very different things.

She drew in a deep breath, sitting up taller, and said, "I'm glad it's not just me. Can we watch more of the clips?"

He nodded curtly and hit play.

As they watched, she could smell the rainforest, feel the damp earth giving way beneath her feet, and instead of the coiled connection binding them together right now, she felt the thrum of it, as it had been in the rainforest. Felt it weaving around them like a web, capturing the very essence of who they were, drawing them closer until there was no space between them at all. She mentally gathered all those images and feelings and filed them away in the recesses of her mind, where they couldn't steal her every thought, just as she'd done with Jock and Archer's rift when she was in college.

"This is a great part," Flynn said when they came to the clip where they were going to collect water.

She startled anew when the scorpion jumped out from under a leaf, which made them both laugh.

"Well, you two seem to be getting along better," Karen said

from the doorway, surprising them. "I take it the trip went well?"

They both sat back, putting space between them.

"We made it back alive. That's a plus," Sutton said nervously.

"I never doubted you would with Flynn at the helm," Karen said with a painfully serious expression.

"The trip went great." Flynn nodded toward the monitor. "We got excellent footage, and Sutton was incredible on the fly. I thought it would be good for her to see the clips before they're edited."

"What do you think, Sutton?" Karen asked.

"I think it's really good. I'm excited to see how the episodes turn out, and I'm interested in how the viewers will respond to it. It's very different from what our audience is used to. Flynn's a better survivalist than he is a cameraman."

He shook his head, eyeing her. "You've always got to ride me, Steele."

She felt her cheeks burn but couldn't stop her smile from peeking through or the challenge from blurting out. "Excuse me, but the reason we had to go on that assignment in the first place was because of *your* unyielding need to ride *me*."

Karen looked between the two of them. "At least now you're smiling when you give each other a hard time. Can I take that as a win and assume things will be less contentious between you two? Or shall we move this into my office?"

"We're good," Flynn said at the same time Sutton said, "Take it as a win."

"Great. I look forward to seeing that footage. I'll let you get back to work, and we'll catch up at the team meeting on Friday."

As Karen walked away, Sutton shoved Flynn, whispering, "Riding you? *Really?*"

"What's wrong with that?"

"You know damn well what's wrong with it," she whispered. "You might as well have said that I like to *fuck* you." She mouthed the word *fuck*.

Amusement rose in his eyes. "Ms. Steele, do we need to revisit the definition of appropriate workplace conversation?"

She narrowed her eyes. "I should've put a tarantula in your underwear when I had the chance."

Chapter Eighteen

BY WEDNESDAY NIGHT Flynn was edgy as shit. Keeping things professional around Sutton was proving to be more difficult than he'd anticipated. Innuendos slipped out without warning, and while she rolled with them, her ever-ready snark and confidence only made him want more. He missed their open camaraderie, their intimate conversations, inside jokes, and flirtatiousness.

Hell, he missed *her*.

He thought watching the videos he'd taken of them on his personal video camera would ease those unfamiliar feelings, but it was only making it worse, bringing back the fun they'd had and the adorable way she scowled at him when he annoyed her. He watched her leg bobbing as she wrote in her journal by the waterfall in that torturous pink-and-white bikini. He couldn't remember the last time he'd wanted any kind of reminders of a woman after they'd been together, but with Sutton, he'd gathered them like a squirrel hoarding nuts for the winter.

His phone rang, and he snagged it from the coffee table, seeing his grandfather's image on the screen. Flynn shared his height and hair color, though his grandfather had lost a couple of inches as he'd aged, and his hair was now snow white and thinning on top. He still wore it collar length and slicked back and kept his beard trim.

Flynn had caught up with the rest of his family, but he and his grandfather had been playing phone tag. Hitting pause on the video, he answered on speakerphone. "Hey, old man."

"Hey, whippersnapper. How's my boy?" His grandfather's voice had always been as rough as sandpaper, with a warmth all its own. Hearing it now took the edge off Flynn's nerves.

"You do remember that I'll be thirty-four soon, right?"

"Yeah, yeah. You'll always be my curious boy. How're you doing?"

"Hanging in there. What's kept you so busy?"

"A little of this. A little of that."

Flynn grinned. "Why are you so evasive lately? What're you keeping from me?"

"I can't say, but you'll be the first to know when I can."

"Does Gram know?"

"Loose Lips Lucy? Heck no."

"*I heard that.*" His grandmother's voice rang out in the background. "*Miss you, Flynny.*"

Flynn laughed. "Tell Gram I miss her, too."

"Flynn said he misses you almost as much as he misses me," he said loudly, then snickered.

"You're a troublemaker."

"I've got to stay on her good side. She's making shortbread cookies for our flight tomorrow. I don't want her withholding my goodies."

"*I can still hear you,*" his grandmother said.

"Busted. Where are you headed?"

"I'm taking your grandmother on a cruise to Alaska."

"You hate cruises."

"But there's nothing I won't do for your grandmother."

"*Except relax and retire,*" his grandmother called out.

Flynn chuckled, hoping he'd be just like his grandfather when he was older. Always up for another adventure.

"I'll rest when I'm dead," his grandfather grumbled. "I got your message about the change of assignment. How'd you and Glamour Girl make out?"

"Better than I thought we would. She gave me shit every step of the way, but she held her own."

"The best women always do. You've said she was feisty. I think I'd like her."

Flynn kicked his feet up on the coffee table, imagining the conversations his grandfather and Sutton could have about him. "I think you would, too, Gramps. Turns out she's a pretty cool person."

"We already knew that. She's put up with you for all this time. And you? How'd you do on the trip?"

"It was a rough one. Making sure Sutton was safe added a whole new level of pressure. I think I developed about ten more senses."

His grandfather laughed. "Despite all the grief you two give each other, you've become comrades in arms. You've shared tough, meaningful assignments in harsh environments. That builds a bond unlike any other. I remember the first time your grandmother came on an assignment with me. This was before we were seeing each other, when she was my field assistant. There weren't many women in the field back then, and I remember worry lodging in my chest like a fist, tightening at every little thing. It didn't relent until we were back home three or four months later."

"Damn. Guess I'm lucky it was just a few days." The time

they'd had together was a double-edged sword. He wanted more time with her, but then he'd be even more messed up when they had to end it. "Sutton nearly stepped on a bushmaster. That was terrifying, but I handled it." He told his grandfather what had gone down with the snake, and his grandfather was silent for so long, he looked at the phone to make sure he hadn't lost the signal. "You still there, Gramps?"

"Yeah. Give an old man time to process his grandson's near-death experience."

"Get outta here. I was fine."

"You wait until you have kids and grandkids of your own. Then you'll understand. You might not want to mention that stunt to your mother or your grandmother."

"I didn't mention it to Mom or Dad, and you can leave it out when you tell Gram."

"You know I will. You never fail to amaze me, Flynn. I want you to know that."

His grandfather believed that you should never leave things unsaid to the people you love, because you don't know what tomorrow will hold. But the little boy in Flynn still wanted to believe there would never come a day when the people he loved wouldn't be around, and he refused to accept anything less. "Tell me yourself the next time you see me."

"Smart-ass."

"I learned from the best."

"You've far surpassed me and your parents in bravery, knowledge, *and* smart-assery, boy. I hope Sutton realizes how lucky she was that you were there, and I hope you realize how lucky you were to have pulled that stunt off."

"She does, and I do, too. But you know I'd do it again."

"I was going to say as long as you learned something, it

sounds like it was a good experience all around. But now I'm not so sure."

"It was a great experience." He heard his grandmother talking in the background but couldn't make out what she was saying.

"It's good to catch up, Flynn. I've got to go. Your grandmother says I need to pack."

"Have fun on your cruise."

"Hm? Oh yeah, right. The cruise. We will. Love you, boy."

"You can't lie worth shit, Gramps. Be safe out there."

"I'm not the one jumping in front of snakes. I make your grandmother do that."

Flynn laughed. "Night, Gramps." He ended the call, and his phone rang right away. He put it to his ear. "What'd you forget?"

"Um…*nothing*. It's Sutton."

Happiness spread through his chest like fucking wildfire. "Hey." There was no masking the surprise in his voice. "Sorry. I just hung up with my grandfather. I thought you were him."

"I'm sorry to call out of the blue, but you're the only person I know who could *possibly* understand this, and I thought you'd get a kick out of it. But if you need to call your grandfather back—"

"No. I'm good. We were just touching base. What am I going to get a kick out of?"

"My embarrassing actions. I'm taking a walk in my neighborhood, and I was scrolling through my phone when a cat darted out of a yard. All I saw was this brown blur, and for some reason, in my head, I was back in the rainforest. I screamed and scrambled off the sidewalk kicking and swatting at *nothing*, because of course the cat had already run past."

They both laughed.

"My neighbor came outside to see what happened, and I was *so* embarrassed."

"Well, you're not alone in doing strange things after trips like that. When I got back from living with the tribe, I went to stay with Seth for a little while in New York City. But his apartment was too quiet, and I couldn't get used to sleeping indoors, much less in a bed, so I slept on a blanket on his concrete balcony. That's probably the only time I'd ever seek out traffic noise."

"Traffic noise is a *horrible* substitute for rainforest sounds."

"No kidding. You want to know the best part? His neighbor saw me and warned him that a vagrant was camping out on his balcony."

She laughed. "Okay, *that's* pretty bad."

"I don't even know how the guy saw me. He must've had binoculars."

"So your brother has a creeper for a neighbor?"

"Not anymore. He's moved since then."

"That makes me feel a little better. I swear, if I were on the island and a cat ran at me the way it did tonight, I'd think my brothers were pranking me."

He sat back, so fucking glad to hear her voice. "Do they still prank you a lot?"

"Not as much as they prank each other, but when we were younger it was constant. If they weren't putting fake spiders in our clothes or hiding under our beds and making monster noises that sent us screaming into our parents' bedroom, they were dragging one of us out to the vineyard at night to help them hunt vampires or werewolves, only to leave us alone in the dark while they slipped into costume and came charging out five minutes later."

"Holy shit." He laughed. "That's epic."

"You don't know the half of it. Jock and Archer have always loved horror movies, and one of their favorite pranks on me lasted a few horrifying *weeks*. They found this creepy antique doll somewhere, and I was terrified of it. Every night they'd wait until I was sleeping and put it on the rocking chair in my room, tuck it under the covers next to me, or prop it up on my dresser. I swear, I'd wake up and that thing would be staring at me."

"That's awful. What did you do?"

"I yelled at them, but the first dozen times or so, they denied it, and I was only six or seven, so I believed them. They told me the doll was possessed and not to tell my parents, or it might do bad things to me. Then they helped me hide it at the bottom of the trash can outside or they'd dig a hole in the yard and we'd bury it. But every morning, it was right there in my bedroom. I'd go crying to Jock or Archer, and they'd play the heroic big brothers and get rid of it again."

He wanted to get his hands on Jock and Archer and scare the living shit out of them. "Jesus, Sutton. No wonder you're afraid of the dark."

"I'm *not* afraid of the dark."

"Sorry. *Uneasy* in the dark."

"We were in the rainforest! That's different."

"Okay. You're totally cool in the dark. *Got it.* Tell me this. Did they prank everyone like that or just you?"

"Nobody was or is safe around them. I have no idea how my parents didn't lose their minds. When Jock and Archer were young, they poured ketchup on themselves and all over one of our father's saws, and then Archer lay in the yard, while Jock, covered in what looked like blood, ran inside screaming that

Archer was dying."

"That's just cruel."

"You think that's bad? You should hear what they did to Levi when he was a kid…"

Sutton proceeded to tell him about how her brothers' pranks had escalated over the years. She described pranks on friends and family, and their significant others, and went on to tell him all the ways she and her sisters and friends had gotten back at her brothers. Even her parents and grandmother had gotten in on the pranking fun.

"I don't know if I should be impressed with your family or worried that your brothers take things so far."

"Probably both, but I'm just glad they're pranking again. I missed it during those difficult years. Did you guys ever prank each other?"

"Not like that. Remember, there were times when we traveled when we had only each other to play with, but we did a few pranks."

"Like…?"

"Nothing too bad. We put cellophane over the toilet and soap on the doorknob, so when Noah peed it splashed on him and he couldn't get out of the bathroom. And Clay pissed me off once, so I put a snake in his bed."

"How is that any nicer than what my brothers did?"

"It wasn't poisonous." He laughed, remembering how angry Clay had gotten. "Besides, I got in so much trouble, I never did it again."

"Good. What else did you do?"

"When we moved back to Ridgeport full time, Victory had a sleepover with some girlfriends. Clay and I eavesdropped and heard who they had crushes on, so we had our friend call and say he was one of the boys they liked. He asked Vic and her friends to sneak out at midnight to meet them. As soon as the girls started sneaking out, we called the police and said we thought someone was breaking in. Needless to say, Vic didn't try to sneak out again."

"That's *so* mean. Did they know you did it?"

"No. We told the police we lived next door, and Vic wouldn't talk to our next-door neighbor for weeks after that. The poor guy had no idea why."

"I don't care what you say, Braden. You are every bit as bad as my brothers."

"No, I'm *not*. Those are childish pranks compared to the shit your brothers do."

"I don't know about that. Does your family have a *thing* like ours has pranks?"

"Kind of, but you'll think it's lame."

"No, I won't. Tell me."

"We sit around the bonfire and make up stories. Everyone takes a turn, building on whatever the person before them said. We've been doing it since we were little."

"That's not lame. It sounds fun. What kind of stories?"

"They run the gamut. Funny, creepy, mysterious, outrageous. But for some reason, Seth *always* brings it back to a pig making a ham sandwich in a deli."

She laughed. "How can that fit into every story?"

"It can't, but somehow it does. I told you he was a dork." He heard crickets. "Are you still out walking?"

"No. I got home when I was telling you about the Christmas prank. I'm sitting outside on my deck. I think the rainforest ruined me."

He didn't like the sound of that. "Why?"

"Because I grew up in a big, noisy family, and then I went to college and joined the Ladies Who Write sisterhood, which is like a sorority, and I lived with a bunch of girls. So when I first moved into my own place, it was hard to get used to being alone. Eventually I not only got used to it, but I loved my solitude. Then we went to the rainforest, where the noises never stopped, and you were always right there, and now it's too quiet again," she said softly. "I think I need to download a rainforest-noise app."

He felt her absence, too, and it was killing him not to admit it. "I just taped you snoring, and I play that at night."

"You did *not*."

He cracked up.

"I can't believe how long we've been on the phone. It's almost midnight."

He didn't want the call to end. "We're good at keeping each other up all night."

"*Mm-hm.* What were you up to tonight?"

He didn't want to pretend he felt nothing for her, when he felt more than he had in as long as he could remember. He'd probably get struck by lightning, but he had to admit the truth, even if they couldn't take it anywhere. He sat up and leaned his elbows on his knees. "Honestly? I was thinking about you."

She went quiet.

He gritted his teeth against her extended silence. "Sorry, Sut. I probably shouldn't have admitted that."

"It's not that," she said softly. "I was going to read tonight, but I couldn't stop thinking about you. That's why I went for a walk. To clear my head."

This was fucking torture. "How's that going for you?"

"Not great."

The mix of sadness and annoyance in her voice cut him to

his core. "I know this sucks. But we're doing the right thing."

"I *know*. What I don't get is why *you* of all people?"

"Hey, that's not very nice."

"You know what I mean. There are millions of men in the world. Why do I have to get hung up on my boss?"

"Just look at the long list of pros on your pros and cons list."

"You mean the two items on that side, both of which are sexual?"

"Two. *Twenty*. Same-same."

She snort-laughed, which made him laugh.

"I've been watching the videos we made of us on my personal camera. We had a lot of fun together."

"*Please* tell me you deleted the dirty ones."

He could lie, but he wouldn't lie to her. "Not yet."

"*Flynn*. You promised you would," she said with a hint of amusement and irritation.

"I will. I just haven't gotten that far. I was watching the PG-rated clips of you scowling at me for every little thing."

"I'm sure you deserved it."

"Probably."

"*Definitely*," she challenged.

He scrubbed a hand down his face, wishing she were there with him. "I'd ask if you want to come watch with me and decide for yourself, but while we might start out watching the videos, I think we'd end up outdoing them."

"*Flynn…*"

Her breathy plea nearly had him changing his mind. "I think we'd better get off the phone."

"Yeah," she said just above a whisper.

"It was nice talking to you, Steele."

"You too, Braden."

Chapter Nineteen

LATE FRIDAY AFTERNOON, Sutton sat in the conference room with the rest of the *Discovery Hour* team, trying to focus as they discussed ideas for upcoming assignments. But her lust-addled mind kept going over the last few days like a never-ending rerun. After Wednesday evening's phone call with Flynn, she was having an even harder time keeping her feelings under control. She'd tried to avoid him at work yesterday, but it was like fighting a magnetic pull. He managed to treat her like he always did in the office, as well he should, but now that the tension was gone, it made it even more difficult. She was starting to wonder if she'd ever really disliked him at all.

It didn't help that he'd texted her last night when she was lying in bed, asking if she was still awake. Her reply had been met with a phone call and Flynn's deep voice in her ear. *Evening, Steele.* She'd gone straight to a tease. *Is it appropriate to call a subordinate when she's lying in bed?* His response, *It's more appropriate than being in bed with her,* had ignited the ever-present fire simmering between them. They'd managed to keep their conversation out of the danger zone, but it didn't matter what they said. The undercurrent of desire was as thick as tar, sucking her in deeper with every rough laugh and low-spoken word. It had been after two in the morning when they'd finally ended the call. She'd ached with missing him. When she'd closed her eyes, all she'd seen was Flynn. All she'd wanted was him. There was no getting any sleep until she'd taken the edge off, and not for the first time—or, she was sure, the last—it was Flynn's gruff, dirty talk that had pulled her through.

"Have a great weekend, everyone," Karen said, drawing Sutton from her thoughts.

She stole a glance at Flynn across the conference table. He looked striking in a dark blue T-shirt. He caught her looking and flashed a coy smile that made her body hum.

Bastard.

She picked up her notebook, which sadly did not contain nearly enough notes about the meeting, and headed out the door. Flynn sidled up to her in the hallway, making her pulse quicken.

"Steele."

"Braden."

"That color pink looks nice on you."

"Thank you."

He lowered his voice and said, "It reminds me of the bikini I took off you with my teeth."

Her body flamed, which she was sure was his intent. Just as she'd hoped to get his attention with the pink blouse and above-the-knee formfitting black skirt. She met his gaze. "That was so long ago, I barely remember it."

His jaw tightened.

"What are you doing tonight?" she asked, hoping his plans included more than just a phone call with her. She was going into the city to have dinner with Leni, but she'd be back in Port Hudson by eleven.

He dragged his gaze down the length of her and back up again, making her tingle from chest to toes, and cocked a brow. "Not what I want to be doing. I've got dinner plans this evening. How about you?"

She remembered the last thing he'd said before ending their call last night—*I need to find a way to get you off my mind before I lose it.* She'd taken it as a joke, but now she wondered if he'd made a date to do just that. She was hit with a pang of jealousy. But she wasn't about to let it show. "I've got plans, too. I hope my dinner date likes my blouse as much as you do."

His eyes narrowed.

"Have a good evening, Braden." She spun on her heel and walked away, refusing to allow the emotions surging through her to rise to the surface.

TWO HOURS LATER Sutton was still fuming and hurt as she spilled her guts to Leni while they headed down the busy city sidewalk on their way to a restaurant. The people rushing past, skyscrapers looming, and the cacophony of traffic reminded Sutton of the story Flynn had told her about sleeping on Seth's balcony. What kind of cruel trick of fate was *this*? He was in her head, and like it or not, he'd already rooted himself in her heart. She was counting on Leni to help her get him out of her head. Leni had a way of getting to the crux of problems and figuring out a way to move past them. But she knew her heart would be a harder sell.

"I can't believe you didn't tell me any of this before *now*," Leni said, looking as sharp as ever in a black pantsuit and crisp scoop-neck white blouse, auburn waves hanging loose over the shoulders of her blazer.

"I was still processing it."

Leni gave her a give-me-a-break look. "You slept with your boss. What is there to process?"

"*Everything.*" She lowered her voice as people walked past. "We were supposed to leave all of that in the rainforest, but every time we see each other, it's like someone poured gasoline on a flame. I swear, Leni, when I see that man, my heart doesn't just race. It gets too big for my chest, and my body's like, *Yes! Finally!*" She sighed heavily. "But now he's out with someone else, so what the hell do I know?"

"Don't be too hard on yourself. Good sex will do that to a girl."

"It's *never* been like this."

"You're just not used to meaningless trysts. But he shouldn't be stringing you along. That's wrong on every level."

"That's just it. I don't think it was meaningless for either of us, and I don't think he's stringing me along. We went from not wanting to be anywhere near each other to being together twenty-four-seven, talking about our lives and families and what made us who we are. I've never connected with a guy like that, and I *liked* it. I like *him*. We can't even go one night without talking for *hours* on the phone. That says something, and not just about me."

"Maybe you're caught up in a romantic fantasy or something, or your biological clock is ticking too loudly. I don't know. But you're a reporter, Sutton. You deal in facts, so open your fucking eyes. You said he's out with someone else."

"*I know.*"

"Then why are you hanging on to the idea of him? You

might have thought it was meaningful, but he obviously didn't. He's a guy. He's horny. Accept that. It's time to move on."

"I don't think he's like that. When we got together, he told me he hadn't been with anyone for more than a year."

"And you believed him?" Leni asked incredulously.

"You weren't there. You didn't hear the way he said it or see the look in his eyes. I know you don't trust easily, but have a little faith in my judgment."

They stopped behind a group of people at a crosswalk, and amusement rose in Leni's eyes. "Says the girl who slept with her *boss*. A man who is now entertaining someone else."

"Yes. I know. I hate this. I'm not a gullible person, Leni. You know that. But if I've completely misread our connection, what does that say about *me*?"

"Nothing bad. Think of it this way. Jules is a heart-on-her-sleeve kind of girl, and before Raz, I kept mine behind barbed wire. When it comes to this kind of thing, you've always been right in the middle of us. You look before you leap, but there's no stopping your heart from getting involved. Unfortunately, you made an agreement with a man who isn't like that, whether he sold you another bill of goods or not. Want me to give him hell?"

"God *no*. Although I should blame *you* for all of this."

"This should be good," Leni said sarcastically.

Sutton lowered her voice as they followed the crowd across the street. "How many times did you say, *Just fuck him already and get it over with?*"

"I clearly should've known better. But in my defense, when you called me from that assignment in Portugal, you lost your train of thought the second Flynn took off his shirt. Remember? I thought if you two hooked up, you'd get him out of your system. Now I guess we're moving on to plan B."

"We have a plan B? What is it? Shock treatments?"

"That would be plan C. Plan B is burying your misguided feelings in good food, strong drinks, and a hot guy."

"Food and drinks, yes, but I'm done with men."

"Wake up and smell the payback, baby. The least we can do is post a picture of you and a hot guy on social media for the jerk to see."

"I doubt he's ever looked at my social media."

"Leave it to me. I'll make sure he sees it." Leni opened the door to the restaurant. "This place is amazing. You're going to love the food."

While Leni spoke to the hostess, Sutton took in the elegant candle-style chandeliers and two-story brick walls, one of which was lined with circle-head windows. She glanced at the back of the restaurant, where she could see a bar through three arched entranceways, and her gaze caught on the sandy-haired, broad-shouldered beast of a man sitting at a table by the farthest archway. Her stomach sank. Flynn held a drink in one hand, his attention on the brunette sitting across from him. Her back was facing Sutton, but her hair fell just past the shoulders of her black dress, and she was leaning forward, like she wanted him to catch every word she said.

"There's about a forty-minute wait," Leni said. "What's wrong?"

"Look who's here."

Leni followed her gaze. "We can go someplace else, but how about I give him a piece of my mind first."

"I love that you would do that for me, but I don't need you fighting my battles, and we're not leaving. You were right. I need to face the facts, and this forces me to do it."

"Are you sure? There are plenty of other places to eat."

"I'm positive. You and I are going to have a good time…and a gallon of alcohol. I might have to sleep on your couch. What are the chances that he'd come to this restaurant?"

Leni pressed her lips together, her brow wrinkling.

"*What* is that look for?"

"This is Seth's restaurant."

"Leni," she whispered harshly. "Why did you take me to Seth's restaurant after everything I just told you?"

"Because it's good, and I didn't think he'd come here. Doesn't he live by you?"

"Leni?"

They turned at the deep voice, which belonged to a gorgeous man with wavy dark brown hair, scruff, and black-framed glasses.

Leni's eyes lit up. "Seth. *Hi.* I didn't know you were in town."

Seth? This was Flynn's nerdy brother? Now she wished she really *had* googled pictures of his brothers. Without thinking, Sutton quickly cataloged his outfit. He wore a tan cardigan like her grandfather used to wear, with the top and bottom buttons undone, a plaid shirt, one side of which peeked out from under the hem of his sweater, light-gray skinny slacks, and white sneakers. He was with two other good-looking brown-haired men.

"I came back to celebrate my brother's birthday." Seth smiled at Sutton. "I recognize you from *Discovery Hour.* You're Leni's sister Sutton, right?"

"Yes, I am." Sutton offered her hand, and he shook it. "It's nice to meet you."

"You as well. I've heard a lot about you," Seth said.

Her nerves flamed. Had Flynn told him what had happened between them?

"So have I," the younger of the two other guys said as he stepped forward. He looked casual in jeans and an untucked white linen shirt with the sleeves rolled up. "Hi, I'm Seth's brother Noah, and you are even more beautiful in person than you are on television." He offered his hand, revealing leather and beaded bracelets around one wrist.

"Thank you." She shook his hand, noticing his similarities to Flynn. He had the same strong jaw and blue eyes. His hair was longish on top and shorter on the sides than Flynn's, though his jaw was just as scruffy. But he had a playful air about him and lacked the edginess Flynn possessed.

"Beauty must run in the family," Noah said, eyeing Leni. "It's nice to meet you, Leni. You are stunning, too."

"Thank you," Leni said. "My fiancé thinks so."

"All right, Noah, back off." Seth clapped a hand on his shoulder. "She's engaged to Duncan Raznick."

"Seriously?" Noah cocked a brow. "We know Dunc. He grew up with our cousins in Pleasant Hill, Maryland. The man's clearly got great taste in women."

"Excuse our baby brother. He was raised with monkeys," the third guy said. "I'm their brother Clay."

"It's nice to meet you," Sutton said.

"I recognize you from the underwear ads," Leni said.

Clay flashed a megawatt smile. "That's nice to hear. Women are rarely looking at my face in those ads."

Sutton laughed.

Leni rolled her eyes. "Whose birthday is it?"

"Flynn's," Seth answered. "He's over there with Victory."

His sister? He's not on a date? Sutton shot a glance at Leni, who caught it ever so coolly, cautiously giving her a look that said not to get too excited. *Too late.* Although she wondered why Flynn hadn't mentioned his birthday to her.

"He thinks he's having dinner with me, Clay, and Vic," Seth explained. "We're surprising him with Noah. Why don't you join us?"

Sutton waved them off. "That's okay. We don't want to intrude on family time."

"You're not intruding," Seth assured them. "The more the merrier, and I think Flynn would be upset if we didn't invite you."

I don't know about that.

"Leni?" Seth urged. "It'll be nice to enjoy a meal without talking about work, and I'm sure Vic would love to see you."

"I'd like to catch up with her. What do you think, Sutton?" Leni looked at her, brows raised in question, but her eyes said, *Let's go get the scoop on Flynn.*

Sutton's heart raced. She was torn between wanting to spend time with Flynn and wondering if everything Leni said about him was right, even though it didn't feel that way. Would it be better to cut those hopeful ties now? "I don't know—"

"Come on. It'll be fun," Clay promised.

Noah slung an arm around her. "We can get to know each other better."

They were already on the move toward the table. She eyed Leni, who shrugged, as if to say, *guess we're joining them.*

Flynn looked up as they approached, and for a heart-stopping second his eyes locked on Sutton, sending her insides into a whirlwind. But those hawk eyes narrowed, his jaw tightening, turning that whirlwind into a gust of second guesses.

WHAT THE HELL? Your date is with my fucking brother?

Flynn pushed to his feet, his blood running hot. He couldn't take his eyes off Noah and Sutton. He hadn't even known Noah was in town. He was vaguely aware of Victory moving around him to hug the auburn-haired woman who was with them and Seth and Clay saying, "Surprise!"

Clay clapped Flynn on the back. "Good to see you back in one piece."

"Thanks, man." Flynn pointed to Sutton and Noah. "What's going on here?"

"*What?* Oh, nothing," Sutton said anxiously, ducking out from under Noah's arm.

"The night's young. We could make something happen." Noah waggled his brows.

"Now, there's an idea," the auburn-haired woman chimed in.

Flynn's jaw clenched tighter.

"We just ran into Sutton and Leni out front, and I invited them to join us to celebrate your birthday," Seth explained.

"Happy birthday, bro." Noah pulled Flynn into an embrace. "Surprised to see me?"

"You could say that." Flynn had the urge to set Leni and the rest of them straight and stake his claim on Sutton. Jesus, she'd gotten so deep under his skin, he couldn't even think rationally.

"Happy birthday," Sutton said tentatively. "We don't have to sit with you if you'd rather we didn't."

"Don't be silly. It's nice to see you, Steele. I'm glad you're here."

"I knew you would be," Seth said with a big-ass grin.

A heads-up would've been nice.

As Seth snagged a waiter to arrange a larger table, Flynn turned his attention to Leni. She shared Sutton's porcelain skin and dainty features, but she gave off a protective vibe over Sutton that seemed to be directed toward him. Either Sutton had shared what they'd done, or Leni was as good at reading situations as Seth claimed she was. "It's nice to finally meet you, Leni."

Leni gave him an assessing once-over. "So you're the *snake*…slayer."

Sutton shot her an imploring look.

Flynn didn't know what that was about, but he didn't have time to ponder it. There was a flurry of activity as their table was rearranged, and they took their seats. As the others settled in, Flynn lowered his voice for Sutton's ears only. "I thought you had a date."

"I did. With *Leni*," she whispered. "I thought *you* had a date."

"I never said I had a date. I said I had plans." *Plans that were supposed to help get my mind off you for a night, but apparently the whole fucking universe is working against me.* It had been torture trying to keep himself in check at work, and their nightly calls had already become his favorite part of the day. He wasn't about to give them up. He wanted a hell of a lot more, and *this* wasn't helping.

They made small talk as they ordered drinks and dinner, and there was no missing the interested glances Noah and Clay were giving Sutton. Seth held up his glass in a toast. "To our crazy-ass brother. Here's to another safe year around the sun, Flynn. Happy birthday."

Everyone clinked glasses and drank.

"Why didn't you tell me it was your birthday?" Sutton asked.

"It's just another day," Flynn said.

"Flynn isn't a fan of birthdays," Seth said.

"He hasn't been since our parents forgot his when he was eight," Victory added.

"They forgot your birthday?" Sutton asked.

"Yes, but that isn't why I don't like them," Flynn argued.

"Yes, it is," Clay said.

"How'd they forget?" Leni asked. "I mean, that's kind of a big deal."

"Our childhood wasn't typical," Seth said. "Our parents were traveling to Indonesia with five little kids, and our days sort of blurred together. When we got settled and they realized they'd missed Flynn's birthday, my mother made a big deal of celebrating, but he hasn't enjoyed them since."

"Aw, that's so sad." Sutton reached over and patted his cheek. "Was your little heart broken?"

"No, but our mother's was." Flynn looked at his siblings' amused expressions. "Don't you guys remember Mom crying when she realized she forgot it?"

"No," Seth said, and his siblings agreed.

"Then you blocked it out," Flynn said.

"Is that why you don't like birthdays?" Sutton asked.

"I don't know," Flynn admitted. "It seems silly to celebrate them when we didn't do anything other than being born. We should be celebrating our mother tonight. She did the hard work."

"We can't celebrate with Mom. She and Dad are traveling across Europe," Seth said.

Flynn took a drink. "I know." Their parents had been planning this trip for a year. "I sent her flowers at the hotel."

"Aw, that's really sweet," Sutton said.

"Thank you." Flynn looked smugly at his siblings. "See? Someone understands."

"I said it was sweet," Sutton said. "But make no mistake, I'm a total birthday girl. Give me *all* the cake and the hoopla. I want gifts and cheers and everything else that comes with it."

Everyone laughed, but Flynn remembered what she'd said about it being hard to stand out in her twin-filled family. He wondered if her affinity for birthdays had less to do with gifts and cake and more to do with having her family's attention for the day.

"So, Sutton. What was it like being stuck in the rainforest with Flynn?" Noah asked.

"I thought it was going to be kind of a nightmare." Sutton sipped her wine, eyeing Flynn. "But it wasn't that bad."

"You mean he didn't try to control your every step?" Noah asked.

"*Well…*" Sutton laughed softly.

"He'll never change," Noah said.

"You were a wild kid with the attention span of a gnat," Flynn reminded him. "I had to rein you in or you would've gotten hurt."

"It wasn't just him," Clay chimed in, and Seth nodded in agreement.

"Flynn was always bossing us around and lecturing us about safety," Victory said. "But, Noah, you didn't seem to mind. You followed him around like a puppy."

"Because he did cool shit," Noah said. "All Clay wanted to do was play ball, and you and Seth were doing boring big-kid stuff."

"Here we go again." Seth glanced at Sutton and Leni. "Excuse us while we hash out our childhoods."

"We know a little something about bossy brothers," Leni said.

"If it makes you feel any better, Flynn is still a bossy know-it-all," Sutton said with amusement. "I got my fair number of lectures while we were in the rainforest. But I'm thankful he's so knowledgeable. He saved my life."

Leni lifted her glass. "To the snake slayer."

"I thought I heard you say that earlier," Clay said. "Dude, did you wrestle an anaconda?"

Flynn shook his head and glanced at Sutton, the amusement in her eyes telling him she was thinking of their private anaconda joke, too.

"No, that was me," she said lightheartedly. Then her voice turned serious. "But I was inches from a deadly pit viper and shaking in my boots. I was sure I was going to die, but Flynn didn't hesitate to get between us and kill it. Your brother knows how to wield a machete." She looked at him, conflicting emotions battling in her eyes. "That was the bravest thing I've ever seen anyone do."

Flynn's jaw muscles were getting a workout tonight. It took everything he had not to reach for her. "Anyone here would've done the same thing."

"Like hell they would," Victory said. "We'd all be hiding behind you. You're a rare breed, Flynn. Even if you are a pain in our ass sometimes."

Noah batted his lashes. "Oh, Flynn. You're my *hero*."

"Jackass." Flynn threw his napkin at Noah.

Everyone laughed.

"Yeah, well, his bravery knows its limits. This is the same guy who threw up the first time he kissed a girl," Clay said.

"What?" Leni leaned forward, looking at Flynn. "Is that true?"

"Yes," Sutton said with a laugh.

"He told you about that?" Seth cocked a brow at Flynn.

Yeah, I know. She's different. I wanted her to know the real me.

"We had a lot of time to talk in the rainforest," Sutton explained.

"Dude, you were alone in the rainforest with this gorgeous woman, and you told her stories about kissing girls and puking?" Noah laughed.

"Is it any wonder he's still single?" Victory said.

"I'm her *boss*," Flynn gritted out.

"Sucks to be you," Clay said. "Sutton, I'm not into jungles, but I have no trouble playing the field."

Flynn shot him a warning stare. He hated having his hands tied while his brothers got to flirt with her.

Sutton smiled at Clay and said, "I bet you're good with your hands, too," inciting more flirtatious banter that Noah was all too happy to get in on.

Flynn had never been jealous of his brothers, but as he listened to them joking around, he couldn't help but wonder which pictures of them Sutton had seen when she'd googled them the other night. The green-eyed monster dug its talons in. They'd all been blessed with good genetics, but the competition around the table went far deeper than looks. Flynn might joke about Seth being a nerd, but there was a reason he'd been featured as one of Forbes's most eligible bachelors *twice*. His oldest brother was savvy in business and in his personal life. It wouldn't matter what he wore; he exuded an air of authority that few could pull off without coming across as arrogant. He was also easygoing in a way Flynn could never be. But Seth knew what had gone down between Flynn and Sutton, and he'd never cross that line with her. Their brothers, on the other hand, were clueless about it.

Flynn looked across the table at Clay, laughing at something Leni had said. *Mr. Perfect.* That's what the media called him. Not only did he reek of a charm all his own, but he'd also honed the ability to let things roll off his back. Then there was Noah, who on the cusp of thirty had the same playful nature he'd possessed as a kid, drawing women like flies.

Their dinners arrived, and the lighthearted banter continued, with one embarrassing story about Flynn after another. Despite his brothers' flirting, which he'd never let go farther, he was having a good time and enjoying the way Sutton took it all in stride. They laughed a lot, but they managed to have some serious conversations, too. Victory and Sutton talked for a long time, and it was great to see his sister having fun for a change. She asked Sutton about her previous position as a fashion editor, which led to a discussion about Seth's retail operations, and Leni's marketing prowess, which had helped kick some of them off. Seth offered the girls a shopping spree at any of his locations, and the three women spent twenty minutes talking about when they should take him up on it.

Sutton asked Noah about his endeavor in Colorado, and she and Leni even talked with Clay about having watched his team play a time or two with their brothers. Sutton and Leni bragged about playing flag football with their family, a sight Flynn would pay to see.

All in all, it was a pretty great night.

After their plates were cleared away, Flynn sat back, grateful for his family, and said, "Thanks for a great birthday. I appreciate you all showing up, and Sutton and Leni, thanks for joining us."

"Just wait for the after-party," Clay said. "We're heading to a club when we're done here."

Flynn was not a nightclub guy, but before he could remind them of that, Noah took center stage.

"You're coming with us, right, ladies?" Noah urged. "I'm looking forward to getting Sutton out on the dance floor."

Flirt all you want, little brother, but the only dancing you'll be doing with her is vertical.

"If you guys go, I'll go," Victory said to Sutton and Leni, shocking Flynn. She disliked nightclubs more than he did. He was sure she'd back out.

Sutton and Leni exchanged a glance.

"Sure." Sutton stole a glance at Flynn. "Sounds fun."

"Sutton's a fantastic dancer, Noah. I hope you can keep up," Leni said.

"That will not be a problem. Unlike the rest of these guys, I've got rhythm and I know how to use it." Noah winked at Sutton.

Christ, Noah. Really? "Why don't we get the check and get out of here?"

"We're not quite done yet." Seth nodded toward a group of waiters and waitresses heading in their direction with a cake illuminated by candles.

Flynn uttered a curse.

"We love you, brother, and we want everyone to know it," Seth said as they set the cake in front of Flynn.

Everyone in the place looked over as they sang "Happy

Birthday." Flynn was going to give Seth hell for this, but one look at Sutton singing with the others, her radiant smile aimed at him, made him wonder if he should thank Seth instead—and lock up Clay and Noah someplace far away from her.

"Make a wish," Victory urged.

There was only one thing Flynn wanted, and she was sitting right next to him.

Chapter Twenty

MUSIC BLARED IN the crowded club, competing with the thunderous roar of Flynn's inner caveman as he stood at the bar waiting for his drink, eyes locked on Sutton dancing with Noah for the umpteenth time. Flynn had been enjoying watching her dance with Leni and Victory before Noah and Clay had sidled up to them. Noah wasted no time moving in on Sutton with his dirty dance moves. Not that Flynn blamed him. Sutton was a fucking goddess on the dance floor, swaying to the beat in that sexy blouse and curve-hugging skirt, her every move more seductive than the last.

"Here you go." The bartender set a glass in front of Flynn, jerking him from his thoughts.

"Thanks." He tossed a twenty on the bar and downed the drink in one gulp. He was tempted to order several more to try to drink the ache away, but there wasn't enough alcohol on the planet to numb the emotions coursing through him.

As he headed back to the table, he saw Clay cut in on Noah and Sutton. Noah looked annoyed but turned around to dance with Victory and Leni. Clay leaned in closer to Sutton, saying something that made her smile. Her gaze skirted over the crowd, finding Flynn. With a wicked glint in her eyes, she danced more seductively. Her alluring lips curled into a sinful smile that made his cock take notice. He knew what those lips felt like wrapped around it.

Fuck. Maybe he needed those drinks after all.

"You okay?" Seth asked.

"What do you think?" Flynn bit out as he took his seat.

"I think you're looking a little Hulkish again."

"No shit."

"You know they're your brothers, and they respect you. If you clue them in, they'll back off."

"She's a big girl. She can do what she wants." Flynn watched her and the others coming off the dance floor.

"It sounds like your good friend Denial is messing with your head again. Do yourself a favor. Rephrase that statement to *she can do* whomever *she wants*, and then tell me how you feel."

Flynn glowered at him. "Why are you fucking with me? Aren't you the one who said workplace hookups never end well?"

"Yes, but I'm getting the feeling she isn't just a hookup for you," Seth said seconds before the others joined them.

It would be so much easier if she were.

"You guys are missing out," Noah said as he sat beside Flynn. "These girls can dance."

Flynn pulled out the chair on his other side for Sutton.

"Thanks, Noah. You and Clay have great moves, too." Sutton sat down and grabbed her drink, smiling at Flynn before taking a sip. She was bright eyed and a little sweaty, her hair tousled. She looked sexy and wild, so different from the woman she was in the office and similar to the one Flynn had come to know in the rainforest.

"Some of us more than others," Clay chimed in.

"Do you compete in everything you do?" Leni asked.

As the others chatted, Flynn leaned closer to Sutton, putting his hand on her leg beneath the table. "You looked great out there. Are you having fun?"

"*So* much fun," she said.

"Of course she's having fun," Noah interrupted. "She was dancing with me. Sutton, we make a great team. We should do more stuff together. You like to explore, right? We should go on an adventure sometime."

"That could be fun, Sutton," Leni urged. "You love adventures."

Are you fucking kidding me?

Sutton stole a glance at Flynn, her eyes dancing with mischief, then turned those gorgeous eyes on his younger brother. "What kind of adventure do you have in mind?"

Flynn ground his back teeth.

"The best kind," Noah promised. "Where we explore and discover new things about each other, like what floats our boats, new kinks, you know. All the fun stuff."

Flynn's hand curled into a fist. "Her schedule is booked for the show."

"Not *every* day," Sutton said coyly. She leaned her elbow on the table, resting her chin in her hand, gazing at Noah. "Where would we go?"

"Someplace where your only predator is of the handsome two-legged variety." Noah smiled smugly. "Well, some might say three-legged."

Victory barked out a laugh. "Does that line *ever* work for you?"

"That was pretty bad, Noah," Seth agreed.

"Give me a break, Seth. You know the Braden curse is not

an urban legend," Noah said.

"Oh yeah?" Sutton stole another glance at Flynn with a challenge in her eyes. "Does that mean you're packing an anaconda? Because I saw one of those in the rainforest, and they're mighty impressive."

Flynn eyed her. *What kind of game are you playing?*

"Now I'm curious. Are all Bradens created equally?" Leni asked, her sharp gaze moving around the table.

"Some of us are better at *exploring* than others," Flynn gritted out.

"Yeah, except you were always more interested in playing in the dirt with creatures than getting down and dirty with women," Clay chimed in. "Leni, to answer your question, some of us are more experienced where it counts."

"Says the man who has always been more interested in playing with his own balls," Seth said.

The girls cracked up.

"I know I've been out of the dating game for a long time, but is this what flirting has turned into?" Victory flipped her brown hair over her shoulder. "Going straight from dancing to kinks?"

"The world just keeps getting better," Noah said.

"Now you understand why I had pretty much given up on men before Raz and I got together," Leni said.

"It's a shit show out there," Sutton said. "You can only fake it until you make it for so long before giving up."

"There's no faking it with me." Noah winked.

"Sounds like I'm not missing much," Victory said.

"Didn't you say that one of your clients offered to fly you out to Bali on his private plane?" Seth asked.

Victory rolled her eyes. "Yes, and he's a total player. I have no patience for that. What happened to regular guys who do crossword puzzles and like to have quiet dinners?"

"I do Wordle," Clay said.

"I do crosswords," Seth said.

Victory scrunched her face in disgust. "Gross. You guys are my brothers."

The song "Waterfalls" by TLC came on, and Sutton exclaimed, "I *love* this song."

"Great," Noah said. "I'll dance with you."

As Noah pushed to his feet, Flynn put a hand on his shoulder, shoving him back down to his chair. "Sit your one-eyed-viper ass down." He took Sutton by the arm. "Let's go, Glamour Girl." He led her out to the dance floor.

"I thought you didn't dance," she said.

"It's not really my thing." He hauled her into his arms.

She blinked up at him with a furrowed brow. "Then why are we on the dance floor?"

"Because *you* are my thing." He held her gaze, sliding his hand to the curve of her back, pressing their bodies firmly together. "You can flirt with my brothers as much as you want, but don't think for a second that I'd let it go any further than that. I'm done following the rules. You're coming home with me."

"It's about time you noticed," she said with a smirk.

"I think everyone in the damn place noticed."

"A girl's got to do what a girl's got to do to get the attention of the *only* man she wants."

The knots in his chest loosened a little. "You're a wicked woman, Steele. Was your plan to drive me crazy? Because you've been driving me nuts since I heard you moan into your coffee on Tuesday morning."

"We both know that's a lie."

"I don't fucking lie."

She brushed her fingers along the back of his neck with a playful smile. "You already admitted that I've been driving you crazy since the day we met."

"You're damn right you have. Those moans have gotten to me since day one. Hell, I almost showed up at your place with that coffee I sent you the morning after we got back into town just to hear you moan while you drank it."

Her brows knitted. "*You* sent me the coffee? I thought Leni did."

"I sent you two. I knew how badly you'd been craving it."

Her gaze softened, but that softness quickly morphed into heat. "That was awfully thoughtful of you. In case you're wondering, this is what I sounded like when I drank it." She leaned closer, moaning seductively.

"You little vixen. I ought to take you right here and show every man in the place who you really belong to."

"Mr. Braden, that is *not* appropriate talk for a boss to their subordinate," she said with feigned, wide-eyed innocence.

He tightened his hold on her, turning his back to his family's table, and lowered his mouth beside her ear. "Then I won't tell you my birthday wishes, since they're definitely not work appropriate." He slicked his tongue along the shell of her ear and nipped her earlobe, earning a sexy gasp.

"I'd much rather you showed me, anyway."

Chapter Twenty-One

SUTTON HAD THOUGHT her nerves would ease on the drive from the city to Port Hudson, but as she followed Flynn's old Land Cruiser down the woods-lined road toward his house, her mind started playing tricks on her, and the butterflies in her stomach turned into a swarm of bees. She'd relived every kiss, every sensual touch, and sinful sound they'd shared in the rainforest so many times, she had them memorized. But what if it was different now that their lives weren't in danger? What if it was awkward or they couldn't find their way back to where they'd been?

She turned onto a gravel road behind Flynn, and a few minutes later a rustic cabin with a wide front porch came into view, and Flynn parked in front of it. Her nerves flared anew as he stepped out of his truck, rising to his full height, taking her breath away. His muscular legs ate up the distance to her car. She swallowed hard as he opened her door, feeling foolish for having been staring instead of getting out of her car.

"Hello, sexy girl." He took her hand, bringing her to her feet, the warm, happy smile that she'd discovered and had become familiar with in the rainforest curved his lips, easing the sting of those bees in her belly. He took her face between his rough hands, looking at her like he hadn't seen her in weeks, and said, "*God*, I've missed you."

Her heart stumbled at the longing in his voice. She felt the same way, but fear of being hurt, of not knowing what this was to him, held those words back. "You see me every day."

"No, babe. I see you every day through the veil of pretending not to really see you. I miss the way you look at me when we're alone and the way your voice changes when it's just us. I miss your laughter and the cute expression you get when I flirt with you. I miss the way you feel in my arms, and I miss the feel of your lips on mine. I don't think I've ever missed anyone or anything as deeply as I miss you."

The sincerity in his voice and his words erased her fear and filled her heart to the brim. Before she could tell him that she missed him in all the same ways and more, he pressed his lips to hers in a tender kiss as familiar as that special smile, pushing away her nervousness and bringing a rush of exhilaration.

"Sutton," he murmured against her lips, and buried his hands in her hair, taking her in a deep, passionate kiss that made her knees buckle.

She clung to him as their lips parted, savoring the feel of one strong arm circling her waist, drawing her tight against him like he wasn't going to chance her getting away, and oh, how she loved that. He pressed a kiss to her forehead, then rested his forehead on hers, and exhaled a breath so full of desire and *relief*, it drew the truth. "I can't stop thinking about you, either. About *us*. I know we were only together for a few days, but I miss it. I miss our closeness. I miss you, Flynn."

"I'm glad to hear that, because I'm done pretending that I don't want to climb through the phone and see your face every night." He took her hand and pressed a kiss to the back of it as he led her down to the cabin. He opened the door. "Fair warning. Once you're inside, I might not ever let you leave."

"I'll take my chances." She stepped inside. Flynn's cabin was as rugged as he was, all dark wood and expansive windows, with substantial furniture, an open kitchen, stairs that led to a second story, and an entire wall of bookshelves filled from end to end. "I like your place, and with shelves like that, I'll happily be the Belle to your beast."

"You haven't seen the best part yet." He strode across the room and opened what she thought was a door, but then the wall folded accordion-style, opening the entire living room to a deck that was built over the water.

"Wow."

They went to the deck, and she took in the smell and sounds of the lake, the chirping of crickets, and the feel of the cool breeze kissing her cheeks. Moonlight illuminated the inky water, which spilled out as far as the eye could see. Lights were strung between poles on the corners of the deck, though they were turned off at the moment, and two cozy-looking loungers sat off to one side, a table and chairs on the other. The deck stepped down to a walkway that led to a second deck off another room, and a boathouse. "This is incredible. You really do have a boat."

"Mm-hm."

"I wondered what your place looked like."

"A little different from the tent you imagined?" His arms circled her from behind, and he kissed her cheek.

She leaned back against his chest, feeling like she could breathe for the first time since they'd come home. "I knew you didn't live in a tent, but I couldn't picture you in a house, either. You're too…"

"Too much like Mowgli?"

She heard the smile in his voice. "*Yes*. But this feels right."

"This, as in *us*, or this, meaning my cabin?"

"Both," she confessed. "But the doors and the deck and the lake aren't the best part of your place. You are."

He tightened his grip on her, his scruff tickling her cheek as he pressed his warm lips to it again. "Do you know how many times I've pictured you right here?" He kissed her neck, his hands skimming down her hips. She felt his heart beating sure and steady against her back and closed her eyes, anticipation stacking up inside her. "How often I think about doing this with you out here?" He remained behind her as he unbuttoned her shirt, placing tantalizing kisses along her neck. Cool air washed over her chest as he unhooked the front clasp of her bra and palmed her breast, growling in her ear. "And *this*." He emphasized his words by teasing her nipple, sending prickles of heat over her skin.

"*Flynn*," she panted out, breathless and needy.

"That's exactly how I've heard you say my name when I fantasized about doing this to you here." He tugged her skirt up with his other hand, rubbing her through her panties.

"Oh*god…please*."

"Don't worry, sweetheart, I *will* please you." He pushed his hand into her panties, his hard length pressing against her ass, thick fingers sliding between her legs. "You're so wet for me. Your pussy missed me, too."

A thrill seared through her at his dirty talk. "*So much*" came out in one heated breath. He pushed two fingers inside her, using his thumb on her clit. Electricity arced through her. "*Flynn*—" She reached back, grabbing his outer thighs to combat her wobbly legs. He sealed his mouth over her neck, loving her flesh with his tongue and teeth as he drove her out of her freaking mind. He worked her faster, thick fingers pumping, thumb circling so perfectly, she rose on her toes, on the verge of detonating. "*Flynn, please.*"

"Tell me, Sutton. Whose face did you see when you came with your toy?"

"Whose do you think?" she panted out.

He slowed his efforts, and she whimpered. "I'm a greedy bastard when it comes to you. I need to hear it. Tell me whose voice you heard whispering in your ear about how sweet your pussy was? About how tight and hot you felt? Whose cock did you fantasize was driving into you?"

"*Yours*" came out strangled. "But I didn't want it to be."

His hand stilled. "Why the hell not?"

"Because I thought we were *done*. But I never looked at pictures of your brothers. I knew they wouldn't do anything for me."

"Fucking right they wouldn't. Because we both know the only person you want touching you *here*"—he cupped her sex— "is *me*." He ground his hips against her ass. "And my cock only wants you."

His proclamation burrowed deep inside her, and "*Yes*" tumbled out with a vehemence and surety she hadn't even known she'd felt until that very second. He quickened his efforts, applying just the right amount of pressure to send her up onto her toes again. "There's only you, Sutton," he said gruffly, as if he knew how those words would strip away any doubts. "You've been in my head for so fucking long, there's no room for anyone else."

"That's only fair," she panted out, clinging to her sanity by a shred, "since you've monopolized my thoughts, too."

"That's what I want to hear." He sank his teeth into her neck and squeezed her nipple, setting her off like a bomb.

"*Flynn*—" shot from her lungs, her inner muscles spasming around his fingers as he masterfully took her higher. She was trembling, barely breathing, soaking in his gruff voice—*That's it, sweetheart, ride that high*—until she was so consumed with pleasure, she thought she might pass out.

When the last of her climax rolled through her, he turned her in his arms, taking her in a soul-searing kiss that carried her right back to that needy place.

"That was birthday wish number one, sexy girl."

She let out a surprised giggle as he scooped her into his arms and carried her into the living room. "We should celebrate your birthday every day."

He flashed a wolfish grin as he set her down on the couch and took off her heels. "I like the way you think, Steele." He kissed her again, deeper and more possessively. Those midnight-blue eyes held her captive as he hiked her skirt up her thighs and brushed one thick thumb over her damp panties. Tantalizing sensations slithered through her core, and she closed her eyes.

"Open your eyes." When she did, he stripped off her panties. "Spread those legs, sweetheart. It's time to grant me wish number two." He guided her legs over his broad shoulders and lowered his talented mouth where she needed it most, sending currents of pleasure throbbing through her. She bowed off the cushion, and he gritted out a curse. "I'd *almost* convinced myself you couldn't possibly have tasted this sweet." She barely caught her breath before his wicked mouth was devouring her again, his expert touch making her writhe and rock. Desire swelled inside her like a thundercloud ready to burst, until it was pulsing beneath her skin. "I'm going to think about how sweet you taste every time I sit on this couch."

She closed her eyes again, digging her nails into his shoulders at the thought of him thinking of her like that. "Look at me, Steele. I want to see the pleasure in those gorgeous eyes." She opened her eyes and was greeted by two pools of smoldering passion. "That's it. You're so fucking beautiful." He held her gaze, teasing her with his tongue, gradually quickening his efforts, his greedy sounds heightening every sensation.

"*Ohgod, Flynn…Don't stop.*" She grabbed his hair, holding him there. He slowed his pace, every stroke of his thick fingers sending sparks through her core as his tongue and teeth worked their magic on her most sensitive nerves. He let out a guttural growl, and as if it had snapped his restraint, his fingers fucked her faster, he sucked harder, and the world spun away. She cried out in sweet agony, consumed by a hailstorm of pleasure as he ravaged her. A stream of sounds flew from her lungs, each one amping up his efforts, earning more of those gratified noises, until she finally floated down from the high.

Her entire body was on fire, so overly sensitive, she inhaled sharply with his every touch as he kissed her inner thighs and loved his way up her body. He lingered on her breasts, licking, sucking, and kissing until she was begging again, desperate for more. *God*, what he did to her. He slicked his tongue around her nipple, eyes gleaming with emotion, and ran two fingers along her lower lip. "Your mouth is mine."

"It's like it's my birthday."

He pushed those fingers between her lips. "Show me what you're going to do to my cock." His dirty demand sent an erotic thrill through her. She closed her mouth around his fingers, swirling her tongue and sucking, loving the hungry sounds he made. She reached for the button on his pants, but he caught her wrist. He pushed to his feet, bringing her up with him. "I've waited a long time for this visual feast," he said as he undressed her.

"So have I." She started to unbutton his shirt.

He grabbed his shirt with both hands and tore it off, sending his buttons flying. She laughed as he tossed it away. He made quick work of stripping off the rest of his clothes and drank in every inch of her nakedness.

"Look at my beautiful girl." He ran his fingers along her slick heat and up the center of her body, his words wrapping into a bow and burrowing into her chest. "I want to take you so many ways tonight." He drew her against him, palming her ass, his eager erection pressing temptingly along her stomach. "But first I need this." His mouth came hungrily down over hers, his tongue sweeping and plunging. She closed her mouth around it and sucked. His cock jerked against her as a guttural growl fell from his lips, and he grabbed her hair, tugging her head back, eyes blazing.

She whispered, "Happy birthday," and pressed her lips to his chest, trailing her fingers over his nipples. Her mouth followed, and he hissed out a curse. Loving that sound, she lingered there, teasing, soaking in his greedy noises. His muscles corded tight with every touch of her lips as she kissed a path down his stomach and wrapped her hand around his thick length. Their gazes held as she lowered herself to sit on the couch. He stood in front of her, big and broad, desire practically oozing from his pores.

"I have been thinking about doing this since the rainforest," she confessed. Every time they'd done it, they'd stopped before he came, both too eager for more. "We're not stopping until I get everything you have to give, so don't hold back. Got it,

Braden?"

"*Christ*, Sutton." He threaded his hands into her hair, wrapping it around his fingers, his chest expanding with his heavy breaths. "You're like my every fantasy rolled into one incredible woman."

Invigorated by his praise, and intent on making him lose control, she slicked her tongue along his length and around the broad head. His skin was salty and warm, his cock heavy in her hand. His gaze remained trained on her, growing more intense by the second as she got him nice and wet and took him in deep, stroking him tight.

"Fucking hell, you feel good." His hands tightened in her hair, sending stings of pleasure racing down her body. She worked him faster, sucking and humming around his cock, earning more curses and praise. She craved all of it. She craved *him*. "Relax your throat. I want to fuck it." She did, taking him painfully deep and wanting more. "That's it…*God*…So fucking good." She stroked him tighter and cupped his balls with her other hand, earning a primal sound that made her sex clench with need. "Fuck…*Sutton*." His warning was clear, but she wasn't done. She withdrew his cock and teased the head with her tongue, and he gritted out, "*You're killing me.*"

"Just think of how enjoyable of a death it will be." Her voice was thick with need. He made her feel safe, and she had a fantasy of her own to live out. "It's your turn to watch." She sat back and spread her legs, reaching between them to touch herself. His eyes locked on her fingers sliding through her wetness.

"*Jesus.*" He stroked his cock, watching her work herself into a panting, needy mess.

On the verge of coming, her eyes fluttered closed, but she

forced them open again, not wanting to miss a second of the hunger in his eyes.

"I need to fuck you," he growled.

"Fuck my mouth and we'll both come. You can have the rest of me after."

The guttural sound erupting from his throat as he grabbed her head nearly carried her over the edge. She used one hand on herself, the other to stroke him, his powerful hips thrusting, his cock hitting the back of her throat. His moans and fervent praise—"*So good…that's it…fucking perfect*"—made her feel wanted and sexy. Caught in a web of arousal, she chased their mutual pleasure. Her name flew rough as rocks from his lips seconds before her orgasm crashed over her and the first warm jet of his hit her throat. They didn't slow down, and as she'd requested, he didn't go easy, feverishly driving into her mouth, his pleasure-drenched sounds accompanying her muffled moans.

When his cock slipped from her lips, her body quivering, Flynn dropped to his knees, wrapping his strong arms around her, and rested his head on her chest. "*Damn*, Sutton. What are you doing to me?"

She could ask the same of him. She'd never been so openly trusting with her heart or her body. Part of her couldn't believe how bold she'd been. But that part was only a sliver compared to the rest of her, which was so full of *them*, she didn't have room for anything else.

Chapter Twenty-Two

FLYNN AWOKE FROM a deep sleep to the sound of Sutton's adorably soft snores against his chest and his phone vibrating on the nightstand. He snagged his phone and saw Victory's name on the screen. She never called that early unless something was wrong.

Sliding a pillow under Sutton's head, he carefully climbed out of bed and headed into the living room. "Hey, Vic. You okay?" He opened the door to the deck, leaving the rest of the wall intact, and stepped outside, bristling against the cool morning air.

"Yeah, I'm fine. I just wanted to talk to you."

"It must be important for you to get me out of bed at the crack of dawn." He paced the deck.

"Can't I just miss my brother?"

"Not likely when you just saw me a few hours ago." He and Sutton had hung out with everyone for a little while after their dance last night. When Sutton had said she was going to head back to Port Hudson, just as they'd anticipated, Leni and Victory had wanted to take off as well, which made it easy for Flynn to say he was beat and was heading out, too, without raising eyebrows.

"Speaking of last night, did you enjoy your birthday?"

He raked a hand through his hair, thinking about how the night had started with needing a distraction from thoughts of Sutton and how it had ended like a dream, making love to her in his bed. "I had a great time. How about you? I was surprised you wanted to go to the club."

"So was I, but it was your birthday, and I was having fun catching up with Leni and getting to know Sutton. I like her."

"That's good. I like her, too."

"I know. I could tell."

"That's why you called."

"So? She's fantastic, Flynn. I *really* like her, and by that I mean, I like her for you."

He scoffed. "I can't remember the last time you weighed in on my personal life."

"I know. I wasn't sure if I should say anything, but I couldn't just sit back and bite my tongue when the chemistry was crackling around you two."

"Vic—"

"Just hear me out, and don't try to pretend you weren't eyeing her all night. Noah and Clay may have been oblivious to the daggers you were casting, but I'm your big sister. I've always seen things you probably wish I didn't, and last night you were looking at Sutton the way you've only looked at the *most* exciting things in your life since you were a little boy. You looked at her like she was uncharted territory that you'd stop at nothing to explore. You haven't had that look in your eyes for so long, I wondered if you ever would again."

So did I.

"I don't know if you two already have a story, or if you just want one, and I don't need to know. But I want you to be happy, Flynn, and if Sutton is your once-in-a-lifetime like Harvey was mine, then take it from someone who knows how fast something precious can be taken away. Don't waste a second of the time you have."

"Vic—"

"Let me finish. I know you're her boss, but Harvey was my boss, too, and he tried to fight what was between us for a whole *year* before I finally broke down his walls. If he hadn't been so worried about what people would think, we could have had all that time together. Do you know what I'd do to have another year with him? I'd give anything for another *hour*."

"I know you would, Vic. I wish I could bring him back for you." She never brought up Harvey, which told Flynn how strongly she felt about him and Sutton, and that made him feel good all over. But her phone call also brought to light how he needed to get control of the way he looked at Sutton before someone at work caught on.

"*Flynn?*"

He turned around at Sutton's sleepy voice as she padded out of the bedroom, looking adorably sexy in his orange Syracuse T-shirt she'd slept in, her hair a tangled mess. He stepped inside. "I'm right here, babe." The second *babe* was out of his mouth, he realized his mistake, but he couldn't have stopped it if he'd wanted to. He wasn't one of those guys who used endearments with just any woman, but with Sutton it came naturally.

Sutton mouthed *Sorry*, and headed for the kitchen.

"*Babe?*" Victory said accusatorially. "Is there a woman at your house? Did I totally read you wrong? Are you seeing someone? Or did you pick up some random chick last night? Never mind. I don't want to know."

"Chill out. It's Sutton."

"It *is*?" Victory practically cheered.

Sutton glanced over, her brow furrowed in question. He mouthed, *It's Victory.* She winced.

"I can't believe you answered the phone if you were in *bed* with Sutton," Victory said.

"I figured it was important or you wouldn't have called so early."

"You are a supremely thoughtful brother, but *please* feel free to ignore my call next time."

"How about you just wait for a decent hour to call unless it's an emergency?"

"Fine," Victory relented. "Tell Sutton I said hi, and go have fun. I'm happy for you!"

"Vic, please don't mention this to anyone. We have a lot to figure out because of work."

"I never would. *Wait.* Does Leni know?"

"Jesus." He moved the mouthpiece away, turning to Sutton, who was rifling through his cabinets, no doubt in search of caffeine. He loved seeing her there, comfortable enough to make herself at home. "Sut, does Leni know about us?"

She turned with a guilty expression. "She knows about the rainforest, but not about last night."

"You guys hooked up in the rainforest?" Victory asked excitedly. "No wonder you looked like you wanted to rip her clothes off."

Shit. "Goodbye, Vic." He ended the call, mulling over his damn transparency. He watched Sutton peer into his refrigerator and felt himself smiling. He definitely needed to learn to mask that. "If you're looking for hazelnut creamer, sorry, but you won't find any. I had no idea I'd see you last night, much less that you'd end up in my bed."

She closed the fridge. "That's okay. I have some in my purse."

He'd have found that annoying when they'd first met, but now he thought it was cute.

"Sorry about before. I didn't realize you were on the phone."

"That's okay." He set his phone on the coffee table and headed into the kitchen. "Vic noticed the way I was looking at you last night. She was calling to say she liked the idea of you and me getting together."

"Really? I like her a lot, and I like your brothers, too. You guys give each other crap the same way my family does, but…" Her brows knitted. "Is this too risky? Are we making a mistake? I mean, if Victory noticed, who else will?"

That's the million-dollar question. "No, we are *not* making a mistake."

"Then why do you look like you're planning a war?"

He softened his tone. "I don't."

"You kind of do," she said sweetly.

"I'm just trying to figure things out, that's all. Vic's call was a good reminder that we have to be careful." He was hit with a horrible thought. "Why? Do you feel like this is a mistake?"

"*No,*" she said quickly, bringing relief. "But this thing between us is new, and who knows where it will lead. I don't want you to get in trouble, and everyone knows the boss always gets blamed for this type of relationship, even if I kissed you first."

He had been hiding, keeping himself out of the spotlight, since he won that reality show, and he realized with a start that with Sutton he didn't want to hide. But what he wanted and what needed to happen were two very different things.

"I'm well aware of that, but I'm not giving you up." He

kissed her softly. "We'll just play it safe and keep our relation-ship off everyone's radar until we figure things out."

A coy smile reached her eyes. "Does this mean we get to be each other's dirty little secret?"

"You like that idea, don't you?" He gathered her in his arms.

"It might be fun."

"I have a feeling anything with you would be fun, but I need to learn how to look at you like I *don't* want you. Think you can ugly yourself up and start bitching at me?"

She laughed softly. "Well, I am wearing orange, which I believe we both agreed wasn't my best color."

"We were wrong about that. But as gorgeous as you are in my shirt, I think it'll look better on the floor." He stripped it off her, and holy hell. She had no panties on. "Well, well, look at this beautiful gift I've been given." He backed her up against the fridge, earning a sexy smile as he lifted her arms over her head and wrapped one of his hands around both of her wrists.

"What do you think you're doing, Braden?"

"Thinking about what a lucky guy I am." He skimmed his free hand down her chest, over the swell of her breast, and traced around her nipple with his fingertips, loving the way her breath caught. "Did it get you hot, prancing around with no panties on, waiting for me to notice?"

"Wouldn't you like to know?" she said with an arch of her brow.

"Damn right I do." He brushed his lips over hers, his fingers trailing down her body. He slid one finger over her clit and through her wetness. The breath rushed from her lungs. "*Mm. My girl is already wet for me.*" He lowered his lips to hers in a slow, sensual kiss that took her up on her toes, her moans making him ache for her. He continued teasing her with slow strokes over her clit and through her swollen sex, in a languid rhythm that had her hips pressing forward and her moans turning to whimpers. "What do you want, sweetheart? A little of this?" He pushed two fingers inside her, and she gasped. He reclaimed her mouth, kissing her deeply and passionately, while stroking that magical spot inside her, until she tore her mouth away, crying out as she shattered against his hand.

When she came down from the peak, her cheeks flushed, eyes fluttering open, so full of emotions, his chest constricted. "I'm so glad you're *mine.*"

"Then show me how glad," she pleaded.

He shed his boxer briefs and lifted her into his arms. As he lowered her onto his cock, her legs wrapped around him, and she panted out, "*Flynn,*" as "*Sutton*" fell from his lips. He captured her mouth, pumping his hips, holding her ass and moving her along his length. She was so tight and hot and excruciatingly perfect, he gritted out, "I need more of you."

He carried her into the bedroom, taking them both down to the bed. She smiled up at him with so much lust and trust and happiness, he wanted to bathe in it. He lowered his mouth to hers and began moving in a slow rhythm, savoring the feel of her tight heat swallowing every inch of him. She felt incredible, but it was the way she moved with him, totally in sync, and kissed him like she'd never get enough that brought an inescapable feeling of oneness.

He wanted to grab hold of that feeling and never let it go.

He broke their kiss, needing to see her face, and knew in an instant that she felt it, too. With that unforgettable sight imprinted in his soul, he reclaimed her mouth, and they both sparked hotter. They groped and clawed, bit and nipped, his growls and her pleas filling the room. She hooked her heels around his legs as he drove into her. But it still wasn't enough. God, would anything ever be? He pushed his hands under her ass, lifting her hips, and angled his body, driving in deeper. She gasped, her pussy tightening like a vise around his cock.

"*Again*," she begged.

"You're fucking incredible." He lifted her hips higher, taking her even deeper, every squeeze of her inner muscles sending him closer to the edge.

"*Kiss me*," she pleaded, pulling his mouth to hers. Their tongues tangled, their bodies rocked, and they lost themselves in a new, seductive beat as erratic as a summer storm. He buried his fingers in her hair, reveling in the sounds she made, the feel of her hands exploring his body, the sensual way she moved, and the sweetness of her mouth. Desire seared through his veins as her thighs flexed beneath him. Her fingernails cut into his flesh, and she cried out into their kisses as her orgasm claimed her. He tried to stave off his release, but he was too far gone and tore his mouth away on a curse. He gritted out her name, following her into ecstasy, their bodies slick from their efforts, their moans and curses filling the air.

When he was bled dry, he dipped his head beside hers, cradling her beneath him as their breathing calmed and the haze of lust abated. He had no idea how he'd pretend she meant nothing to him at work, when he wanted her all to himself—a litany of endless days and passionate nights like they'd had in the rainforest. Suddenly the weekend felt like a ticking clock, the work week looming like a villain, and as Victory had suggested, he didn't want to waste a second of it.

He kissed Sutton's cheek, lips, and forehead and lifted his face to look at her. Her eyes fluttered open, a sweet smile curving her lips. "Stay with me."

"I don't think I could move even if I wanted to," she said just above a whisper.

"I'm serious. Spend the weekend with me. We'll take my boat out, I'll let you check out my book collection, and I'll even cook you dinner. Then we can spend tomorrow doing anything you want."

Her eyes narrowed. "Does dinner include worms of any kind?"

"Only if you're lucky."

Her grin gave him her answer before she said a word. "That sounds wonderful, but I can't just *stay*. I have to go home to get clothes."

"We can make it a clothing-optional weekend."

"I am *not* going on your boat naked."

"My loss." He rolled them onto their sides, keeping her close. He didn't care if she wore a parka. He felt like he'd won the lottery. The woman he adored was *his* for the weekend. "I guess I can let you escape long enough to pack a bag. That'll give me time to get provisions." He kissed her softly. "Like hazelnut creamer for the morning."

"Books *and* hazelnut coffee?" Her eyes lit up. "Careful, beast. I might never leave."

As he lowered his mouth to hers, he whispered, "My evil plan is working."

Chapter Twenty-Three

THE BRISK MORNING gave way to a warm afternoon, perfect for a lazy day on the lake. Flynn's boat might be new to Sutton, but the sun glittering off the water and the gentle sway of the boat were soothingly familiar. The water had always had a calming effect on her, quieting the chaos of life, but being with Flynn made the experience feel new and different, like an adventure in relaxation. He'd surprised her and had stocked up on her favorite snacks and, as promised, hazelnut creamer. He'd even packed them lunch. She had to remember to mention that to Leni. They'd talked when she'd gone home to change earlier, and the last thing Leni had said was *Tell him if he's not good to you, his family will find his body at the bottom of the lake.* Flynn thought Archer was out of control, but Leni's protective instincts were just as fierce.

They'd been out on the water for a long time, chatting and relaxing, and had cut the engine in the middle of the lake to eat lunch and soak up the sun. Sutton so comfortable and happy, she couldn't imagine being anywhere else. But she was still trying to wrap her head around the fact that they were together like this, sitting on opposite ends of the cushioned bench, her legs between his, as he read *Gulliver's Travels* to her.

As if they did this every weekend. They'd each brought other books, but she'd missed having him read to her.

She admired him in his cargo shorts and T-shirt as he read. His hair brushed the edge of his sunglasses in the breeze. He held his most treasured book in one hand. His other hand rested on her calf, his fingers absently stroking it. She'd never had this type of comfortable togetherness with a guy. She'd lived her life aiming for the career she'd always wanted, and everything she did was with that goal in mind. The journalist in her wanted to understand everything about how they got here and who she was when she was with him. But the woman in her reveled in not having all the answers about her and Flynn and just allowing herself to be in these beautiful moments with him, discovering new things about herself as they were unearthed by their coupledom.

Flynn looked up from the book, giving her leg a squeeze. "Are you bored?"

"Not at all. Are you?"

He shook his head.

"I never imagined you as the kind of guy who could sit back and relax like this. I pictured you as restless. Always on the move."

He smiled. "Disappointed?"

"*No.* This is wonderful." She could sit there all day with the sun warming her face and the water kissing the sides of the boat. "Is this what you usually do on the weekends?"

"It depends. I've spent my life on the move, so when we're not traveling for the show, I tend to stick close to home. I do enjoy taking the boat out and doing a little fishing, but I also like going for hikes and just sitting on my deck reading. What about you? What do you usually do on the weekends?"

"Kind of the same thing minus the boat, and the hikes, and the fishing."

They both laughed.

He squeezed her calf. "What do your weekends look like, Steele? I won't judge you if it's all hair and nails and big shopping trips."

"I wouldn't change if you did judge me. Sometimes that's what my weekends look like, but usually I just run errands, read, and catch up with friends and family. I like to go for walks, and Dawn and Andi live in my neighborhood and go to the same yoga studio I do, so some weekends we'll take a class together." She motioned around them. "But if I lived in a place like this, I'd probably never leave. I didn't see any other houses on the way in or along the shore. Do you own all this land?"

"No, but I own acres, and the properties abutting mine are in a trust, so they'll remain undeveloped."

"You're so lucky. You have your own private oasis. You could do so much with this if you wanted to."

"Like what?"

She looked around, pondering the question. "You could make your own wilderness camp for kids who like to explore, like you did."

"That's not a bad idea at some point. Maybe when I retire. But I don't know if I'd want to give up my privacy."

"I didn't think about that. It would definitely change the vibe of this place. Did you always want to live on the water?"

"Not necessarily on the water, but I need to be near nature the way you need caffeine."

"I totally get that kind of need. Why here and not in Massachusetts? Was it because of the show?"

"No. I just got lucky that it worked out that way. I bought

this place a few years after I became old news. I had been traveling for so long and doing it under a fake identity. I started to feel like I had lost part of myself. I wanted a home base, someplace of my own to feel grounded. I love Ridgeport, but it's a small town, and I didn't want to feel like a bird in a cage. Victory, Seth, and Clay were already living in New York, and I wanted to be near them but close enough to my parents and grandparents that I could see them, too. I happened to be visiting Seth when this place came on the market. A week after closing on it, I heard about LWW launching their World Exploration Network, and I got a job working as a location director for one of their travel shows. It was great. I got to travel and had this place to hide out in when I was back in town. Eventually I moved up the ranks and came up with the premise for *Discovery Hour*. The rest is history."

"It's like you were meant to find this place."

"Even more so now." He scooted closer, guiding her legs over his, and leaned in for a kiss.

She loved their easy affection. "You've accomplished so much. What's next for you?"

"Honestly? I don't know, and I'm not in a hurry to figure it out. I'm enjoying spending time with my family, and I love my job. I get to see cool places with even cooler people. Like a certain blonde who looks fantastic in orange." He ran his hand up her calf. "I'm happy with my life. I want to stay close to family, continue to travel, and maybe have a family of my own one day. Who knows. What about you?"

"What about me?"

"I keep thinking about you as a little girl, reporting the Silver Island News from that cardboard box. You had big dreams, and you're making them happen. That's got to feel good."

"It feels amazing. I've learned so much about reporting and different cultures—and the *world*—since coming to *Discovery Hour*. I mean, one month we're digging up ninety-thousand-year-old remains of a brown crab, and the next we're eagle hunting in Mongolia. Who knew a job I took as a stepping stone could turn out to be so much more than I ever imagined?"

"Don't forget christening the rainforest."

She laughed. "That, too."

"So, what's next? Where will Sutton Steele be in five years? Do you want a family?"

"I want it all. A great career, traveling, family." She thought about the résumé she'd sent to GNN, and a knot formed in her stomach. She decided not to mention it since they hadn't gotten back to her yet, but she wanted to be honest with him. "What we're doing is important, and I love it. Even more so now that we're getting along, but I've always dreamed of being a cutting-edge reporter headlining global issues and news, and eventually becoming a respected journalist like Tom and Barbara were, but I know I have to pay my dues and work my way up the ladder."

"If you could report on anything right now, what would it be?"

"Off the top of my head? I need a minute to think about it." She thought about all the stories she'd wanted to report on over the last few months and settled on the one she was most curious about. "I read a story the other day about the issues the world's children will face in the coming year, and it covered everything from violence to the climate crisis. I'd love to do a deep dive into the issues children have endured globally over the years and show how they've changed and how they've impacted them, and how different the issues are in the US versus in other countries.

What happened to the kids in other countries who faced war and famine and other issues? Where are they now? And has anything changed for better or worse for children in those areas?"

"*The effects of a fragmented world on children.* That sounds like a great story. Do some research. See what you can put together, and let me take a look."

"But we have a full docket of shows for the next ten months. You can't just change it because I want to do a story."

"It's my show. I can do anything I want. Write it up, and we'll see if it's worthy of shifting things around."

She cocked her head, astonished. "You're serious?"

"One hundred percent. You have a goal. Let's see if you've got what it takes to get there."

"Doesn't it bother you, as my boss, to know that I have other aspirations?"

"Babe, I've been doing what I want my whole life. You've dreamed of doing a specific job since you were a kid. It would only bother me if you didn't follow your heart."

What if it takes me to California? She pushed away the thought. She couldn't allow herself to get lost in *what if*s when their relationship was so new, no matter how hard she felt like she was falling for him.

"You've worked hard, and you've come a long way in the last year and a half."

She shook her head. "I had no idea what I was walking into when I took this job. In my mind, I just saw *reporter* in neon lights. You of all people know how green I was."

"I also know how determined you were."

"Yes. I have mastered faking it until I make it."

A wicked grin slid into place. "Not with me."

"Yes, I did. Just not in the bedroom…or in the waterfall, or on the rocks, or in the tent, or on your couch."

He laughed and pressed his smiling lips to hers. "I sure like you, Steele."

"That's good, because it would be weird if this was how you treated your enemies."

"Some people say kill them with kindness. I find exhausting them with orgasms to be more effective."

"So *that's* your evil plan? To kill me with passion since you couldn't get me fired."

"Not today." He ran his hands up her hips and lifted her onto his lap. "I'm not done exhausting you yet."

HOURS PASSED WITH fun banter, steamy kisses, and a sexy sun-drenched siesta that left them both a little euphoric. Evening found them back at the cabin making dinner. Fries were in the oven, and Flynn was flipping burgers on the grill. Sutton came in to use the bathroom, and on her way back outside, she stopped to scour his bookshelves, taking in the plethora of adventure novels, geographical and cultural literature, and a host of other fiction and nonfiction works. Interspersed with the books were framed pictures of Flynn and his family. She admired one of him and his brothers, arm in arm, all four of them caught laughing, and another of Flynn and Victory with a dark-haired older man who had his arm around Victory. Flynn and Victory were looking at the camera, but the other man was gazing lovingly at Victory. Sutton had a feeling that was Harvey and felt a pang of sadness.

She studied a picture of an older couple that had to be Flynn's parents. His father had thick, wavy salt-and-pepper hair, and gazing out from behind glasses were the same keen eyes as Flynn's. Flynn's mother was tall and slim with fine lines around her eyes and mouth. She had a mix of dirty-blond and gray hair that hung past her shoulders, a welcoming smile, and a warm gaze that reminded Sutton of her own mother.

Another photograph caught her attention, and she took it off the shelf, studying the thick-chested, older man with hair the color of sand and snow brushed away from his face and a trim mostly white beard. He had a kind face, and he was laughing, holding the tiny knees of a young, messy-haired Flynn riding on his shoulders. Flynn wore a green backpack and held a magnifying glass in one hand. His other hand was wrapped around the man's chin. He couldn't have been more than five or six years old, with Chiclet teeth and a carefree light in his eyes. Beside them was a woman who was also laughing. She had short light brown hair streaked with gray, a thick waist, and so much love in her eyes, it felt tangible. She had one hand on the older man's back, the other touching one of Flynn's little hiking boots. Sutton wondered what they were laughing at.

"Snooping?" Flynn asked as he walked in from the deck.

"You caught me." She held up the picture. "Is this you and your grandparents?"

"Yeah. Those are my dad's parents. I used to hang all over my grandfather."

"You were adorable, and it doesn't look like he minded."

"I was a pest, but he put up with me. He still does." He pointed to a picture of another older couple sitting on a bench near a garden. The woman's hands were folded neatly on her lap, and the man had a serious look about him. "Those are my mom's parents."

"Are you close to them?"

"Sort of, but not as close as I am to my dad's parents. My mom's parents live in Illinois and have very old-fashioned values. They're good people, and I love them, but they've never really understood how we were raised." He pointed to the picture of the younger couple. "That's my mom and dad."

"I could tell. They look nice, and happy."

"I think they are. They're always holding hands, and the way they look at each other is pretty special. They still travel a lot, but I see them when they're around."

She pointed to the pictures of him and Victory. "Is that Harvey?"

"Yes. He was a good man," he said thoughtfully.

"I don't see any pictures from your travels. Do you keep them someplace else?"

"I don't have many of them."

"Why not?"

"At first I was hiding, and I didn't want pictures. I've always believed in living in the moment, you know? Taking in what you could. When I reclaimed my identity, I enjoyed my experiences, but I have memories. I didn't need pictures. I wasn't traveling to show off or share it with others."

"Then why did you take so many videos of us with your personal camera?"

He rubbed his scruff, shaking his head. "I need to learn to lie if I'm going to keep hanging out with a reporter."

"Why?"

"Because you caught me. One day my memories are going to fade, and I never want to forget that trip."

She felt a little giddy at that, but it was such a big confession, she didn't know how to respond, so she said, "*Oh.* I like knowing that," and let them both off the hook, moving on to a safer subject. "Do you have more pictures from when you were growing up?"

"I've got a ton. My mother's a photographer, remember? She gave us all photo albums from when we were growing up." He plucked a couple of them off the bottom shelf. "We can look at these after we eat. Why don't you take them out, and I'll grab the rest of the food and meet you out there."

"Okay." She turned to walk out, and he tugged her back.

"Forget something, Steele?" He leaned in for a kiss, then swatted her ass. "Now you're free to go."

She was grinning like a fool as she headed outside. The lights sparkled against the night sky, giving the evening a romantic flare. She set the albums on the lounge chair and heard a noise she couldn't identify coming from inside the house. She wondered what Flynn was up to. She gazed out at the water, and a few minutes later, he joined her, carrying a tray with their veggies and fries, all the fixings for hamburgers, rolls, and two enormous milkshakes.

"Are those chocolate shakes?" There was no hiding her excitement as he set the tray on the table.

"No, they're chocolate–peanut butter shakes. I remember you dreaming about them in the rainforest."

"Is this all part of your evil plan, too? Spoiling me to make sure I never leave?" She sidled up to him as he took the burgers off the grill.

"Yes. I'm going to need a list of all your favorite things." He sealed that request with another kiss.

An hour later Sutton sat between Flynn's legs beneath a blanket on a lounge chair by the water, looking through one of the photo albums of a young Flynn and his family. There were adorable pictures of Victory holding Flynn when he was an infant, of Flynn sleeping on his father's chest, and as a toddler lying with his mother in a hammock. She marveled at the photos of Flynn and his grandfather wearing similar hats and jackets, crouched by plants as if inspecting them, and of Flynn, Seth, and Clay wielding sticks like swords, while Noah played with a truck in the grass. Sutton nearly melted at a picture of Flynn at maybe seven or eight years old, and Noah, who looked to be about three or four, sitting on a hill with a full moon behind them. Flynn had a book open on his lap, and Noah was shining a flashlight on the pages.

"I remember this one." Flynn pointed to a picture of himself hanging from a tree branch by his legs above a mud puddle, his striped T-shirt bunched around his ribs, his long hair hanging inches from his face. Below him sat a furious Victory in the middle of the puddle, covered in mud. Her mouth was open like she was yelling, and Clay was a few feet away, bent over in hysterics.

"What did you guys do to her?"

"*Nothing.* I was just hanging there, minding my own business, and Clay came tearing through the bushes like a bat out of hell. He jumped the puddle, and then Victory burst through the bushes, running after him. She slipped on her ass." Flynn laughed. "She was so mad."

Sutton laughed and shook her head. "As a sister who's endured plenty of crap from my own brothers, I feel for her."

"Yeah, but she's tough. She got him back. She dumped a bucket of mud on him while he was sleeping."

"*Oh no.* Your poor parents had to clean that up."

"Hey, if you raise kids in the woods, they're going to get

dirty." He turned the page, revealing a picture of himself at maybe three or four years old, sleepy eyed and pink cheeked, sitting on his father's lap by a window. His head was tilted back, and his father's eyes were closed as he kissed the top of it.

"*Aw.* That's such a sweet picture."

"I was on the third day of a fever. My mom said I wouldn't leave my father's arms."

She gazed up at him over her shoulder. "It had to be hard for them to see their wild boy so sick."

"Either that or they were enjoying the downtime."

"They were *not*."

He hugged her. "Yeah, probably not."

They continued looking through the pictures, and Flynn told her stories about many of them. When they came to one taken at an archaeological dig site, she took a minute to study Flynn's young face. He and his siblings were lined up like ducks in a row, sitting on their knees, peering into an excavated area where three men, including his grandfather, were working.

Sutton gazed up at him again. "Why didn't you follow in your grandfather's footsteps?"

"Several reasons, but mainly because his goal was to explain the past and figure out how we got here, and mine was to understand the present and to try to make the future better, whether it was helping protect tribal lands or bringing to light threats to species of animals or issues affecting earth or people. My grandfather calls the stories we tell stories of the heart." He brushed a kiss to her forehead. "You and I aren't so different, Steele."

She was learning that on many levels.

They looked at pictures of Flynn and his siblings riding bikes, climbing trees, and hiding in forts made out of branches, and of their family sleeping in tents, sitting around bonfires, and with dozens of people from other cultures, dressed in varying garb, at enormous tables piled high with food.

"Are these people you lived near?"

"Yeah, mostly."

"I haven't seen any pictures of holidays. Do you celebrate them?"

"Sort of, but not in the way people here are used to, with tons of presents and lights and cutting down trees."

"What does your family do?"

"Since we traveled among different cultures, my parents adopted celebrations of family and friends as a way of being more inclusive. In many of the places we lived, the communities were small, and they didn't have much, so celebrations revolved around spending time together, preparing and eating meals as a group, sitting by bonfires telling stories, singing, and playing music. My dad plays the guitar, and he taught us all to play, but Seth and Victory are the only ones who do it well."

"So that's where the bonfire tradition came from."

"It is. We grew up with homegrown fun, taking part in whatever traditions and cultural activities were going on at the time."

"That sounds wonderful. Did you exchange gifts?"

"Sort of. My siblings and I made gifts for each other, and every year my parents made us each a map of wherever we were, and they'd give us a list of hints, sending us on a treasure hunt that would lead to our gifts from them. Each map is different and contains clues to find the gifts, but we have to work together to figure them out because they all tie into each other. When we were kids, it would take us days to find them, and I think we fought half the time, but it was fun."

"What kind of gifts did you get?"

"They were never what we expected. My parents have a knack for remembering things we mentioned that they couldn't make happen at the time. Like when Noah was four, and all he wanted was to sleep by himself under the stars. The treasure hunt led us to directions for building a treehouse, and we all built it with my parents, just so Noah could have his night under the stars. Of course, my dad stood guard at the bottom of the tree that night, but Noah didn't know it. And when Clay was six or seven, he was obsessed with going to a pro-football game. We were living overseas, and it was more than a year later when the treasure hunt led us to tickets to a football game for Clay. I swear they never forget a damn thing."

"Except your birthday," Sutton said carefully.

Flynn held her tighter. "That seriously wasn't a big deal until I heard my mother crying over it."

"Maybe it meant so much to her because your family is *all* about family, and she didn't want you to feel like you weren't important."

"I'm sure that's exactly what it was. That year, the treasure hunt led us to an invitation for an extra birthday celebration for me."

"I was wondering if there was more to the birthday story. I love that they did that. Did you guys ever mind that the gifts were for one of you more than all of you?"

"Not that I remember, but the gifts were for all of us. We all went to the football game, because we were supporting Clay, and they all got cake and ice cream at my extra birthday party. The fun was the treasure hunt, really, and we didn't have much growing up. We lived minimally because of the extensive travel, so we didn't have big expectations. I think with kids, it's more about how things are presented over time. My parents acted like what we did was normal, and it was for us, so we didn't begrudge each other. We were happy for each other. Or at least I was for them."

"I love that. When did they stop making treasure hunts?"

"They didn't."

"They *still* make them?"

"Yup. The teenage years were hairy, trying to get us to work together, but we made it through. Now the maps are much more elaborate. It's not like we're all in one location, and at the heart of the holidays is family, so if my grandparents or one of us happen to be traveling, chances are we're all going to end up where they are."

"What about when you lived with the tribe? Did you do the treasure hunt? Did they all come there, or did you end up with them?"

"No. My brothers and sister weren't trained to go to a place like that." Shadows rose in his eyes.

"Do you regret spending that time with the tribe?"

"I'm not happy about missing those years, but I don't regret it. Sometimes you have to do what's best for you, and remaining under the radar was what I needed at the time. Thankfully, my family understood that."

"I think it's pretty incredible that you knew yourself well enough at that age to realize what you needed, and your family sounds wonderful."

On the surface, their families were nothing alike. His had traveled the world, as she'd seen proof of in the beautiful photographs of huts and trails and animals in jungles and plains and everything in between. The settings were all vastly different from the quiet island where she'd grown up, but the love of

Flynn's close-knit family was palpable in every picture and every story, just as it was with hers. She found herself falling for the family she barely knew just as she was falling for Flynn.

FLYNN WAS ENJOYING sharing stories about his life with Sutton, but he wanted to know more about hers, too. "What are your holidays like? Do you spend them on Silver Island?"

"Yes. Every holiday is a big community event, and we all get together for them. At Christmas all of the main streets and shops are decorated, and Jules makes personalized wreaths and gives them out to the other shop owners. There's a holiday festival that takes place a few weeks before Christmas. It starts with a night of hot chocolate and sledding at the annual tree lighting in Majestic Park. There's an event every weekend after that leading up to Christmas, like a flotilla, and horse-drawn sleigh rides down Main Street, and caroling. The Silver House hosts a fancy holiday dance and charity auction that benefits the local hospital. Everyone comes to it."

"That sounds incredible."

"It's a big deal, and a lot of fun. Jules and Grant got engaged at the tree lighting two years ago."

"Is that when they pranked your dad?"

"Yes." She laughed. "I told you no one was safe from pranks. Jules and Grant got married over the holidays, and Leni and Raz got engaged. Holidays with my family are the best they've ever been now that Jock and Archer are getting along, and after Levi got engaged to Joey's aunt Tara, he and Joey moved back to the island."

"Hold on. Your brother got engaged to his daughter's aunt? As in her biological mother's sister?"

"Yes, and I *know* how odd that sounds. But Joey's mother is not a nice person, and Tara is amazing. She's a lot younger than Levi, but she's been in Joey's life since Joey was born, and she's been in love with Levi since she was a kid. They're *so* good together. I know he's loved her for years, and Joey adores her."

"Then good for them. I wasn't judging him, I was just making sure I heard you right. You said Archer's getting married soon. Are Levi and Tara getting married, too?"

"Yes, later this summer, and Archer and Indi are getting married in three weeks at my family's vineyard where my grandparents and my parents got married. Jock and Daphne got married there, too."

"Gotta love traditions." He hugged her tighter. "Guess I'll have to stock up on time with you before then, so I don't have withdrawals."

She turned with a sweet smile. "That makes two of us."

"Don't worry, Steele. We'll make excellent use of the time we have before then." He kissed her. "Are you looking forward to the wedding?"

"I am. There were so many years when I worried that Archer would be unhappy forever, and now he's with Indi, who we all love. I haven't seen him this happy since before my grandfather died."

"How long ago was that?"

"A long time ago. I was fifteen, so Archer was eighteen. Archer was with him in the vines when he died. It was awful. We were all devastated when we lost him, but I think Archer lost a piece of himself, too. He was the closest to him, and they were so much alike. My grandfather loved hard, but he didn't have a lot of patience, and he could be abrasive, which is Archer to a T."

"It sounds like Archer and I aren't so different after all."

"Because you were abrasive toward me?"

"No. That was only because I wanted you and shouldn't have wanted you. We're alike because if I'd lost my grandfather at eighteen, it would've messed me up big-time." He reached around Sutton, turning a few pages in the photo album, and stopped at a picture of his father and grandfather lying on the floor looking at a map. Flynn was lying on his grandfather's back, his skinny arms crossed beneath his chin, as he peered over his grandfather's shoulder.

He tapped the image of his grandfather with his index finger. "I can face a lot of things in this world, but losing that man is not one of them."

"I wondered if you ever thought about that."

"Not a day passes that I don't. He's in his eighties, and he's active, but you know… Do you worry about losing your grandmother?"

She was quiet for a beat. "All the time."

"Well, if that happens, you won't have to go through it alone." He kissed her temple.

"Thanks. Neither will you." She rested her head against his chest.

They sat in comfortable silence, serenaded by the sounds of the crickets and the water, and Flynn was enveloped by a sense of contentedness. He rested his chin on her shoulder and whispered, "You know, Steele, you're not so bad after all."

"I'm glad you think so, because I'm pretty sure I'd like to keep you around for a while."

Chapter Twenty-Four

SUTTON PACED HER office, reading the script for the voice-over she was scheduled to narrate later that afternoon. *Imagine the rainforest drying up because it's unable to generate its own rainfall to sustain its ecosystem. We're nearing that tipping point, and this is why—*

"Knock, knock?"

Her pulse quickened at the sound of Flynn's voice. She looked up from the script and found him standing in the doorway with Ray, the audio technician. She heard other people in the hallway and tried not to let the emotions coursing through her show, but it was like trying to hold back a tsunami. It had been a week and a half since she'd met Flynn's siblings and had spent her first weekend at his place. They were playing platonic colleagues at work while sneaking steamy kisses and satiating their desires behind closed office doors every chance they got. The first couple of times they'd hooked up at work, she was shocked she'd done it. But that shock had faded fast. The risk of being caught was an unexpected aphrodisiac, heightening every sensation. She'd begun craving their office hookups, and they'd since perfected the act of quickies. Most evenings found them hiding out at Flynn's cabin, having dinner by the water, taking walks, watching movies, reading, or just being together, all of which Sutton loved, and their nights were spent in each other's arms, burning up the sheets or talking until the wee hours.

"Are we interrupting?" Flynn asked.

"No. I was just going over the script. What's up?"

"Ray has a schedule conflict this afternoon," Flynn said.

"Sorry, Sutton, but I just got a call about a conference at my kid's school." Ray was a single father of a teenage son who was always getting into trouble. "Is there any chance you can do it earlier?"

"Sure. I've got a call at three, but I can do it anytime between now and then."

"How about in twenty minutes?" Flynn suggested. "I want to go over a few tweaks with Sutton first."

"Sounds good to me," she said.

"Great. Thanks, guys. I appreciate it," Ray said. "I'll go get ready."

As he walked away, Flynn stalked into her office with a wolfish grin that made her stomach flip-flop. He pointed to the script as people walked by her office, brows knitted as if he were giving her directions, but his low voice was pure lust. "I can't stop thinking about *breakfast* this morning."

Her body flamed with memories of him down on his knees in the kitchen as he'd made her come and of riding him on a kitchen chair where he'd given her two more toe-curling orgasms. *Good Lord*, she could still feel him inside her, still feel the sting on her scalp as he'd tugged her hair, demanding her mouth, and kissed her senseless. She felt herself go damp.

"*Tweaks?* Really?" Driving each other crazy in the office had become a dangerous and addictive game. She loved the way they toyed with each other at work, but cooling off after they turned up the heat was never easy. "I have to perform in twenty minutes."

"I have no doubt you'll give a *peak* performance. You always do." The corners of his mouth tipped up. "I just like knowing you're thinking of me."

She had visions of closing her office door and seeing if it was as much fun to ride him on her office chair as it was in the kitchen. But while they'd fooled around behind closed doors when they could steal a few minutes, it seemed like everyone was in the office today. As much as she wanted him, she wasn't about to risk it, and she knew just how to get back at him for revving her up. "I'll keep that in mind," she said loud enough for anyone in the hallway to hear, then turned her back to the door and lowered her voice. "The question is, what should I do about my wet panties?"

The muscles in his jaw clenched.

"I guess I'll just have to slip them off. I might even have to take things into my own hands to ease the tension before narrating."

"*Sutton*," he said gruffly.

"Is it *hard* thinking about my fingers doing the walking?" She whispered, "I'm wet just thinking about you imagining me doing it."

"You're playing with fire."

Having fun, she arched a brow. "Burn, baby, burn."

"Skip yoga tonight, and come to my place." Since she lived in the same complex as Dawn and Andi, they'd decided staying at her place was too risky.

"I can't. I promised Andi and Dawn I'd go." She'd skipped yoga last week, and she hadn't spent time with them since she started seeing Flynn. She was determined to go tonight, if for no other reason than not wanting to be one of those women who changed her life for a man. Even if said man was pretty darn incredible. She leaned closer, enjoying taunting him. "Don't you like me limber?"

"You know I do." He inserted himself between her and the door. His arm circled her, and his hand slid down to her ass, resting there like a branding iron, scalding her through her thin skirt. "Then come over after."

Karen appeared in her doorway behind him, and Sutton quickly stepped back. "Oh, good. Flynn. I was looking for you. Do you have a minute?"

"Can you give me five? I want to go over a few things with Sutton."

Sutton heard the tension in his voice, and from the way Karen's brows were slanting, she had a feeling she'd picked up on it, too. This was perfect payback. "No need. I understand what you want, *Braden*," she said sharply, for Karen's benefit. "I'll do my best to satisfy all your *tweaks*. Now *please* get out of here and let me prepare."

As he strode out of the room looking like a top that was wound too tight, Karen said, "Are you riding her too hard again?"

It took all of Sutton's willpower not to laugh.

SUTTON LAY ON her back in Savasana, the final resting pose in her yoga class, trying to focus on the guided meditation the instructor was reciting and not how much she wanted to see

Flynn. She'd never been clingy, and she didn't feel like she was clingy. She just missed him and loved being with him. It was nice to be with someone smart and interesting, who she had things in common with and wasn't afraid to talk or debate or share his feelings. He understood her in a way others didn't. Their amazing sex was icing on the cake.

"And now, start moving your fingers and toes…" The instructor's soothing voice eased them back to the present. "When you're ready, roll onto your right side and come up to a comfortable seated position."

Sutton was more than ready to go as she sat up. She glanced at Dawn and Andi, who looked as relaxed as if they'd just had massages.

"Thank you for sharing this space with me." The instructor steepled her hands, closed her eyes, and bent forward. "Namaste."

The class did the same, and then there was a murmur of voices as everyone rolled up their mats and thanked the instructor.

As Sutton headed out with Dawn and Andi, Dawn took out her ponytail holder, shaking her long blond hair free, and said, "I always leave yoga feeling like I've had great sex."

Sutton and Andi looked at her like she'd lost her mind as they pushed through the glass doors and headed into the parking lot.

"I must be doing yoga wrong," Andi said.

"Me too. I didn't feel any thunder down under either," Sutton said.

"You know what I mean," Dawn said. "But speaking of thunder down under…The jig is up, Sutton. Who's the guy?"

Worry hit her like a splash of cold water. "What guy?" She

was dying to tell them about her relationship with Flynn, but she knew she couldn't risk it.

"She thinks you're seeing someone," Andi said.

"Why would you think that?"

"You missed yoga last week, and every time we text you, you're out." Dawn stopped beside her car and parked a hand on her hip. "And last weekend you turned down a chance to be my taste tester for a new recipe, and we all know the only thing better than my goodies is thunder down under. So if you're not getting my goodies, you're definitely getting someone else's."

Sutton didn't think it was possible, but Flynn's *goodies* brought even more pleasure than Dawn's baked goods. "As much as I hate to admit it, I've just been busy. Now that Flynn and I are getting along better, I've been working late and trying to keep up the good mojo."

"I told you," Andi said to Dawn.

Dawn sighed. "Well, that's a bummer. I was hoping you'd found someone great."

I have. I just can't tell anyone other than Leni and Victory about him.

She had gushed like a schoolgirl to Leni, telling her how crazy about Flynn she was. Leni, being her overprotective sister, had been cautiously happy for her. Victory, on the other hand, had texted Sutton a few days after she'd called that first weekend and had caught them together. She'd told Sutton she was thrilled for them and couldn't wait to get to know her better. It had been hard to coordinate their schedules since Victory was traveling on and off, but they'd planned a girls' day with Leni the weekend after Archer's wedding, and Sutton was looking forward to it.

"Sorry to disappoint you," Sutton said, and headed to her

car. "But I love you for wanting that for me."

"Yeah, right. We all know you love me for my goodies," Dawn teased. "Have a great night."

"You too!" Sutton waved and climbed into her car.

Fifteen minutes later, she walked into her townhouse. She was toeing off her shoes when her phone chimed with a text.

Flynn: *Hey, Glamour Girl. Are you nice and limber?*

Sutton: *Oh yeah. I'm hot and sweaty, too. Too bad you're not here to reap the benefits.*

She pulled off her tank top and took a selfie in her sports bra, then sent it to him.

Flynn sent a flame and a devil emoji.

Flynn: *I hope you practiced the pretzel pose, because I have ideas.*

Sutton: *They didn't cover that one. I'll have to ask my instructor about it.*

Flynn: *It takes finesse. I'll give you a private lesson. I'm adept at other couple poses you might like.*

Sutton: *You've piqued my interest. Do tell.*

Flynn: *There's the Balls Deep Braden. It's similar to Downward Dog, with a twist.*

She laughed, but her body heated up at the thought of it.

Sutton: *I think I might like that one.*

Flynn: *Then there's Thighs Wide Open. It's especially good with one of my other favorite poses. Downward Tongue.*

Heat swirled through her.

Sutton: *Now you've got my attention.*

Flynn: *I think you'd enjoy the Happy Big Daddy. It's similar to the Happy Baby but with more moving parts.*

Sutton: *Oh my. Yes, I can see myself enjoying that.*

Flynn: *Then there's the Cat's Meow, which pairs well with*

another favorite.

Flynn: *Double Penetration.*

Sutton's eyes widened. She'd never done anything like that, but the thought of Flynn touching her where she'd never been touched before turned her on.

She sent a hot-faced emoji.

Sutton: *Too bad you're not here, or I'd show you one of my favorite poses, the Happy Ending. I guess I'll have to see if one of my battery-operated boyfriends wants to join me in the shower.*

Flynn: *Open your door.*

Sutton: *Is that a back-door-pose reference?*

A knock at her front door made her jump. She peered out the peephole and saw Flynn standing there in a hoodie, his jaw tight. The feral look in his eyes ignited flames beneath her skin. She opened the door and he charged in, clutching a bouquet of pink flowers and sending her heart into a wild flurry. "You brought me flow—" He dropped the flowers, taking her in a penetrating kiss, setting off an explosion of pent-up desire, and lifted her into his arms. She wound her arms around his neck. "Well, hello to you, too, *beast*. Where are you taking me?"

"We have a playdate with your *little friend* in the shower." His voice was gruff and lustful. "Just point me in the right direction."

She'd never used toys with a man before, and she was surprised that instead of embarrassment, heat seared through her at the prospect of *playing* with Flynn. She pointed to the stairs. He kicked the door shut, and as he carried her upstairs, she said, "How'd you get here so fast? Isn't it risky for you to be here?"

"I was parked around the corner. I wanted to surprise you after yoga, and figured Andi wouldn't see my car if it wasn't in the neighborhood." He carried her through the master bedroom toward the bathroom. "We were texting as I was walking here."

Her heart swelled. "You thought of everything."

He set her on her feet and took her face between his hands, his gaze a tortured mix of desire and something deeper. "All I wanted was to bring you flowers and hang out with you tonight. I didn't have sex in mind, but *Jesus*. We text, and I turn into an animal, and then I see you, and…" He pushed one hand to the nape of her neck, his other hand sliding down to her bottom. "I can't look at you without wanting to be closer."

"I'm guilty of that, too, so if you're afraid I'll think you're only in this for sex, don't be."

She grabbed the front of his hoodie, tugging him into a kiss that quickly turned urgent and greedy. He toed off his shoes, and they stripped each other bare between feverish kisses. He turned on the shower and returned his glorious mouth to hers. When steam floated out the open shower doors, they stepped beneath the warm spray, devouring each other with renewed fervor. Anticipation billowed inside her as their hands roamed over their slick flesh. He lowered his mouth to her breast, his other hand teasing between her legs, sending scintillating sensations through her core. She wrapped her fingers around his cock, earning a sexy growl. He teased her until she was panting, her thoughts fragmenting.

"I need my mouth on you." He sank to his knees and pushed her legs apart, holding her open as he feasted on her. Her back hit the tile, and she grabbed his hair with both hands, riding his mouth, her hungry moans echoing around them. He knew exactly how to make her come. He was a master at it, and she was just as hungry for him. It didn't take long before she was hanging on by a thread. When he took her clit between his teeth, she lost it, crying out as her hips shot forward. He continued feasting on her and slid two fingers inside her, stroking that other sensitive spot, taking her to new heights, magnifying every pulse of her orgasm.

When she finally came down from the high, she was breathless, but managed to say, "My turn." She fisted his thick shaft and wasted no time, lowering her mouth over his cock, taking him in deep.

"Aw, *fuck*, baby. I love your mouth." She stroked and sucked and hummed around his length, until his entire body flexed. "Sutton, I'm not going to last if you keep doing that." She slowed her pace, not wanting their fun to end. His eyes blazed into her. "Where's your toy, babe?" His gaze moved over the shelf.

Her nerves flared as she pushed to her feet. "It's…the rose."

His brows slanted as he reached for the rubber rose and looked it over. "This is different."

"It *licks*." Her cheeks burned as she turned it on, and the tongue at the center of the rose petals began flicking. Just seeing that toy in his big, rough hand, and his wicked grin, made her ache with anticipation. She pressed the button again, speeding up the licking action.

"Damn."

She grinned. "Jealous?"

"We both know my tongue is better." He threaded his hand into her hair, drawing her into a smoldering kiss that was as tender as it was possessive. His fingers tightened in her hair, and she felt the rose touch the apex of her sex, sending a zing of electricity through her. She clung to him as he found the spot that made it hard to think. "Is this what you use when you think of me?" His voice was low and demanding.

"*Yes*," she confessed.

He pressed it a little harder on her clit, and she sucked in a breath. His eyes narrowed. "Did you use it thinking about me *before* we went to the rainforest?"

She panted without answering, her entire body trembling with need. He removed the toy from her clit, and the breath rushed from her lungs. "Flynn, *please*."

"Tell me, sweetheart. Did you pretend it was me licking your pussy before we got together?"

"Yes. Every time. It was always you."

He took her hand and moved it to the head of his cock, rubbing her fingers over the bead of liquid at the tip. "Feel what knowing that does to me."

"I'd rather taste it." She dipped her head and sucked the broad crown.

He hissed out a curse and tugged her back up by her hair, crushing his mouth to hers in a punishingly hard kiss as the rose touched her neediest nerves. His tongue plunged, fucking her mouth as he applied more pressure on that flicking rubber tongue, sending the world spinning away. He swallowed her cries, continuing his masterful seduction through the very last pulse of her climax. Then he drew back with a predatory gaze that made her entire body want to be owned by him.

He turned her around. "Bend at the waist and put your hands on the wall, beautiful."

The endearment was soft, but there was no mistaking who was in control. She pressed her palms to the wet tile, her inner muscles clenching with need. He ran his hand over one ass cheek. "Hold on tight, sexy girl." He teased his cock along her pussy, and he pushed the head inside her. She closed her eyes as he thrust slowly, burying himself to the hilt, and stilled. He leaned over her back, pressing a kiss to her spine as he brought the rose to her clit. "Feel good, baby?"

"God, yes."

She tried to rock against his cock, to make him thrust again, but he grabbed her hip, stilling her. "I want you needy." He gyrated his hips, remaining buried deep inside her. The constant flick of the tongue and the feel of his thick length hitting that magical spot inside her with every gyration sent shocks of pleasure skating through her. "I love how your pussy swells around me."

"*Flynn*, please," she panted out.

He pressed the rose tighter against her clit, while his other hand moved from her hip and caressed her ass. His fingers slid between her ass cheeks, and he teased her tightest hole. All her inner muscles clenched tight, and he gritted out, "Fuck that feels good." He began pumping his hips, still teasing her with the rose and with his finger on her other hole. The feel of the water raining down her back, sliding between her ass cheeks, the rose licking her clit, and his cock stroking that hidden spot, had her standing on the edge of a cliff, breathless and greedy for more.

Her head dipped between her shoulders. "Feels so good, Flynn."

She rocked back with his every thrust, wanting him to take more of her. Craving what she'd never had. He pressed his finger harder against that tight entrance, rubbing, teasing, until she was out of her mind with need. When his finger breached the tight rim of muscles, pleasure surged through her. "*Ohgodyes. Don't stop.*" She clawed at the wall, moans streaming from her lips as his finger pumped into her ass. She felt like a bundle of live wires.

"You're so fucking sexy. You like it when I fuck you everywhere, baby?"

"Yes. *Harder*," she pleaded.

He fucked her harder and faster with his finger and his cock, while the rose worked its magic. Pleasure chased down her limbs, through her torso, all the way to her fingers and toes, hurtling her into oblivion. She cried out, bucking and moaning, ravaged by overwhelming sensations. Then she was soaring, enveloped in pleasure so all consuming, she was sure she'd died and gone to heaven.

When she finally started coming down from the high, Flynn said, "Again."

"I don't think…" she panted out. "I can."

He wrapped one arm around her, palming her breast as he straightened her spine without breaking their connection. He rolled her nipple between his finger and thumb, bringing such delicious pleasure, her head lolled back against his chest. "Do you want to come with me?" he asked, his voice thick with need.

"Always," she panted out.

"Then you will, baby. Trust me." He kissed her cheek and put the rose on the shelf. Taking one of her hands in his, he pressed it to the wall, and laced their fingers together, holding it there. Her legs were so shaky, she was pretty sure his cock and that hand were the only things holding her up as he thrust deep and slow, using his other hand on her clit. The new angle heightened every sensation. Every slide of his cock brought a gust of pleasure, drawing greedy noises. Their laced fingers curled together into a fist. "I need to see you," he gritted out. "I need to *kiss* you. I can never get close enough." He spun her around, and in one swift move, he thrust inside her, pinned her hands to the wall, and devoured her mouth. Every thrust took her higher, filling her so completely, she felt him *everywhere*. Tingling in her limbs warred with heat and lust whipping through her, creating a hurricane of sensations. Her senses reeled and skidded. She was overcome with pleasure, crying out, bucking wildly as Flynn surrendered to his own powerful release, and there in the shower, surrounded by their pleas and moans, they rode the waves of their orgasms until they were both too spent to move.

Chapter Twenty-Five

A LONG WHILE later, after bathing each other and sharing dozens of kisses and laughs, they were sitting in Sutton's living room eating sushi and looking through her middle school yearbook. Flynn turned the page and found her seventh-grade photo. She was a freaking adorable bright-eyed little girl, with her blond hair gathered over one shoulder and that brilliant smile beaming off the page.

"Hey, Braden. This is a definite pro."

He looked up from the yearbook, drinking her in for the millionth time. She looked relaxed and happy sitting cross-legged on the couch in his T-shirt, her hair still damp from their shower. He had no idea which pros and cons list she was referring to, but being with her tonight was a definite pro for him. He couldn't have stayed away if he'd wanted to. "Eating sushi is the pro? What list are you working on?"

"The pros and cons of sleeping with my boss. Eating sushi *after* having great sex with you." She popped another piece of sushi into her mouth.

"It's a pro for me, too, but I'm feeling slightly objectified," he teased. "Do you have my sparkling personality on your list, or just my sexual skills?"

"Sparkling is debatable, but I do have several of your personal attributes on there. And no, they're not all sexual."

"Really?" He wondered what they were.

"Yes, and I'm not telling you what they are, so don't even ask."

He chuckled. "Mind reader. I wonder if seventh-grade Sutton ever imagined she'd get this lucky."

"Seventh-grade Sutton was the head of the newspaper club. She had big aspirations of being the next Barbara Walters, and she was *not* going to sleep with her boss to get there."

"The newspaper club, huh? Let's see." He turned the pages until he found a picture of the newspaper club. There were five girls and two boys sitting on the front steps of the school. A black man with glasses sat behind them smiling proudly. The teacher who ran the club, no doubt. Sutton was easy to spot, sitting beside a blond-haired boy. Her hair was pinned up in a ponytail, and she wore a blue sweater, blue plaid skirt, and sandals. "You were stylish even at that age. Are you still good friends with these kids?"

"Most of them. The girl sitting next to me is Deirdra de Messiéres."

"The one in that picture?" He pointed to one of the photographs on the wall she'd shown him earlier, of her, Leni, Deirdra, and Deirdra's sister Abby, sitting on the beach when they were teenagers. Her walls were covered with beachy paintings, cool bamboo planters, and loads of pictures of family and friends, each of whom she'd pointed out while they'd waited for their sushi delivery.

"Yes, that's her. We've always been close. She and her fiancé travel a lot, so I haven't seen her much lately, but I see her sisters since they live on the island. Abby owns a bistro that her father used to run, and my aunt Faye works with her."

"You have extended family on the island?"

"Just my aunt, who technically isn't my aunt anymore. It's a long story, but basically, she was married to my father's brother, who's a real ass, and they lived in Colorado. For years my mother tried to convince my aunt to move to the island, and she finally did last year. But her kids are spread out between New York, Harborside, and Colorado."

"Will they be at the wedding?"

"Yeah. It'll be nice to see them. Anyway, Abby and Dee's half sister, Cait, is a tattooist. See this guy?" She pointed to the dark-haired boy in the picture. "That's Jamison Remington. Cait is engaged to his brother Brant."

"Remington. That's one of the families your family is close to, right?"

"You don't forget a thing, do you?"

He cocked a grin. "You should put that in my pro column."

"Maybe I will." She pointed to the blond boy in the picture. "See this guy? That's Fitz Silver. He gave me my first kiss, and he was the first guy to ever get to second base with me."

"Ah, the truth comes out. You dated one of the highfalutin Silver boys."

"He's *not* like that. He's a really good guy."

"How long did you go out with him?"

"A few weeks, maybe. But we were in seventh grade, and dating meant hanging out with our friends and holding hands."

"Sounds like he held more than your hand," he teased. "Lucky kid. I'd've loved to have been your first kiss."

"Why? I wasn't very good at it."

"I wasn't either. We could've learned together." That earned a dreamy smile.

As he turned the page, a paper slipped out. He picked it up, taking in the printed picture of a blue-footed booby with one blue foot and one red foot. The bird was caught midstride, with the blue foot up in the air, leaning to one side as if it were tipsy, its pointy beak leading the way. He recognized the picture.

"Oh my gosh, that's my blue-footed booby! I love that picture. I did a report on them in seventh grade, and when I read it to the class, I went all out. I wore a white sweater with brown sleeves, because the bird had a white body and brown wings, and I painted my toenails red on one foot and blue on the other."

"Always going the extra mile. Where did you get this?"

"I don't know. Online somewhere. I probably cited it in the report. Why?"

"My mother took it. It was published in a nature magazine."

Her eyes widened. "No *way*."

"I'll show you." He grabbed his phone from the coffee table and navigated to his mother's website, where he searched blue-footed booby and showed her the picture, along with information about where it had been published.

"That's crazy. Tell your mother I said thank you. I got an A on that paper, and I swear it was because I loved that picture so much."

He was starting to think that maybe his and Sutton's paths had been fated to cross. "I'll be sure to tell her."

She was eyeing his salmon with the same expression she'd worn ten minutes ago when she'd been salivating over his tuna roll and had plucked a piece off his plate and replaced it with a piece of eel she didn't care for.

"Would you like a piece of salmon?"

"Do you mind? It looks delicious."

"Babe, I like sharing food with you. You don't have to ask. Just take what you want." He moved his plate closer to her.

"In that case." She leaned in and kissed him. "You just got another point in the pro column for sharing your food."

He'd take every tally he could.

She popped a piece of salmon into her mouth and motioned to her plate. "Take whatever you want."

He cocked a grin.

She laughed. "You are insatiable."

"Only for you, babe." He leaned in for a kiss.

They finished eating as they looked through the rest of the yearbook and read what her friends had written in it. About half of them mentioned Sutton's pros and cons lists. "Did young Sutton make a really bad decision or something?"

"No. Why?"

"I'm just curious about why you started making pros and cons lists."

"They've just always been my thing. I don't know why I started, but after Jock and Archer had their falling-out, I was glad I made them and made my big decisions based on facts and not solely on emotions like they did."

"That seems like a good way to approach problems, when it's feasible."

"It's always feasible."

"Is it?" He arched a brow. "You're with me, and I'm pretty sure that's an emotional decision, because the facts are stacked up against us."

Her eyes narrowed, and she pointed her chopsticks at him. "That's true. You know what? You're the only person who gets me crazy enough to forgo my lists."

"I think we have that in common. Not that I make lists, but

I usually think rationally, and most of the time it's impossible to do that with you."

"What exactly are you saying?" she asked playfully. "That we're bad influences on each other?"

"No. I think we're good influences, and you should add that I help you make spontaneous decisions to our pro column."

She smiled. "That's very clever."

"Sometimes I use my head for good and not evil." He tapped his temple and sat back, taking in her living room, which was as feminine and striking as she was. Cream couches and lavender upholstered chairs were accented with cream, salmon, and deep purple throw pillows. French doors along the back wall led to a deck, and he remembered she'd sat out there the night she'd called him while she was out for a walk and had run into an errant cat.

That cat had opened a door for them, giving her a reason to call him, and he was grateful for it.

He glanced across the room at a cozy-looking window seat with more decorative pillows tucked between built-in book-shelves. A book lay on the cushioned bench. He imagined Sutton lounging there in the sunlight, reading. "I really like your place. It suits you."

"Thanks."

"That reading nook is awesome." He pushed to his feet and went to check out the book.

"The nook and the bookshelves are what sold me on the townhouse."

He picked up the book, which had a picture of a handsome guy on the cover. "*His Wicked Ways*. This sounds interesting." He started paging through it.

"I forgot that was there. It's nothing." She jumped to her

feet, hurrying over to him.

"Nothing huh?" He started reading aloud. "*This isn't going to be like a high school blow job, buttercup. I'm going to fuck your mouth, and—*"

"Stop!" She tried to grab the book, but he lifted it out of reach.

"Do you have a highlighter? I'd like to take notes."

Her eyes shimmered with amusement, but her cheeks pinked up. "Shut up and give it to me." She held out her hand expectantly.

"Why? Do you want to study up for our next rendezvous?"

She pushed her hand closer to him. "*Braden*, the *book*, please."

"Fine." He handed it to her. "I'll look for a copy this weekend."

She rolled her eyes, but she was still smiling. "What's this weekend?"

"I was thinking about taking you up to Salvation Falls. Have you been there?"

"No."

"You'll love it. It's a cool town, with a massive lake on one side and miles of forest on the other. There's a great bookstore and lots of shops, and a café that has the best sandwiches you've ever eaten. Best of all, it's far enough away that I can hold your hand and kiss you without worrying someone will see us."

"That's quite a sales pitch." She set the book down on the cushion and crossed her arms, amusement rising in her eyes. "Are you asking me on a real date?"

"Yeah, I guess I am. I love spending time with you at my place, and being here is nice. Even if I had to park several blocks away and wear a hoodie so nobody recognized me."

Her brow furrowed. "Sorry."

He drew her into his arms. "It's okay. I'd do it a hundred times over to see you. But I spent a lot of years hiding, and I don't want to hide all the time with you. I know we have to be careful, and I wouldn't suggest this if I thought it would jeopardize our jobs. What do you say, Steele? Want to spend an afternoon with me knocking around Salvation Falls like a real couple?"

"I don't know." She put her arms around his neck, stroking the back of it as light as a feather, the way he loved. "I guess that depends."

"You have stipulations? Is there a mental pros and cons list being developed?"

"No. I'm just wondering if that date is in lieu of our nights of debauchery?"

He cocked a grin. "What's the matter, sweetheart? Suddenly the idea of using your toys alone isn't quite as fulfilling as the real thing?"

"A lady never tells."

Chapter Twenty-Six

FLYNN HAD BEEN hiking in Salvation Falls many times and had spent time in the town, but it felt different, more alive and interesting, being there on that sunny Saturday afternoon with Sutton. She was as enamored with the lake and the two-story brick shops, funky signs, and colorful murals on the sides of buildings as he was. They'd been there all morning, making their way through the shops along the main streets, chatting and holding hands. They stopped at Bite Me, the café he'd told her about, for lunch and shared a basket of sweet potato fries with their delicious sandwiches. Based on the smile that had taken up permanent residence on Sutton's beautiful face as they walked out of the café, he knew getting out of town had been the right choice. It had taken them a little while to trust that they could be openly affectionate without worrying about work, but now it was second nature for both of them.

"I'm stuffed," Sutton said as they reached for each other's hands.

He leaned in for a kiss, loving having the freedom to do it and being able to look at her without second-guessing his own expression for the sake of others. "Too stuffed to hit the bookstore? It's right around the corner."

"I'm never too full to walk around a bookstore."

As they headed down the street, the rumble and roar of motorcycles rang out, and a pack of them came over the hill. They watched as about two dozen bikers wearing black leather vests drove past.

"They're Dark Knights, like Levi," Sutton said excitedly.

"How can you tell?"

"They have the logo on the back of their cuts. Is there a chapter nearby?"

"Yeah. The Salvation Falls chapter has a huge presence here. They do a lot for veterans, kids, and the community as a whole."

She tipped her chin up. "I like this place even more now. I'll have to mention it to Levi."

"Is there a chapter on the island?"

"No. He's still a member of the Harborside chapter, so he goes back for their meetings. They've been a big part of his and Joey's life. They helped him through some rough times."

"From what I hear, they do that for a lot of people."

They headed around the corner, and her eyes lit up the way he'd hoped they would when the sign for the bookstore that took up half the block, the Imaginarium, came into view.

"Now, *that's* a bookstore," she exclaimed. "Look at the sign. It's gorgeous." The sign was a work of art, with colorful flowers, funky houses, and long-limbed trees peppered with funny-looking animals and animated people reading in different positions.

"The same local artist who painted some of the murals on the buildings made it. Denver Whiskey. In fact, he's a Dark Knight."

"He's really talented. I'll have to ask Levi if he knows him."

Flynn pulled open the door to the bookstore and followed her in.

Her gaze danced over the large number of displays, aisle after aisle of books and reading chairs and comfortable couches that formed conversation pits. "Did Denver paint those signs, too?" She pointed to the elaborate signs hanging above each aisle, indicating the genres shelved there. They featured the same style of people and animals as the sign out front.

"Yeah. Pretty cool, huh?"

"They're so *fun*. I bet they have a great kids' section here. Maybe I can find something for Joey and Hadley to take with me next weekend."

"How old are they again?"

"Joey is nine going on twelve, and Hadley is four and wants to be a writer, just like Jock."

"That's wicked cute."

"They both are." She smiled up at him. "You might be in trouble. I could spend all afternoon here."

"That's just one more reason we're so good together. *Go.* Shop to your hearts' content. We'll find each other by nightfall."

"No pressure in a bookstore? That's a definite *pro*." Her smile brought a wave of happiness as she went up on her toes, meeting him halfway in another kiss. "I'll be in women's fiction if you need me. Where are you starting?"

"Horror. I want to check out Jock's books. You said the first one was called *It Lies*?"

"Good memory. He published that one under Jack Steele. The second one, *Eyes on You*, is more of a romantic suspense, and he published under the name Jock for that one."

"Why did he switch it up?"

"I think he did it to honor who he is now. He hasn't been Jack in a long time."

"That's a big part of the healing process, accepting changes within yourself. Good for him. I'll catch you on the flip side, then." He stole one more kiss and watched her walk toward the women's fiction sign with a bounce in her step. He'd kissed her a hundred times already, and he knew they'd kiss a hundred more before the day was out. He was stocking up to hold himself over for all the workdays to come. He hadn't realized how much he'd needed this time with her.

Over the next hour, as they searched for books, Flynn never let too long go by between stolen glances at his glamour girl, gorgeous in white shorts, a peach short-sleeve top with a lace neckline, and strappy sandals. He liked watching her, whether she was paging through books, narrating a scene at work, or just sitting by the water with him. He was painfully aware of the fact that eventually they'd have to figure out what to do about work, but there was too much at stake to jump the gun, regardless of what he felt for her.

After picking out several fiction novels and a few nonfiction titles, he rounded the end of an aisle and nearly bumped into Sutton.

"Whoop. *Sorry.*" She juggled a stack of books.

"Here, babe. Let me help you." He reached for them.

"It's okay. I've got them." She settled the books in her arms. "I was just talking to a woman who lives nearby, and she said there's an arts and crafts fair in the town square this weekend. Do you want to check it out? She said it's only a few blocks away."

"Absolutely. Looks like you found some good books. Are you ready to go, or do you want more time?"

"I'm ready." As they headed up to the register, she said, "You have to see the adorable journal I got for Hadley. It's the pink one, second from the top."

"Great minds think alike." He plucked a matching pink journal from his stack of books. "I looked for something for Joey, but I don't know enough about nine-year-old girls to pick something out."

"*Flynn.*" She looked at him a little dreamily. "You didn't have to do that, but you do have good taste."

"I considered the yellow journal for Hadley."

"So did I, but"—

"I didn't like the drawings that were in it," they said in unison, and laughed.

"The pink elephants are definitely the cutest," he said.

"She's going to love them."

He put his books on the counter and reached for hers.

"I've got these." She turned to the side so he couldn't grab them.

He stepped closer, holding her gaze. "Steele, put the books on the counter."

"No. I can pay for my own b—"

He silenced her with a kiss. "Give me the books, beautiful. We're on a date, remember? It's okay to relinquish control and let me buy you a few things."

"*Okay,*" she relented.

"That's my girl." He put the books on the counter, and the woman behind the register nodded approvingly.

When they left the bookstore, Sutton said, "Thank you again for buying those. You're really stacking up the pro column lately."

"What's this *lately* crap?" he teased. "I saved your life. That's got to be worth a few points."

"Yes, but most of those points were used to make up for the points you lost by making me eat worms."

"That's fair." He dipped his head beside her ear, whispering, "I should've had you go straight for the anaconda."

THE DIN OF music, laughter, and conversation hung in the air at the arts and crafts fair. Children clung to balloons and danced around a folk band in the center of the brick-paved town square, while fairgoers moved in and out of canopied vendor booths and stood in line for popcorn and other goodies. As they meandered through the booths checking out arts and crafts, homemade furniture, jewelry, and clothing, their affection came as easily as their conversation and banter. Sutton felt like they'd escaped into a bubble of happiness that nothing could pop, which was exactly how she felt when they were at Flynn's cabin.

"Everyone here is so talented," she said as they left a stained-glass vendor. "How did you find this town?"

Flynn took her hand. "It was listed on a hiking website. There are miles of trails in the woods, and a number of waterfalls. We should come one day and take a hike."

"A hike with you without any deadly animals? Now, *that* sounds fun."

"We might get lucky and see a black bear." He stole another kiss, as he'd been doing all day. "Stick with me, Steele. I'll show you all the hidden gems."

If she had it her way, she would be sticking with him for a

long time.

They walked all the way down one side of the square, which was enormous, checking out every table, talking to the artists, and sharing kisses. As they made their way up the other side, Flynn stopped to talk to a leather artist, and Sutton walked out of the booth to take it all in. She loved being out and about with him, enjoying the sunny afternoon and discovering new things about each other and the little town. She spotted a booth up ahead with pink and black flags around the canopy, black-and-silver sparkling tablecloths, and a sign that read SHINY THINGS FOR COOL KIDS. Maybe she could find something for Joey there.

She headed back to Flynn. He was still talking with the artist, so she waited until there was a break in their conversation. Then she said, "There's a booth up ahead for kids that I want to check out for Joey. Meet me there?"

"Sure." He gave her a quick kiss. "I won't be long."

"Take your time." She walked up to the other booth and was thrilled to see all sorts of trinkets, sunglasses, hair clips, and jewelry for kids.

"Good afternoon," the woman behind the table said. Her dark hair framed her friendly face, and she wore a black-and-silver sparkly tank top and jeans. "I'm Erin."

"Hi. I'm Sutton. How are you?"

"I'm wonderful, honey. Thank you for asking. Are you looking for something special today?"

"Yes, a gift for my niece. She's nine."

"Nine is such a fun age. What's she like?"

"She's a firecracker, and she's into skateboarding, photography, and riding her dad's motorcycle."

"Oh honey, you came to the right place. I raised a very

similar daughter, and I had a heck of a time finding things she liked. At that age, my Sailor was into anything with wheels. Roller skates, skateboards, bikes, and just like your niece, her daddy's motorcycle. She still is, but she's in her twenties now and has been into classic cars for about the past decade. She knows more about them than all her brothers put together."

"That's impressive."

"They don't think so." She laughed and waved her hand. "I'm kidding. They're so doggone proud of her. Sailor makes a line of charms I think you'll like for your niece." She motioned for Sutton to come to the other end of the booth. "I have to keep these locked up, because tiny, shiny things are too enticing for little hands."

Erin opened a glass display case and took out a tray of charms. "These are all sterling silver and hand painted. Take a look through and see if anything catches your eye. If you find some that you like, I have silver and gold bracelets and necklaces. But if your niece is rough and tumble like my Sailor was at that age, you might want to go with a leather cord instead of a chain, or maybe a thin braided leather. They're heartier, and I find they hold up well for active kids."

"That's a great idea. Thank you." Sutton looked through the charms and was floored at the intricate detail of tiny classic cars, motorcycles, bikes, skateboards, footballs, tennis rackets, and dozens of other sports and hobby-related charms. There were flowers and hearts and others as well. She chose a silver-and-black motorcycle like Levi's, a skateboard that looked like Joey's, a camera, and a tiny silver heart.

Flynn came up behind her as Erin wrapped her purchases. "Hey, Steele. Did you find something?"

She told him about the charms. "I can't believe I found all

those charms. She wants to be a photographer like Tara, a biker like her dad, and a pro skateboarder. I wasn't sure if she'd like a necklace or a bracelet, so I'm getting a leather cord necklace. She can wrap it around her wrist several times, or Levi can shorten it if she wants to wear it as a bracelet."

"I'm sure she'll love it. Can I borrow your wrist for a moment?" He lifted her hand.

"Why?"

"Because I made you a little something." He put a beautiful bracelet on her, with two thin tan leather cords that had fancy knots evenly spaced around it. Between the knots were two slim gold beads with an iridescent glass bead between them. The glass beads alternated between pink and blue, and he fastened it with a gold button that had flowers on it.

"You *made* this? Just now?" She had to tease to keep her emotions from taking over. "Like a…friendship bracelet?"

His gaze was soft and warm, and not at all teasing. "Something like that."

"I love it. It's beautiful. Thank you." She hugged him.

"I'm glad. I wanted to give you something so you'd always remember our time in the rainforest together."

Did he really think she could forget a minute of the time they'd spent together there?

He took her hand in his and touched the bracelet. "The two leather chords symbolize us, and the tan color is so you never forget the worms we ate."

She laughed softly.

He brushed his thumb over a knot. "These are lovers' knots, and the pink glass beads remind me of you, how feminine you are, and of that unforgettable pink bikini." He touched a blue bead. "Your favorite color beads are for our waterfall."

She got choked up.

"And the seven knots and two gold beads represent the seventy-two hours we spent there." He touched the button, his gaze flicking briefly to Erin, who was watching them with a tender expression. His lips curved up in a secret smile that reached his eyes. "These flowers are for the pink flowers I put out for you while we were there."

Her heart swelled to near bursting. "I love it even more knowing why you chose each piece."

He held her gaze, his thumb gently stroking the back of her hand. "I know you're a glamour girl, and you might be more into diamonds and gold, and I love that about you. But that's all the world sees, and I'll always see you as you were in the rainforest. In all your natural beauty and resilience."

She threw her arms around him, struggling to keep tears at bay. "I love it so much. Thank you."

"Don't worry. I don't expect you to wear it all the time. I just wanted you to have it."

She held his gaze. "I'm never taking it off."

"I wouldn't either," Erin said. "That was just beautiful. My husband, Jacob, better step up his game."

Sutton laughed. "Erin, this is Flynn, my…?" *Boss? Boyfriend?* She glanced at him.

"I'm her dirty little secret." He put a finger over his lips and whispered, "*Shh.* Don't tell anyone."

"Your secret is safe with me." Erin winked. "Here you go, honey." She handed Sutton the bag. "I put my daughter's card in the bag. If you run into any problems, just reach out to her."

"Will do. Thank you for all of your help. It was nice to meet you."

"It was a pleasure meeting both of you as well. Enjoy the

rest of your day."

As they walked away, Sutton couldn't stop looking at her bracelet or the man who made her feel special with every little thing he did and said. "I really love my bracelet, and this town, and this whole day." *I want a million more days like this with you.*

"I could get used to doing this with you, too, Steele." He tucked her beneath his arm and kissed her temple.

How did he always know what she was thinking? As they meandered through more booths, she said, "Going to places like this is one of the things I miss about living on the island."

"Do they have a lot of craft shows?"

"They have quite a few, and the Winter Walk, which is like a giant sidewalk sale. But each town has its own events throughout the year, so there's always something going on."

"Then we'll do more of this so you don't miss it so much. What else do you miss?"

"Small-town stuff. Knowing people everywhere I go, which also has its downside, but mostly it's nice. I miss friends and family, and I swear Joey and Hadley are more grown-up every time I see them."

"You should get home more often."

"I've been a little busy banging my boss lately," she whispered as they walked out of a booth.

He drew her into his arms, flashing that sexy grin. "Maybe one day you'll want to bang your boss *on* the island."

Was he trying to make her heart explode today? "As much as I would love that, and as much as I love my family, they'd send you running for the hills."

"I doubt that."

"You have no idea, Flynn. Jules would practically alert the

media that I was bringing a guy home, and she'd be planning our wedding the second we stepped onto the island. God only knows what my brothers would do to you. They kidnapped Raz and held him over the edge of a cliff when he came home with Leni. My parents would be sweet and interested and treat you like family and get all up in your business, and my grandmother would try to convince you to become a dancer at Pythons. They're like a giant whirlpool of warmth and good intentions. They'll suck you in and never let you go."

"The kidnapping is questionable, but all in all? That doesn't sound so bad to me, Steele."

As her mind spun and her heart soared, he lowered his lips to hers and kissed her breathless.

Chapter Twenty-Seven

THE WEEK PASSED in a blur of busy days and steamy nights. Sutton felt like she was living on cloud nine as her and Flynn's lives continued to blend together. They were wrapping up the final edits for the rainforest episodes, the research for their next assignment was well under way, and she and Flynn were making plans for future outings together. On top of all of that goodness, it was Friday afternoon, and Sutton was leaving in half an hour to catch the ferry to the island. Archer was getting married tomorrow afternoon, and tonight she and Indi and all the girls were getting together at her parents' house. She wished Flynn was going with her, but she didn't want news of their relationship overtaking her brother's wedding weekend.

"Ready to do the last one?" Ray's voice came through the speaker in the sound room where she was finishing narrations.

She gave him a thumbs-up, the bracelet Flynn gave her sliding down her wrist. As always, it brought memories of that day and a smile.

Half an hour later, she headed out of the sound room, excited to get on her way.

"Great job, Sutton." Ray looked up from the equipment. "Have a good time at your brother's wedding."

"Thanks. I'm sure I will. I'm glad your son is doing better."

"Me too. But we'll see how long it lasts."

He turned back to the equipment, and she headed toward her office to gather her things. As she turned down the hall, she nearly bumped into Flynn, coming out of the supply room. In the space of a breath, those sexy blue eyes searched the empty hall, and he tugged her into the supply room and locked the door, kissing her like they hadn't seen each other in a month. She was just as ravenous for him, their hands searching, bodies grinding.

He tugged up her skirt as she worked open his jeans. "I already miss you," he rasped against her lips, sending her heart into a wild flurry. She palmed his thick length, and he groaned as she taunted, "What are you going to do about it?" His wolfish grin amped up her greediness for him. He shoved his jeans down as she stepped out of her panties, and their mouths fused together. She clung to him as he lifted her up and lowered her onto his cock, sending pleasure searing through her. Their moans were stifled by their brutal kisses, as they pounded out an urgent beat. Her back hit the wall, and he used it for leverage, taking her rougher, and soon they both spiraled out of control. Their bodies thrust and rocked as they swallowed their sounds of passion, until they collapsed, breathless and trembling, in each other's arms.

He buried his face in her neck and nipped at her flesh. Her whole body shuddered with pleasure. "*Jesus, Steele.*" He lifted his head and gazed into her eyes with so much emotion, her body thrummed anew. "I will never get enough of you."

"Can I get that in writing, please?"

He grinned and then he kissed her, long and slow and so perfectly, she was tempted to try to get him hard again. But she had a ferry to catch, and they were careful not to spend too long behind closed doors when they snuck away like this.

Several quick kisses later, Flynn hung back in the supply room as she hurried out and headed for the ladies' room.

After cleaning herself up and touching up her makeup, she headed into her office, and found a manila envelope on her chair. She recognized the strong, determined strokes of Flynn's handwriting across the front, which mirrored the man himself—*MS. SUTTON STEELE—PERSONAL AND CONFIDENTIAL*. She opened the envelope and withdrew a gorgeous gunmetal-blue leather journal with her name embossed on the front cover and a pretty silver button stud enclosure. There was a note sticking out of the top.

Steele, I noticed you were nearing the end of your journal when we were in the rainforest. I thought you'd like this one. I took the liberty of jotting down a few notes about our trip so you wouldn't forget any of it. Feel free to share them with your family. Braden

She ran her hand over the soft leather, falling a little harder for him as she opened and read what he'd written.

THE AMAZON RAINFOREST

- *YOU WERE CONSTANTLY WET.*
- *IT WAS ALWAYS RAINING. YOU THOUGHT YOU'D GET TWO INCHES, BUT YOU GOT NINE.*
- *I MADE SURE YOU HAD WOOD EVERY NIGHT TO KEEP THE FIRE BURNING.*
- *YOU WERE A REAL TROOPER. ALWAYS WILLING TO DO THE HARD STUFF AND GET ON YOUR KNEES TO STOKE THE FLAMES.*
- *WE HAD A ROUGH START BUT ENDED UP HAMMERING*

THINGS OUT.

- *I RODE YOU OFTEN, AND YOU WERE EAGER TO GET ME OFF.*
- *REMEMBER HOW THIRSTY WE WERE AT THE WATERFALL? WE SURE TOOK A DEEP DIVE THAT DAY.*
- *DON'T FORGET TO TELL THEM HOW NICE YOU WERE TO ME. I MEAN, STROKING MY HEAD AT NIGHT? SO SWEET.*
- *YOU MIGHT NOT WANT TO MENTION THE ANACONDA AT THE RIVER.*

Silently laughing, she closed the journal and clutched it to her chest, unable to believe he was the same man she'd wanted to strangle a month ago. She put the note and the journal back in the envelope, put it in her tote bag, and went to shut down her computer. As it was shutting down, her phone chimed. She fished it out of her bag and was surprised to see a notification from her personal email account from Global News Now. She'd mentally written off the opportunity with them. She opened and read the message.

Dear Ms. Steele,

We have reviewed your résumé and would like to set up a time to meet with you next Thursday when our management team will be in New York City...

She scanned the rest of the email with her heart in her throat. GNN was interested in her? This was big. *Huge.* It could be the stepping stone she needed to becoming the journalist she one day hoped to be. But now that she and Flynn were getting along and he'd just given her the chance to do a story about something that was important to her, did she really want to leave *Discovery Hour*—and Flynn—and move across the country?

Her chest constricted.

They couldn't even spend one night apart without losing their minds. She needed to think this through, and she was going to miss her ferry if she didn't hurry. She'd have time on the ferry to go over the pros and cons of accepting the interview and make a decision. Normally, she and Leni would take the ferry home together, and she could have run it by her. But Indi was Leni's best friend, and Leni had taken the day off to spend it with her.

Sutton put her phone in her bag and headed for Flynn's office to thank him for the gorgeous journal and get one last kiss goodbye.

Andi came around the corner just as she reached Flynn's empty office.

"Hey," Andi said. "If you're looking for Flynn, he just went into a production meeting."

"Oh, okay. I'll just leave him a note. Have fun this weekend." Andi and Dawn were going to visit their brother Dash and his wife, Amber, in Oak Falls, Virginia.

"I'm sure we will. Dawn's excited about hanging out with those hot Jericho brothers. Have fun at the wedding."

"Thanks." As Andi headed down the hall, Sutton hurried into Flynn's office and scrounged his desk for a piece of paper. She snagged a notepad from under a stack of documents, and her blood went cold at what she saw written on it. There in black-and-white, in Flynn's blocky, right-leaning handwriting, were all the reasons she wasn't qualified to be a higher-level journalist. It became harder to breath as she scanned the list. *She's excellent on the fly but needs more life experiences to warrant the respect of a professional journalist. Interviewing skills aren't sharp/direct enough to push people into revealing hard truths.* She scanned the next few things he'd written, each one cutting like a knife. When she reached the last two lines, she had to read it twice to believe Flynn had really written them. *Walters and Brokaw were trusted to give accurate, honest information. Sutton needs to report 100% honestly. Not half-ass it (tp in rainforest).*

Her hand shook, her mind spun, and she tried to drag air into her lungs. She'd trusted him, and this was what it had gotten her? It didn't make sense. Why was he letting her research the effects of a fragmented world on children if he didn't believe she could do a good job of researching or reporting about it? His voice blared through her mind like a foghorn. *You have a goal. Let's see if you've got what it takes to get there.*

He expected her to fail.

She felt sick.

Was everything he said, all his support, fake?

Tears threatened, and her heart felt like it was being torn in half. She had to get out of there before she lost it. She dropped the notepad on his desk, and her bracelet slid down her wrist. She hadn't taken it off since he'd given it to her, but now it felt like a lie burning through her skin. Struggling against tears, she took it off with trembling fingers, and dropped it on top of the notepad. She grabbed the envelope with the journal he'd given her in it and left it on the chair, willing her tears not to fall as she straightened her spine and held her head up high.

Faking it like the expert she'd become, she hurried out of his office, leaving too big a part of herself behind.

Chapter Twenty-Eight

SUTTON HAD HOPED being on the water would help bring her down from the jagged emotional cliff she'd been perched on since reading Flynn's godforsaken list, but she hadn't gotten that lucky. Her nerves were fried. She'd spent the first twenty minutes of the ferry ride in the ladies' room. First trying to stop her tears and then fixing her makeup *again* and putting on a brave face. She didn't even have to make that pros and cons list about the interview with GNN. She'd replied and accepted it right after she'd found a seat.

Now, as the ferry docked on Silver Island, she gazed out at the colorful cottages and cedar-sided homes dotting the lush landscape. Her parents' winery flags waved on the hill in the distance, just south of Silver Monument, and Flynn's voice trampled through her mind—*Maybe one day you'll want to bang your boss on the island*—bringing a stabbing pain to her chest.

Refusing to give in to the hurt, she shouldered her tote bag and picked up her small suitcase, following a stream of people to disembark. Thankfully, it was the middle of June, the thick of tourist season, and she hadn't recognized a single person on the crowded ferry.

As she made her way down the ramp, she spotted Jules

waving from the dock, looking cute in a red dress with white polka dots. "*Sutton! Sissy!*" Jules hollered. "Over here!"

If Sutton let on that she was unhappy, Jules would spend the rest of the weekend trying to make her feel better, and that was the last thing she needed. She waved, forcing a smile that she hoped would satisfy her overzealous sister.

"Welcome home!" Jules ran over as she came off the ramp and threw her arms around her, hugging her too tight. "I've missed you!"

"I've missed you, too."

"You look funny. Are you okay?"

"Yeah. Just a little tired."

"The ferry *always* makes me tired. It's such a relaxing ride. You'll wake up once you see everyone. All the girls are at Mom and Dad's. Leni and Indi are half a bottle of wine into the night already. They spent the day at that fancy spa in Chaffee." Chaffee was an artsy town on the island. "I swear it's like they think this is their last chance to be silly or something. As if getting married changes anything other than adding a pretty ring to your finger, taking your favorite person's last name, and knowing you'll spend the rest of your life with your best friend. Come on. I'm parked over there."

As they headed for Jules's Jeep, Sutton wished her love life were as easy as Jules made her own out to be. As she climbed into the passenger seat, she said, "Who's spending the night tonight?"

"Just you and Leni and Indi. The rest of us have men to go home to."

Sutton swallowed against the emotions clogging her throat. She wasn't in the mood for a party and was relieved to hear that it would just be the three of them overnight. "What are the guys doing tonight?"

"Dad took them out to dinner. But Raz isn't here yet. He's coming from LA and should be here around one tomorrow." Jules drove out of the parking lot. "You're lucky you haven't been home this week. Archer is so freaking nervous, he's been a total grouch."

"He's always grouchy."

"Trust me, he's worse. He's a total groomzilla."

"The ceremony is just the family. What is he up in arms about?" Sutton's phone vibrated with a call, sending her nerves into a panic. The sight of Flynn's name on the screen made her feel like she'd swallowed a bowling ball. She didn't have the bandwidth to deal with excuses, and she didn't need to break down in front of Jules. She sent the call to voicemail and turned off her phone, suffering in silence as Jules went on about the wedding.

"*Everyone* is going to be at the reception, and Archer wants every little detail to be perfect for Indi…"

When they pulled up in front of their childhood home, a rambling two-story with weathered cedar-shingle siding, peaked roofs, and a built-in gazebo anchoring the right side of the wide porch where Sutton had spent many hours reading throughout the years, it brought a modicum of comfort. As did the winery and its sixty beautiful acres next door.

"Everyone is excited to see you," Jules said as they walked up the front steps. She pushed open the door, and they were greeted by the sounds of laughter and conversation floating out from the kitchen.

Joey's adorable freckled face peered out of the living room at the end of the hall. "Aunt Sutton's here!" She bolted toward Sutton in striped leggings and a cute green shirt with a bear riding a yellow skateboard on it, her cinnamon hair flying over her shoulders.

Hadley ran after her calling out, "Aunt Sutton!" She was as cute as a button in a pink dress with a matching headband in her wispy blond hair.

Sutton set down her bags, and the girls threw their arms around her legs. It was hard to be upset with two adoring girls beaming up at her. "How are my favorite nieces?" As she crouched to hug them, her mother and grandmother headed up the hall from the living room.

"Good!" Joey and Hadley said in unison.

"Hey, where's *my* auntie love?" Jules teased.

The girls ran over and hugged Jules as Leni, Indi, Daphne, and Tara came out of the kitchen.

"Hi, sweetheart." Her mother wrapped her in a warm embrace, hugging her tight, drawing her emotions closer to the surface. "I'm so glad you're home."

"Me too," Sutton said as she moved to hug her grandmother. "Hi, Gram. How are you?"

"I'm just dandy. I've got wine and time with all my lovely girls."

"She's talking about me," Leni teased. "I'm the lovely one."

"We know," Indi said, bumping Leni's hip with hers.

"Did you bring us anything?" Joey asked.

"*Joey.*" Tara shook her head. The tall, slim blonde looked pretty in shorts and a blue tank top, her curls hanging loosely down her back.

"Presents?" Hadley chimed in, bouncing on her toes.

"I *might* have brought you each a little something," Sutton said coyly, and grabbed her tote bag.

Daphne, a curvy blonde, touched Hadley's shoulder. "Had,

what did we tell you about begging for presents?"

Hadley's smile fell. "That it's not nice, but it doesn't *feel* mean."

The adults tried to stifle their laughter as Daphne crouched in front of her daughter, in her jeans and peach top, and said, "It's not mean, honey. It's just that we don't want the people to think we only care about them for the gifts they bring."

Hadley blinked wide eyes up at Sutton. "I don't only care about presents."

"I know that, Had," Sutton reassured her.

"But I like them," Hadley added, making everyone laugh.

Daphne rolled her eyes and pushed to her feet, but she was smiling at her precocious little girl who once could do little more than scowl.

"I like presents, too," Sutton said, and immediately regretted it, because her mind zipped back to Flynn and the beautiful gifts he'd given her. The sting of what he'd written on that notepad came rushing back, and she tried to shove it down deep and focus on her nieces. "Hadley, since you want to be a writer like your daddy, *w*—I got you these journals to write in." *I, I, I. Not we!*

"Thank you! Look, Mama! Elephants!" She showed her journals to Daphne, who gushed over them and mouthed *Thank you*, to Sutton.

"Joey, I know you don't wear much jewelry, but I thought you might like this. It's a necklace that can also be worn as a bracelet, and if you don't want to wear it, you can just hang the charms in your bedroom or something." She handed the leather cord necklace with the charms to Joey.

"A skateboard *and* a motorcycle *and* a camera charm! I love it! Thank you!" Joey hugged her again. "Look, Tara!" She put it on and showed it off to everyone else. "Can we go play, Grandma?"

"Of course, honey," her mother said, and Joey and Hadley hurried toward the living room. "Sutton, honey, we were waiting for you to eat dinner. Who's hungry?"

Everyone else said they were, and they headed into the kitchen. The counters were littered with platters of food and several bottles of wine. There were pigs in a blanket, skewers of grilled chicken and vegetables, miniature sandwiches, pasta salad, Greek salad, chips and salsa, and three different types of heart-shaped cookies.

"This looks great, Mom," Sutton said as everyone loaded up their plates.

"Thank you for thinking of Joey. That was a really nice necklace," Tara said. "Where did you find it?"

"Flynn and I went to this—" *Shitshitshit.*

All eyes turned to her. Leni looked amused. The others looked as shocked as Sutton felt betrayed by her loose lips.

"I found them at an arts and crafts festival," Sutton said. "There were so many vendors, and the buildings—"

"Hold on, Sutton, dear," her grandmother said. "You're going to have to rewind to the part about you going there with your jungle boy."

"He's not my jungle boy, and this is Indi's night. We're not here to talk about me." Sutton took a bite of a cookie.

"Oh *nonono*, Sutton," Indi said. "My day is tomorrow. Tonight I'm just carrying out a long-held tradition of not screwing my soon-to-be husband the night before the wedding."

"Yeah, and we want to know about you and your hunky boss," Jules said.

"Are you two dating? Or did you go to the craft fair as

friends?" Tara asked.

"Good question." Daphne pointed a skewer at Sutton. "Are we talking enemies to friends or enemies to lovers?"

Sutton put down the cookie. "I'm going to need wine for this conversation."

"I've got you." Leni poured a full glass of wine and handed it to her.

Sutton guzzled half the glass, trying to figure out what to say and where to start.

"I think it's safe to say our Jane climbed Tarzan's vine," her grandmother said with a smirk.

Sutton closed her eyes for a beat, trying to figure out where to start, knowing they'd pester her until they got the full scoop. The sooner she got it out, the sooner they could move on. "I might have slept with him in the rainforest."

"Might have?" Leni scoffed. "I'm pretty sure you and Flynn scared the animals."

"I knew it!" Jules exclaimed. "I could tell by how nicely you talked about him on our video call. I'm so happy for you!"

"Don't be," Sutton said flatly. "He's not what he seems."

"I thought you said he wasn't a jerk to you in the rainforest," Tara said.

The truth brought a pang of longing. "He wasn't. We got really close while we were there, but we knew we couldn't keep seeing each other after we came back because he's my boss. We tried to stay away from each other, but we ended up texting or talking every night for hours. Then Leni and I ran into him a few weeks ago when he was out with his brothers and sister for his birthday. We got together that night, and we've spent every night together since then."

"That sounds promising," her mother said.

"I thought so. We meshed, you know? Everything with us was in sync. I really thought we had something special. I've never felt that way with anyone, and with him, the most unlikely person on the planet, it just happened. He said and did the nicest things. But…" She shook her head. She didn't want to say it. Saying it would make it real, and part of her still didn't want to believe it. Another part of her, she realized with surprise, wanted to protect Flynn, and that upset her even more.

Her mother put her hand over hers. "It's okay, honey. You don't have to talk about it."

"But she *should*," her grandmother said. "Matters of the heart are unlike anything else. They have a way of twisting and turning in our heads until we don't know what's real and what's not. It's best to just get it out there."

The others nodded in agreement. Sutton met the caring gazes of the women she knew would always have her back and forced herself to tell them what happened. "I trusted him. I know that's stupid, given our history, but I did. I told him about my idols and where I wanted to be in five years, and he acted *so* supportive. He asked what I'd want to report on if I could report on anything. It wasn't something *Discovery Hour* would typically take on, which should've tipped me off, but it didn't."

She paced the kitchen, her voice escalating. "I was so caught up in him, when he said to write it up so he could see if I had what it took, I thought he really believed in me. When we were at that craft show last weekend, he made me a beautiful leather bracelet with knots and beads, and every piece had a meaning that was about *us* and our time in the rainforest together. It was so romantic. And then at work today, he left a beautiful leather journal on my desk with my name embossed on it, and he wrote

317

all this cute stuff in it about us. I thought he was my person and I was his."

"*Aw*. That's so sweet. Can I see the bracelet?" Jules asked.

"*Jules*. This doesn't have a happy ending," Leni said sharply. "Let her finish."

"Oh, right. *Sorry*," Jules said.

"It's okay. I don't have it anyway." A dull ache lodged in her chest. "When I went to his office to thank him for the journal, he wasn't there, so I was going to leave a note. That's when I found a list he'd made of all of my shortcomings. He wrote down all the reasons why I don't have what it takes to be the type of journalist I want to be. And it *wasn't* a short list. I left the journal and my bracelet on his desk and took off." Tears of anger and hurt burned, and she choked out, "Who makes a list like that about the person they're seeing?"

"An asshole, that's who." Leni seethed. "Who the hell is *he* to make that kind of judgment, anyway? He's just some dumbass survivalist. He doesn't have journalistic experience."

"He's not a dumbass," Sutton choked out, feeling protective of him again, which pissed her off even more. "*Discovery Hour* was his concept."

"So what? That doesn't make him qualified to judge you like that," Indi said, quick to agree with Leni.

"You don't get it," Sutton snapped, and revealed another hurtful layer. "He was *right* about all of it. He knows what he's doing, but that's not the point. The point is, he didn't mean all the nice things he said to me. He was acting, or playing a game, or…I don't *know*."

"Oh, honey," her mother said. "I'm so sorry."

"You and me both. I fell for him, Mom. Hook, line, and sinker." Tears welled in her eyes.

"I can see that." Her mother drew her into her arms.

"I thought we were building something special." Tears slid down her cheeks. "I really thought we could have what all of you have." She stepped out of her mother's arms, swiping angrily at her tears, and guzzled the rest of her wine.

"I'm sorry, sissy." Jules hugged her, shedding tears of her own, which made Sutton feel even worse. "He's a big, fat jerk for doing this to you."

"Maybe the list wasn't about you," Tara said hopefully.

"It's definitely about me. He called me out by *name* on it," Sutton seethed.

"Have you talked to him about it? Could you have misconstrued what you saw?" Daphne, always the peacemaker, asked.

Sutton shook her head. "No. I'm sure I didn't, and I'm *not* going to talk to him about it. I don't want him to know how bad he hurt me."

"Your boss hurt you?" Joey asked as she and Hadley came into the kitchen.

Shit. Sutton swiped at her tears. "No—"

"Yes, he did. The little shit," Leni said.

"*Mama,* Aunt Leni said a bad word," Hadley tattled.

"I know, honey. She's upset that someone hurt Aunt Sutton," Daphne explained.

Hadley scowled and crossed her arms. "I'm upset, too."

"I'm fine, Had," Sutton said lamely, feeling guilty for allowing the kids to get mixed up in her heartache.

"Is he the boss that was trying to get you fired?" Joey asked. "The one Leni said you should bag?"

There was a collective gasp, and their grandmother giggled. Their mother glowered at her. Sutton wished she'd been more careful about their conversations and said, "Yes."

"I think you should put the meanie back in the body bag," Joey said, sparking a round of laughter.

Pieces of that particular conversation came back to Sutton. Leni had said she should *bag* Flynn, and Sutton had said something about putting him in a body bag. When Joey had asked what she'd meant, she'd said it was a place where you put arrogant bosses when they pissed you off.

"Hear! hear!" Leni said, and took a swig of her wine. "Sutton, it's a good thing you applied for that other job. Have you heard back yet?"

"They emailed today to schedule an interview for next week. I said I was interested. I'm just waiting to get a date and time."

"Good. You'll show Flynn Braden what Steeles are made of," their grandmother said.

"I just don't get it," Tara said. "Why would he do that to you if you guys were so close?"

"Because he's a"—Leni looked at Hadley—"a big, fat jerk."

"*Hello?* Where is everyone?" Bellamy Silver's voice sounded in the hall.

"We're in the kitchen, Belly!" Jules called out.

Bellamy, a petite brunette lifestyle influencer, and Jules's bestie, walked into the room, looking as stylish as always in black shorts and a white cap-sleeve top, her dark hair sweeping across her shoulders. "I knocked, but no one answered."

"Sorry, honey, we were talking and didn't hear you." Their mother went over and hugged her.

"I didn't know you were coming by," Jules said. "Is everything okay?"

"Everything is *fine*," Bellamy reassured her. "I'm super excited about the wedding. I'm sorry to crash your sisters' night. I promise to only take a minute. I just wanted to talk to Sutton before wedding craziness takes over. Since *The Bachelor* turned me down, which I still can't fathom. I mean, look at me. I'm cuter than half the women on that show. I'm submitting my application to LWW's new reality show, *InstaLove*. I was hoping Sutton wouldn't mind reviewing my submission since she used to be an editor."

"Sure," Sutton said. "I'd be happy to look it over for you. Just email it to me."

"Awesome. Thank you! Do you have any connections that might help nudge me up the list?" Bellamy asked.

"No, sorry. That's a whole different division."

"Bummer. Okay, I'll email it to you. One more thing." Bellamy hiked a thumb over her shoulder. "There's a hot guy out front who claims to be your boss. I know you said your boss was a total jerk, so I didn't invite him in. But *wow*, Sutton, he is *gorgeous*."

Panic flared in Sutton's chest. "Flynn is *here*? Why is he here?"

"The man must have a death wish," her grandmother said.

"He said he had to talk to you." Bellamy's brows knitted. "You look upset. I can take him down to Rock Bottom for a drink if you want." She winked.

"Nobody's drinking with *him*. He hurt Sutton," Jules snapped.

"In that case, I'll get rid of him," Bellamy said. "Why do they waste hotness on a-holes?"

"Don't bother, Bellamy. I'll take great pleasure in getting rid of him." Leni walked into the hall.

Sutton went after her. "Leni, *stop*. I can handle my own business."

Anger and hurt warred inside her as she strode out the front door with her cavalry on her heels. Her heart thundered at the sight of Flynn standing in the walkway, unfairly handsome in jeans and a dark T-shirt, looking uncharacteristically perplexed. Every fiber of her being ached to go to him as she descended the porch steps. But she forced herself to stop several feet away and crossed her arms, steeling herself against those feelings.

FLYNN HAD BEEN gutted, and a little pissed, when he'd found that Sutton had left the gifts he'd given her in his office. But that pain was nothing compared to the hurt in Sutton's eyes right then, which nearly dropped him to his knees. He'd spent the last two hours out of his mind with worry as his texts and voicemails had gone unanswered. But now, as Leni and several of the women he recognized from the pictures on Sutton's walls filed out of the house looking furiously at him, he was rethinking showing up there. Leni held a golf club, glowering at him like she intended to use it, and Jules held an umbrella, which he had a feeling was also meant for him, since the sky was clear.

Sutton lifted her chin, those sad eyes trained on him. "What are you doing here, Braden?"

He held up the bracelet. "I believe you forgot something."

"The only thing I forgot was that you weren't to be trusted."

"You have some nerve showing your face on our island," Leni seethed.

"Yeah!" Jules barked. "Nobody hurts our sister and gets away with it." She slapped the umbrella in her palm.

Sutton turned to look at her. "What are you going to do with that? Hold it over him in case it rains?"

"Leni took the only good weapon! But I can use this." Jules swung the umbrella like a bat, and it opened, causing her to squeal and wrestle it closed.

"*Jules!*" Leni barked.

Flynn tried to keep a straight face.

Joey stomped over to Sutton, shooting him a death stare. "Aunt Sutton doesn't need *you* to get her fired. She can do that on her own! Why don't you climb back into that body bag and leave her alone before I get my daddy to beat you up."

"*Joey!*" Tara chided her.

"Yeah, go away, you meanie!" Hadley sported that killer scowl he'd heard about.

"*Hadley!*" Daphne leaned down, speaking quietly to her daughter.

Flynn held up his hands. "I don't want to get your aunt Sutton fired, and I didn't mean to hurt her."

"*Right.* I wasn't meant to find your notes," Sutton snapped. "Why did you pretend to believe in me and say all those nice things about my reporting skills?" Her voice escalated, eyes glistening with tears, gutting him anew. "Why did you act like you really liked me? Is this some kind of sick game for you? Leading women on and then secretly shooting them down?"

"Sutton, I would *never* pretend to have feelings for you, and I complimented your reporting skills because you're a phenomenal reporter and I believe you're going to be a better journalist than all your idols put together."

"*Stop.* Just stop lying already," she seethed.

"*Babe.*" He stepped forward, and so did Leni, lifting the golf club. He held his arms out, palms up. "You can hit me with that thing as many times as you want, but I'm going to say what I have to say to your sister." He returned his attention to Sutton.

"I told you that I would never lie to you, and I meant it. You'll know if I ever lie. All Bradens suck at lying. I'm talking universal suckage. If I were to lie to you, I'd get all twitchy and forget what I was saying. But that's not *why* I won't lie to you. I won't lie to you because I respect you too much, and I care about you too deeply, to ever try to pull the wool over your eyes about anything. I never denied that I wanted you gone when we first started working together. I worried your lack of experience would sink the show, and that show was my baby."

"Bastard," Leni fumed.

Ignoring that comment, Flynn didn't take his eyes off Sutton. "But you chipped away at those misconceptions, rising to every challenge, and as I told you in the rainforest, I learned that the harder I pushed you, the harder you'd push yourself to go above and beyond what's expected. You've already surpassed reporters who have far more experience than you do." He saw some of the tension easing from her shoulders. "Babe, I am truly sorry that I hurt you by making that list. But as someone who lives by her pros and cons lists, I'm hoping you'll understand why I made it. I make lists, too. But as a survivalist, I analyze situations to see how I can be one step ahead at all times. I make lists about what I have to work on to get there. I wrote that list after you told me your goal. *Not* because I don't believe in you, but because I *do*. It's my job as your boyfriend to help you achieve your dreams. To me that means helping you hone your skills to become the best damn journalist that ever walked this earth."

"I *love* that. You were trying to help her," Jules said, and others murmured their agreement.

Tears slid down Sutton's cheek as he took another step, bringing them close enough to touch. "You're a force of nature, sweetheart. But you're human, like the rest of us. We're always learning and growing, and nobody gets to be the best without the help of others. If you don't want me to be one of the people who helps you, then tell me and I promise I'll back off. But please don't end us because I made the mistake of wanting to help you."

"It *hurt* to find that list," she said shakily and angrily.

"I'm truly sorry. I should have talked with you to see if you wanted my help, and if you did, then I should have made the list *with* you, not *for* you. I adore you, Sutton, and I love us and what we're building together. I swear on my grandfather's life that I have *no* secret agenda."

Her brow furrowed, and the trust he'd seen in her eyes so many times over the past month rose to the surface.

"It hurt like hell to find those gifts you left behind, and I know you well enough to know that leaving them hurt you, too. That tells me how bad I screwed up. I'm sorry, Sutton. I want to be with you. I want to cheer you on as you climb your mountains. But if you need time to make a decision about whether you want to be with me, to write up a pros and cons list or talk with your army of defenders about it, that's okay. I'll wait as long as it takes, because you're worth waiting for."

A collective "*aw*" and a symphony of sniffles rang out around them.

Tears streamed down her cheeks, and the energy rolling off her was no longer heavy with anger. "I don't need to make a list or talk to anyone to know I want to be with you. I'm sorry I assumed the worst, but that was a horrible, hurtful list."

"*No*, it wasn't. It was horrible that you found out about it the way you did, and it was hurtful because we're our own worst critics, and you're so smart, you probably already knew those were things you had to work on. Seeing it coming from me is what hurt."

She looked up at the sky, blinking against tears.

"But that list was *not* a judgment. I'm on your side, Sutton. That was a list of things we could work on together to get you where you want to be. And it hurt, and that sucks. But I *told* you I'm not a mollycoddler. I'm a results guy, and you're my girl. I want you to succeed, but from now on I will not do anything like that without asking first."

"You better not."

"I won't." He reached for her hand. "We're both used to being on our own, and we're learning how to communicate and trust and navigate our relationship while hiding it half the time. That's not easy. Hiding, even from others, builds mistrust, so I'm going to work extra hard to prove to you that you can trust me on every level. But if I can't make lists, then you need to promise you *will* make them."

"Why?"

"Because you're not allowed to make any more assumptions where we're concerned. Facts first. Pros and cons lists only."

She nodded, fresh tears spilling down her cheeks. "Okay."

He drew her into his arms, whispering for her ears only, "I'm so sorry, sweetheart," and then he kissed her, feeling all their broken pieces coming back together.

"Yay!" Jules cheered. "Love wins."

They broke the kiss on a laugh, and as he gazed into Sutton's eyes, he knew Jules was right, because those three special words vied for release.

"Thank goodness. I was holding my breath," her mother said.

"Me too," Daphne said.

"I'm just over here tearing up," Tara said, wiping her tears.

"Grandpa would like this young man," her grandmother said.

That got Sutton's attention. "He would?"

"Yes indeed. He respected men who didn't waste time or mince words," her grandmother said.

"Hear that, sweetheart? Since I have your granddad's approval, will you please do me the honor of wearing your bracelet?"

"What do you think?" She held out her wrist, grinning from ear to ear as he put it on her.

He laced their fingers together and kissed the back of her hand.

"Do we like the meanie now?" Hadley asked.

"Yes," Joey answered. "I guess Aunt Sutton doesn't need to bag her boss after all."

He and Sutton exchanged a heated glance, and she said, "Well, I wouldn't go that far."

Everyone laughed, and Flynn drew her into another kiss.

"Okay, Romeo. Keep it in your pants," Leni teased.

"I'll get out of your hair." He looked at the women who he had a feeling would do anything for Sutton and said, "Thanks for letting me intrude. I've heard a lot about each of you, and I hope at some point we'll have a chance to get to know each other better."

"You're not staying?" Sutton asked.

"I don't want to intrude on your family time."

"You're *not*." Sutton held his hand tighter and glanced at Indi. "Do you mind if he comes to the wedding?"

"Of course not," Indi said.

"That's really nice of you, but I didn't bring clothes for a wedding."

"That's okay," Jules said. "There are clothing shops in town. You can pick something up before the ceremony."

"It's an afternoon wedding, and not too fancy." Sutton looked at him hopefully. "Unless you don't want to stay?"

He tapped his jaw, as if contemplating it. "Let's see. Go home to an empty house and think about you all weekend, or attend the wedding of two of your favorite people *with* you? That's a tough choice."

She laughed softly. "Is that a yes?"

"That's a yes. Just tell me where to book a room."

"Oh, honey. I'm sure you and Sutton want to be together. You can share her room here," her mother said.

He looked at Sutton. "Is that okay with you?"

"More than okay," she said.

"Then I guess I'm staying."

Jules cheered, and everyone spoke at once, introducing themselves and hugging him. Even Leni embraced him and said, "You better have meant every word you said, or I'll seven iron the hell out of you."

He met her steely gaze. "You're a good sister, Leni. I'm glad Sutton has you watching out for her."

She looked momentarily confused, as if she had been awaiting a smart-ass retort. Then she closed her mouth, respect rising in her eyes.

"I bet you're hungry," her mother said. "We have loads of food and wine, and with these girls, there's always great conversation. Why don't you join us?"

He glanced at Sutton. "I don't want to interrupt your girl time. I can find something to keep me busy."

"You should stay," Indi said. "It's not a bachelorette party, and it'll give us a chance to grill you before the Steele brothers get their hands on you."

He arched a brow at Sutton, and she nodded. "I guess I'm staying."

As they headed inside, Bellamy and Sutton's grandmother flanked them. "So, Mr. *Discovery Hour*," Bellamy said. "Just how good are your connections with the producers of *InstaLove?*"

"Excuse me?" He glanced at Sutton.

"It's a new LWW reality dating show," Sutton explained.

"This night just got a whole lot more interesting," her grandmother said.

HOURS LATER THEY lay in Sutton's childhood bedroom, nose to nose, arms around each other, legs tangled together. Flynn was relieved they'd gotten past their misunderstanding and thrilled he'd had a chance to meet Sutton's family and friends, even if under not-so-great circumstances.

"I'm really glad you're here," Sutton said softly, her hand sliding down to his butt.

"Thank you for asking me to stay, but you'd better keep those hands to yourself before you get us both in trouble."

She pressed her hips forward, rubbing against his erection. "It doesn't feel like you want me to keep my hands to myself."

"You know I can't get within ten feet of you without wanting you, but we're not exactly quiet lovers, and I don't need your amazing parents thinking I'm here as your sex toy." He kissed her smiling lips. "I loved meeting everyone and seeing you with them. It's obvious how much they all adore you."

"I'm pretty lucky. Everyone loved you, too."

"*Almost* everyone," he teased. "I think Leni's withholding final judgment until I prove myself worthy of her smart, beautiful sister."

"I told you she was protective."

"I'm not worried. But I am sorry about earlier. I hate the idea of you spending even one minute thinking I don't believe in you. I know you've spent your life feeling like you had to work extra hard to stand out, but you've always stood out to me. Not just because you're beautiful. At first, maybe, but once we started working together and I got to know your fierceness, it was so much more. I promise you, you will never have to compete for my attention or worry that I don't think you're the most incredible woman alive. Because to me there's only you." He kissed her again. "You can trust me, sweetheart, and if you ever doubt that, talk to me before you waste a second being unhappy."

Her eyes watered. "I've never had anyone like you in my life before."

"Neither have I."

"It's a little scary. I'm used to gathering facts and learning everything there is to know about situations before diving in headfirst, but with you, I'm throwing caution to the wind. We're risking everything at work."

"I know we are." He felt a little guilty for their secret office trysts. It wasn't fair to jeopardize her career that way. "I'll try to keep my hands to myself in the office from now on."

"*No.*" She grinned. "I like that part of us, and we're careful. It's just scary opening up and…"

"Developing feelings so fast?"

She nodded.

He tucked her hair behind her ear. "You're worried about getting hurt."

"Aren't you?"

He thought about it before answering, and the truth surprised him. "I'm less afraid of getting hurt than I am of losing you."

"Don't they go hand in hand?"

"Yes, but it's not the heartbreak that scares me. It's believing I didn't want or need a life partner, that I was fulfilled by all the places I've gone and the things I've done, and then finding you and falling head over heels and realizing that everything else pales in comparison to how it feels to be with you."

"*Flynn*," she whispered, her eyes tearing up.

"I hope that doesn't scare you off."

"How could it, when I feel the same way?"

Their mouths came together in a slow, sensual kiss, and he moved over her. She smiled up at him, whispering, "I thought we weren't doing this."

"I guess your parents will just have to be okay knowing I'm your boy toy."

Chapter Twenty-Nine

FLYNN PULLED ON his shirt Saturday morning and leaned against the doorframe to the bathroom that adjoined Sutton's childhood bedroom, watching her put on lotion. Her hair was wet, and she had a towel wrapped around her. They'd just made love in the shower, and still he wanted to strip that towel off and love her until they were both too tired to move.

She glanced at him. "Get that look off your face, Braden."

"What look is that?" He closed the distance between them and wrapped his arms around her from behind, gazing at her in the mirror. "The look that says I can't get enough of you?" He kissed her shoulder.

She turned, wrapping her arms around his neck. "As much as I love *that* look, this house is about to become mayhem central, and getting caught with our pants down won't work to your advantage." She went up on her toes and kissed him.

"Duly noted. What's today's plan?"

"I thought we'd head into town after breakfast to find you some clothes for the wedding, and I was hoping to show you around the island since the wedding isn't until four."

"So we have all day together?"

"Most of it. I need to meet Indi and the girls here at two to get ready. You can help the guys set up for the wedding, or borrow my father's car and go somewhere, or just chill here at the house if you want."

"It all sounds good to me." He slipped his hands beneath her towel and squeezed her butt.

She wiggled out of his grasp. "Go get some breakfast before you get yourself in trouble. I'll be down after I get dressed and dry my hair."

"Breakfast sounds good." He raked his gaze down her body. "Lose the towel, baby. I'm starved."

She giggled and shooed him out the door.

He tugged her in for one last kiss, then gave her ass a swat, earning a pink-cheeked glare. "See you downstairs, Steele."

He followed the scent of bacon and coffee to the kitchen. Shelley and Steve stood by the stove with their arms around each other and their hands on each other's butts, talking between kisses. "*Uh*, sorry." Flynn turned to go back upstairs.

"Flynn, honey, come back," Shelley said, pretty in jeans and a forest-green T-shirt.

He headed back into the kitchen. "You sure? I didn't mean to interrupt a private moment."

"Son, we raised six kids," Steve said as he cracked eggs into a pan on the stove beside another pan of sizzling bacon. A maroon Top of the Island Vineyard polo shirt was stretched across his thick chest. He was a good-looking man with short dark hair flecked with gray, a neatly trimmed beard, and a friendly demeanor. "We gave up private moments a long time ago."

"Would you like some coffee or juice?" Shelley poured batter into a waffle maker, nodding toward the coffeemaker.

"Sure. Coffee would be great. Just point me in the direction of the mugs."

She reached into a cabinet and handed him one.

"Sutton is just drying her hair." He poured a cup of coffee. "Breakfast smells delicious. How can I help?"

"You can take the muffins out of the oven," Shelley said. "The mitts are in the drawer next to Steve."

He set down his coffee mug, snagged mitts, and opened the oven. The heavenly scent of freshly baked muffins wafted out as he withdrew two trays. "Blueberry and chocolate chip? My favorites. You've been busy this morning."

Steve peered out the window and said, "Here comes Archer. Flynn, whatever happens, just go with it."

"Okay." He looked questioningly at Shelley, who wore a coy smile.

The kitchen door opened, and there was no mistaking Archer Steele, with his military-short dark hair and trim beard, massive biceps, barrel chest, and his father's sharp jawline. "Hey, Mom. Dad."

"What are you doing here, honey? You're not supposed to see Indi before the wedding," Shelley said.

He scoffed. "We're done with that. I've had enough time without her. Where's my girl?" He turned serious eyes on Flynn. "Who are you?"

Flynn opened his mouth to answer, but Steve cut him off. "Archer, this is Miles. Miles Long, a friend of your grandmother's from bingo. He's coming to the wedding with her."

Oh shit. Let the pranks begin. "How's it going, man?" Flynn extended his hand.

Archer's face contorted into a mask of rage. "Are you fucking kidding me?"

"Archer, watch your language in front of our guest," Shelley chided.

"Mom, you're okay with this?" Archer fumed.

"Honey, who am I to tell my mother who she can spend her time with?" Shelley played it off like a pro. "She's got needs like everyone else."

"Needs? She's..." Archer gritted his teeth, his chest puffing out like a silverback gorilla as he closed the distance between him and Flynn, glowering. "What are you, a *stripper?*"

"I prefer exotic entertainer."

"And I'd prefer if you got the hell out of this house and stayed the fuck away from my grandmother. How old are you, anyway?"

"Thirty-four." Flynn flicked his hair out of his eyes, cocking an arrogant grin, and ran his hands down his abs. "A damn hard thirty-four if you ask me."

Archer's eyes narrowed, his jaw grinding like he was going to spit nails. "Do you get off preying on old ladies? You know how pathetic that is?"

"Did you just call my woman old?" Flynn threw his shoulders back, puffing out his chest, too. "Watch yourself, dude."

"She's my *grandmother,*" Archer seethed.

"I'd say that makes you a lucky guy. Lenore is quite a woman. *Very* loving."

Archer gritted his teeth. "You—"

Shelley shoved a plate of waffles between them. "Here you go, Miles. You need to keep your calorie count up to keep up with my mother."

"Don't forget the protein." Steve put eggs on Flynn's plate and winked.

Archer bit out, "*Dad,* what the hell are you doing?"

Leni came into the kitchen. "Hey, Archer. I see you met

Romeo."

"You're cool with this shit, too?" Archer growled.

"Well, I wasn't until I saw them together last night," Leni said as she poured coffee into a mug. "And yeah. Now I am. He's really into her, and I haven't seen her this happy in years. He must be rocking her world in more ways than one."

"Seriously, Archer, don't you think you're overreacting?" Steve asked. "Everyone is allowed to have some fun, and love comes in all forms."

"All of y'all have lost your fucking minds." He grabbed Flynn by the collar, hauling him toward the kitchen door. "You go near my grandmother again and I'll fucking—"

"Grandmother?" Leni asked, wide-eyed.

"Hey! Get off him!" Sutton ran into the kitchen and tried to pry Archer's hand off Flynn's shirt.

"You too, Sutton? What the hell? He's sleeping with Grandma!"

Flynn shrugged, trying not to laugh. "What can I say? Lenore's hot."

"That's it, motherfucker." Archer cocked his arm as Indi came into the kitchen. Sutton yelled, "Stop!" Indi screamed, "Archer, don't!" and Steve caught Archer's fist before he could throw the punch, gloating, "*Gotcha*, son."

Archer's furious eyes moved over them.

"Sorry, dude. I was just a pawn. I'm Flynn. I'm here with Sutton."

Archer's expression went from rage to confusion to fury, and he wrenched his arm free from Steve's grip. "Her *boss*? You're the asshole who's been trying to get her fired?"

"Archer, don't be a dick," Sutton seethed.

"It's okay, Sutton. I was that asshole when you first started working with me." Flynn put his arm around her and met Archer's ice-cold gaze. "Then I realized the error of my ways. Now I'm the guy who's falling head over heels for your sister. But based on the stories I heard last night, it sounds like you were the same with Indi, and look at you now."

"He's right," Indi said, sliding between Archer and Flynn and wrapping her arms around Archer.

"Yeah, whatever, man," Archer grumbled. "Just watch yourself."

"Hey, Flynn," Leni said, drawing everyone's attention to her as she snagged a muffin. "I bet you're having second thoughts about coming to the island now, aren't you?"

He gazed into Sutton's beautiful eyes and knew he'd do whatever it took to make her his. "Not even a little."

AFTER A DELICIOUS, banter-filled breakfast, Flynn and Sutton headed to Main Street to get him clothes for the wedding. Sutton was glad she'd never brought a guy home to meet her family before. Somehow it made walking around her hometown hand in hand with Flynn even more special. Not that she'd brought him to the island, but she was glad he'd come. She still couldn't believe he'd come all that way to make things right and hadn't hesitated to fight for her in front of everyone last night. If that didn't tell her how real his feelings were, nothing could.

"This is a cute town. The shops remind me of Ridgeport," he said as they walked from the car toward the men's clothing store. "I'd like to take you there one day and introduce you to my parents."

Her heart soared, but she couldn't help teasing him. "I don't know, Braden. That's a big step."

"Almost as big as playing the part of Grandma's boyfriend."

They both laughed.

"When I saw Archer going after you, I thought you'd run for the hills," Sutton said carefully.

"It would take a lot more than your hotheaded brother to scare me off." He leaned in and kissed her, and she filled with happiness. "What do you say, Steele? Want to meet my parents and see all my old haunts?"

"I would love to."

"Great. They'll be back in a few weeks. We'll talk to them and plan something. In the meantime, show me all your old hangouts and where your milestones happened."

"You're looking at one right now. After I graduated from my cardboard-box newscasting, I would go with my mom when she ran errands and interview the shop owners to practice reporting."

"See? Always going the extra mile to get things right. That's adorable."

"I'm sure it was annoying to the people I interviewed, but they never let on. They went along with it, answering my questions and telling customers they'd be with them in a minute, as if I were someone important and not just a kid."

"You were a kid on a mission. That's impressive, not annoying. I can't wait to talk to some of them."

"Seriously? Are you dead set on embarrassing me today?"

"No, babe. On hearing how cute you were." He pulled open the door to the men's store. "What color is your dress?"

"Seafoam green. Why?"

"Staking claim to the prettiest girl on the island comes in many forms." He took her hand, leading her to the ties.

Half an hour later they walked out with a change of clothes and everything he needed for the wedding, including a seafoam-green tie and shiny black shoes. They wandered through the rest of the shops, and when the people she knew greeted her with hugs and enthusiastic hellos, Flynn took a few minutes to get to know each of them. She liked the way he didn't rush them along and was at ease with the people in her community and added that to his pro column, which was getting mighty long. He asked a few of them about her reporting practice, and they relayed fond memories, which made her feel good and not like she'd been an annoyance to them.

They crossed the street and walked through the park. Sutton showed him the boulder she used to sit on and read when she was a kid and the hills they'd sledded down. They walked to the library, where she'd spent ages when she was younger, and stopped for coffee at the Sweet Barista, which was owned by her friend Keira Silver. Sutton introduced him to Keira, and the second he turned his back, Keira mouthed, *He's so hot,* which made her laugh. Then they drove by her old schools and Abby's Bistro, and she showed him Silver Monument and Majestic Park, where the town Christmas tree was located.

"The annual holiday festival I told you about takes place in the park the weeks leading up to Christmas," she said as they drove away.

"I'd like to come to that with you this year."

She wanted to bundle that up like a promise. "I'll pencil you into my date book."

"That won't do. Write that sucker in with permanent marker."

They drove down to Rock Harbor and parked at the marina. "This is where the flotilla takes place."

Flynn took her hand as they headed down toward the docks. "I bet it's gorgeous. Is this where Archer and Zev keep their boats?"

"Yeah. They're just past the boathouse. I'll show you. Is Zev here?"

"No. He's visiting family this weekend."

They descended the steps, and as they neared the boathouse, Roddy Remington walked out of the office carrying a massive box of lights. Roddy had always reminded Sutton of a young Jeff Bridges with thick gray-brown hair that brushed the collar of his vibrantly colored shirt, which was opened nearly to his navel, as usual.

"*Sutton.* What a nice surprise. I figured you and the girls would be busy as bees today." Roddy wrapped her in a bear hug.

"Hi, Roddy. I'm meeting them at two to get ready. Roddy Remington, this is my boyfriend, Flynn Braden." Her pulse quickened with the word *boyfriend* in a way it hadn't when she'd introduced him in town. Roddy had always been like a second father to her, and she found herself hoping for his approval.

"It's a pleasure." Roddy offered his hand, and Flynn shook it. "Are you related to Zev and Carly Braden?"

"Yes, sir. Zev's my second cousin. You're one of the men responsible for bringing Sutton's dad to the island, right? I've heard a lot about your family."

Roddy laughed low and knowing. "Stick around long enough, and you'll have stories of your own to tell."

"I'm already penning a list."

"Dad played a prank on Archer this morning, and Flynn was at the center of it," Sutton said.

"Ah, so you've survived the Steele initiation." Roddy chuckled. "Congratulations, son. Sutton's pretty special, and you'd've had a hard time on this island if you'd failed that test. I look forward to getting to know you better. Where are y'all headed?"

"I was going to show Flynn Archer's boat."

"I'll walk with you." Roddy picked up the box. "I'm heading down there now to meet some of the boys to decorate it."

"That's nice of you," Flynn said. "Want me to carry that box?"

"No thanks, son. Gotta keep these old muscles working."

"You're decorating his boat?" Sutton asked. "Archer doesn't let anyone touch that boat."

"I wasn't born yesterday. I'm well aware of that fact." Roddy shrugged. "But I'm just the lights guy."

They made their way down to the boat. Sutton pointed to Archer's boat, and Flynn whistled. "That's a beauty."

"I didn't think anything could measure up to the boat or the winery vines in Archer's eyes until he fell for Indi," Sutton said.

"Ain't that the truth," Roddy added.

"Hey, gorgeous!" Wells hollered from the deck where he was hanging a JUST MARRIED sign off the railing.

"Hi, handsome," Roddy hollered back, and they laughed.

"That's Wells Silver," Sutton explained. "Leni dated him in high school. He's a good guy, but a bit of a player."

"Is he the brother of the guy who was your first kiss?" Flynn asked.

"That'd be Fitz Silver," Roddy said, and headed up the boat ramp chuckling.

"Got to love small-town gossip," she said as they followed him onto the boat. Wells, Grant, and their friend Brant, one of Roddy's sons, came over to greet them. Wells and Brant were as clean cut as Grant was shaggy haired. "Hi, guys."

"Good to see you, beautiful." Brant, a blue-eyed boatbuilder, kissed her cheek. "Give me that box, old man." He took the box from Roddy and set it down.

"Hey, Sut." Grant hugged her, his serious gaze curiously assessing Flynn.

"Get in here." Wells tugged her into his arms, hugging her tight. "Damn, you even smell good."

She rolled her eyes and tried to ignore the nervousness in her stomach as she introduced them to Flynn. "Guys, this is my boyfriend, Flynn. Flynn, this is Roddy's son and one of our close friends, Brant, Jules's husband, Grant, and his brother—"

"Wells Silver. Nice to meet you, man." Wells shook his hand with a rascally look in his eyes. "You're Sutton's *boyfriend*, huh? What's with all these outsiders stealing our island girls?"

"Ignore him," Grant said. "You won my wife over last night. It's nice to meet you."

"She's a trip," Flynn said.

"It's nice to meet you, man," Brant said, and shook Flynn's hand.

"You too," Flynn said as Jock and Levi came out of the cabin.

"Hey, Sutton," Jock said, exchanging a look with Levi that she couldn't read as they made their way over.

Her nerves flamed, and she turned to Flynn. "That's Jock and Levi. Jock has the darker hair, and Levi's the one with the tattoos."

"Guys, this is Flynn, Sutton's boyfriend," Grant said with a serious lilt.

Her brothers gave him a once-over as they shook his hand and exchanged greetings.

"Flynn? Aren't you Sutton's boss?" Levi asked.

"That sounds dicey," Roddy said. "Brant, Wells, let's go take care of these lights."

Wells laughed. "You think I'm missing this?"

"Yes. I am her boss," Flynn said. "And yes, I didn't think she was qualified for the reporting job when we started working together, but your sister has blown me away every day since."

"That sounds dirty," Wells said under his breath.

Jock glowered at Wells.

"You're done, little brother." Grant clapped a hand on Wells's shoulder and dragged him away to join Roddy and the others.

"Listen, Flynn, we all make mistakes," Jock said. "Sutton's a smart woman. If she's with you, then so am I. Life's too short for extra drama."

"I'm with Jock on that," Levi said.

Sutton felt like she might cry and hugged her brothers. "Thank you."

"I appreciate that." Flynn looked at Sutton, adoration gleaming in his eyes. "I think the world of your sister."

"We know." Levi cocked a grin. "We were just messing with you about the boss thing. Daphne and Tara gave us the scoop on you last night."

"I really enjoyed meeting them, and your daughters. They're both firecrackers. Hadley scowls like a pro. If Sutton hadn't already filled me in, I'd've thought she'd learned it from Archer."

Jock shook his head. "She was already a queen scowler when

I met her. Daphne said by the time they left last night, Hadley was following you around."

"She was," Sutton said. "It was the cutest thing."

"She just wanted my cookies," Flynn explained. "So, y'all are decorating the boat?"

"Yeah, we are," Jock said, and he and Levi exchanged smirks.

Sutton crossed her arms. "What are you *really* up to? Are you pranking them?"

"Who, *us?*" Levi asked incredulously.

"We'd never do that on their wedding day," Jock said. "Weddings are sacred."

"*Mm-hm.* I don't even want to know." She reached for Flynn's hand. "Come on. Let's grab lunch before I have to be back."

"Hey, Flynn, you can hang with us when the girls are getting ready and help set up for the wedding," Jock offered.

"Sounds good."

Sutton narrowed her eyes, pointing at them. "Don't you dare do anything bad to him."

"Levi, didn't we just say life is too short for extra drama?" Jock asked.

"Yes, brother, I believe we did," Levi said.

"I can't…" Sutton shook her head. "Let's go, Flynn."

"See you later," Flynn said.

As they walked away, Levi said, "We look forward to it."

Chapter Thirty

JULES AND LENI'S childhood bedroom was bustling with activity as the girls put the final touches on their hair and makeup, and Tara moved stealthily around the room taking pictures. Indi looked stunning in a sleek and simple backless ivory spaghetti-strap, mermaid-style silk gown. Her blond hair spilled over her shoulders in gentle waves as her sister, Meredith, and their mother, Monica, fawned over her. Since she and Archer were having an intimate family wedding, there was no best man or maid of honor, no groomsmen or bridesmaids, which meant no bridesmaid gowns.

All the girls looked beautiful in dresses of different styles and lengths. Joey and Hadley were coloring at the table. Joey was adorable in a fluffy pale blue dress with her biker boots, and Hadley was pretty in pink all the way down to her sandals. She and Daphne wore matching cap-sleeved dresses with shiny ribbons around their waists. Sutton felt the tug of longing that had been happening more often since Hadley had come into their lives, and Flynn's voice whispered through her mind. *I'm happy with my life. I want to stay close to family, continue to travel, and maybe have a family of my own one day.* She wanted all those things, too, and she was pretty sure she wanted them with him.

But she was getting ahead of herself. She turned toward the full-length mirror, taking one last look at her seafoam chiffon dress with a fine mesh overlay and plunging neckline. She turned her back to the mirror and looked over her shoulder at the lace-up back.

"Let me take a look, honey." Her grandmother moved behind her, stylish as ever in gorgeous wide-legged black pants with a matching cropped, short-sleeved silk jacket overtop a pale yellow blouse, with one of her colorful signature silk scarves. Her makeup was impeccable, her pixie styled to a T. Her pearl accessories pulled it all together.

Her grandmother fiddled with the ties on the back of her dress, then turned her by the shoulders and looked her over from head to toe. "Sweetheart, that beautiful man of yours is going to lose his mind when he sees you in that dress."

"Thanks, Gram. I hope so."

"What is this *hope* nonsense?" Leni asked, coming over to join them. She looked like a million bucks in a dark wine sleeveless dress that had a ruffled slit along one side. "We all look hot, and all of our men are going to lose their minds."

"I know mine is," Jules called out as she fiddled with her hair. "I tried my dress on last night just so he could strip it off me." She looked sexy in a pale yellow dress with a fitted bodice and slim shoulder straps.

"Oh *my*," Indi's mother said.

"What? That's the best part of getting a new dress," Jules said. "Right, Tara?"

Tara blushed a red streak. "*Mm-hm.*"

"Heck yeah it is," Leni agreed.

"You'll have to excuse my girls, Monica," their mother said.

"They get it from me," their grandmother said, making them all laugh.

"I guess that's where I get it from, too," Indi said. "Sorry, Mom, but I cannot wait to get to the boat and have my *husband* rip off my dress."

"The first flaw in your thinking is that Archer will wait that long," Leni said. "We all know he's going to drag you into a dark corner of the vineyard or his office in the winery."

"He totally is," Sutton said.

"I hope so." Indi giggled. "And don't tell me you don't hope Flynn is going to do the same to you."

"I plead the Fifth," Sutton said, and her mind skipped happily down that sexy street.

"Honey, there's no mistaking the way you two have been looking at each other," her mother said.

"That man practically salivates every time he looks at you," Daphne said.

"It's called passion, dear," her grandmother said. "It's no wonder you two went head-to-head for so long. Passionate people can't turn it off. Their passion carries over from their work and family to *all* the things they care about."

"That's true," her mother said. "Look at Leni's protectiveness and Jules's need to spread happiness like fairy dust."

"Exactly," her grandmother said. "And, Sutton, you've been passionate about reporting and making a difference since you were a little girl. I think you and Flynn tried to smother the fire in your bellies that was meant for each other with hatred, and it didn't work, because there was no hate."

"You know what they say," Jules chimed in. "There's a thin line between love and hate. Maybe you've loved each other this whole time."

"No, we definitely *did not*." Sutton looked at her grand-mother, and although she'd always been private about her intimate life, she wanted to tell the truth. "But I think Gram's right. All those times we challenged each other, we were stoking the fire, until we couldn't hold back anymore. But everything has moved so fast. We went from hate to"—*love?*—"being crazy about each other in the snap of a finger, and now I can't imagine my life without him. That's scary."

"Love is supposed to be scary," Meredith said. "If it weren't, we wouldn't want it as badly as we do."

"The man came all the way here last night to win you back, Sutton," Indi reminded her. "That's the equivalent of Archer showing up at that first brunch with my parents."

"That was serious weak-knee stuff, sissy," Jules said.

"I know. I was there." Sutton looked around at their caring gazes. "So you guys don't think I'm nuts for feeling this way so fast?"

"I totally think you're nuts," Leni said. "You went into the Amazon rainforest with some guy you barely knew. No sane person does that."

Sutton's brow furrowed. "So, what are you saying?"

"Honestly? That I'm kind of jealous," Leni exclaimed. "*I'm* the brave one, and there's no freaking way I'd ever do that."

Everyone laughed.

"Seriously, though, Sut," Leni said more gently. "I think I know why you haven't dated in forever. Your heart was tied up in Flynn before either of you knew it."

Sutton thought so, too.

"But the jury is *still* out on him," Leni warned.

"How can you say all that nice stuff and then add that to it?" Daphne asked.

"Because someone has to make the guys think their balls are on the line," Leni said.

"*Leni*," her mother chided.

"What? It's true," Leni insisted. "So they never forget how special we are."

"Honey, look around you," her mother said. "Do you see a single weak woman in this room? Because what I see is a room full of strong, loyal, compassionate women, who not only stand up for themselves but for each other."

"Darn right we are," Jules exclaimed, and everyone concurred.

Leni looked at Sutton and said, "As true as that may be, a little backup never hurt."

"You're never going to change, and I love that about you." Sutton hugged her. "Just so you know, Flynn does, too."

"Great," Leni said sarcastically. "There goes my street cred."

They all laughed.

"And now Flynn's going to be waiting for you at the bottom of the stairs," her grandmother reminded her.

Sutton thought of all the years she'd been getting ready for events with her sisters, and other than high school dances, she'd never had anyone waiting downstairs for her. "I've got butterflies."

"That's how you know it's real," her mother said. "I still get butterflies when your father walks into a room."

"You're making me nervous. Let's stop talking about me. This is Indi's big day," Sutton said. "Indi, have you and Archer decided on where you're going for your honeymoon yet?" They'd decided to take their honeymoon in the winter when her cosmetic shop and the winery were slower.

"We're still tossing around ideas," Indi said. "We don't care where we go, as long as there's a king-size bed and room service."

Daphne made a gagging sound. "Excuse me." She ran into the bathroom, and everyone exchanged concerned glances.

"Did she eat something bad?" their mother asked.

"I didn't see her eat anything. I hope it's not the stress of coordinating the wedding," Indi said. "She's been working so hard."

Their mother knocked on the bathroom door. "Honey, are you okay?"

They heard her retching.

"Is Mama sick again?" Hadley asked.

"Has she been sick today, Had?" Leni asked.

Hadley nodded. "She's been sick a lot. Daddy talks to her belly, and it makes her feel better."

Their eyes bloomed wide.

"Does he do that a lot, Had?" Sutton asked.

Hadley nodded, eyes trained on her coloring book. "Every night."

The bathroom door opened, and all those wide, happy eyes turned to Daphne.

"What? Did I get something on my dress?" She looked down at her dress.

"Hadley told us that Jock talks to your belly," Jules exclaimed. "Are you…?"

Jules looked at Hadley, and Sutton was glad Jules knew enough to keep that last part under wraps, leaving Hadley out of the secret.

"Oh gosh. *Um*…" Daphne looked happy and worried at once, smiling and nervously covering her mouth.

"That's a yes," their grandmother said.

Daphne winced. "We were waiting until after the weekend to tell everyone because we didn't want to steal Indi and Archer's thunder."

"You're not stealing it; you're *sharing* it. I'm so excited for you," Indi exclaimed.

"In that case…" Daphne's eyes danced with delight. "We're having *twins*."

Jules squealed, and everyone talked at once, hugging and congratulating Daphne.

"No wonder you've been sick. That's a double dose of hormones," their mother said.

"Peppermint tea helped me with morning sickness," Meredith said.

"I'll try anything," Daphne said.

"How is Jock handling the news?" their mother asked.

"He's over the moon, but he checks on me every hour. Sometimes it drives me a little crazy, but after all he's been through, I understand. And after going through my first…with a man who wasn't excited about any of it, I don't mind being driven a little crazy."

"I'm so happy for your little family." Their mother hugged her. "And for our big family."

"These little ones are going to be so loved," their grandmother said.

"They already are." Daphne was beaming. "You should see how many books on babies and pregnancy Jock bought. The man is obsessed."

"Aunt Daphne, you're having two babies?" Joey asked.

"Are we getting a baby, Mama?" Hadley asked excitedly.

"*Shoot*," Daphne whispered. She crouched between Joey's and Hadley's chairs. "Yes, we're having *two* babies. They're growing in Mommy's belly, and you're going to be a big sister, Had."

"I'm gonna be a big sister?" Hadley exclaimed. "I'll be a *good* sister!"

"I know you will, baby," Daphne said. "I guess I have to stop calling her baby."

"Nonsense," their mother said. "Children grow up, but in our hearts they're always our babies."

Everyone made a big deal over Hadley becoming a big sister, and Hadley beamed at them, rattling on about things she'd do with the babies.

"Tara, can we tell them our news since Daphne said she's having *two* babies?" Joey asked.

Crimson spread over Tara's cheeks. "I think you just did," she said, sparking more excitement as everyone converged on her and congratulated Joey on becoming a big sister.

"Should we move your wedding date up?" Daphne asked.

"Actually, we were hoping to put off the wedding until after the baby is born so we can focus on Joey and getting ready for our new little one."

"I think that's a fabulous idea," their mother said.

"When are you guys due?" Sutton asked.

Daphne said, "November fourteenth," at the same time Tara said, "November ninth."

"Fall babies. How wonderful," their grandmother said. "But, Daphne, twins may come early."

"I know," Daphne said.

"I need to get pregnant right away so our babies can grow up together!" Jules exclaimed. "We should *all* get pregnant!"

"No, we should not," Leni said. "Some of us have things to accomplish before we have babies, but I'm super happy to be an aunt again."

"*Three* times," Indi said.

Sutton felt another pang of longing as they chatted about babies, and Joey and Hadley went back to coloring.

Leni lowered her voice, asking Tara, "How's Levi taking it? Were you guys trying?"

Tara shook her head. "I was afraid to tell him, but I couldn't *not* tell him. One night we were sitting on the deck, and I just blurted it out. He got teary eyed, and I thought he was upset." Her eyes teared up. "But he was just overwhelmed with happiness. He wants a big family, too. I'm glad Joey is just as happy as we are."

"Oh, honey. We all are." Their mother hugged her, and everyone chimed in with their support.

There was a knock at the door, and everyone froze.

"Can we *not* say anything until after the wedding, please?" Daphne pleaded. "Jock would feel horrible if he took any attention away from Archer."

"Same with Levi," Tara said.

"Of course. Mum's the word," their mother said as she went to the door.

Their father stood on the other side, handsome in a dark suit with a coral tie that matched their mother's dress. He whistled, raking his gaze down their mother's body. "You are even more beautiful than the day I married you." He leaned in for a kiss, and there was a collective, "*Aw.*"

Sutton warmed at the love she'd never tire of seeing between her parents.

Hadley and Joey popped to their feet, and Joey said, "Grandpa, do you like our dresses?" They twirled in circles.

"They're almost as pretty as you are." He scooped Hadley

up and pulled Joey into a one-armed hug.

"We're gonna be big sisters!" Hadley exclaimed. "Mommy and Aunt Tara have babies in their bellies!"

Shock and joy lifted his features. Tara gasped, and Joey said, "Hadley! That was a secret!"

"It's my fault! I should have talked to her." Daphne rushed over to them. "Hadley, honey, we're not talking about the babies tonight. It's time for Indi and Archer's wedding, and the babies need to be our special secret until tomorrow, okay?"

With a mask of seriousness only a grandparent could pull off, her father said, "That's an awfully big secret for such a little girl to hold in. I'm not sure Hadley is big enough to keep a secret like that."

"I *am* big enough!" Hadley insisted. "I'm gonna be a *big* sister. I can keep a *big* secret."

"I don't know, Had. You're going to see a *lot* of people tonight," he said. "Are you sure you can lock it up and throw away the key?"

She nodded and pressed her lips together, then twisted her fingers beside them like she was locking them and pretended to throw the key away.

"I'll make sure she doesn't tell anyone," Joey offered.

"Thank you," Tara and Daphne said in unison.

"Now that that's settled, who's ready for their grand entrance?" her father asked as he put Hadley down, and she and Joey cheered, "Me!" and jumped up and down.

As Indi and the others decided the order for descending the stairs, Sutton sidled up to her father. "Dad, please tell me the guys didn't do something horrible to Flynn."

His expression warmed. "Darlin', that fine young man is downstairs waiting with bated breath to see you."

"No bruises or kick-me signs on his back?"

"Not that I saw. Just a look of something pretty special in his eyes. You look beautiful, angel."

She warmed with the endearment, but a worry crept in. "Thanks, Dad. Are you disappointed in me for getting together with my boss?"

He looked at her with disbelief and compassion. "Darlin', I have never been disappointed in you a day in your life. I know you wouldn't be risking everything you've worked so hard for if you didn't think he was worth it."

She got choked up, but managed, "Thanks, Dad."

"You've worked hard at being *the good one* your whole life."

"I haven't…" The look on her face told her denying it would fall on deaf ears.

"Don't think your mom and I haven't noticed and appreciated it." He embraced her, whispering, "But you've only got *one* life, angel, and you deserve to be happy."

"Let's go, you two," Leni said. "We've got a wedding to put on!"

There was a rush of commotion as they made their way into the hall. Tara and Joey were the first to go downstairs, so Tara could take pictures of everyone else. Levi's whistle rang out, followed by appreciative murmurs. The butterflies in Sutton's stomach swarmed as she waited her turn. More whistles and compliments floated up the stairs as the others headed down.

When it was Sutton's turn, she took a deep breath, making her way slowly down the stairs, holding the railing because she didn't trust her wobbly knees. Flynn's handsome face came into view. The look of adoration in his eyes was inescapable. The thrum of their connection, which she knew so well, wrapped around her like a lasso, filling her with surety and happiness, sending her anxiety skittering away.

Flynn took her hand as she came off the last step, boldly taking a long, lascivious look at her, while Tara took pictures, and her brothers watched on. His lips curved into a wolfish grin. "*Damn*, Steele. You sure clean up nice."

She arched a brow, drinking him in, in his new shirt and slacks, and the tie that matched her dress perfectly. "You're not so bad yourself, Braden."

He drew her into his arms, his big hands blazing on her bare back as he whispered, "Seafoam green is my new favorite color. I bet it'll look great on your bedroom floor." He pressed a kiss to her cheek and tucked her beneath his arm, leaving her heart full and her body reeling as they stepped back to let Meredith's husband and children move forward.

Chapter Thirty-One

FLYNN SAT WITH Sutton by the vineyard with her and Indi's families, waiting for the ceremony to begin. He had a pocket full of tissues, thanks to Steve, who had passed them out to all the men when they were setting up for the wedding. Flynn had always found weddings to be overblown. As if a couple's entire relationship would be judged based on a few hours and a show they put on for others. But after helping Sutton's father, brothers, sisters' significant others, and friends prepare for the wedding, hanging lights, setting up tables and chairs, and erecting easels with beautiful photos of Archer and Indi—as many laughing as arguing—Flynn's only thought was, *This is how to put on a wedding.* It was simple, elegant, and all about family and friends. They'd adorned wine barrels with beautiful flowers that trailed down the sides and strategically placed more barrels around the perimeter of the patio to be filled with ice for bottles of champagne. Tables were draped in white, decorated with gorgeous white lilies and red roses, and twinkling lights were strung in the trees around the patio and along the stone wall between the vineyard and the winery. The bottoms of glass vase centerpieces were encased in small rustic wine barrels that Grant had made, each one featuring a photo of Archer and Indi with their friends and/or family.

Flynn glanced across the lawn at Archer, standing with the officiant by the vines in front of a stunning wooden arch Levi had built and they'd decorated with more lilies and roses. Archer was probably one of the gruffest men he'd ever met, and he definitely had a flash of temper when it came to protecting the people he loved, but Flynn had learned that Sutton was right. Beneath Archer's beastly exterior was a big, loving heart. When they were setting up for the wedding, he'd told Flynn about his grandfather and how much it meant to him to get married on the grounds where his grandfather had taken him under his wing. They'd talked about Flynn's grandfather, too, and Archer had left him with one piece of advice. *Don't assume he'll always be there.*

Flynn tucked that thought away for now, as Tara, pretty in a pastel-blue halter dress, took a picture of Indi's brother, his wife, and their baby girl and turned their way, snapping pictures of Sutton's family. Levi was sitting with Joey, to Flynn's left, watching Tara with a palpably loving expression. Flynn peered around Sutton at Leni and Raz, who were whispering to each other, and just beyond them Jock sat with Hadley on his lap, beside Daphne. Hadley had one arm around Jock's neck, and she was touching Daphne's belly. He was glad he hadn't missed this. Sutton might have felt a little lost among her paired-off siblings, and if he had it his way, she'd never feel lost again.

He laced his fingers with Sutton's, and whispered, "Archer looks nervous." He nodded in her brother's direction. Archer's hands were opening and closing, and he was staring at the back door of the winery, as if he could will Indi to walk through it.

"He's probably afraid Indi will get cold feet."

He squeezed her hand. "That's not going to happen. She's

crazy about him."

"I know." She leaned in and kissed him.

"And I'm pretty crazy about you."

"I know that, too," she said cheekily.

As he moved to kiss her, the "Wedding March" started. Everyone turned to watch as the winery doors opened, and Indi walked out on her father's arm. She looked beautiful in a white silk gown and a long lace veil. Archer drew his shoulders back, standing taller, watching her every step. Flynn tried to imagine what that must feel like, watching the love of his life on their wedding day. He didn't have to try too hard. All he had to do was picture Sutton in a beautiful white gown.

He held her hand a little tighter, as Indi's father hugged her, then gave Archer an approving nod and went to sit down. Now it was Sutton squeezing Flynn's hand. Archer stood in front of Indi and lifted the veil, revealing—*Bellamy?* Gasps rang out, Archer's hands fisted, and his face turned to fire, as Bellamy said, "Hi, future hubby!"

Archer whipped around, storming toward Jock and Levi. "I'm going to kill you."

Jock and Levi scrambled to their feet, waving their hands, saying it wasn't them, and Indi ran out from the vines and snagged Archer's wrist, shouting, "Bananas! Bananas!"

"What's going on?" Flynn asked Sutton, but she was laughing too hard to answer, as were Leni and the other girls.

"Fuck bananas," Archer fumed. "They're *dead*."

"It was me!" Indi threw herself between him and his brothers, pushing at his chest, while his bulging muscles threatened to shred his suit coat. "It was my prank, not theirs! I promise! It was me, Archer! It was me!"

"Dude, she's *not* lying!" Jock held up his hands in surrender, walking backward.

"Look around you," Levi insisted.

Jules and Bellamy were high-fiving and giggling, and the other girls were doubled over in their seats, cracking up. Even their parents and Sutton's grandmother were chuckling. If looks could kill, the girls would be flat out as Archer shot visual daggers at all of them. He turned those cold eyes on Indi. She flashed the sweetest, happiest, most loving smile. Like balm to a wound, Archer's hands unfurled, and his angry eyes softened.

"It was me. Jock and Levi refused to prank you on our wedding day."

"Smart men," Archer snarled. "I should marry Bellamy just to get back at you, you sexy little brat."

Indi stepped closer to him. "You wouldn't dare."

"No shit," he gritted out. "Now get your ass down there and let's try this again."

"Daddy Dock!" Hadley shouted. "Uncle Archer said a bad word!"

As Jock and Daphne hushed her, Indi arched a brow at her future husband and said, "Excuse me, but where is my *please*?"

Archer closed his eyes for a beat, his chest expanding with a deep inhalation. When he opened his eyes, love radiated from them. "Please let me have this moment to watch my future wife walk down the aisle."

Her smile widened, and ten minutes later Archer got his wish, turning all those chuckles to sniffles and tears as he and Indi exchanged vows and rings, and the officiant said, "I now pronounce you husband and wife. You may kiss your bride."

Whoops and cheers rang out as Archer kissed the living daylights out of Indi.

Chapter Thirty-Two

ALL OF THEIR close friends and some of their extended family had shown up for the reception, which was in full swing. The first dance had long passed, toasts had been made, and dinner had already been eaten and cleared away. Lights twinkled against the clear night sky, and conversation, laughter, and music filled the air as Sutton danced with Leni, Indi, and Keira to "I Gotta Feeling" by the Black Eyed Peas.

Jules and Bellamy twirled into their group, and Jules belted out, "*Tonight's gonna be the best night! We're living it up.*" She shimmied her shoulders. "*I got my honey. He's gonna get it up. I'm gonna ride him, like, oh yeah, baby. On the couch, gonna ride him hard, make a baby. Gonna have an O-O-O-O—*"

They all cracked up and threw their hands in the air, bouncing up and down, singing Jules's lyrics and laughing. Sutton looked toward the bar, where her brothers had dragged Flynn and Raz off a little while ago. She spotted Flynn and Raz watching them. Flynn was holding up his phone like he was taking a video of Sutton and the girls. She amped up her sexy dancing, whipping her hair around and swinging her hips. Then she turned to the girls and pointed to Flynn and Raz. As Sutton and the girls danced their hearts out, Flynn and Raz ate it up.

When the song ended, Jules and Bellamy ran over to Tara, who was taking pictures, and the rest of them headed off the dance floor together.

"That was fun." Leni fanned her face. "But I need a drink."

"Yeah, right. You just want some *Razz*matazz." Indi waggled her brows.

"Who can blame her?" Keira said, her light brown hair falling over the shoulders of her plum-colored dress. "That man is freaking hot."

"I thought you swore off men because they created drama," Sutton asked.

"I did, but that doesn't mean I lost the ability to ogle them," Keira said. "Don't think I haven't noticed your cousins. Talk about tall, dark, and handsome glasses of champagne. *Gimme, gimme.* I swear they get better looking every time I see them."

Sutton followed Keira's gaze to three of her aunt Faye's sons, Reggie, Jesse, and his twin, Brent. She and Flynn had seen their brother Finn, his twin sister, Fiona, her husband, Jake, and their baby, Cannon, earlier. Talk about six degrees of separation, Jake was another relative of Flynn's.

"And don't get me started on *your* man, Sutton," Keira said, drawing her attention back to the conversation. "I can't believe it took you a year and a half to get with him. If that guy were trying to get me fired, I'd've jumped his bones ages ago just to win him over."

"That's a load of crap," Leni said. "You would've decked him."

Sutton nodded in agreement. "You totally would have."

"They're right," Indi said. "You might be petite, but you've got *big* opinions, and you don't hold back."

Keira lifted her chin proudly. "What can I say? I went to the

Leni Steele School of Attitudes." She looked over Sutton's shoulder and leaned in, lowering her voice. "Here come the matchmakers."

Sutton turned as her mother approached with her aunt Faye, who was big and beautiful, like her mother, and could pass for her mother's blond sister. They were with Keira's mother, Margot Silver, and Gail Remington. Margot and Gail looked like they were from different worlds. Margot was tall and lean and always impeccably put together, from her perfectly coiffed light brown bob and expensive jewelry to her designer dress and thousand-dollar heels, though she was anything but pretentious, and Gail was the epitome of laid-back, with her wild gray and brown curls and free-flowing earthy fashion.

"Hello, ladies," Margot said, beautiful in a long black dress with lace shoulders.

"Hi," they said in unison.

"We heard about your prank, Indi," Gail said. "That was gutsy."

"I *had* to do it." Indi grinned proudly. "My *husband* is the king prankster. It's only fitting that I prove myself to be the queen."

"Well, sweetheart, you definitely did that," Sutton's mother said. "Are you enjoying the reception?"

Indi's eyes lit up. "*Yes.* I'm so glad everyone could be here to celebrate with us."

"As if we'd miss one of our boys' weddings?" Gail said.

"Sutton, your new beau is quite a catch," Margot said.

"He was telling us about your time in the rainforest. How exciting was that?" Gail asked.

"It was terrifying, but it was also exciting," she admitted.

"Especially the nights," Leni chimed in.

"*Oh*, is *that* where you two got together?" Faye asked.

Sutton gave her aunt a deadpan look. "Don't pretend my mother hasn't already filled you in. I know how things work around here."

Her mother and the ladies shared a confirmatory glance and giggle.

"Well, you *are* like our daughter, too," Faye said.

"I'm not complaining, Aunt Faye. I'm just saying there's no need to pretend."

"You're right, honey. Why pretend?" Margot eyed Keira. "Sweetheart, did you see Faye's boys? They sure have grown into handsome young men. You know, Jesse and Brent *are* in the restaurant business. You have that in common with them. Right, Faye?"

Keira rolled her eyes.

"Yes, and I have to admit, I'd really like to see my boys get married," Faye said. "Reggie is getting a little long in the tooth."

"Wouldn't it be lovely if Keira and one of your boys got together?" Margot suggested. "We could be related."

Sutton and Leni chuckled.

"Mom, *please* stop. I told you, I'm not dating right now," Keira said. "I think I could use that drink now, girls. Excuse us." She stalked away.

"She is relentless," Indi said as they made their way toward the bar.

"Tell me about it," Keira said. "Ever since Jules and Grant got married, she's been hungry for more weddings. She tried to set Wells and Fitz up with tourists a few weeks ago."

"I'm sure they didn't mind," Leni said.

"Keira!" Five-year-old Ritchie Lacroux ran over and grabbed Keira's hand, blinking wide, excited eyes up at her from beneath his thick, wavy hair. "Will you dance with me?"

Keira's smile reached her eyes. "I would love to dance with you. Sorry, girls, looks like I'll get that drink later."

"You *know* Ryan put him up to that," Leni said as they watched their friend walk away. Ritchie's uncle Ryan Lacroux was his legal guardian, and the hottest cop on the island. He was raising him for his brother, who had substance abuse issues. Ryan had been stopping by Keira's café, the Sweet Barista, for months, asking her to make special treats for his nephew. Keira said there was nothing more to it, but Leni and Sutton thought otherwise. Unfortunately, Keira saw Ryan as drama waiting to happen.

Sure enough, Ryan sidled up to Keira and Ritchie as they reached the dance floor and put a hand on Keira's back. She extracted herself by moving to Ritchie's other side and glanced over her shoulder at Sutton and Leni with a wincing expression.

"Fifty bucks says they end up together," Leni said.

Sutton watched the three of them dancing. "But she hates drama as much as you do, and kids are cute little bundles of drama."

"And yet I ended up with a guy who creates drama everywhere he goes by simply existing." Leni raised her brows.

"That's true," Indi said.

Sutton looked at Leni like she'd lost her mind. "That doesn't sound like a profitable bet for us."

"Damn it." Leni leaned closer as they walked toward the bar. "Let's get the guys to bet with us."

"And make it a hundred bucks," Indi said.

As they approached the bar, Sutton watched Flynn doing a shot with her brothers and warmed all over. She hadn't realized how badly she'd wanted her family to like him or how big an impact it would have on her if they did.

Flynn looked over, and their eyes connected with that pulsing heat she swore had become a part of them. A hopeful future played out in her mind. She imagined meeting Flynn's family, sitting around a bonfire with them making up stories, attending Levi and Tara's wedding together, and at some point, Raz and Leni's wedding, too. She pictured taking the ferry home together in the fall to meet Daphne's and Tara's new babies.

"There's my glamour girl." Flynn reached for her hand, drawing her from her fantasy into a kiss. "I missed you," he whispered in her ear.

Oh, her heart…

"I missed you, too. Are you having an okay time?" she asked quietly.

"I'm having a great time, and I'm glad you're with me now. That table of women over there has been checking me out for the past half hour."

He motioned with his chin to a table of her grandmother's friends sitting to their left, drinking wine with mischievous expressions. The ladies waved to her. Sutton waved back and said, "Take it as a compliment. They're the original Bra Brigade crew, and they're definitely checking you out."

He glanced at them. The ladies lifted their wineglasses as if toasting. "They're not shy, are they?" He flashed a friendly smile and waved.

"Sutton, are you going to let him flirt with the Bra Brigaders?" Raz asked.

"You're just mad that they've got fresh meat to check out," Levi teased.

"Speaking of fresh meat," Sutton said, looking at her brothers. "Thank you for not pranking Flynn."

Archer lifted his chin. "It turns out Miles Long is a pretty cool guy."

"What the hell, Archer?" Raz held up his palms. "I got kidnapped and held over a cliff, and this guy gets a cool stripper name?"

"That wasn't *my* doing," Archer said.

"That was all Steve," Flynn said. "I was just standing there offering to help with breakfast and he saw you coming and said to go with it."

"Nice one, Dad," Jock said, sharing a nod with Levi.

"Our fucking father," Archer grumbled. "I really thought our grandmother had lost her mind."

Flynn laughed. "I spent some time talking with Lenore last night. She's as lucid as we are, but I thought you were going to let me have it."

"I was *this close*." Archer held up his finger and thumb, an inch apart.

"I'm glad you didn't try to rearrange Flynn's face." Sutton smiled at Flynn. "I happen to be very fond of it."

"Thanks, babe." Flynn kissed her.

"Okay, enough mushiness," Leni said. "Archer, how does that ball and chain feel?"

Indi looked amused.

"Pretty fucking great," Archer said.

"You might want to ask him again tomorrow," Indi said. "He freaked out when I brought my toothbrush over before we moved in together. Lord only knows what will happen when he wakes up and sees a ring."

They laughed.

"To Archer, that ring on your finger is a symbol of ownership," Jock pointed out.

"I wasn't talking about *my* ring," Indi said, inciting more chuckles. "Hey, Archer, the girls and I were just waging a bet about Keira and Ryan getting together. Want to get in on it?"

Archer scoffed. "Definitely. They'll never get together. Keira's anti-men."

"But she loves Ritchie," Indi pointed out.

"I'll take that bet. She's always giving Ryan hell," Levi said.

"Jock?" Leni arched a brow.

"I think she's playing hard to get," Jock said.

"Bullshit," Archer said, sparking an animated debate.

Eventually, bets were placed, and Archer whispered something to Indi that made her blush. He hugged her against his side, puffing up like a proud peacock, and said, "Excuse us. We have some *business* to tend to."

"Don't mess up the vines," Jock said as they walked away. "I hear the vintner goes apeshit on anyone who touches them."

Archer flicked him the bird as they walked away.

"I still can't believe he's married," Levi said.

"I can," Sutton said. "They belong together. The question is, when are Leni and Raz heading down the aisle?"

Raz looked lovingly at Leni. "Sometime in the next year. We're just waiting to hear about my filming schedule."

"Maybe we can have a double wedding," Flynn suggested, drawing curious gazes.

Sutton's eyes flew open wider, her emotions reeling. Did she hear him right? Was he serious? Did she want him to be? It was too fast. Wasn't it?

"Hey, that'd be great," Raz said. "Right, Len?"

Leni's brows knitted, but a smile tugged at her lips. "If it's what Sutton wants." Always the protector.

Everyone was looking at Sutton. Her mind spun.

"I…*um*…" Her stomach knotted up, and she looked at Flynn, trying to read his expression, but he just looked…*happy*. "We haven't talked about—"

Flynn's lips quirked. "*Gotcha.*"

The breath rushed from her lungs. "Give a girl a heart attack, why don't ya?" She tried to ignore the pang of disappointment moving through her as her brothers cracked up.

He hugged her. "Sorry, babe. I had to get in on the pranking."

"Gotta love a guy who pranks on the fly," Jock said.

"Damn, Flynn," Raz said. "Way to burst my bubble. I was getting excited."

"You're such a marshmallow when it comes to love," Leni teased him.

Raz pulled her into his arms. "Only since falling for you."

"That's what love does to you. I'm a softie for Tara, too," Levi said.

"That's what she said." Leni laughed at her own joke.

"I think that can be said for all of us," Jock added. "*Not* in the way Leni took it."

Flynn whispered, "Me too, for you," in Sutton's ear, sending a shiver of delight through her.

"Ohmygod. You guys are *so* mushy," Leni said. "I need a shot if we're going to make it through any more of this."

They toasted to Archer and Indi, and with only the six of them within earshot, Leni and Sutton congratulated Levi and Jock on their growing families, and they toasted to them, too. They toasted new friends, honoring Flynn, and then they joked around before going their separate ways to chat with friends.

Flynn and Sutton mingled their way around the reception.

When the song "Beautiful Things" by Benson Boone came on, Flynn took Sutton's hand and led her onto the dance floor.

He twirled her in his arms, gazing deeply into her eyes, and as Benson sang about not wanting to lose the woman he loved, Flynn said, "Did I freak you out with what I said about a double wedding?"

She swallowed hard, so crazy about him, she could barely see straight. "I wouldn't say I was freaking out. I was just surprised that you were thinking in that direction. But then you said you were joking, so…"

"I was joking, but would it scare you to know I'm hoping we'll get there someday?"

Goose bumps chased over her skin. "No. I hope we will, too."

A smile crept across his handsome face. "Good."

He kissed her, and then she rested her head on his chest as they swayed to the music, reveling in the surety of them and the feel of his heart beating against her cheek.

Hadley and Ritchie ran by giggling, and Joey followed as the song came to an end and a faster one came on. Flynn twirled her again, and she laughed. He gathered her in his arms, swaying seductively, as if it were a slow song. His hands slid down to the small of her back, and every ounce of her longed for his touch.

"I'm really glad I pissed you off, Steele."

She arched a brow. "Why is that?"

"Because I got to spend this time with you, and meet your awesome family, and see you with them and with your friends. I like learning things about you and seeing who you are with the people you love most. I want to experience everything with you."

Her heart felt like it might burst. She wanted to experience everything with him, too. "Everything?"

"*Everything*," he whispered.

"Then what do you say we get out of here?"

"Won't your family get upset if we leave?"

"Are you kidding? My family is probably celebrating the fact that I finally brought a guy home."

"A great guy," he teased.

"The *best* guy." She went up on her toes and kissed him.

SUTTON CLUNG TO Flynn's hand like she was never going to let him go, and he hoped she never would as they hurried to the edge of the patio. She snagged a bottle of champagne from a barrel of ice and made a beeline past the stone wall, stealing glances over her shoulder.

She was so damn cute, tugging him between a row of vines. She shoved the champagne bottle into his hands. "Hold this." Using his arm for leverage, she quickly took off her heels and plucked them off the ground. She snagged his hand again, hazel eyes glittering in the moonlight. "*Let's go!*"

They ran to the end of the row, and she didn't slow down as she said, "*This way*," and bolted to the left.

Driven by lust and love and everything in between, they ran hand in hand, the salty sea air filling their lungs as they passed row after row of vines, laughing and slowing only long enough to steal a few kisses. They ran all the way to the end of the vineyard and kept going until they got to a hill.

"Up here!" She led him through a group of trees, ducking

beneath branches as they hurried along what looked like remnants of an old path. They wound through more trees, eventually coming to a grassy knoll. Sutton dropped her heels and grabbed her side, trying to catch her breath.

He set down the bottle. "I had no idea you could run like the wind."

"It's been a long time." She laughed and blew out a breath.

"It's beautiful here. Is this your secret make-out spot?"

"No. It's my secret reading spot. I've never shown it to anyone. Not even Leni." She lowered her gaze briefly, her long lashes fluttering as she lifted her eyes to his again, full of desire. "But I'd like it to be our secret make-out spot."

She looked so beautiful, wearing her heart on her sleeve. He slid an arm around her waist, drawing her closer, and threaded his other hand into her hair. "I'm honored. Do I get to defile the untouchable Sutton Steele on Silver Island?"

"Shut up and kiss me," she said through a laugh.

His lips came down over hers, sweet and slow, savoring their connection. She moaned, going up on her toes, trying to take as much as she gave. Every slide of their tongues, every sinful sound she made, lured him deeper into her, until her breaths became his, and he ached to be inside her. Reaching behind her, he untied the back of her dress and slipped it off her shoulders. It puddled at her feet, and goose bumps rose on her skin. He helped her step out of the dress and held her against him, taking her in deep, passionate kisses. His hands moved over her body, warming, caressing, *loving* her until her flesh was hot, and she was groping him, begging for more. He tugged off his tie, and together they worked the buttons on his shirt free. He reluctantly broke the kiss to toe off his shoes and take off his clothes, slowing only long enough to spread out his shirt and strip off her panties.

She sank down to her back, and as he came down over her, his heart spoke. "You look so beautiful wearing your heart on your sleeve." Their mouths came together as their bodies became one, sending rivers of pleasure washing over him. Her mouth fell open with a gratified "*Oh.*"

"God, Sutton. How can we feel this good?"

Her eyes found his again, so full of want and need, it clawed at him. He thrust deeper into her, their mouths colliding. He pushed his arms beneath her, cradling her as they found their rhythm. Their kisses were deep and smoldering, their thrusts passionate and eager. But it was the whole of them, the world they were creating, the feel of her softness against his hard frame, the trust they put in the hands of each other, that had him holding her tighter, loving her harder.

He rolled them onto their sides, hiking her leg over his hip, and cupped her ass. Driving into her slower, deeper. His heart thundered, his emotions as raw as they were powerful. He dipped his head beside hers, grazing her shoulder with his teeth. "*Flynn,*" she said pleadingly. Her fingers dug into his flesh as he quickened his efforts. "I've got you, baby." He held her tighter, loving her more forcefully. Her inner muscles tightened around him, testing his restraint. She panted out, "*Ohgodohgodohgod.*"

"Ride me." He held her hips as he rolled onto his back, still buried deep inside her. He thrust as she pressed her hands to his chest, arching like a goddess in the moonlight as she rode him. Her hair bounced over her breasts. He moved one hand to her clit.

"Oh, *yes*—"

"That's it, baby. Fuck me like you own me."

Her eyes blazed wickedly into his, and they both went a

little wild. He groped her breast, pinching her nipple, and she cried out, "*Again.*" He did it again, and she rode him faster. Just when he felt her thighs tense and her inner muscles clamp down around his cock, *she* pinched *his* nipple, sending a bolt of lightning straight to his balls, severing his restraint at the same moment as her climax consumed her. Every sensation felt new and explosive as they thrust and moaned. Their bodies grew slick despite the cool air, and they lost themselves in a world of pleasure.

When the last aftershock rocked through them, he gathered her in his arms, cocooning her from the chilly air.

"Can we stay right here forever?" she whispered against his neck.

He closed his eyes, soaking in those sweet murmurs. "Absolutely."

Chapter Thirty-Three

THEY DIDN'T QUITE make it forever, but they lay tangled together beneath the stars until the air grew too cold, and Sutton was shivering. Flynn helped her dress, and then he picked up his shirt and held it up for her. "Put this on."

"No, you need it."

"Sutton, I'm fine. I'm always hot around you."

"Lucky me. Thank you," she said as he put it on her.

She looked like a naughty waif in his shirt. He dressed and draped his tie around his neck, wrestling with the feeling that like all their nights together, he wasn't ready for this one to end. All too soon, they'd be back at work again, pretending not to be tumbling down that unexpected hill.

"Can we just sit for a few minutes and drink some champagne?" she asked. "I'm not ready to go back yet."

"It's like you read my mind." He opened the champagne, and they sat on the hill. "To us." He handed her the bottle.

"To us." She took a sip, then handed it back to him.

He took a sip. "What's the plan tomorrow?"

"There's a brunch at my parents' house with Indi's family, and I thought we'd leave after that. I mean, if you can stick around for it."

"There's no place I'd rather be."

"Good." She leaned her head on his shoulder.

He put his arm around her, and they sat for a long time, sipping champagne, gazing out at the gorgeous views of the island and the lighthouse in the distance, its beam sprinkling light over the dark water. For the hundredth time while he was with her, he was struck by an unmatched sense of closeness. Only this time, he had the urge to share it.

"Hey babe, do you mind if I take a picture of us?"

"Why would I mind?"

"Just making sure. I asked Tara if I could see the pictures from the wedding when she's done doing her thing, so I can buy some, but I'd like to send one to my family tonight."

"You want to buy pictures from her?" she asked with surprise.

"*Yes.* You looked so happy with your family. I figured you want some of them, and I know I do." He took out his phone and snapped a picture of them with their heads leaning together, and then he took one while he kissed her, making her laugh, which of course he caught in another picture.

"Can I see them?"

She leaned against him as they scrolled through the pictures, his heart swelling at the light in her eyes in every single one of them.

"We're not a bad-looking couple," she said softly.

"Are you looking at the same pictures I am? How can you look at your beautiful face and say we're *not bad* looking? You're the prettiest woman everywhere you go, and you shine in pictures as brightly as you do in person." She blushed, and he hugged her against his side, kissing her temple. He sent the picture in a group text to his family.

"You're not going to send a message with it?"

"I think the picture speaks for itself."

"Will you send them to me?"

"I think I can manage that." As he texted them to her, his phone vibrated with a string of texts. "Here we go." He and Sutton read them together.

Grandpa: *Try not to muck it up before I get to meet her.*

Noah: *Keep your hands off my woman.*

Clay: *You know she's pretending she's with me.* He sent a devil emoji.

Sutton laughed softly.

Seth: *I'm glad to see you're still going strong. I'm happy for you both.*

Mom: *We can't wait to meet her.*

Victory sent a smiling emoji surrounded by hearts, and *Don't wear her out. We have a shopping date coming up.*

He pocketed his phone.

"Aren't you going to reply?" she asked.

"No. I just wanted them to know we were happy."

"I'm pretty sure Victory knows that already."

"Are you sharing secrets with my sister, Steele?"

"Maybe," she said playfully.

"Good. I'm glad you two are becoming friends. Maybe you can convince her to get out and enjoy life a little more. Maybe she'll even meet a new guy."

"From what I've seen, the right things happen with the right people without any interference from others." She drank some champagne and handed him the bottle.

"You might be right." He took a drink. "Look at us."

"That's what I'm talking about. I'm really glad we didn't like each other for so long."

"Speak for yourself. I was totally digging you from day one. I told you that."

"But you didn't *know* me. That was a physical attraction."

"It was primarily physical, but it didn't take long before you hooked me in with your fierce determination and smart-mouth challenges. But why are you glad we didn't get along?"

"Because if we'd been friendlier to each other, Karen wouldn't have sent us to the rainforest alone, and we could've missed out on all this."

"You mean great sex with your dick of a boss?"

"Well, my boss *is* very talented with that particular body part."

They both laughed, and he held up the champagne. "To my dick and the challenging woman who likes it." He took a swig and handed her the bottle, noticing she was shivering again. He picked up her heels and pushed to his feet. "Come on, Steele. Let's get you into a warm bed." He reached for her hand, helping her up.

"You're always trying to get me naked." She pressed a kiss to his bare chest. "You sure you're not cold?"

"What did I say about when I'm with you?" He gave her ass a pat. "Let's get you home."

The reception was over, and the winery was dark when they got back. As they crossed the lawn between the winery and Sutton's parents' house, they heard giggling and saw Indi and Archer climbing into Archer's truck. Flynn squeezed Sutton's hand. "Guess they had a good time."

"They probably christened every office in the winery. I feel bad for the cleaning crew."

They went in through her parents' kitchen door, and Flynn quietly put away the champagne as Sutton went down the hall to use the bathroom.

"Are you hungry?" Sutton asked when she returned.

"Just for you." He pulled her into his arms and kissed her.

"You have the *best* answers." They went down the hall, and he grabbed her ass as she ascended the staircase ahead of him. She giggled and swatted his hand away, which made him laugh, too. She shushed him, whispering, "I don't want to wake anyone up."

"Does that mean we can't knock on Leni and Raz's door, yell fire, and run away?"

She grinned, and he could tell she was considering it.

He tugged her down the hall. "Come on, Steele. I want to see if that dress looks as good on the floor as I think it will." Unable to wait, he backed her up against her closed bedroom door right there in the hall. "What is it about you that drives me so crazy?"

"Does it matter?" She went up on her toes, meeting him in a scorching kiss that had his body thrumming again. She grabbed hold of his hair, and he growled against her mouth.

"*Fuck.* You know what that does to me."

"Yes, I do," she said coyly. She turned to open the door, and when it opened, something flew toward them. Sutton screamed, stumbling backward into him as the creepiest porcelain doll Flynn had ever seen swung in the doorway from a noose around its neck. Its glass eyes seemed to stare through them. Its face was a web of cracks and burns, and the tip of its nose and its painted-on hair were chipped. It held a tiny rubber knife in its hand, which was missing one finger, and there was a note pinned to its tattered, burned, and filthy jumper that read FLYNN IS MINE.

Her parents and Leni and Raz ran out of their rooms. Leni

hollered, "*What happened?*"

"Our asshole brothers happened." Sutton pointed to the doll. "I'm going to *kill* them. They nearly gave me a heart attack."

Leni and Raz were doing their best to stifle their laughter.

Sutton glowered at them.

"I'm sorry, babe." Flynn pulled Sutton into his arms, caught between amusement and wanting to slaughter her brothers, and realized Leni was eyeing *them*, not the doll, as was her mother. Sutton's hair was a tangled mess, with pieces of grass in it. The back of his shirt she wore had grass stains, and he was shirtless. There wasn't much he could do about that now.

"Dad, where did they find that frigging doll, anyway?" Sutton fumed. "I thought you got rid of it."

"Yes, Steve," her mother said. "I thought you burned that thing ages ago."

"I *did*." Her father was dragging her desk chair over to take down the noose.

"It does have burn marks," Leni said.

"I think it's time for some serious retaliation," Flynn said.

"I want in on that," Raz said.

"We have to come up with something good, and we have to do it when they least expect it," Flynn said.

Her father climbed down from the chair, giving him a serious look. "I don't know if that's a good idea. You'll be opening yourself up to even worse pranks."

"What could be worse than scaring your daughter?" Flynn challenged.

"I don't know, but they always seem to outdo one another." Steve lowered his voice. "You need the original pranksters on board for this."

Leni gasped.

"Who are the originals?" Flynn asked.

"You're looking at one of them," Sutton said. "My dad and his college buddies started the whole pranking thing."

"Roddy and Alexander?"

Her father smirked.

"*Steven*," her mother said sternly. "This is *not* a good idea. I do not want tomorrow ruined."

"I give you my word, darlin'," her father said.

Sutton's phone chimed in her room. She snagged it from the dresser and came back out to the hall. "It's a group text from Archer. *Disco lights and baby shark? Really assholes? I'm going to kill you!*" She looked at Flynn. "That's what the guys were doing on his boat! I knew they were up to something!"

Raz chuckled. "They told me they had a friend make some kind of device that they put under the mattress, so when Archer and Indi got into bed, it set off disco lights and music."

Everyone laughed.

"On that note," her father said. "I think I'll go get rid of this doll."

Sutton exhaled loudly. "Thanks, Dad."

After Steve went downstairs and everyone else went to their rooms, Flynn and Sutton went into hers. He closed the door, and as he drew her into his arms, she buried her face in his chest. "They're such jerks."

"They're brothers, babe. You know they love you. How about I help you forget about the creepy doll?"

She looked up at him with hopeless eyes. "Even you and your magic anaconda can't make me forget that thing."

"But it'll be fun trying."

Chapter Thirty-Four

SUTTON SAT IN her office Monday reading the email from GNN confirming a time for her interview. She was on the fence about accepting, and she wanted to talk to Flynn about it. But she'd have to wait until tonight when they were alone. She closed her personal email program and dove into research.

Hours later, Flynn stalked into her office, those devastating blue eyes twinkling with secret emotions, sending her heart aflutter. With the exception of the creepy doll fiasco, the weekend had been like a dream come true. Having Flynn all to herself and not having to hide their affection or emotions were the best feelings *and* the worst kind of taunt. Now that she'd had a taste of that freedom, she wanted more of it. She didn't mind being back at work, but that part of their reality sucked.

He lifted his chin, speaking earnestly. "*Steele.*"

"Yes, *Braden?*" She feigned annoyance. "Are you hoping to ride me again today? I know you take great pleasure from it."

His eyes narrowed, but his lips quirked. "I do enjoy giving you a *hard* time. But that's not why I'm here. I'm hitting the Beehive for lunch, and I thought you might want to come along to discuss our upcoming projects."

A thrill darted through her, but so did worries. The Beehive was frequented by a lot of LWW staff. "I'm not sure that's a good idea."

"A working lunch." He placed both palms on her desk and leaned closer, whispering, "I want to spend time with you. Now, tell me you will go to lunch with me if you have to, and move that sexy ass of yours."

She smiled and immediately fell back into the role of friendly*ish* colleagues. "If I must." She stood and smoothed her pencil skirt over her hips, reaching for her purse.

"My treat."

Her brows knitted in question.

"It's a write-off," he reassured her.

"Once again, you've thought of everything." She slipped her phone into her pocket and locked her purse in her desk.

"That's why I'm the boss," he said as they left her office.

"As arrogant as ever."

It was a sunny day, and it felt even brighter walking down the street with Flynn, as if there was a spotlight on them. Her anxiety about being caught was messing with her head. She wanted to go back to the weekend, when they could hold hands or touch or kiss without worrying.

Flynn opened the door to the café, waving her in. "After you."

"Thank you." They went to stand in line, and his cell phone rang.

"Excuse me." He put his phone to his ear. "Hello?" He shook his head, his lips tipping up at the corners. "You've got the wrong number. There is no Miles Long here, and I'm not an entertainer for hire."

"Ohmygod," she said as he ended the call, stifling a laugh.

"That's the fourth call today."

"I'm so sorry. My brothers are idiots."

"No, they're not." He smiled. "They're smart and their pranks are good, but they're going to pay for this and for that psycho doll prank."

"Did you and Raz decide on a prank?"

"Not yet, but we're brainstorming with your dad and his buddies."

"Lord help us all."

As Sutton studied the specials on the chalkboard behind the counter, a familiar voice caught her attention. She looked over her shoulder as Karen stepped into line with Aubrey Stewart, one of the original founders of LWW, and the head of the media division.

Sutton's stomach knotted. She felt like there was a sign on her forehead outing her and Flynn as a couple. He touched her lower back, and she nearly jumped out of her skin. She shifted, putting distance between them.

"Why are you so jumpy, Steele?" He motioned to the line having moved forward.

She gave him a tight smile as Aubrey appeared on his other side.

"I thought that was you two," Aubrey said. She was tall, blond, and an absolutely brilliant businesswoman. Everything she touched turned to gold.

"Hi. It's nice to see you. We're just having a working lunch, talking over projects," Sutton said nervously. "Future projects."

"How's it going, Aubrey?" Flynn asked.

He was so calm, cool, and collected, it made Sutton's nervousness even more noticeable.

"I'm well, thank you. Flynn, I got your message about wanting to meet with me. I'll get back to you soon with a date and time. I'm hearing wonderful things about the two of you. Karen mentioned you two nailed your Amazon assignment, but then I saw the footage, and *wow*. That was impressive reporting, Sutton."

Sutton beamed with the compliment. "Thank you. Flynn was great out there, and his filming was incredible."

"Sutton deserves all the credit," Flynn said. "She's a real go-getter. She wasn't afraid to get down and dirty."

Sutton shot him an incredulous look but quickly schooled her expression.

"That's good to hear, about both of you. I heard about the pit viper, Sutton. I'm so sorry you went through that."

"It was terrifying." Sutton flashed back to the cold wave of fear that had consumed her, giving her a distraction from her current worries. "But Flynn knew just what to do."

"I have to tell you, I was on the fence when Karen told me her plan about sending you two there," Aubrey said. "But from what I'm hearing, and seeing you two having lunch together, it appears it was the right thing to do. Sometimes you just have to go with your gut. Flynn, you went above and beyond our expectations, and, Sutton, I knew we made the right decision, moving you into the reporting position."

Guilt coiled tight and painful in Sutton's chest with thoughts of her impending interview. "I truly appreciate the opportunity. I've learned so much."

As the person in front of them paid for their lunch, Aubrey said, "I know Flynn can be a real ballbuster, but with him pushing your limits and making sure you hit your peak on every assignment, there's no telling how far you'll go." She smiled at Flynn. "Keep it up, Flynn."

He cocked a grin. "That's not a problem."

"Enjoy your lunch."

Aubrey walked away, and as they stepped up to the counter, Sutton whispered, "Did everything she said sound dirty?" *Like she knows what we're up to?*

"No. You just have a one-track mind." He put his hand on her lower back and leaned down like he was going to kiss her.

They both froze.

He gritted out a curse and cleared his throat, pretending to brush something off her back. "I think I got it."

"Thanks," she managed, her heart thundering against her ribs. She wanted to look over her shoulder to see if Karen and Aubrey were watching them, but she was afraid to.

They got their lunches and sat at a table by the windows, but Sutton was too nervous to eat. She pushed her salad around in the bowl, trying to figure out how to talk to Flynn about the interview, which now seemed like a really *good* idea. She glanced across the café at Aubrey and Karen chatting animatedly at a table. If they'd noticed anything, they hadn't let on.

"Are you okay, Sut?"

"No," she said softly. "I hate this. My nerves are shot."

His jaw ticked.

"I want to go back to Silver Island, where we don't have to pretend."

"Me too. Sorry about what I did by the register. I thought we could just enjoy lunch together. I didn't think I'd forget like that."

"It's not your fault." She took a deep breath. "Flynn, I need to tell you something."

"That sounds ominous."

"It's not. Or maybe it is. I don't know. The day we went to the rainforest, I submitted my résumé to GNN." His brows slanted, but she continued before she could chicken out. "They got back to me Friday, and I was so upset after seeing that list on your desk, I accepted an interview. Their management team will be in the city Thursday. I was thinking about canceling, but after what just happened, I think it might be best if I go through with it. I don't want you to risk your career because of me."

His expression turned serious. "Take me out of the equation. Are you interested in the job?"

Take him *out* of the equation? He was part and parcel to it. He was the reason she'd applied.

He must have seen her struggling, because he said, "Sutton, this is your career. You've worked your whole life toward one goal. Let's focus on what's important. Are you interested in the job?"

"I don't know. *Yes*, I guess. It's an anchor position, but the description said it would include reporting on location and offers growth."

"Just like your idols. You should definitely explore it." He sat back and took a drink, looking comfortable, while her insides were twisting into knots. "GNN is in LA, but we could do long distance. Unless you're trying to tell me something."

"I'm *not*. I hate all this sneaking around, and I couldn't live with myself if someone found out about us and you lost your job."

His jaw muscles worked double time. "Don't worry about me. I've lived my dreams. It's time for you to live yours. Take the interview, and knock their socks off."

Chapter Thirty-Five

SUTTON TOOK THURSDAY off for her four o'clock interview with GNN, and what had started as *let's meet for lunch* with Leni and Victory, had turned into lunch and a two-hour shopping trip. The music streaming through the speakers in the upscale boutique did little to block out the din of confusion in Sutton's mind about the interview. She plucked a dress off a rack and draped it over her arm with the other outfit she'd chosen and headed for the dressing room.

"Oh, good. You're back," Leni said over her shoulder. She was standing in front of the three-way mirror, her auburn hair spilling down the back of a sleek forest-green dress. "What do you think of this?"

"It's gorgeous, and it looks classy on you, but isn't that the first dress you tried on?"

"*Yes,*" Victory said from behind a dressing-room curtain. "She keeps going back to it, as if she can't afford a hundred of them."

Leni checked herself out in the mirror. "I just want to be sure. Not all of us have closets big enough for seven people's clothes."

"Again, it's not like you and Raz can't afford it." Victory

came out from behind the curtain, looking elegant with her hair twisted up in a bun, wearing cream wide-legged slacks and a snug black sleeveless shirt with a one-shoulder cutout.

"*Wow*, Vic. You look incredible," Sutton said.

Leni moved from in front of the three-way mirror, motioning for Victory to step up to it. "That's a seriously hot outfit. You could take it straight from the boardroom to the bedroom."

Victory strutted over to the mirror. "The boardroom, yes, but it's been so long since I've had a man in my bedroom, I'm not sure I'd know what to do with him."

"Well, if you're looking, you'll have guys lining up in that outfit." Sutton hung the clothes she'd carried in on a hook in a dressing area and closed the curtain to take off her clothes.

"No, thank you," Victory said. "My life is perfect just the way it is. I go to the gym, and to work, and to my favorite restaurant every Thursday night."

"Flynn is worried that you don't have enough fun." She put on a short-sleeve salmon-colored dress and began buttoning it.

"I know. My whole family is," Victory said. "My brothers push me to get out there and meet someone, but I already met the love of my life, and he's gone. I'm not looking for a replacement."

"I get that," Leni said. "Now that I'm with Raz, I can't imagine being with anyone else."

Sutton wrapped the thin leather belt around her waist and stepped out from behind the curtain. "Same with me, so please don't think I'm pushing you."

"I don't." Victory gave her a quick once-over. "That's a great color on you."

Leni peeked out from behind a dressing area curtain. "Oh, it is."

"Flynn and I are hoping to visit your parents when they get back to Ridgeport. Do you think this will be okay? Not too dressy or too casual?"

"It's perfect, but my parents wouldn't care if you showed up in sweats. They're really down to earth. They only care that you treat Flynn well and you guys make each other happy." Victory stepped away from the mirror, allowing Sutton to get a better look at herself.

"That's what Flynn said, but I still want to make a good impression." Sutton looked herself over. "I love the flow of this dress. I think I'll buy it."

"I'm going to get this outfit, too." Victory headed back into her dressing area as Leni came out of hers and said, "I'm taking the green dress."

"Hallelujah," Victory called out.

"I have one more to try on. I'll only be a minute." Sutton headed into her dressing area and took off the dress. She put on her white blouse and tried on a charcoal suit with bold blue windowpane checks and a cinched, belted waist. She slipped on her heels and went to take a look.

Leni and Victory were waiting for her, their eyes widening with appreciation.

"Now, *that's* a suit," Leni said.

"I love windowpanes," Victory said, the two of them circling Sutton, eyeing her from head to toe. "You should wear that to the interview."

"You definitely should," Leni agreed. "You look smart. With your personality, and that suit, you'll win them over."

Sutton's stomach twisted. She looked in the mirror, taking note of her creased brow and the uncertainty in her eyes.

"What's wrong?" Leni asked.

"You don't like it?" Victory asked.

"No, it's beautiful. I just…" She looked at them, needing to talk to someone about what she was feeling, and blurted out, "I'm not even sure I want the job."

"Why?" they both asked.

"Because now that Flynn and I are getting along, I like everything about my job, and I love working with Flynn. We make a good team."

"Oh boy." Leni sighed. "Here we go."

"What does that mean?" Sutton asked with irritation.

"It means you've worked your ass off to get a job like the one at GNN, and now you're thinking of throwing it away because you're falling for Flynn. If he's the right guy, he'll support you no matter where you're living."

"He *is* supportive in *every* way. He's encouraging me to go for this job, and if I get it, he's willing to do a long-distance relationship. He wants me to pursue my dreams."

Leni planted a hand on her hip. "Then why would you stagnate your career? It's not like you're going to become a world-renowned journalist working at *Discovery Hour*. It's a great place, but it's not GNN."

"I know it's not, but Flynn's giving me a chance to report on more important stories, so who knows what the future holds?"

"I think that's the point Leni is making," Victory said. "You don't know what the future holds on either side. You've worked hard to get where you are, and Leni doesn't want you to throw it away for any man."

"Exactly," Leni said.

"On the other hand, Leni," Victory said firmly, "Flynn sees her potential, and it sounds like he's trying to nourish that."

"Yes, but he can't take her as far as GNN can," Leni pointed out.

"That's true," Victory said. "But as a businesswoman *and* someone who is madly in love with her fiancé, surely you can see where she's coming from."

"Of course I can, but Raz's schedule takes him away for long stretches, and we make it work without either of us giving up what we want."

"I didn't say I was giving it up," Sutton said. "I said I wasn't sure what I wanted."

"Does that mean you'll blow the interview on purpose?" Leni asked.

"*No.* I'm just confused."

"Maybe you should talk to Flynn about that," Victory suggested.

"I can't. That would put him in a terrible position. It's my decision to make, and I will. I just needed to get that off my chest. Part of me wishes he'd ask me not to go."

"Trust me, you do *not* want that," Leni said. "You'd eventually resent him for holding you back."

"I know I would." Sutton looked up at the ceiling, trying to hold back tears of frustration. "But that doesn't mean my heart doesn't want it."

Victory put a hand on her shoulder. "Here's the thing, Sutton. You *should* be confused right now. Any smart woman would be. But your head and heart aren't separate. They both got you where you are in your career, and nobody else can tell you what's right or wrong for you. Leni has a valid point about not making a decision based on a guy."

"Would you have left your job working with Harvey?"

A shadow washed over Victory's eyes, but it was gone as

quickly as it had appeared. "What I would or wouldn't do doesn't matter. Everyone's situation is different. I feel for you, and I believe that true love can endure anything. I think you should go to the interview and give it your all. See if you like the management team, weigh the opportunity. You might come out of there with stars in your eyes and be thankful you did your best. You can still turn it down if you don't want to go. Either way, you can't clear the confusion you feel without taking that first step."

Sutton swallowed hard and nodded. "You're right. Thank you. I needed to be talked off the ledge."

"*Hello,*" Leni snapped. "We both said the same thing. Why will you listen to her and not me?"

"Because it's hard to think when I'm being bowled over. You're like a bullying wave, and Victory is a gentle wind."

"That's because you're not doing business with her," Leni said.

Victory batted her lashes at Leni. "Cutthroat in business, comforting in life. Harvey lived by that statement."

Sutton's chest tightened. "I'm really sorry you lost him."

"Me too."

"Me three," Leni chimed in. "But it's almost time for Sutton's interview. Are you going to buy that suit and wear it out?"

"If I want to nail this interview so I have a decision to make, according to the advice of my incredibly wise and pushy sister and my new rational friend, yes, I am. Let's do this."

IN THE CAB on the way to the interview, Sutton's phone

vibrated with a text.

Flynn: *Good luck, Steele. You'll blow them away.*

Sutton: *Thanks! I hope so.*

Three dots danced at the bottom of the screen. She waited for his text, but the dots disappeared. He might be her boyfriend, but he was still her boss. Was she asking too much of him to be supportive and understanding as her boss? A new weight of worry settled on her shoulders.

Sutton: *Not that I'm dying to leave DH. I love my job.*

Sutton: *But it's good to have options.* She added a smiling emoji.

She closed her eyes, breathing deeply and reminding herself not to assume the worst.

Flynn: *I agree. See you tonight.*

Ten minutes later, Sutton strode purposefully into the room to meet GNN's management team, two professionally dressed men and a sharply dressed woman. "Good afternoon," she said, offering her hand. "I'm Sutton Steele, your next frontline reporter."

Chapter Thirty-Six

AS THE SUN hovered over the horizon and evening settled around him, Flynn paced the deck waiting for Sutton to arrive. She'd texted a little more than an hour ago to say the interview had gone well, and she'd tell him all about it tonight. Of course they loved her. Why wouldn't they? She was a brilliant, driven reporter with a great personality. He was happy for her. He meant what he'd said about following her dreams, but that didn't mean he relished the thought of living across the country from her.

The sound of tires on gravel had his pulse ratcheting up.

He lit the lanterns he'd set out, and as he made his way inside, the front door opened, and Sutton walked in. Her beautiful eyes instantly found his, a hopeful smile lifting her lips. In that moment, everything became clear. He wanted to give her the world. To make things easy and pave the way to the future she'd always dreamed of and more. But he knew that while he could give her unconditional love and endless support, there was another level of fulfillment that could only come from within her. Pushing his own inner turmoil aside, he made room for what mattered most. Supporting her in that endeavor, regardless of the sacrifices.

"There she is. GNN's next big ace in the field." He closed the distance between them, drinking her in.

"It's not a sure thing."

"Well, *I* am a sure thing, so at least there's that." He nipped at her neck, earning a sweet giggle. "You look incredible. Am I losing my mind, or are you wearing a different outfit than the one you laid out last night?"

"Is there anything you don't notice?"

"Not about you. Charcoal just became my second favorite color."

"What's your first favorite?"

He arched a brow. "Nude."

"And here I thought you left all the *cheese* in the rainforest." She laughed.

"Lucky for you, I've got plenty more where that came from." He set her shopping bags and tote on the table by the front door and took her hand. "Come on, Steele. It's celebration time."

As he led her around the couch and his surprise came into view, Sutton's eyes lit up. He watched her taking in the antique lanterns illuminating the picnic blanket he'd spread out on the deck with the seafood medley for two he'd prepared, the champagne he'd chilled, and the bouquet of colorful wildflowers he'd picked.

"*Flynn.*" She sounded awestruck. "What are we celebrating?"

"Your successful interview."

She looked at him with disbelief. "You did all this just for the interview? You even got champagne."

"It's a big day for you. One you'll remember twenty years from now, when you're the first name out of people's mouths when they talk about great journalists."

She looked like she might cry. "What if I had bombed the interview?"

He slid his arms around her, pulling her closer. "Then I would have gotten you drunk and made you forget about GNN."

She laughed and put her arms around him. "And I thought pink flowers around my poop hole were romantic. Thank you."

He kissed her. "Why don't you kick off those heels and get comfy, and then you can tell me all about your interview."

After she changed her clothes, they ate dinner, and Sutton told him about the people she'd met and the topics they'd discussed, vacillating between excitement and uncertainty. "I'd be covering domestic and international events, and I'd be in the thick of it. Traveling, interviewing influential people and maybe one day even world leaders."

"That's exactly what you're striving for."

"It is. But as we were talking, it made me realize how much I'm enjoying the human-interest stories we're working on. Bringing to light discoveries and plights that don't get the attention they deserve."

"Stories of the heart are small potatoes compared to where you want to be, documenting wars and world events." They weren't small to him, but in a selfish world divided by political, social, and economic wars, they were seen as small by many.

"I know, but there's a lot to think about. They asked me about my goals and aspirations, and I think I handled it okay. That's always such a hard question, because I want to show I'm driven without making them think I'm looking for instant growth."

"I'm sure you did fine. What did you tell them?"

"Basically the same things I told you. That I'm striving to become a well-respected journalist, and I know I have to pay my dues and earn the respect of the public, but I'm passionate about what I do and confident in my abilities."

Flynn listened with admiration and knew her interviewers had probably done the same. "That's a perfect answer. How do you feel about the interview?"

"It was intense, like they were assessing every answer I gave them."

"That's good. That means they were interested."

"They're definitely interested." She sipped her champagne, her gaze shifting nervously to the water, then back to him. "They said I'm their top candidate. They want me to go to LA a week from Monday for a site visit to meet the rest of the staff."

The weight of his emotions bore down on him, but he was determined not to let them show. "That's fantastic, babe."

"You think so?" she asked tentatively. "If I get the job, I'd be thousands of miles away."

"There's no *if* about it. You're going to get this job."

"You don't know that."

"Yes, I do, because I believe in you in the same way I believe in us." He took her hand in his. "It doesn't matter how many miles life puts between us, or the obstacles we have to overcome. A connection like ours is one in a million. I have no doubt we can get through anything."

Warmth pushed away the worry in her eyes. "You always make me believe everything is going to work out the way it should."

"Well, a wise woman did once tell me I was a know-it-all." He leaned in for a kiss and picked up his champagne, holding it up in a toast. "Here's to you, my beautiful Steele, changing the world one headline at a time." As they clinked glasses and drank to Sutton's success, he tried to ignore the ache of longing that was already taking hold.

Chapter Thirty-Seven

SUTTON SMILED AT the couple stepping into the posh hotel elevator.

They didn't return the eye contact.

She was starting to wonder if she'd become invisible in the last twenty-four hours, or if not noticing other human beings was a West Coast thing. She'd first noticed her new invisibility cloak when she'd arrived in LA last night for this morning's site visit with GNN. Nobody had made eye contact with her in the airport, on the sidewalk, in the coffee shop, or just about anywhere else. She was either invisible outside of the meeting with GNN, or she was so mentally and emotionally exhausted, she was sporting a serious resting bitch face and people were keeping their distance.

That could be it.

Especially tonight. The last week and a half had been a roller coaster of the highest highs with Flynn, personally and professionally, and gut-wrenching anxiety about the site visit. On the heels of that, she'd thought the site visit would take an hour or two, but she'd been at GNN *all* day and had walked out with an offer in hand.

An offer for an amazing job she wasn't even sure she wanted.

The elevator doors opened on her floor, and she headed down the hall to her room. Her phone rang as she opened the door. She dug her phone out of her tote bag and saw her grandmother's name on the screen. Anxiety prickled her skin. *Fake it until you make it.*

Mustering her best positive attitude, she answered the call as she toed off her heels. "Hi, Gram."

"Hi, honey. I couldn't wait any longer to call. I hope I'm not interrupting."

"You're not. I just got back to my hotel." She walked over to the windows and gazed out at the traffic below.

"How did it go?"

"It was great. The offices are gorgeous, and everyone's really nice. I had lunch with the woman I'd be working for, and I can tell she's tough, but that's okay."

"You've been around tough people your whole life. You can handle her, unless she's witchy."

"She didn't seem to be. She was just very serious, and she offered me the job, so she must have liked me."

"Of course she did. That's wonderful, honey. You must be excited."

"It's a great offer, and they're excited about working with me, which is nice. But it's a big decision. I need to think about it for a few days."

"Good girl. Let them sweat it out. Have you told Flynn?"

"Yes. I called him the minute I left the building." She hadn't told him she had misgivings about the job. She didn't want to worry him when she didn't know what those misgivings were. Something just felt *off.* "He's thrilled for me." She'd hoped his excitement would spur the same in her, but it just left her feeling even more unsettled.

"I knew he would be. He seems to have your best interests at heart. It's good that the company is excited and Flynn is thrilled."

"It *is*," Sutton said cheerily.

"Well, color me impressed. You're in LA for one day and you're already giving Academy Award–worthy performances."

Sutton's shoulders slumped. Of course her grandmother would see right through her act.

"Spill it, girlie. What's really going on?"

"I don't know, Gram," she admitted. "I should be on cloud nine. I just got an offer for the job I've always wanted, I'm head over heels for the most supportive man on the planet, and he's not only thrilled about the job offer, but he's also really happy with the fragmented-world piece I've been working on. What is it about life-changing decisions that makes me want to throw up?"

"I think the answer is in your question."

"I don't know what that means, and I don't have the wherewithal to figure it out. Being here is exhausting. The traffic is insane. A drive that would've taken fifteen minutes in Port Hudson took almost an hour, and don't get me started on the price of coffee, or the sheer number of people there are in this place."

"Nobody said success was going to be stress-free or cheap."

Sutton rolled her eyes. "*I know.*"

"Oh, honey, you know all major life changes are stressful. If they weren't, you'd never know the excitement of anticipation. It's just the fear of the unknown tickling your ribs. Are you worried that you might not be able to handle the job?"

"No. I know I can." *But I didn't get the same flutter of ex-*

citement that I do with my current stories.

"Good, because you've been working toward this your whole life. But it is very far away. Maybe that's what's got you feeling ill at ease. You're used to hopping on a ferry and coming home when you're mad or sad or just need to feel grounded. Are you anxious about being that far from family?"

"Kind of, but it's not like I can't handle it."

"Then there's only one more thing I can think of that might have you on edge. Are you worried that if you move, your relationship with Flynn won't survive?"

"Not really." She sat on the bed and fiddled with the bracelet Flynn had made for her. She'd worn a pink blouse for the sole purpose of matching with the bracelet. They hadn't said those three special words yet, but she felt them in every aspect of their relationship, from stolen moments at work and inside jokes to their lovemaking and late-night chats. "We've talked about it, and we're both willing to do whatever it takes to make it work." She sighed. "I don't know what it is. Something just feels *off*. It's probably just me. I'm exhausted. I think I'm going to take a hot bath and find something mindless to watch."

"That's probably a good idea. You've gone through a lot of changes lately. A little rest will do you good. If you want to talk it through, I'm always here, and just remember, whatever is supposed to happen will happen."

I wish I knew what that was. "Thanks, Gram. I love you."

"I love you, too, honey."

Sutton ended the call and went to fill up the tub.

EVENING FOUND HER curled up on the hotel bed in shorts and Flynn's Syracuse T-shirt, watching the season of *Wilderness Warrior* that Flynn had won and trying not to think about the decision she had to make. She sipped the milkshake she'd ordered from room service and opened her second package of peanut butter crackers, watching in awe as Flynn navigated the grueling heat and deadly wildlife of Kenya, Africa, facing water buffalo, wild cats, snakes, dehydration, and other terrifying animals and conditions. Unlike other survival shows, there was no cameraman or group of contestants banding together. Flynn was dropped in the Serengeti alone with a medical pack, a video camera, a week's worth of rations, and a bottle of water. She'd watched the first three episodes already, and not once had he shown a moment of weakness, while the other contestants had shown many.

It was strange and exciting seeing Flynn with short hair, youthful, unmarred skin, and eyes that exuded the cool bravado and arrogance of a twenty-one-year-old who believed himself to be indestructible. His confident swagger reminded her of Noah. At thirty-four, Flynn was as confident as a warrior, though he'd learned the realities and dangers of the world. His eyes were wiser, the shadowed lenses of that younger man who had reached his dream and then realized the dream wasn't all it was cracked up to be.

Was that what was happening to her?

Her phone chimed with a text, startling her back to the moment. She smiled at Flynn's name on the screen and paused the show. It was after nine in California, after midnight for him. She knew he'd planned on working late with Ray on trailers for upcoming episodes.

Flynn: *Just got back from work. My place is lonely without you.*

She was lonely without him, too, and it had only been a day.

Sutton: *I miss you, too. How did it go with Ray?*

Flynn: *Great. The trailers are fantastic. I can't wait for you to see them.*

Flynn: *How is your night? What's GNN's newest star doing to celebrate?*

Sutton: *Spending the evening with a guy who's a lot like you. He's a survivalist but a bit younger.*

Flynn: *Is he someone you'll be working with?*

Her heart squeezed, because she wanted him to be.

She looked at Flynn's frozen image on her laptop screen. She'd paused the show when he was holding a pencil-thin speckled bush snake that was wound between his fingers and around his wrist. His hair was a mess, his face was dirty, and he sported a scruffy beard and mustache, but his bright eyes lit up the screen.

She took a picture of the screen and sent it to him.

Flynn: *I can't believe you're watching that.*

Sutton: *I love seeing you at that age. You were so brave. I can see why you were so popular.* She added a hot-faced emoji.

Sutton: *But you're even better looking now.*

Flynn: *Have you always had a thing for older men?*

Sutton: *No. It was a taste I acquired in the rainforest.*

Flynn sent a devil emoji.

Sutton: *I know that show changed your life and not all for the better, so if it bothers you, I'll stop watching. But I like seeing who you were back then.*

Flynn: *It's fine.*

Flynn: *That show changed me, not just my life, but it also put me on a path that led to us. That makes thinking about that time a little less painful.*

She wondered if he had any idea how much knowing that meant to her. She sent three smiling emojis surrounded by hearts.

Flynn: *I'm beat, babe. I've got to get some sleep. I have an early meeting with Karen and Aubrey.*

Sutton: *Is everything okay?*

Flynn: *Yeah. Just program stuff. Nothing to worry about. See you tomorrow night? My place?*

Sutton: *Definitely. I can't wait.* She added a kissing emoji.

She sat back against the pillows, marveling how just texting with Flynn calmed her as much as being near the water did. She pulled her laptop closer and pushed play on the show, smiling to herself as she watched Flynn, wishing she'd known him then and that they'd had all those difficult years together. She didn't think she'd have pushed him to take those jobs he didn't want. She would have wanted him to be happy. Would he have still gone into hiding? Would he have wanted her to? If he had, would she have dropped out of school to go with him?

Her brain told her nothing would have stopped her from completing that goal, but her heart wasn't so sure.

A notification from her personal email account popped up. She paused the show and opened the program, surprised to see an email from Flynn.

Steele,

Congratulations on the job offer. I knew you'd nail it. Now I can say I knew you when...

Braden

There was a video attached to the email. She opened it and

hit play.

"Addicted to you" by Picture This began playing, and breathtaking views of the rainforest taken from the bush plane bloomed before her eyes. She'd been so stressed during that flight because of the tension between them, she hadn't even noticed the views. Even when they'd watched the footage together at work, the tension between them had escalated, and she'd seen it through the eyes of a reporter. But now, as lyrics about hoping she wanted him and being addicted to her rang out, she saw it through the eyes of a woman who had set out on a journey scared half out of her mind with a man she was certain was trying to get her fired—and had returned questioning everything she'd thought she knew about herself *and* him.

I KNEW YOU WHEN YOU COULDN'T STAND TO BE WITHIN FIFTY FEET OF ME appeared at the top of the screen, and footage of Sutton stalking angrily toward the forest appeared. She'd been terrified and had tried so hard not to let him see it. He'd muted their conversation in the video, but as she turned to face the camera with an expression that was a cross between fuming and calling him an idiot, she remembered him calling out to her, asking where she thought she was going.

That image blended into a montage of monkeys, the ocelot behind her as she reported, collecting water from the rocks. There was a shot of a strangler fig, and BUT WE BROUGHT OUT SOMETHING IN EACH OTHER WE DIDN'T KNOW EXISTED appeared at the bottom of the screen.

She smiled to herself as more images appeared of her laughing and sticking her tongue out at him in the pouring rain, looking like a drowned rat, and eating chontacuro worms. Then her back was to the camera again and she was wrestling with the tent. She remembered how frustrating that had been. She'd been wet and hot and overwhelmed.

The music faded to the background as she stalked toward the camera, glowering, and said, "*Know what's not fun? Being hungry, thirsty, and wet and thinking you're going to get wood so maybe we can get more comfortable. But I'm still wet, and you have no wood.*" Flynn's laughter rang out, drawing laughter from her in real time.

The music grew louder again, lyrics about being obsessed with her and how he'd come running and take her away to someplace where nobody could find them. The camera panned down to Flynn's feet walking through the woods, pink flowers sailing to the ground beside them, leading to the bathroom hole he'd dug for her.

She teared up as images of them in the tent appeared, illuminated by the dim light of his phone lying on the tent floor beside his head. Flynn was holding the camera above them, and she was sleeping on his chest. His smile spoke volumes, and the emotions in his eyes drew tears from hers.

The video morphed into images she'd taken with his video camera of bugs crawling along plants, snakes hiding, and a sloth hanging out in a tree as they walked through the forest. WE WERE FORCED TO WORK TOGETHER appeared across the screen, followed by clips of them fishing with the net, of her plucking the fish out, and the two of them eating them by the fire. Then they were walking again, and images of the sun peeking through the treetops appeared. I KNEW YOU BEFORE YOU WERE DEFILED IN A WATERFALL flashed across the screen, and she appeared with her back to the camera as she pushed plants aside, revealing the waterfall they'd found for the very first time. She spun around with sun-kissed cheeks, eyes dancing with joy, and a smile that leapt off the screen.

Her heart skipped, remembering the thrill of that moment and how overwhelmed she'd been when she'd realized he'd planned it for her.

Footage of the waterfall appeared, and then she was lying on the rocks in her bikini, her knee bent, foot bouncing, as she wrote in her journal. The music faded, and Flynn's voice appeared from off-screen. *Have you made your pros and cons list about us yet?* He'd edited it so it went directly to her looking at him as he said, *Let me help you. Pro. Never has trouble getting wood.* She smiled playfully and said, *I wrote something about you being a dick. Does that count?* He pointed the camera at himself as he lowered himself to sit beside her and said, *That's how she says she loves me,* and then he was kissing the living daylights out of her.

Sutton swiped at her tears as more images played out of her sleeping on the rocks, Flynn's treasured copy of *Gulliver's Travels* on his lap, and of him reading it aloud in the tent as she held the flashlight for him. That morphed into a montage of videos on his boat, his deck, cooking dinner, and of her wearing his T-shirt as he chased her around his cabin with the camera, both of them laughing.

The music faded on a video of her sleeping on his chest on a lounge chair on his deck and his handsome face as he whispered, *I knew you before you were mine, Steele, and I hope I'll never know a time when you're not.*

Tears slid down her cheeks as the music played softly, and selfies of them from the last few weeks swam across the screen.

Chapter Thirty-Eight

SUTTON AWOKE TO a vibration against her chest in the dark hotel room. She pushed up on one elbow, glancing at the clock—*3:15*—trying to get her groggy brain to function. Her laptop was precariously perched on the edge of the bed. She'd watched the video Flynn had sent her twice before texting to thank him, and they'd ended up on the phone, reminiscing about their trip to the rainforest for another half hour. Afterward, she'd tried to watch another episode of *Wilderness Warrior,* but her nerves over the job offer had gotten the better of her, so she'd watched old videos of her journalistic idols. She must have fallen asleep while watching.

She pulled her laptop closer and sat up to answer her vibrating phone. "Hey, Flynn. You okay?"

"Yeah. Sorry to wake you. How do you feel about Alaska?" He sounded wide-awake and excited.

"*Um.* Curious, I guess. Why?"

"Because that's where we're heading, babe. Get your cute little ass up. You've got to get to the airport."

Anticipation brought her to her feet. "What's going on? Do we have a story?"

"We sure do. I just got a call from my grandfather."

"Isn't it like two in the morning in Alaska?" Her brain scrambled to keep up. "Are your grandparents okay? I thought they were on a cruise."

"He never sleeps, and they're fine. They haven't been on a frigging cruise for the last six weeks. My grandfather put together an expedition along the Yukon River to learn more about the landscape and habitat of dinosaurs up north."

"He's sneaky. Way to go, Grandpa. I can't wait to meet him."

"He's stoked about meeting you, too."

"What did they find? Dinosaur bones?"

"No bones, but they found an impression of dinosaur skin and several fossilized footprints. He's giving us the first chance at the story."

"That's amazing."

"He and my grandmother rented a cabin, so we can stay with them tonight if that's cool with you."

"Sounds perfect." She pulled open the curtains and scribbled down the flight arrangements Flynn gave her.

"I'll meet you at the airport in Alaska. A bush pilot will fly us out to meet my grandfather."

"I can't wait!"

"To see me, or to report the story?"

"Both!"

SUTTON MADE GOOD use of the long flight to Alaska. She researched Flynn's grandfather, who was far more impressive than she'd imagined. He had more publications than anyone she knew, and he'd been making archaeological and paleonto-logical discoveries, big and small, for decades. She also researched the history of dinosaurs in Alaska and read reports about previous expeditions that had taken place there. But her thoughts kept trickling back to the job offer from GNN. What should feel like a beacon of new opportunities loomed over her like a storm cloud waiting to break.

When she'd watched the videos of her idols last night, she'd found that while her respect and admiration for them had magnified over the years, the issues they'd reported on, while important world news, didn't cause the same kind of thrill she felt about her work at *Discovery Hour*. She returned to the pros and cons list she'd started when they'd asked her to come for the site visit, but for the second time in recent weeks, she didn't feel like her tried and true lists were showing her the right answers. She didn't know why she was having a change of heart after so many years of working toward a singular goal, but she spent the last two hours of the flight watching more videos of her idols and clips of people talking about them. The renowned journalists were praised for their integrity and achievements, but it was reiterated many times over that achieving that level of success came at great personal costs, like lack of privacy, having a target on their backs for criticism, and giving up family time. She'd known that, of course, but hearing it time and time again had her thinking about what she really wanted. She knew the chances of achieving that level of success were slim, but if she took the job, it would be with that goal in mind, and she'd give her all to attain it.

By the time she landed and connected with Flynn and the tech crew, she was armed and ready for the assignment and more unsure than ever about the job offer. She was also pumped up on coffee and adrenaline. It took a great deal of willpower to act within the confines of a professional relationship with Flynn around their peers, and she hated every second of it. But that suddenly felt like a small price to pay for the excitement of their new assignment.

The crew was flying out with another bush pilot to get bird's-eye-view footage of the expedition location. Sutton and Flynn headed out to meet their pilot.

"I did a lot of research on the flight." Her hair blew across her face. Wishing she had a hair tie, she turned toward the wind so it would blow away from her face as they walked. "I was surprised to read that scientists haven't ever taken a close look at this stretch of the river."

"That's why my grandfather put the expedition together. He said he's been studying a forty-year-old research paper focused on the sedimentary rocks lining the banks along the middle section of the river for years. It's the only paper of its kind, and he used it to determine field sites."

"Amazing."

"It's pretty cool." A sexy glint appeared in his eyes. "But what's amazing is that your lips have never looked more tempting."

How did he go from work to *that* so seamlessly, and why did it instantly make her body hum with desire? "Maybe if you're nice to me, I'll let you taste them later."

"I'm about to be very nice to you." He stopped walking and shrugged off his backpack.

"What are you doing?"

His eyes took on an intensity that felt serious and soft at once, making her pulse quicken. "Now that we're alone, I wanted to take a minute to say that I'm really proud of you.

Getting an offer from GNN is no small feat. I know how hard you've worked to get this far, and now there's no limit to how far you'll go. Which is why I want to give you this."

She was floored he was thinking about her and the job offer as they embarked on such an exciting assignment, but when he withdrew the familiar leather book cover that protected his treasured copy of *Gulliver's Travels*, her thoughts stumbled. "I can't accept that. It's from your grandfather."

"I want you to have it." He put it in her hands and covered them with his own. "It's brought me luck for all these years, and now I have the career I want and the girl I'm crazy about. Now it's your turn to reach for the stars, and this will keep you safe and help get you there."

"I…" Tears burned her eyes. She blinked rapidly, trying to keep them at bay. "I haven't accepted the job yet."

"I know, but you will and you should. It's what you've always wanted."

Her hair whipped across her cheek. She tucked it behind her ear and clutched the book to her chest, wishing she could hug Flynn, and at the same time, wishing her thoughts weren't so jumbled so she could figure out if she wanted the job or not. But she felt the pressure of the pilot waiting for them, and all she could manage was, "Thank you."

"Come on, Steele. Let's not keep our pilot waiting." He shouldered his backpack and led them to a rugged-looking man with a white buzz cut and a trim mustache who looked to be in his sixties, standing by the bush plane.

"You must be Flynn and Sutton," the man said with a friendly smile that helped calm her nerves.

"Yes, sir," Flynn said.

"Gregg Lange. It's a pleasure." He shook their hands.

"It's nice to meet you." Sutton glanced at the plane. "Is this our ride?"

"Yes, ma'am. Are you comfortable on small planes?"

"I guess that depends on the pilot." She smiled to let him know she wasn't really worried about the flight. It was her looming decision and Flynn's gift that were consuming her thoughts.

"Makes sense. Bush pilots are like air cowboys. Especially in the remote places you two go. But don't you worry. I've been doing this for longer than you've been alive," Gregg reassured them. "Let's get your bags loaded."

Flynn took out his personal video camera, tossing Sutton a wink, and then handed Gregg his bag to put in the luggage compartment. When he closed the compartment door, Flynn said, "Would it be okay with you if I got a shot of you and Sutton before we board your plane?"

"Absolutely." He stood beside Sutton.

"Sorry. He's obsessed with that camera," Sutton said, secretly loving that Flynn wanted to savor their memories.

AS THE PLANE took off, Flynn turned the camera on Sutton gazing out the window. Through the camera's eye, he drank in her delicate features and the porcelain skin he knew every inch of by heart. He was going to miss doing assignments with her after she started her new job. Hell, he was going to miss everything about her.

The plane slanted a little. Her fingers curled around the book he'd given her. As the plane leveled out, her gaze shifted to her lap. A sweet smile appeared as she ran her fingers over the leather cover. Her hazel eyes flicked in Flynn's direction, and her brows lifted. "*Really?* Would you put that thing away?"

"You know me better than that." He winked. "Why don't you read to me?"

Her smile widened, and she unzipped the cover. She ran her fingers over the red-and-black hardcover. "Are you sure you want me to have this?"

"I've never been more sure of anything in my life."

"Won't your grandfather be upset?"

"Nope." He'd told his grandfather his plan that morning, and his grandfather had said he'd seen it coming. Flynn had asked him how, and his grandfather had just barked out a laugh, as if it were a stupid question. He shouldn't be surprised. They'd spoken a few times while his grandfather was supposedly on a cruise, and they'd spent most of that time talking about Sutton.

Her fingers found the pink tassel at the top of the bookmark he'd made for her, and she opened to it. Her brows knitted as she studied the bright pink flower petals he'd dried and pressed inside the laminated bookmark. "Are these from the rainforest?"

"Yeah. I thought you might want—"

A thunderous *crack* exploded around them, and the plane lurched, shaking violently. The color drained from Sutton's face as the plane careened to the right, and Gregg's harsh voice rang out, identifying himself over the radio. Flynn grabbed her hand, the concern in Gregg's voice escalating, "*Multiple mechanical failures…*"

"Flynn!" Tears streaked her cheeks as the nose of the plane lifted, shaking so hard it sounded like it was going to burst apart.

"It's okay. Look at me, Sutton. *Focus* on me," he shouted over the metallic rattling. He was shattering inside at the terror in her eyes and the reality that the plane was going down.

"Are we going to die?" Sobs burst from her lungs.

"*No*. We're are *not* dying today. Do you hear me? We just found each other. We are *not* dying."

The plane careened to one side, and Gregg hollered, "We're going into the trees. Get down."

"Flynn!"

He put a hand on her back, pushing her chest to her legs, and assumed the same position. Their eyes locked, and he spoke fast. "Keep looking at me, baby. You're going to be okay." *God, please. Take me, not her.* "I love you, Sutton. You are my world."

"I love you, t—"

The plane tore through the tops of trees, the deafening sounds of Sutton's screams and wrenching metal exploded around them as the plane took a nose dive, and then the world went black.

The End

Gotcha! This is a Steele novel, after all. Turn the damn page!

Chapter Thirty-Nine

SUTTON TRIED TO make sense of her disorienting surroundings. It took a minute for her brain to fire and realize the plane had crashed. Panic consumed her. Her head was throbbing. She was upside down, suspended by her seat belt, and she couldn't see. Something was pressed against her face. "*Flynn,*" she croaked, tasting blood, and saw him out of the corner of her eyes. "*Flynn!*" Panic engulfed her anew. He was upside down, a branch pinning him at an awkward angle, and blood dripped from his head. *Please don't be dead. "Flynn! Wake up! Flynn!"* She reached up to move whatever was against her face, and a sharp pain seared through her wrist. She cried out, hot tears spilling free.

"*Sut…?*" Flynn's voice was strained, but it hit her like a lifeline.

"Flynn? Oh God. Flynn! Are you okay?"

"I'm fine. I'm right here." His fingertips touched hers. "Don't make any sudden moves. I don't know how stable we are. It looks like we're pretty high up in the trees."

"Oh my God." Sobs burst from her lips.

He pushed his hand closer, catching two of her fingers between his fingers and thumb. "Focus on me, baby. Try…to calm down. Tell me…where…you're hurt."

"I think it's just my wrist, but I can't see. Something's against my face."

"It's the book, but there's a sharp branch on the other side holding it in place. *Do not* try to move it."

"Okay." Her breathing was so erratic, she thought she might pass out.

"Deep breaths, Steele. Yoga breaths." She closed her eyes, trying to slow her breathing.

"*Gregg?*" Flynn said, his voice strained and harsh. Then louder, "*Gregg.*"

There was no response.

Sutton's chest constricted. "Is he…?"

"I don't know. Don't think about that. I'm sure help is on the way. He radioed."

The plane shifted and creaked, and she screamed as their fingers slipped apart.

"*Sutton*," Flynn said sternly. "You *have* to try to calm down."

"The book shifted. I can't see you anymore," she said frantically. "It's freaking me out."

She heard him grunt, and then his fingers curled around hers. "I'm here, baby. You can feel me. Concentrate on that. Do *not* move that book, the branch will impale you."

More sobs burst free.

"Sutton, baby…think about the waterfall. Remember how pretty…it was?"

"Yes." She closed her eyes, shaking all over. "I remember."

"You were so beautiful that day. So happy and relaxed, driving me in…sane in that damn pink bikini." He panted loudly. "Remember how much fun we had?"

"*Yes*," she managed, but more sobs hit her. "Flynn, I'm scared. I don't want to die."

"You're not going to die, baby. You're going to get out of this…and go to LA to be everything you ever dreamed of, and I'm going with you."

"No—"

"*Don't* argue with me. Listen. We don't have to live together if you're not ready…but you're it for me, Sutton. I love you. I want every day with you…cheering you on while you set the world on fire. I pitched a show for you to Karen and Aubrey, covering more of the stories you want to handle…but you got the offer from GNN so fast, we didn't have time to discuss the details. That's what our meeting was supposed to be about today."

She closed her eyes against her sobs, choking out, "You were? For me?"

"I'd do anything for you. I know it's fast, but you are my love, my *life*. You *are* my heart story, baby. The only one that matters, and I'll wait a lifetime if that's what it takes until you're ready to be with me full time…but I'll be damned if I'll miss you from across the country."

She couldn't stop the flood of tears. "You don't have to wait. I want every day with you, too. I'm not going anywhere. I don't want to report about wars and political issues. That *was* my dream, but it's not anymore. Those things make me sad. I don't want to be Barbara Walters or Tom Brokaw and move far away from you and my family. I want to be Sutton Steele, doing what I love, and I want to be with you. I know we can't keep working together, but I'll find something closer to—"

The sound of a helicopter drowned out her voice, filling her with hope. Flynn shouted, "Hear that, baby?" just as the branches snapped, and they plummeted toward the ground.

Chapter Forty

FLYNN ENDED THE call with his parents and set his phone on the book that had saved Sutton's life. She was sitting beside him on the emergency-room bed, clinging to his hand as she spoke to her parents on the phone, reassuring them that they were okay. They'd been there for a few hours, and they were waiting to be discharged. Flynn had stitches on his head, gnarly scratches on his chest, three broken ribs, a broken arm, and a sprained ankle. Sutton had miraculously gotten out almost unscathed, with a fractured wrist and stitches on her arm. Gregg had been knocked out with the initial impact. He had a broken leg and several lacerations. They were keeping him overnight for observation, but he was going to be okay. All three of them suffered a multitude of scratches and bruises, and Flynn knew they'd feel like they'd been hit by trucks tomorrow. But he was so fucking glad they'd made it out alive. When the plane had plummeted toward the ground, he'd thought they were goners. But it had gotten caught between two trees. According to the rescuers, they'd initially been about forty feet up in the trees, and they'd ended up about fifteen feet lower.

"I will, Mom. I love you guys." Sutton ended the call, turning troubled eyes to Flynn. "They send their love."

He kissed the back of her hand. "We'll go see them as soon as we get back."

She nodded, fresh tears sliding down her cheeks. "I was so scared."

He gently drew her against his uninjured side, knowing it could be a while before the trauma subsided. "I know, babe. You're safe now."

The curtain opened, and his grandparents walked in, eyes clouded with worry, brows furrowed. Tears sprang from his grandmother's eyes as she carefully put her arms around both of them. "Thank goodness you're both okay."

"We're okay, Gram." Flynn looked over his grandmother's shoulder at his grandfather. His jaw was tight, blue-gray eyes struggling not to water.

"It took me a frigging hour and a half of bitching to get them to let us back here," his grandfather said.

"We're here now, Bradshaw. That's what matters." His grandmother put her soft hands on Flynn's and Sutton's faces, her gaze moving between them. "We needed to see for ourselves that you two were okay. Sutton, honey, it's nice to finally meet you. But next time maybe don't make quite an entrance."

Sutton smiled and swiped at her tears. "I'll try not to."

"Why do you always gotta try to outdo me, boy?" His grandfather's voice was thick with emotion as he stepped forward. "I get a story, and you try to beat me into the evening news."

"I learned from the best, old man."

"Showing off for your girl, no doubt." He winked at Sutton. "Not that I blame you. She's prettier than you are, Flynn."

Flynn took Sutton's hand again. "Sutton, meet my grand-parents, Bradshaw and Lara Braden."

"It's nice to finally meet you both."

"I've been itching to meet you, sweetheart," his grandfather said. "You've had this boy tied up in knots for a long time. I have to admit, I never thought coupledom would settle him down, because I don't believe in settling, but I thought it might quiet things for a bit. I can see I was wrong. That's two life-threatening situations you two have gotten yourselves into in under as many months. I'm not a cat with nine lives, you know. I'm an old man, and these near heart attacks add up."

"We'll try to keep them to a minimum," she promised.

"*Pfft.*" His grandfather waved a hand dismissively. "If you think I believe you, then you must think I don't know my grandson. He would never be with a woman who wasn't just as much of an adventure seeker as he is." His gaze moved to *Gulliver's Travels* on the bed beside Flynn. "I told you that book was lucky."

"You have no idea how lucky, Gramps. If not for the book, Sutton wouldn't be sitting here right now." She definitely had an angel watching over her. The book had somehow remained in place when the plane dropped, protecting her when the branch that had pinned him and had been aiming at her face had snapped.

The curtain opened, and the nurse walked in, eyeing his grandparents. "I guess I didn't get the invitation to the party."

"Are you going to spring these two from this joint?" his grandfather asked.

"Yes, sir," the nurse said. "Are you taking care of them to-night?"

"Yes, we are," his grandmother said.

The nurse told them what to watch for and how to care for their injuries. "They should take it easy for a while."

"We'll rest tonight, but we need to record a show tomorrow," Sutton said.

Flynn and his grandfather exchanged a knowing look, and Flynn couldn't hold back a chuckle. He grabbed his ribs, wincing.

"Then I guess that's what we're going to do," his grandfather said.

The nurse frowned. "The doctor advised—"

"Save your breath, honey," his grandmother said. "I've been trying to reason with them for years."

The nurse gave them their discharge papers and said she'd come back with crutches for Flynn.

"Oh, honey, you're so busy. I'll come with you and grab those crutches so you can help other patients." His grandmother followed the nurse out.

"I'll bring the car around so you don't have to hobble too far." His grandfather opened the curtain and glanced over his shoulder, setting a loving gaze on Flynn. "Love you, boy."

"Tell me when y—" Flynn stopped himself from finishing that sentence, Archer's words echoing in his head. *Don't assume he'll always be there.* "You know what? I love you too, old man."

"I know you do, kid." He smiled at Sutton. "I might not know you one on one yet, but I know you through my grandson's heart, which means I love you too, Sutton."

Tears welled in her eyes. "I feel the same."

With a nod, he walked out, pulling the curtain closed behind him.

"I love them," she said softly, and leaned her head on his shoulder.

Flynn's heart swelled. "And I love you." He kissed her head.

She tipped her beautiful face up, eyes so full of love, he

could feel it. "Tell me again."

"I love you, Glamour Girl, and I'm going to tell you every day for the rest of our lives."

Chapter Forty-One

FLYNN'S GRANDFATHER'S VOICE was as gritty as gravel and as warm as a summer day, reminding Sutton of the man sitting on the other end of the couch facing her, their legs meeting in the middle. The man who owned every ounce of her heart. Flynn had one hand on her foot, his other arm in a sling, and even though he was battered and bruised, he wore the most serene, contented expression as his grandfather read *Gulliver's Travels* to them. Lara, Flynn's incredibly kind, witty grandmother, a plump woman with short gray hair, sat in a rocking chair by the fireplace, knitting and stealing glances at them, as if she couldn't believe they were really there.

Neither could Sutton.

Gratitude and the weight of what they'd survived hung in the air. She got teary eyed just thinking about how close to death they'd come. Flynn's phone chimed with a text. Their phones had been blowing up with texts and calls from their families and friends all day. A few hours after they'd arrived at the cabin, their parents had called to check on them, and they'd video chatted with both sets of parents. Flynn's parents, Belinda and Charles, were lovely. His mother was easygoing and, for lack of a better word, earthy. She wore no makeup, and her hair hung loose and a little wild past her shoulders, the natural gray taking over the blond, and his father looked similar to his grandfather, but with shorter, thicker, salt-and-pepper hair, glasses, and a serious edge that reminded her of Flynn.

"Excuse me, Gramps." His grandfather stopped reading as Flynn squeezed Sutton's ankle. "It's Karen. Are you up to a video call?"

Anxiety prickled her nerves, but she nodded. "Might as well get it over with." Someone from their crew had contacted Karen earlier, and she'd texted both Sutton and Flynn when they were in the hospital, checking on them.

He typed out a response to Karen as they shifted their legs over the edge of the couch and Sutton scooted closer.

His grandmother hurried over with a pillow and put it on the coffee table. "Here, sweetheart. Put your foot up. It's best to keep it elevated."

"Thanks, Gram." He handed the phone to Sutton. "Would you mind holding it for the call?"

"Sure." She took the phone, and he put his hand on her leg. Just like that, her anxiety came down a notch. She hadn't even realized she'd needed that support.

Karen's video call came through a minute later, and her worried face appeared on the screen. Her dark hair was pinned up in a ponytail, her face void of makeup. She looked younger and less threatening than she did at work. "Hey," she said with far less of an edge than Sutton was used to. "How are you guys?"

"Thankful to be here." Flynn squeezed Sutton's leg.

"Yes, very," Sutton answered, her eyes getting teary again. God, she hated that.

"I can't imagine how scary that was. I want you both to take the next two weeks off and relax. I emailed you both the names and numbers of therapists in Port Hudson who specialize in trauma. When you're ready, I highly suggest you talk with someone."

"Thank you," Sutton said as Flynn drew in a deep breath, his hand weighing heavier on her leg.

"I appreciate that," Flynn said. "But we need to talk to you about something." He looked at Sutton, and his heart shone brightly for all to see as he returned his attention to Karen. "Sutton and I are seeing each other. I'll be submitting my resignation tomorrow."

"*What?*" Karen and Sutton snapped with shock.

"No, you're *not*," Sutton insisted. "I'm resigning. *Discovery Hour* is your show."

"So I'll start another show."

"*No.* You can't just walk away from something that means everything to you."

"*You* mean everything to me—"

"Both of you stop talking," Karen demanded, and they both looked at her. "First of all, why are either of you resigning? LWW doesn't have a no-intracompany-dating policy."

Sutton could do little more than blink as she processed that new information.

"It doesn't?" Flynn asked.

"*No.* If we did, I'd have been fired six months ago when I started seeing Ray," Karen said vehemently.

"You're seeing Ray?" Sutton asked.

"Yes. We don't broadcast it, but I thought everyone knew."

"I had no clue," Flynn said.

"Well, now you do," Karen said. "Look, you've both been through a lot. The last thing either of you need is more stress.

We can talk about this in more detail when you're back in the office. But, Sutton, I know you want to report on bigger issues, and Flynn, Aubrey and I are interested in exploring the idea you had for *Heart Stories*."

Sutton turned curiously to Flynn. "Heart Stories?"

He squeezed her leg again. "That's the name of the show I pitched for you."

Tears sprang into her eyes again.

"Well, I'll be damned," his grandfather said.

"Sutton." Karen's softer tone drew her eyes to the phone. "You're a strong reporter, and we don't want to lose you. But this industry is relatively small, and I'm aware of the offer from GNN."

"I'm not taking it," she said quickly. "I realized I don't want to report on the types of stories they cover."

"Maybe not, but I know you have bigger aspirations, so I'd like to suggest that you and Flynn discuss the idea he pitched, since it sounds like you weren't aware of the details. Then, when you're back in the office, we can all discuss it and brainstorm, and see where it goes."

"That would be incredible. Thank you." She beamed at Flynn, her heart overflowing.

"Aubrey and I were so impressed by the Amazon footage, we're leaning toward having you two do more shows in that same fashion." Karen's gaze shifted to Flynn. "We think the audience is going to love your dynamic, but with Flynn's aversion to being on camera, that might not work."

"I'll give it some thought," Flynn said, shocking Sutton.

"Okay, well, you two get some rest."

"Wait," Sutton said. "One more thing. I'd still like to do the story about Flynn's grandfather's discovery, if that's okay."

Karen smiled. "No wonder you and Flynn are together. You're like two stubborn peas in a pod. I'll let the crew know they're sticking around for another couple of days."

After they ended the call, it was like a weight had lifted from Sutton's shoulders.

"Are you really going to think about being on camera, or did you just say that to appease your boss?" his grandfather asked.

"I don't have to think about it." He took Sutton's hand and held her gaze as he said, "I enjoyed the hell out of filming with you. I'm definitely willing to do more of it."

Excitement bubbled up inside her. "You *are?*"

"Yes. I only said I'd think about it because I didn't want to make it too easy for her or give her the upper hand in negotiations. You can thank Victory and Seth for teaching me a thing or two about how to negotiate."

"Look at that," his grandfather said. "Our boy is finally done hiding."

"What have I always said, Bradshaw?" his grandmother asked.

His grandfather reached between their rocking chairs and took her hand as he said, "Love is the most powerful impetus of all."

"I think you're right," Sutton said, gazing at Flynn, feeling lighter, happier, more in love than she ever imagined possible. "*Heart Stories*, huh?"

"It seems fitting, since you are my heart story."

"Oh, Flynn." As she leaned in to kiss him, she said, "You're my heart story, too."

Chapter Forty-Two

SUTTON SAT ON her parents' living room floor wrapping gifts with her mother for Hadley and her adorable twin baby brothers, Harrison and Harvey, who they called Hank and who was named for Jock's old friend, and for Joey and her new baby sister, Antoinette, who they called Toni and who Joey named for the skater Tony Hawk. It was the week before Christmas, and Sutton and Flynn were back on the island for the third weekend in a row. Flynn was determined not to miss a single event of the holiday festivals. They'd come the weekend of the Christmas tree lighting and last weekend for the flotilla. Today he was helping her father and Archer load crates of wine into Archer's truck for the annual holiday dance and charity auction taking place at Silver House later that evening.

So much had changed over the past six months, and they'd never been happier. Their siblings had helped her move into Flynn's house after the plane crash, and life had been a whirlwind ever since. Flynn's parents had come to visit, and Sutton had fallen as hard for them as she had for Flynn. She and Flynn had finally made it to Ridgeport, and she'd had fun seeing all his old haunts. They tried to see his parents and grandparents often and got together with his siblings when they could, but lately Flynn's family had been busy, and her and Flynn's new work schedule had made it difficult to coordinate visits. She knew he was missing them.

After months of meetings and negotiations, *Heart Stories* had been approved for production. But viewer response to their rainforest episodes had been overwhelmingly positive, and neither she nor Flynn wanted to stop working on *Discovery Hour*. They'd decided to launch *Heart Stories* as special-assignment pieces to be aired once a month rather than a scheduled weekly show, allowing them to work on both productions. They were launching *Heart Stories* in six weeks with the fragmented-world piece Sutton had been working on.

She loved not hiding their relationship, and that freedom brought them closer together. She'd never realized how working toward the one goal she'd set when she was a little girl and living her life as if there were no other path had stifled her in so many ways. Letting go of the confines she'd always lived within had allowed her to feel freer and happier than she ever had. She and Flynn were working as a team, brainstorming ideas, and coming up with stories, which added another new level of joy *and* frustration. But with Flynn, the pros far outweighed the cons.

"I can't believe it's almost Christmas," her mother said as she wrote a name on a gift tag and taped it to the wrapped gift.

"I can. We've been so busy, it seems like the last six months have flown by. I can't believe our new show airs in six weeks."

Her mother stopped wrapping and looked at her. "I'm so proud of you, honey."

"Thanks, Mom."

"You know, I probably don't tell you that enough. I'm not just proud of you for your professional accomplishments. I'm proud of the person you are, the way you stand up for yourself and others, and the way you love Flynn with your whole heart."

"I don't know any other way to love. I only know what I've seen with you and Dad. I hope Flynn and I are as close as you two are thirty years from now."

"You will be. But you know love has its ups and downs, and if you and Flynn ever decide to get married and have a family of your own, you'll hit trying times like we all do."

Sutton dreamed of marrying Flynn one day, and she knew when the time was right, they'd get there. They both wanted a family, and with three more adorable babies in their lives, and Jules three months pregnant, she'd been thinking about it a lot more often.

She set the gift aside and began wrapping the last present, a camera for Joey. "Can I ask you something?"

"Anything."

"What's it *really* like to be a mom?"

"Oh boy." Her mother sighed. "Do you want the truth or the pretty picture?"

"The truth, of course."

"Well, honey, being a parent is the most rewarding, thrilling, and terrifying thing I've ever done. Imagine holding your fragile new baby who relies on you for *everything* and sledding down an icy cliff littered with massive boulders you can see a mile away and patches of grass so small, you never see them coming, and all the while, your goal is to hit a tiny ramp at the bottom at just the right angle in order to sail over a ravine filled with hungry crocodiles to get your child safely to adulthood on the other side."

Sutton laughed. "Wow, Mom. Don't hold anything back."

"Hey, you asked, and I know you'll take that with a grain of salt. Don't tell Jules any of that."

"I never would." Because Jules had gone through chemo-therapy when she was young, she faced a higher chance of infertility and miscarriage. She'd gotten lucky, getting pregnant so quickly, and Sutton threw prayers up to the powers that be on a daily basis, hoping to keep Jules and the baby healthy.

"Good. Now let me share the good stuff with you. There is something magical in every baby, and there is no greater joy than discovering what that is in each of them. I loved watching you experience things for the first time and develop opinions and your personality, and I love helping you find your way through the ups and downs of life. And you know how cute babies are and how they make you crazy with their infectious giggles. They're worth every gray hair and every frustrated tear."

"Do you ever wish you didn't have so many of us so fast?"

"I've had many moments of feeling like a failure as a parent. I think every parent does. But I can honestly say that I've never once wished any of you away. But I did worry that none of you got enough attention or that I'd say or do the wrong thing. I mean, let's face it, six kids in eight years is a *lot*."

"You're a great mom, and you always were, but I don't know how you stayed sane."

"Who said I did?" She laughed. "There were nights when I was so exhausted, I'd yell at your dad for no reason, or sit in the bathroom and cry. When Jules was diagnosed, my mother had to peel me off the floor, and I can't tell you how many times Margot and Gail did the same. And when your father and I found out we were having Levi and Leni, I bawled my eyes out for you."

"Why for me?"

"Honey, you were my first baby girl after rambunctious

boys. Selfishly, I was loving my time with you. You had just gotten me all to yourself when the boys were at preschool, and you flourished. I knew how demanding twins were and what a toll another set of twins would take on our family. Jock and Archer had each other, but I worried about you getting enough attention. Thank God for your grandmother. She was always there to help me with you kids, but I needed to be with the babies when I was nursing them, and you were always such a good girl. Even at two, you entertained yourself and almost never cried, and frankly, I was concerned that you were *too* good. My mother told me I was right. That was hard to hear, but it was the truth, so I asked her if she'd spend time alone with you, and you *loved* it. You'd pack your toys in your little backpack and wait by the window at the same time every day. You two would go to the park or play in the garden. And as all you kids got older, she'd come get you at what we called the witching hour. When things were craziest."

"I remember that. I enjoyed that time with her."

"I know you did, honey. I wish we had more time together when you were a little girl. I did make time every night to read to you before bed. That was our time. After every story, you'd ask me to stay, and I'd say, *If I stay, I get to snuggle with you. That's a good thing, or what Daddy and I call a plus.* And you'd say, *I'll tell you a story! That's a plus.* I'd tease you and say something like, *Does the story have a bad guy in it? Because that's not a plus.* We'd spend ten minutes making up a pros and cons list, and of course you'd convince me to stay even longer. Those are some of my favorite memories, but then you got old enough to read your own stories, and you didn't need me as much."

Sutton had forgotten about those times, but it was all coming back to her now. "*That's* when I started making pros and cons lists."

"Did you ever have any doubt?"

"I didn't remember the lists until just now. I love that it started with us."

"Me too." Her mother leaned in and hugged her. "I treasure those times." As they sat back, she said, "I hope I didn't scare you about having children."

"You didn't. I'm glad you were honest with me, so when I feel like that, I'll know it's normal." Sutton grabbed a gift tag and a pen. "But I don't think I need to have six."

Her mother laughed.

Sutton heard the kitchen door open, and Flynn's deep voice rang out. "It's cold out there." It had snowed last night.

"Right on time," her mother said quietly as they pushed the gifts under the Christmas tree, which Sutton and Flynn had helped decorate last weekend with their siblings.

Flynn walked into the living room wearing a blue hoodie and jeans. His face was scruffy, his cheeks pink from the cold, and it made the love in his eyes shine even brighter.

"I told you they didn't run off to Pythons," her father said.

"Pythons?" Sutton asked. "Why would I do that when I have my own personal Miles Long?"

"That's what I said." Flynn reached for her hand, drawing her into his arms. "How's the present wrapping going?"

"We just finished, and I found this under the tree." She handed him the envelope containing the gift she'd made for him.

FLYNN LOOKED OVER the envelope. Sutton had very distinguishable handwriting, and it looked like she'd tried hard to disguise it. "You found it, huh?"

"*Mm-hm.* Open it."

She was so cute, all bright eyed and excited, he kept his hunch to himself. "Shouldn't I wait for Christmas?"

"No. It's not a wrapped gift. You should open it now."

He glanced at Steve and Shelley. Steve shrugged, and Shelley nodded.

"Okay." He opened the envelope and withdrew a tourist map of the island calling out all the major landmarks, with a single handwritten line that read, *LISTEN CAREFULLY.* He looked up from the map and saw Sutton holding up her phone, and his mother's voice rang out.

"*Hi, honey. Where would your father and I feel most at home on the island?*" His father's voice took over. "*Don't forget to follow the rules, Flynn.*"

Flynn realized with a burst of excitement what this was, and an unstoppable grin tugged at his lips as he met Sutton's happy gaze and said, "Are we going on a treasure hunt?"

"Sounds like it," Sutton said.

"How fun!" Shelley exclaimed.

"You'll need these." Steve held out his car keys.

"Thanks, Steve." Flynn took the keys and hugged Sutton. "What have you done, Glamour Girl?"

She giggled. "Let's go!"

They grabbed their coats and headed out to the car. The brisk air stung Flynn's cheeks. He studied the map as they climbed into the car. "The wildlife refuge." He started the car. "I need directions, sweetheart."

"This is *your* treasure hunt. Use those skills you're always flaunting around to figure it out."

"Flaunting? Really? You're a wicked girl, and I love you so much." He leaned across the seat and kissed her. Then he pulled out his phone and set the GPS for the refuge.

Twenty minutes later they pulled up to the wildlife refuge. As they got out of the car, Flynn said, "Doesn't Tara's brother manage the refuge?" They'd met Robert Osten, a sandy-haired athletic guy, when they'd come to the island for Tara and Daphne's joint baby shower.

"Yes. Why?"

"The clue said to follow the rules. Whenever we went to a place like this, my parents checked in with the local ranger office so we could all meet them, and they would give us the lowdown on the rules. Come on."

He took her hand, following the signs to the office. Robert looked up from a document he was studying and pushed to his feet. "Sutton, Flynn. Good to see you."

"You too, man." Flynn shook his hand. "Do you by any chance know anything about a treasure hunt?"

"I might've heard a little something about it." He glanced at Sutton, who was grinning from ear to ear, and he pulled his phone out of his pocket. "There's only one rule in this game. Listen carefully." He navigated on his phone, and Seth's voice rang out. "*Hey, Flynn. Congratulations on finding your first clue. Ready for your second?*"

Flynn's pulse sped up as he waited for his brother to give him the clue. When Seth said, "*Charlie McGregor,*" Flynn barked out a laugh.

"Who's Charlie McGregor?" Robert asked.

"He's this kid who went to high school with Seth. He got caught at a massage parlor asking for a happy ending."

Robert and Sutton laughed. "You're out of luck," Robert said. "We don't have those kind of massage parlors here."

"Right." Adrenaline had Flynn's mind going a hundred miles an hour as he studied the map. "But you've got the Happy End. Jules's shop! Thanks, Robert. See you at the dance."

He snagged Sutton's hand, and as they headed back to the car, she said, "You're good at this, Braden."

"Never underestimate a know-it-all."

They drove into town and had to park a block away from Jules's shop because of tourists. They practically ran down the sidewalk. Bells chimed overhead as they walked in. Bellamy waved from behind the register where she was helping a customer, and Jules made a beeline for them. "You made it! Yay!" Her cheeks had gotten fuller with her pregnancy, and she was positively glowing. "Ready for your clue?"

"Absolutely." He pulled Sutton closer as Clay's voice rang out from Jules's phone.

"*Hey, bro. Congrats on finding another clue. Listen carefully. I'm only going to say this once. You, me, tequila. Streaking.*"

"That's *juicy*," Jules said giddily.

Flynn laughed and mumbled, "Fucking Clay."

"You never told me a streaking story," Sutton said.

"It wasn't my finest moment."

"It can't be worse than throwing up with your first kiss," Sutton said.

"Sutton told us that one," Bellamy yelled from behind the counter. "That would've scarred me for life, although Sutton said you're a great kisser."

The customers in the store looked over at Flynn, and he gave them a half wave.

"He's taken," Sutton said.

"Thanks, Jules," Flynn said. "Come on, Sut. We need to go to the police station."

"See you tonight," Jules called after them.

On the way to the station, he told Sutton about the streaking incident. "I was fifteen, and I told Clay, who was sixteen, that I wanted to get drunk. To this day I have no recollection of where he got a bottle of tequila, but he did, and we did shots until we were both blitzed. I have no idea why we thought streaking in December, in six inches of snow, was a good idea. But there we were, streaking through the neighborhood with nothing on but our snow boots, our privates practically shriveling up inside us, when the red and blue lights found us. We thought we could outrun them. It was *not* a good night."

Sutton was cracking up so hard, she was in tears as they headed into the police station. Ryan Lacroux was waiting for them, arms crossed, chin low. "I was surprised to hear you had experience in a police station, Flynn."

"Me too," Sutton said, trying to regain control.

"I learned my lesson," Flynn said.

"I should hope so. We can't have Sutton hanging out with a derelict."

"Yeah, yeah, Lacroux. Do you have a message for me?"

"I do." He tapped his phone screen, and Noah's animated voice rang out.

"*Congrats on another clue, Flynn. Hey, Sutton. Now that you know about my brother's checkered past, hit me up. I've got a clean slate.*" Flynn cursed under his breath, just as Noah's message continued. "*Did you just curse? You did, didn't you?*" Flynn gritted his teeth, and as if Noah were in the same room, his younger brother laughed and said, "*Okay, listen up, Flynn. Go to a place like the one where we both got stomachaches and pooped blue for two days.*"

Sutton and Ryan laughed.

Flynn scrubbed a hand down his face. "Thanks, Ryan. Let's go, Sut. We've got to hit up that ice cream shop in town."

As they left the police station, she said, "Too much cotton candy ice cream?"

"Blue raspberry. Noah bet me five bucks he could eat more than me. I won. I ate five scoops. He got sick after four."

"That skill should definitely go on your résumé," she teased.

He backed her up against the car, boxing her in with his big body. "You know what should go on yours?"

"Knowing you…that I'm good with my mouth?"

"Yes, but I was going to say, best treasure-hunt coordinator ever." He lowered his mouth to hers, taking her in a deep, passionate kiss that had her thinking she should have put a make-out spot on the treasure hunt.

A police siren startled them apart. They turned and found Ryan standing beside a police car with a big-ass grin on his face as he said, "Don't make me arrest you for lewd and lascivious conduct."

"Shit." Flynn laughed and waved him off as he opened the door for Sutton. As she got in, he said, "How funny would it be if we got arrested for that and your parents had to come bail us out?"

"It would definitely be a first for me."

He climbed into the driver's seat and started the car. "Did you get the whole community in on this treasure hunt?"

"Not *everyone.*"

He drove out of the lot. "How did you get my family to make the messages?"

"A lady never tells," she said coyly.

At the ice cream shop, there was a red-haired teenage boy behind the counter. "Can I help you?"

Flynn looked at Sutton, and she shrugged. He looked the kid over. "Ah, yeah, maybe. Do you have a message for Flynn Braden?"

"No," the kid said. "But I have a message for *the wildest Thornberry*."

Sutton laughed.

"That would be me," Flynn said. "Vic hasn't called me that since I was a kid."

The kid took out his phone and said, "Listen carefully, Thornberry. I can only play this once." Victory's voice sounded. "*Hey, Flynn. Congratulations on finding so many clues. While you're here, why don't you get some blue pie in the sky ice cream? I hear it's delish.*" The kid said, "Dude, it's the bomb," as Victory said, "*Listen carefully, Thorny. This homonym can't keep my bad dreams away, but it can bring you answers.*"

"Thanks, kid." Flynn shoved a few bucks in the tip jar, and they headed out of the ice cream shop. "What's a homonym again?"

Sutton shrugged. "You're the know-it-all, Thorny."

He gave her a wry smile and pulled out his phone to look it up. "Words that have the same spelling or pronunciation but different meanings and origins. It can't keep her bad dreams away but can bring me answers. She's obviously referencing her dream fairy. Fairy. *Ferry? Ferry!* It's the ferry! That's it. Let's go!"

They drove to the marina, and when they headed up to the ferry dock, cold air whipped off the water, and the ferry was on its way *out* of the harbor. "Damn it. How often does the ferry run?"

"Every couple of hours."

"Do we need to be on it to find the next clue?"

"No." Her eyes danced with mischief. "The next clue is practically staring you in the face."

"Well, it would be if you were facing the other way, boy."

His heart leapt at his grandfather's voice, and he spun around, shocked to see his entire family standing there.

"Surprise!" they cheered, and converged on them with warm hugs and claps on the back.

Flynn's heart was overflowing.

"You look a little stunned, son," his father said.

"I can't believe you're all here." He glanced at Sutton, falling even more in love with her.

"We missed you," his mother said, hugging him again.

"Not me. I missed Sutton." Noah slung an arm around her. "How's it going, babe? Did you miss me?"

"Every day. Kind of like I miss mosquitoes in the winter," she teased.

Everyone chuckled.

"Still can't get your own woman, huh, little brother?" Flynn reached for Sutton's hand. "Clay, how'd you get time off? I thought you were playing right through Christmas."

"I am. Today and tomorrow are the only days off I've got through the holidays. When Sutton suggested we join you guys, I thought, let's do it."

"And, Vic, I thought you had to be on the West Coast this week."

"Since everyone else could get here, I rescheduled," she said. "I would love to see the island. Do you have time to show us around before the dance?"

"I'd like to see the wildlife refuge," his father added.

"We'd love to meet Sutton's family, too," his mother said.

"I heard there's a whaling museum," his grandfather said. "We'd like to check that out."

"Just point me in the direction of wherever the single women hang out," Noah said.

"How about we get some food first?" Seth slapped his stomach. "I'm starved."

"You're always hungry," Victory said, sparking teasing banter from the others.

"And you're not?" Clay chimed in. "I saw you eat two candy bars on the ferry."

"Don't judge me," Victory said.

"He's just jealous because he has to watch his figure," Noah teased.

As his family joked around, Flynn drew Sutton into his arms and gazed into her beautiful eyes. "You did this, Steele. You brought the crazies to your quiet island."

"I knew you were missing them, so I thought I'd try my hand at carrying on your family tradition."

"God, I love you. This is the *best* gift ever." He lowered his lips to hers in a tender kiss.

"Are you going to show us around the island or make out with Sutton all day?" Clay teased.

Flynn kept Sutton close and glanced at Clay. "Are you really giving me the option? Because…" He cocked a brow, and everyone laughed.

Chapter Forty-Three

SUTTON HAD A great day with Flynn and his family, introducing them to her family and friends as they showed them around the island. They'd loved the little towns, cute shops, and everyone they'd met. Sutton had invited Flynn's grandmother, mother, and Victory to get ready for the dance with her and the girls at her parents' house. They'd had a wonderful time, sipping wine and holding babies. The men had created a lot of fanfare as the women had paraded down the stairs. Sutton loved that they'd gotten to share in that family tradition with her.

The dance was in full swing, and the banquet room at the Silver House was hopping. It had been transformed into a winter wonderland, with elegant chandeliers casting a soft glow over the dance floor, where couples were twirling and swaying. Tables were draped in white and adorned with gorgeous floral arrangements, and holiday trees anchored each side of the stage, their pine needles sprayed with white, wrapped in twinkling lights and gold ribbons. Sutton loved seeing everyone dressed up for the dance and was reminded of shopping for holiday dresses with her grandmother, mother, and sisters when she was younger. Those outings had made the events even more special.

She looked for her mother, thinking about how much she'd

enjoyed their alone time today. She saw her standing by the doors leading to the balcony, talking with Margot Silver, Flynn's parents, and Seth. She looked around at his family mingling throughout the room and loved seeing them getting to know everyone. Flynn's grandmother had been with Sutton's grandmother and the other Bra Brigaders all evening. Clay was surrounded by teenage boys, talking football, no doubt, and Noah was on the dance floor with Bellamy and Keira. She searched for Flynn and spotted him with his grandfather, Jock, and Levi. Her brothers and Flynn were each holding a baby, and Flynn was swaying to the music, gazing at the baby in his arms. Her heart squeezed. He was going to be the best father one day. She looked at her brothers. She hadn't thought they could get any happier than they'd been this last year, but those babies added a whole new level of happiness for everyone.

"You weren't kidding when you said people here knew how to celebrate the holidays," Victory said, bringing Sutton's mind back to their conversation. "I feel like I'm in a Me Time movie." Me Time was an LWW network, sort of like Hallmark with steam.

"I can see it now," Sutton said. "Cutthroat businesswoman meets charming small towner, and they live happily ever after."

Victory scoffed. "Not a chance."

"Sutton, you sound like Jules and one of her dreamy fantasies," Leni said.

"How can you say that? You're marrying a small-town guy," Sutton reminded her.

"He's not an island guy," Leni pointed out.

"What's wrong with island guys?" Victory asked.

"Nothing. We just know them all too well," Sutton said.

Leni nodded toward Wells heading their way, looking sharp

in a dark suit, drink in hand, ogling Victory. "*That's* an island guy."

"The guy with the movie-star looks and that you-know-you-want-me glint in his eyes? No thanks. Not my type," Victory said.

Sutton noticed she didn't stop checking out Wells as he approached.

"Ladies," Wells said. "I don't believe I've had the pleasure of meeting your gorgeous friend."

"Wells Silver, this is Flynn's sister, Victoria. *Victory*," Sutton said.

"It's a pleasure to meet you, Victory," he said.

Victory smiled. "You too."

"I noticed you haven't been on the dance floor yet, and I was hoping to change that," Wells said. "I have a feeling dancing with you will be the highlight of my night."

"I can't believe that. A guy like you could dance with any woman in here," Victory said.

He lifted his brows. "And I choose you."

"Thank you, but I think I'll pass," Victory said coolly, her eyes never leaving his.

He studied her for a beat. "You don't dance?"

"Yes, that's right," Victory said, a small smile curving her lips.

Leni stifled a laugh.

"Lucky for you, I'm a great dancer. I'll show you the ropes." He lowered his voice seductively. "We'll start off with a little swaying action, let our bodies find their rhythm, and ease into more."

"As interesting as that sounds, I was just on my way to get a drink. It was nice to meet you." Victory turned on her heel, nudged Leni, and the two of them stalked off.

Wells watched her walk away. "Now, *that's* a woman."

"She just turned you down flat," Sutton said.

"Verbally, but did you see the way she was undressing me with her eyes?"

"Wells, you're barking up the wrong tree," she said, noticing Flynn heading her way.

"We'll see." He downed his drink. "Suddenly I'm thirsty, too."

Flynn sidled up to her as Wells walked away. He slid an arm around her waist, speaking low and gruff into her ear. "Did you see me with that baby?"

"Yes. I think my ovaries exploded."

"*Mm.* Did it give you any ideas?" He palmed her ass.

"Are you thinking about babies already?"

"Not yet, but I'm looking forward to honing our baby-making skills later."

She turned toward him, grinning. "I like the way you think, Braden."

The music stopped, and they both looked toward the stage, where Alexander Silver was stepping up to the microphone. He was distinguished-looking in his designer suit, with thick dark hair, silver at the temples, broad shoulders, and chiseled features, and he had a commanding presence. "Good evening. It's nice to see everyone tonight. I hope you're enjoying yourselves."

As applause and a few whistles rang out, Flynn hugged Sutton against his side and said, "This should be fun. Come on." They made their way over to their families on the other side of the room.

"Before I bring Mayor Osten to the stage to announce the

winners of the silent auction, I'd like to thank everyone who bid tonight," Alexander said. "As you know, all proceeds will benefit the Silver Island Hospital. Let's give our medical workers a round of applause for all they do for our community."

Another round of applause rang out.

When the din quieted, Alexander said, "Without further ado, please join me in welcoming Mayor Patrick Osten to the stage."

As everyone clapped and cheered, Tara's humble father made his way across the stage waving, his cheeks pinking up. Mayor Osten had short brown hair, a little extra weight around the middle, and he always had a kind word at the ready. He cleared his throat and waited for the crowd to silence. "It is my pleasure to announce the winners for tonight's auction." He put on reading glasses and pulled a piece of paper out of his suitcoat pocket. "The winner of the weekend retreat at the Silver House is Saul and Nina Barker."

Applause rose around them as the sweet older couple made their way up to the stage to collect their gift certificate. They stood with the mayor for a picture, before heading off the stage. Mayor Osten read off several other winners of a case of wine from their family winery, dinner at Wells's restaurant, a chartered fishing trip, and more, working his way up to the larger items.

"The next item is very special. Many thanks to bestselling author Jock Steele for donating it." Mayor Osten motioned for his wife to carry the item up to the stage.

"What?" Jock said loudly. He leaned closer to Daphne. "What did we donate?"

"Congratulations to Davis Barrington, whose family owns the *Silver Island Gazette*," Mayor Osten said as Tara's mother hurried across the stage carrying Jock's treasured antique typewriter. "Davis has won this beautiful antique typewriter."

Applause and cheers rose from the crowd.

"That's my typewriter! I didn't donate that!" Jock fumed. "That was from Harvey Fine! It was his wife's."

"*Shh*," Daphne pleaded. "It's for charity, and you can use the computer. It's just taking up space."

Jock's voice rose above the crowd. "Daphne. How could you do that? You know how much it means to me." Baby Hank started to cry.

"You're scaring the baby." Daphne started crying.

"Hold him," Jock demanded. "I'm getting my typewriter." As they argued, Sutton and Leni ran over to try to calm Jock down, and Mayor Osten continued announcing winners.

"The Steeles have been awfully generous this holiday season. This next item is from my future son-in-law, Levi Steele," Mayor Osten said as Robert Osten wheeled Levi's Harley-Davidson motorcycle into the room. "The winner of this shiny Harley is Wells Silver!"

As whoops and cheers filled the room, Levi hollered, "Who donated my bike!"

"I did!" Tara said. "We have a baby and Joey. You don't need the bike anymore."

"I'm a frigging Dark Knight," he seethed. "I need my bike."

Gasps rang out around them.

"You're embarrassing me." Tara started crying.

"You don't need your bike, Dad!" Joey yelled. "You have us!"

"Watch out, ladies. There's a new biker in town!" Wells ran over and straddled the motorcycle, waving to the crowd as Levi tore away from arguing with Tara and Joey and tried to pull

Wells off with one hand, holding his baby with the other.

"*Levi*," their mother snapped as she and their father rushed over to him.

"Get your hands off Wells," their father demanded.

"Tara made a mistake. I *need* my bike." Levi shot a death stare at Wells. "Get off my bike, or I swear you're done."

"Dude, I paid for this," Wells said.

Jock and Daphne's argument escalated, their voices rising over the crowd, as Leni and Sutton tried to calm them.

Alexander strode over to Levi and Wells. "Levi, do we need to remove you from the room, son?"

Levi began arguing with him as Mayor Osten held up an enormous picture of Archer's yacht and spoke into the mic. "We saved the best for last. This small luxury yacht, complete with a bedroom, bathroom, and bar, goes to Roddy Remington!"

Cheers exploded around them as Archer barreled through the crowd barking, "Like hell it does!"

Indi was right behind him. "I donated it! We have a house and the hospital needs money!"

Roddy rubbed his hands together, ascending the steps to the stage. "I've had my eyes on this puppy for years!" As the mayor dropped the yacht keys into Roddy's hand, Grant grabbed one of Archer's arms, Raz grabbed the other, and Flynn moved between Roddy and Archer.

"Remington!" Archer hollered, thrashing to break free. "You take one step on my yacht and it'll be your last!"

"All donations are final," Mayor Osten announced.

"Like hell they are!" Archer hollered.

"One more thing," Mayor Osten said, and then all at once *everyone* in the room yelled, "Gotcha!"

Sutton watched as understanding dawned on her brothers, who were now searching the faces of their significant others. Tara, Daphne, and Indi were grinning from ear to ear, wiping away their forced tears, and Flynn shouted, "That's what happens when you mess with a Braden's girl! We enlist the big guns."

"Are you kidding me?" Levi said. "You're *all* in on this?"

Wells climbed off the bike. "Hey, man. I'll still buy it from you."

Davis carried the typewriter over to Jock. "Here you go. Write like the wind, my friend."

Jock scoffed. "They got us good."

"*You* put this in motion?" Archer seethed, yanking his arms free and going chest to chest with Flynn.

"Damn right I did." Flynn held his ground. "That doll was one prank too many on the woman I love. You got something to say about it, banana boy?"

There was a collective gasp.

"Hell yes, I do," Archer gritted out.

The entire room seemed to hold its breath, just as Sutton was.

A slow grin lifted Archer's cheeks. "Welcome to the family, Miles."

Relieved laughter fell from Sutton's lips, and from everyone else's, as more cheers rang out, and Roddy hollered, "Archer, check your pocket."

Archer reached into his pocket and pulled out his keys, inciting uproarious laughter. He pointed at the crowd and said, "You *all* better watch your backs now."

TWO HOURS LATER, after tensions had eased and friendships were rekindled, Sutton and Flynn and their families were gathered around a bonfire at her parents' house. They sat bundled up in blankets, eating s'mores, and drinking wine, while Joey and Hadley sipped hot chocolate. The babies were safely tucked into playpens in the house, and Jock and Levi were keeping an eye on them via the baby monitor apps on their phones.

Sutton snuggled closer to Flynn, listening to everyone chat about the pranks and the dance.

"You Steeles really know how to put on a show," Flynn's grandfather said.

"We've had a lot of practice," her mother said. "The first summer Steve came to the island with Alexander and Roddy, the three of them turned this quiet town into one where everyone was watching their backs."

"I haven't heard that story," Jock said.

"Steve, you're not from here?" Flynn's mother asked.

"No. I'm from Trusty, Colorado, where ranchers are plentiful and gossip is as ripe as cow patties on a hot summer day." He chuckled at his own joke.

"I'm familiar with that area. I have distant relatives there. What brought you here?" Flynn's father asked.

"My buddies. I met Alexander and Roddy in college. They'd spent all year talking about how great the island was, so when they asked me to join them for the summer, I jumped at the chance. I got a job at the winery, and one day I was talking to Shelley's father, a man who did not appreciate interruptions, and this feisty sixteen-year-old beauty came barging into his office and called me *college boy*. Then she spews venom about how she's just decked a seventeen-year-old kid working on the vines. Let me tell you, I was hooked from that moment on. Alexander and Roddy warned me away from her. They said she was stubborn as the day was long and wouldn't give the boys around there a second glance."

"He didn't listen," her mother said. "He took it as a challenge."

"Darlin', you stole my heart that day. I wasn't about to walk away." He looked at Flynn's parents and said, "I had to prank this woman ten times before she'd agree to a single date."

"You pranked *Mom*?" Sutton asked.

"I sure did. I rigged her bicycle so when she pedaled, the chain would come off, and I'd happen to be there to fix it."

"So chivalrous," her grandmother said.

"Hey, I had to pull all the stops to win her over," her father said. "I found out that every morning she'd leave the house at six thirty to sit outside and read, so every day I set up a bucket above the door. When she opened it, flowers tumbled down, or confetti, or love notes."

"Aw, Dad. That's so sweet," Jules said. "No wonder Mom fell for you."

"That didn't do the trick. She drove me batty for weeks. I didn't think she'd ever give in," he said.

"In my defense," her mother said. "He was going to college in New York City, and I was a small-town girl. I didn't want to be his summer fling. I wanted to be his forever girl."

"Darlin', you've been that since I first laid eyes on you." He leaned in and kissed her. "She kept me on my toes back then, and still does."

"Sounds like someone else I know." Flynn hugged Sutton, whispering, "You're my forever girl."

She loved hearing that but had to tease him. "We'll see how you feel a year from now."

"Now that we've experienced your family tradition, would you like to see a little of ours?" Seth asked.

"Yes, please," her mother said. "We'd love to."

"We tell stories around the bonfire," Seth explained. "We go around in a circle, and everyone gets to add to the story. Do you want to try?"

"I do!" Joey said.

"Me too," Hadley said sleepily.

"Okay." Flynn nudged Jock, sitting next to him, and said, "You're the storyteller. Why don't you start, and we'll go around the circle."

"I start!" Hadley exclaimed.

"Sounds good, Had," Flynn said.

Jock whispered in Hadley's ear, and she said, "It was a dark and stormy night."

Everyone chuckled.

Jock said, "The caregiver looked out the lighthouse window at the turbulent waves and spotted a rowboat heading to shore."

"In the rowboat was a girl, alone and scared, desperate for safety," Daphne added. "She was drawn to the island."

"I'm next," Jules said excitedly. "When she reached shore, she found a beautiful little town with colorful shops and heard lively music coming out of a house with a red door."

"That was very specific, Pix," Grant said.

Jules wiggled her shoulders. "I like red. It's a happy color. Take your turn."

Grant said, "She peered through the windows and saw people dancing the jig."

Noah jumped right in. "But it wasn't the dancing people that caught her attention—"

"It was the creepy doll hanging from a noose in the corner of the room," Jock called out, and everyone cracked up.

"Nice, Jock," Sutton said sarcastically.

"But she was even more fascinated by the boy sitting across the room drawing a map," Noah added.

"She wanted to know where that map led to," Indi added.

"So she burst through the door and charged across the room," Archer said.

"Is her name Archer?" Indi bumped him with her shoulder, and everyone laughed.

"It's your turn, Gram," Leni said.

"Hold your horses. I've got to think," her grandmother said. "I've got it. The boy looked up at her and said, *I've been waiting for you.*"

"Good one, Gram," Leni praised. "The girl said, *How did you know I was coming?*"

"And he said, *It was written in the stars before the storm,*" Raz added.

"My turn!" Joey bounced on Levi's lap. "Then the boy said, *I was afraid you wouldn't come.*" She patted Levi's leg. "Your turn, Daddy."

"And the girl said, *Maybe I've been waiting for you my whole life, too.*"

"Even the girls in made-up stories are challenging?" Flynn asked.

"They're the best kind," his grandfather said.

"It's Tara's turn," Joey announced.

Tara said, "So the boy said, *I made us a treasure map. Are you ready for an adventure?"*

"And the girl said, *I was born ready*," her mother added.

Sutton watched her father's brow knit in contemplation for a long moment before he took his turn. "The boy opened the window, and they climbed out and ran through the rain all the way back to town."

Noah jumped in with, "But first they took a detour through the woods, where they swung from branches, and the boy wrestled an anaconda to save the girl."

Sutton and Flynn laughed.

"And when they got back to town," Seth said, "they were starving, so they went into a deli, where they found a pig making a ham sandwich."

"Every single time," his father said with a shake of his head.

"You know you love the pig, Dad," Seth insisted. "Take your turn and quit complaining."

"The pig made them ham and pickle sandwiches, which they devoured, and with full bellies, they ran back outside," his father said. "The rain had stopped, and at the end of the road, they saw a rainforest."

"Oh, a rainforest," his mother said. "The boy took her hand and said, *Stick with me. I'll keep you safe while we're on our adventure*, and off they ran." She patted Sutton's leg. "Your turn, honey."

Sutton thought about the rainforest and where she could take this story. "The girl wanted to run away from the scary rainforest, especially since she seemed to forget the boy had a map." More laughter ensued. "But she heard the sound of running water, and she burst through the bushes and found a beautiful waterfall." She turned to Flynn. "You're up."

"The girl turned around to show him what she'd discovered

and found him down on one knee." Flynn slipped off the chair and got down on one knee in front of Sutton. "He was holding up a slice of pickle with the inside cut out, like a ring."

Sutton laughed softly. "Where's my pickle ring?"

"The boy looked into her hazel eyes and saw the girl she'd been, the woman she'd become, the babies they'd have, the adventures they'd go on, and he knew she deserved more than a pickle ring."

"Smart boy," her grandmother said.

Flynn reached into his pocket and pulled out a stunning teardrop diamond ring with a halo of diamonds around it and a diamond band. Sutton's breath caught in her throat.

"Sutton, we had to go into the rainforest to realize we liked each other. It took a plane crash for us to admit what we really felt and what we really wanted. I don't want to wait to see what comes next. You're *it* for me, baby. The sun and the moon and the stars all pale in comparison to you."

Tears slid down her cheeks at the words she'd shared months ago.

"Let's grab the brass ring and create our life together. We'll develop shows, and you'll report on the things that make your heart happy. We'll go on wild expeditions, or stay home and read on the deck. I don't care what we do as long as I get to do it with you. I love you with everything I am, Glamour Girl, and I know I will love you with everything I grow to be until the day I take my last breath. Will you be my *it* girl, baby? The first person I see every morning and the one who falls asleep in my arms every night, drooling on my chest and snoring?"

A nervous laugh bubbled out with her tears.

"What do you say, Steele? Want to make this thing permanent? Will you marry me? Be mine forever, and let me be your *it* guy?"

"Yes!" she cried through the blur of tears. "*Yes*, Braden, I'll marry you. I'll be your it girl, your glamour girl, or whatever girl you want." She threw her arms around him. Whoops and cheers rang out as he rose to his feet, kissing her, his strong arms wrapping around her and holding her tight.

"I love you," he said against her lips, and slipped the ring on to her finger.

"I love you, too."

As he pressed his lips to hers again, Raz said, "We can still do that double wedding!" and Jules shouted, "Now sissy can get pregnant, too!" making everyone laugh.

Congratulations rang out, as they were passed from one hug to the next, receiving too many well wishes to count. Then she landed in Flynn's arms again, gazing into his loving eyes, and there beneath the stars, on that cold winter night, Sutton realized she'd finally found something better than hazelnut coffee. *This* was what she wanted. A life with the families she adored and the man she loved. The man she craved. The man who was sweet, and hot, and never failed to satisfy.

Ready for More Silver Island Romance?

I have two great series to share with you. Flynn's siblings are all getting their own stories. Grab Victoria Braden and Wells Silver's book, FLIRTING WITH TROUBLE, below, and then turn the page to get Clay Braden's book, PLAYING MR. PERFECT, the first book in the Bradens at Ridgeport series.

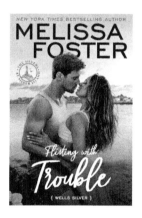

Victoria Braden wasn't supposed to become a widow at thirty-two, much less still be trying to figure out how to move on five years later. She'd planned to drown her sorrows in alcohol on what would have been the anniversary of the day she'd met her late husband, not flirt with trouble and lose herself in a night of passion with playboy Wells Silver. Forgetting Wells was supposed to be easy. But apparently the pushy player didn't get the memo.

Meet the Bradens at Ridgeport

Fall in love with the hot, wealthy, fiercely loyal, and wickedly naughty Bradens at Ridgeport, and join these business-savvy, pleasure-oriented New Englanders as they fall head over heels with their forever loves.

Sleeping with the NFL quarterback dubbed by the media as Mr. Perfect might not have been my smartest move, but I was in the city of love, I'd had a few drinks, and I was jacked up on giddy girl talk and hopeful hearts—two areas in which I never buy into—and I threw caution to the wind. In the morning I want to sneak out, but when I open my eyes, he's already *up*. In more ways than one. Convincing the ridiculously cocky (pun intended) man that I'm not the woman he slept with is impossible. I don't even know who that woman was, and now he's determined to find out. Even if it means using his career-risking injury to his advantage and finagling my professional help. The trouble is, while I'm trying to ignore the sparks flying between us and focus on work, he's more interested in hands-on research.

About the Love in Bloom World

Love in Bloom is the overarching romance collection name for several family series whose worlds interconnect. For example, *Lovers at Heart, Reimagined* is the title of the first book in The Bradens. The Bradens are set in the Love in Bloom world, and within The Bradens, you will see characters from other Love in Bloom series, such as the Snow Sisters and The Remingtons, so you never miss an engagement, wedding, or birth.

Where to Start

All Love in Bloom books can be enjoyed as stand-alone novels or as part of the larger series.

If you are an avid reader and enjoy long series, I'd suggest starting with the very first Love in Bloom novel, *Sisters in Love*, and then reading through all the series in the collection in publication order. However, you can start with any book or series without feeling a step behind. I offer free downloadable series checklists, publication schedules, and family trees on my website. A paperback guide for the first thirty-six books in the series is available at most retailers and provides pertinent details for each book as well as places for you to take notes about the characters and stories.

Save on Bundles & Enjoy Early Releases

Only from Melissa's Online Bookstore

shop.melissafoster.com

See the Entire Love in Bloom Collection

www.MelissaFoster.com/love-bloom-series

Download Series Checklists, Family Trees, and Publication Schedules

www.MelissaFoster.com/rg

Download Free First-in-Series eBooks

www.MelissaFoster.com/free-ebooks

More Books By Melissa Foster

STANDALONE ROMANTIC COMEDY
Hot Mess Summer

LOVE IN BLOOM BIG-FAMILY ROMANCE COLLECTION

SNOW SISTERS
Sisters in Love
Sisters in Bloom
Sisters in White

THE BRADENS at Weston
Lovers at Heart, Reimagined
Destined for Love
Friendship on Fire
Sea of Love
Bursting with Love
Hearts at Play

THE BRADENS at Trusty
Taken by Love
Fated for Love
Romancing My Love
Flirting with Love
Dreaming of Love
Crashing into Love

THE BRADENS at Peaceful Harbor
Healed by Love
Surrender My Love
River of Love
Crushing on Love
Whisper of Love
Thrill of Love

Seaside Secrets
Seaside Nights
Seaside Embrace
Seaside Lovers
Seaside Whispers
Seaside Serenade

BAYSIDE SUMMERS
Bayside Desires
Bayside Passions
Bayside Heat
Bayside Escape
Bayside Romance
Bayside Fantasies

THE STEELES AT SILVER ISLAND
Tempted by Love
My True Love
Caught by Love
Always Her Love
Wild Island Love
Enticing Her Love

THE SILVERS AT SILVER ISLAND
Flirting with Trouble

THE RYDERS
Seized by Love
Claimed by Love
Chased by Love
Rescued by Love
Swept Into Love

THE WHISKEYS: DARK KNIGHTS AT PEACEFUL HARBOR
Tru Blue
Truly, Madly, Whiskey
Driving Whiskey Wild

Wicked Whiskey Love
Mad About Moon
Taming My Whiskey
The Gritty Truth
In for a Penny
Running on Diesel

THE WHISKEYS: DARK KNIGHTS AT REDEMPTION RANCH

The Trouble with Whiskey
Freeing Sully: Prequel to For the Love of Whiskey
For the Love of Whiskey
A Taste of Whiskey
Love, Lies, and Whiskey

SUGAR LAKE

The Real Thing
Only for You
Love Like Ours
Finding My Girl

HARMONY POINTE

Call Her Mine
This is Love
She Loves Me

THE WICKEDS: DARK KNIGHTS AT BAYSIDE

A Little Bit Wicked
The Wicked Aftermath
Crazy, Wicked Love
The Wicked Truth
His Wicked Ways
Talk Wicked to Me

SILVER HARBOR

Maybe We Will
Maybe We Should
Maybe We Won't

WILD BOYS AFTER DARK
Logan
Heath
Jackson
Cooper

BAD BOYS AFTER DARK
Mick
Dylan
Carson
Brett

HARBORSIDE NIGHTS SERIES
Includes characters from the Love in Bloom series
Catching Cassidy
Discovering Delilah
Tempting Tristan

More Books by Melissa
Chasing Amanda (mystery/suspense)
Come Back to Me (mystery/suspense)
Have No Shame (historical fiction/romance)
Love, Lies & Mystery (3-book bundle)
Megan's Way (literary fiction)
Traces of Kara (psychological thriller)
Where Petals Fall (suspense)

Acknowledgments

I hope you enjoyed Sutton and Flynn's love story, and I cannot wait to bring you more Silver Island love stories. In the meantime, if you haven't read my Silver Harbor series, it is also set on Silver Island and features the de Messiéres family. *Searching for Love*, a Bradens & Montgomerys novel featuring Flynn's cousin treasure hunter Zev Braden, and *Bayside Fantasies*, a Bayside Summers novel featuring billionaire Jett Masters, both take place partially on Silver Island as well.

Please note that I have taken many fictional liberties while writing this story and do not recommend anyone take an unescorted trip into the Amazon rainforest, as the threats are vast and varied. But this is a romance, and it wouldn't sit well to have our beloved heroine or hero find a tragic end during the story.

Writing a book is never a solo process, and I often reach out online while researching to find professionals in specific industries. I'd like to thank Sheila Gibson Selman for referring former bush pilot Kevin Hawkins to me. Loads of gratitude go out to Kevin for patiently answering all my questions and providing detailed information that was helpful while writing this story. I'd also like to thank producer Trip Taylor, who is always willing to share his knowledge and, I'm sure, shakes his head when I veer off course with my fictional liberties.

I'm blessed to have the support of many friends and family members and cannot name them all, but I am grateful for each of you and for my hawk-eyed editorial team: Kristen, Penina, Elaini, Juliette, Lynn, Justinn, and Lee.

If you'd like to get to know me better and haven't joined my Facebook fan club, I hope you will. We have loads of fun, chat about books and hunky heroes, and members get special sneak peeks of upcoming publications and exclusive giveaways. www.Facebook.com/groups/MelissaFosterFans

Meet Melissa

www.MelissaFoster.com

Melissa Foster is the *New York Times*, *Wall Street Journal*, and *USA Today* bestselling and award-winning author of more than 100 novels. Her books have been recommended by *USA Today*'s book blog, *Hagerstown* magazine, *The Patriot*, and several other print venues.

Melissa enjoys discussing her books with book clubs and reader groups and welcomes an invitation to your event. Melissa's books are available through most online retailers in paperback, digital, and audio formats.

Melissa also writes sweet romance under the pen name Addison Cole.

Printed in Great Britain
by Amazon